Versions of Us

eve blakely

To those who spark hope

in the darkness...

You are braver than

you know...

Prologue

KRISTEN

"Cliff Haven helpline, you're speaking with Kristen. How can I help?"

I cradle the receiver gently between my cheek and collarbone, tapping on the laptop keyboard in front of me. I hold back a weary sigh as the screen comes to life.

"Do you ever wish you had a different life?" A soft, timid voice comes through the line. One I recognise all too well, although it's been weeks since she's called.

"I think everybody does sometimes, Em."

There's a pause from her end before she speaks again.

"Sometimes I try to think back to a time when everything was easy, and you know what?" I don't miss the way her voice cracks as she continues. "I don't think it ever really was."

"Why do you say that?" I ask cautiously. "Do you want to tell me what's wrong?"

I already know before the question leaves my mouth that I'm not going to get an answer. Most people who call the helpline are just looking for an opportunity to vent, and right now, Em is no exception. Luckily for me, patience has always been one of my strong suits.

"I just keep waiting for better days to come," she says. "Sometimes I feel like the universe is laughing at me. Watching and waiting for me to fail."

"We all have bad days, Em," I tell her. I've had my fair share of them lately too, but I keep that information to myself. "But we survive them. We've survived all of them. Every single one."

"How do you get through yours?"

"*Dum spiro spero*." This time a sigh does escape my lips as my fingertips pitter patter delicately along the laptop's keyboard.

"Huh?"

"It's a Latin phrase. It means 'while I breathe, I hope.'"

I don't tell her that I learned this definition by googling it after seeing it scrawled across a brick wall in colourful graffiti.

She pauses for so long that if it wasn't for the quiet murmur of her shallow breaths, I'd begin to think she'd opted out of this conversation.

"Em? Are you still there?"

"Did you ever think you knew someone? Like really knew them, only to find out they're not at all the person you thought they were?"

I let out another long breath. Her words are like a slap to the face, and I have to fight to maintain my professionalism.

You're preaching to the choir here, sister.

I want to tell her I know exactly what she's talking about, that I fully sympathise with that notion, but this isn't about me. "Do you want to tell me more about this person?"

"My whole life is a lie," she spits, her voice suddenly like acid.

She does this sometimes. Goes off on some sort of cryptic tangent. She feeds me fragments of information in the hopes that I can offer her some inspiring words in reply. I don't think I have any left in me tonight.

"Maybe I'm no better than any of them," she continues. "Maybe I've been deceiving myself."

"Tell me something about yourself," I say, attempting to pull her out of this downward spiral I sense she's falling into.

"I can't. I don't even know who I am anymore." Her voice rises with emotion, and I know I have to step up my game here.

Be the light she needs in her dark moment.

"Sure, you do," I say encouragingly.

"He's a fraud." I hear a faint sniffle and I know she's lost the battle with her tears. "We all are. We're all just pretending."

"It's okay, Em..." I begin to say, but I'm cut off by the dial tone.

She's gone, leaving me guilty and helpless in a dimly lit room, staring out the window at the turbulent ocean below.

I wish I could do more to help her. The truth is that bearing the weight of the problems of others inches further toward impossible when your own load is already so heavy.

The clock on the wall tells me I've been here twenty minutes longer than I needed to be, but I don't mind spending the extra time. Especially when it's for Em. I love volunteering at the helpline, but I can't deny that tonight the hours have dragged.

The chair wheels squeak across the floor as I stand and shrug on my grey, knit cardigan. I sling my black satchel bag over my shoulder and an exhausted sigh escapes my lips, capturing my supervisor's attention.

"It's eleven already?" I hear Jules ask from the back corner desk.

"Twenty past," I answer, wishing the time had passed as quickly for me today as it seems to have for her.

"Big night planned?" she asks.

"Not tonight," I answer.

Jules is in her mid-thirties and divides her time between volunteering here at the crisis centre and being a mother to a baby that barely sleeps. She often jokes about living vicariously through me. I hate to disappoint her, but at twenty-four, my life is just as lack lustre these days.

A few months ago, I might have been able to tell her something different. That I was meeting up with friends for a drink or spending the night with my slightly immature, fun-loving boyfriend, but I'm not nearly as social as I used to be.

Things change.

And I guess, so do we.

Sometimes people disappoint you.

After descending the stairwell that leads to the street, I'm hit with a warm blast of fresh ocean air; a welcome contrast to the dry air con I've been subjected to for the last five hours.

The esplanade stretches out before me, an air of loneliness in its wake as I follow the cobblestone path past the beach in the direction of my apartment.

Distant chatter fills the silence, as patrons from Steve's Tavern gather outside, saying their goodbyes to each other as they call it a night.

The tavern has always been our one lively beacon of energy in this otherwise quiet town and although it's been a while since I've been there, I smile at the memories it resurrects.

Of laughing with friends, wasting time sipping back burning liquid concoctions. The nostalgia stops me in my tracks, intense and overpowering.

I know it won't be the same. Nothing will ever be the same again, but I crave the familiarity anyway.

What the hell. I could use a drink.

I turn on my heel and march toward the tavern's heavy, wooden, paint-chipped door and shove it open, finding myself immersed in its humble atmosphere. It almost feels like home.

Almost.

Muscle memory kicks in and my feet carry me over to the bar. I clamber onto a stool at the end. I've sat in this exact position hundreds of times before, either waiting on drinks, or watching Liv or EJ, or Henley, play on the bar's tiny, modest stage.

It's late and it's a weekday, so the tavern isn't exactly overflowing with people. It doesn't take much to get the bartender's attention.

"You look like you could use a drink," he says when he saunters to my end of the bar.

"I look that bad, huh?" I aim a weak smile in his direction.

"Are you kidding? You look terrible," he teases with a lopsided smirk, earning an eyeroll from me. "I'm joking, obviously. You're always gorgeous, Kristen."

I shake my head at his mockery, though I'm thankful for the slight grin he's managed to get out of me.

He pushes a scotch on the rocks down the bar in my direction. "On the house."

"Thanks, Dylan."

I swirl the glass, gazing into the amber-coloured liquid, watching as golden hues bounce off the clear-cut glass under the tavern's overhead lights.

Old Tommy, the town drunk, sits hunched over at the other end of the bar. I hear Dylan tell him it's time to call it a night and quite frankly, I'm surprised he's made it this late before being refused service.

Dylan treats him with kindness and respect, and I admire him for that. Henley used to take a much more aggressive approach to Old Tommy.

I silently reprimand myself for allowing him to circulate in my thought process yet again. No matter what I do, everything seems to revolve back to him.

Alex Henley.

The guy whose absence has left a hollowness between my ribs, an ache that burns in my lungs. Every moment spent with him that graces my memory hurts, serving only as reminders that the life we could have had together will never be.

We used to run this town. And now I hate how empty it feels without him in it.

I've spent months searching for a distraction, anything to take my mind off his abandonment. But the human mind is a twisted thing, and sometimes we long for nothing but the one thing we can't have.

Even if it's the very thing that's hurt us.

I wish I didn't miss his stubborn, overprotective personality. I wish my thoughts weren't constantly led to wonder about his whereabouts and what he might be doing. But most of all, I wish I knew the truth about why he up and left this town with no real explanation.

And why he left *me*.

Because the truth is, he doesn't deserve any of my longing. He isn't worthy of the way my heart flutters foolishly when I hear his name. He doesn't deserve me, and he sure didn't deserve the patience I wasted waiting for him to become the version of himself that I needed him to be.

I throw the glass back and down the bittersweet liquid, feeling the flare of warmth it sends through me, like a fireball igniting from within.

I haven't always been this self-assured. His leaving broke me in a new way. I'd wallowed in self-pity for a while. Screamed and cried at the unfairness of it all, reduced to a pathetic puddle of caramel honey macadamia ice-cream on his kitchen floor.

But enough is enough.

I can't live like this anymore.

I slam the glass back down on the bar and it lands with a loud clunk.

Alex Henley doesn't get to destroy me. I won't give him the satisfaction.

And heaven help him if I ever lay eyes on him again.

Chapter 1

KRISTEN

"You what?" I stare dumbfounded, wondering if – and if I'm being honest with myself, hoping – I've heard correctly.

"We're engaged?" Liv replies. There's a question within her tone, although there's no mistaking the glint of joy in her eyes.

"You guys are getting married?" I'm genuinely excited as I gape in awe upon my two best friends.

Liv nods, hesitantly at first, as though unsure of whether her announcement will be met with positivity. But when she sees the smile spread across my face, her evident excitement is irrepressible. She holds out her left hand to me, her ring finger adorned with a single elegant diamond on a dainty gold band. It's beautiful, simple. It's the embodiment of Liv herself. It glistens as the dim tavern lights catch on it.

"Oh my god! It's gorgeous!" I gush.

"It's a little big but we're going to see the jeweller in Little Bay tomorrow about having it resized."

Liv retracts her hand, not taking her eyes from the ring until EJ's hand reaches up to cup her cheek. Her head swivels in his direction and he lays a kiss on her lips.

Liv and EJ are the epitome of true love.

Meant to be, forever and always.

I'd known that since Liv first set foot in Cliff Haven. Hell, half this town knew. I'd be jealous if I didn't love them both so much.

Henley shifts beside me. I know he's probably thinking the same thing I am. That this is the beginning. The first of our friends are getting married and, whether we like it or not, this is the start of a sequence of weddings and babies to come and damn we're getting old and am I even ready to be a grown up yet?

Henley's fingers graze my neck as he drapes an arm around me and pulls me into his chest. I dare a glance at him, curious about what I'll see.

I've known him since we were teenagers and he's never really been the romantic type. He isn't the forever doting boyfriend in the typical sense. He doesn't send flowers or open car doors. He's rough around the edges, but he respects me, and I know that inside his hard exterior, there's a great big heart.

I don't have to wonder how he feels about me. I see it in the way his eyes find mine in a crowded room, feel it in his fingertips as they brush the hair at the base of my neck.

I don't expect the corners of his mouth to draw up slightly, yet they do, and he pulls me in even closer, sending warmth up my spine. I turn my attention back to Liv and EJ.

"This is so exciting, you guys. I'm so happy for you," I say, and I honestly mean it.

These two have been through hell and knowing they've overcome every obstacle thrown at them inspires hope for the rest of us.

"Yeah, this is fantastic news," Henley agrees from beside me.

His optimism earns a stunned expression from the rest of us. None of us are able to decipher whether he's simply being polite or if his words are authentic.

"Thanks, man." EJ slides his fingers through Liv's. He looks happier than I've ever seen him.

"How did you propose?" I ask, turning to EJ.

Liv beams as EJ launches into his proposal story. "I took her to the waterfall."

"Ah, the elusive waterfall," I say. We had all heard about the waterfall, but EJ refused to disclose its exact whereabouts. "I was starting to think that place was a myth."

"It's definitely real," Liv confirms, then laughing she adds. "He was so nervous he almost slipped off the rock and lost the ring."

"If you were that nervous proposing," Henley begins, an eyebrow raised, "Just how bad were you shitting yourself when you went to ask Victor permission to marry his daughter?"

"Oh my god. So bad," EJ blurts.

Laughter erupts from the three of us as we watch him squirm in his seat.

"Honestly though, Victor is great. Intimidating as hell. But great," he adds.

We all nod in agreement as Liv gives EJ a sympathetic glance.

Being a semi-retired surgeon and authoritative figure in the medical business world, Liv's dad is a powerful and stern man. But the town has grown to love him just as much as they respect him.

"You know what? I'd say you deserve a drink for your bravery." Henley rises from his seat. "I'll get a round. My shout."

"Dude," EJ scoffs. "My family owns this bar."

EJ's father, Steve, has managed the tavern since we were kids and both EJ and Henley had begun working here casually once they were of legal age. It wasn't until a couple of years ago that Henley took on a full-time position behind the bar.

"I don't care. It's on me." Henley doesn't wait for EJ to protest, instead making his way in the direction of the bar.

He doesn't pause at the counter, rather swings himself over the top of it and begins pouring a couple of beers. The other bar staff don't bat an eyelid. They've seen this before.

"So, obviously you need to be my maid of honour," Liv blurts.

I gasp excitedly with wide eyes. I can't help the high-pitched squeal of joy that leaves my mouth. "Oh my god! Are you serious? I'd love to!"

"I don't know why you're so shocked," Liv laughs. "You're the obvious choice for the job."

"I'm just so excited! I've never been a maid of honour before." I clap my hands together in delight. "This is going to be so much fun. There's so much to plan!"

"Careful, Liv. You have no idea what kind of monster you've just unleashed." EJ jokes.

"Hey!" I retaliate by reaching across the table to give him a light slap on the forearm, then turn my attention back to Liv. "Don't listen to him. I'm not that bad. I just like to be organised."

"I know you do. That's why you're the perfect person for the job," Liv says.

"See?" I give EJ a smug look and a cheeky grin and then to Liv I say, "I'm going to plan the most epic bridal shower for you. I can't wait!"

"Just make sure you don't forget to actually, you know, hand out the invitations. We don't need a repeat of your twelfth birthday."

"EJ!" I shriek, a hand reaching out to slap his forearm again.

Liv's eyes dart back and forth between the two of us, her forehead wrinkled in a frown.

EJ and I have known each other since we were kids and she's aware of our brother/sister-like dynamic, but it's obvious she's utterly confused.

"Umm, what happened with the invitations?" she asks.

I sigh. "There was an unfortunate miscommunication resulting in a very unhappy birthday."

EJ smirks mischievously. "Kristen thought her mum had taken care of distributing the invitations. Her mum thought she'd handed them out at school. I was the only one that showed up."

"It's kind of how we met actually," I say. "Maggie had taken their family dog to the vet clinic…"

"Oscar," EJ interrupts.

"Right. Oscar," I continue. "And they'd gotten talking. EJ's invite was the only invitation delivered by word of mouth. Hence, the reason he showed up."

"Well, to be fair, my mum made me go."

"Shut up!" I try to glare at him but I'm unable to hide the smile that forms at his teasing tone.

EJ is still chuckling at my reaction when Henley returns, his arms laden with a tray of drinks. He eyes him suspiciously, one side of his mouth turned up in a questionable smirk.

"What?" Henley asks.

"I can't help but notice – and please, correct me if I'm wrong…" EJ begins. "You never actually paid for those." He nods towards the assortment of beverages that Henley is now dividing between us on the table.

Henley waves a hand at him. "Take it out of my paycheck."

"Uh huh." EJ rolls his eyes, but his lips twist in a playful grin.

"Anyway, what did I miss?" Henley asks, the legs of the chair scraping along the hardwood floors as he sits.

"I get to be maid of honour," I disclose, my hands still clasped together in exhilaration. I couldn't contain my reaction if my life depended on it.

I expect Henley to roll his eyes or dismiss my excitement but once again I'm caught off guard by the brief smirk that touches his lips before he hides it behind his beer glass.

It may come as a surprise to many that Alex Henley is a softie at heart, but I've known it for quite some time. My eyes find his and there's a secret message in them, meant only for me.

Alex Henley keeps everyone at an arm's length.

Everyone except me.

"Obviously I'm going to need a best man." EJ's voice pulls his gaze away from mine.

Henley clears his throat, eyebrows raised in apprehension. "Oh yeah?"

"Come on, man. Say you'll do it. I'm not asking anyone else."

He nods. "Of course. I'd be honoured."

He steals another glance at me and though I'd never admit it to anyone, I melt.

Honoured? I've seen many sides to Alex Henley. Fun-loving party animal, dark and brooding, and in rare quiet moments, sweet and sensitive. But this right here, is new.

"I'm happy for you, EJ. Really," he says, a seriousness lacing his tone. "This is great news."

"Really? This isn't weird for you?" EJ throws him a sceptical glance.

We all know what EJ is referring to when he asks this question. Henley's parents had never instilled much faith for him in happy marriages. Nor had they ever set a true example of what a happy couple looks like, hence my oversight when it came to Henley's lack of romantic advances. Their constant bickering and arguing finally ended in a messy divorce about two and a half years ago and then one night, over about fifteen beers, Henley had sworn off ever getting married himself.

"Really. Come on. If anyone can make it work, it's the two of you," he says, taking another sip of his beer and then placing it down on the worn-out table with a clunk. "Besides, if I'm best man I get to plan the best part."

Liv's eyes narrow in suspicion as she glances at me, while EJ begins shaking his head, his thumb and forefinger coming up to pinch the bridge of his nose. "No, dude."

"What are you talking about?" I ask, genuinely confused.

"The bachelor party," Henley answers.

Liv and I both exchange a look and groan simultaneously before breaking out into laughter.

"I don't want anything crazy," EJ interjects. "We'll have a poker night or something. Just the guys."

"Uh huh. Sure," Henley says sarcastically with a mischievous wink.

"Anyway," I interrupt, slamming my palms on the table in front. "First things first. When are we having an engagement party?"

Chapter 2

HENLEY

"What's up, little brother?" My sister lays a hard, playful slap on my chest as she shoves past me through the door to my house, her stilettos clattering on the wooden floor.

"Hey, Katie. Why, yes of course. Come right on in," I mutter, more to myself than to her.

She scoffs at my sarcastic remark, helping herself to my refrigerator. "Geez, where is all the food? Please tell me you aren't living purely off Coco Pops and beer."

That was insult number one and I know she has a quota to fill. She has at least four more of those in her before she leaves me alone.

"It's grocery day," I say. "Actually, this isn't a great time. I was just on my way out."

This is a lie, but I'd rather be anywhere else than be subjected to my sister's mockery.

"What's wrong? You don't have time to talk to your big sister anymore?" She closes the refrigerator door then straightens, smoothing out her skirt.

"Quit with the big sister bullshit. You're literally only twenty-five minutes older than me."

Katie and I are twins. We share the same sandy blonde hair colour and blue eyes but that's about where the similarities end. Our personalities are miles apart. Katie is driven, ambitious and smart.

And I'm not.

"I'm showing an open house down in Little Bay. Thought I'd stop by and …"

"Torture me?" I interrupt her, my eyebrows shooting toward my hairline.

"You know me so well." She aims a sly grin my way. Katie loves her career as a real estate agent. Possibly more than she loves anything else. "Actually, it's Dad's birthday next week and I wanted to see if you wanted to chip in and get him that golf club set he's been hinting about."

"Ah, yeah. Sure. Okay." My gaze tilts to the ground, my palm coming up to rub the back of my neck.

I know without a doubt that a new set of golf clubs is more than I can afford, even when I'm only paying half.

Katie, sensing my hesitancy adds, "I mean, you don't have to. If you can't afford it, I'll just get it."

I can't help but notice the curtain of smugness that falls over her perfectly made-up face.

There it is. Insult number two. I can't deny my reluctance is due to the fact that I earn less money than her, but it still hurts.

"No, it's cool," I say. I'm determined not to let her get the better of me. "I'll pick up an extra shift at the bar next week."

Or three.

"Are you still working at that old place? I'm surprised it's still standing." She picks up a pile of unopened mail from my kitchen bench and begins flicking through the envelopes.

And there it is. Number three.

I nod, my lips pursed to form a thin line. "Yeah. Look, if that's all you wanted to talk about, I really should get going. I have errands to run." I grab the mail out of her hands, slamming it back down on the counter.

"Errands?" she eyes me curiously, seemingly oblivious to the fact that she's pissed me off. "What kind of errands?"

Of course, this mystifies her. The fact I might actually have something better to do than sit around here listening to her insult me.

"Well, groceries, as you so kindly pointed out. Then I'm probably going to meet up with Kristen." I spin around, reaching for my baseball cap and wallet.

"Wow. You still haven't scared her away yet, huh?"

I squeeze my eyes shut, my back still turned to her as I stretch the cap over my head. It's getting really hard to bite my tongue here.

"Not yet," I say through gritted teeth.

"Enjoy that. It's only a matter of time before she comes to her senses." She laughs casually, as though she hasn't just said the most hurtful thing she could possibly say to me. "Okay. I'll be in touch with you about the golf clubs." She flicks her straight blonde hair over her shoulder and opens the door.

"Looking forward to it."

"See you 'round, little brother," she says cheerfully as she skips down the front steps two at a time.

"It's been a pleasure as always," I say to the closed front door after I swing it shut.

I throw my wallet back down on the kitchen bench, a frustrated sigh escaping me.

It wasn't always like this between the two of us. Sure, we'd always had different interests, but Katie and I had been inseparable as kids. We spent countless hours plotting pranks and terrorising the neighbourhood. Then at some point, Katie stopped being my partner in crime and started being the bane of my existence.

I haven't always considered myself the black sheep of the family either. But I do now.

If I had to pinpoint the exact moment everything changed, I'd say it was around the time our family made the move to Cliff Haven, no more than a week after our sixteenth birthdays. That was when I realised my sister was going to be more successful than me at pretty much everything. My parents started paying more attention to the things she did, and they seemed to lose interest in trying with me.

Katie has a way of infuriating me like no one else. I feel my nostrils flare as I scan the living room, my eyes settling on the cherry red drum kit in the corner. My own personal stress-reliever when I need to blow off steam.

I march over to the corner of the room, taking a seat on the small black stool. I reach for a set of sticks from the ground in front and I pound the skins until my back is slick with sweat and my arms and shoulders burn.

This thing is my saviour when my temper boils. Drumming keeps my emotions in check like nothing else on this planet but today I'm finding my frustration a little harder to shake.

Katie revels torturing me. And I'm used to it.

But what she said about Kristen cut a little deeper this time.

Because lately Kristen is all I think about.

Chapter 3

KRISTEN

Professor Caldwell paces the front of the lecture room spouting facts about social psychology. We've only been working through this component for a few days, but somehow, she makes it feel like weeks with her monotonous drivel. She seems nice enough, and very knowledgeable but the problem lies within the delivery of the information.

To put it bluntly, she's putting me to sleep.

Psychology has always been the end goal for me, although I can't deny that there have been moments during my academic career where I've questioned whether I'm heading down the right path. Investigating the workings of the human mind can be fascinating and intriguing. It can also be downright dark and disturbing.

But my decision to enter into this course had been made many years ago and the reason for it is one close to my heart.

I remember that day like it was yesterday. It had been my eighth birthday. I realise that a career in mental health and well-being might seem an odd thing for an eight-year-old to be contemplating but my circumstances were anything but normal.

Up until a few months before that birthday, we had lived an ideal life. I was the only child of Pamela and Greg Riley. My mother was a vet nurse, my father the CEO of a major corporation. We resided in a picturesque mansion on a lake.

And we were happy.

That is, until my father was caught sleeping with his secretary. My mother didn't hesitate to pack us both up and move to Cliff Haven, with nothing but a suitcase and a tank of fuel.

It's impossible for a child to fathom the courage required to step out as a single parent and build a new life from scratch, and I'll admit I gave her hell for the first few weeks. I'd blamed her for taking me away from everything I'd known. I missed my friends, despite them turning on me when vicious rumours began to circulate through the school. I guess I hadn't realised yet that Mum was not the enemy.

I received that clarity on my eighth birthday.

Previous birthday parties for me had looked like pony rides and petting zoos, giant pinatas with excessive candy bars and professionally decorated cakes three tiers high. But Mum couldn't give me those things anymore. I didn't even have a single friend to invite. I was unaware of her struggle, too focused on my own, and all I wanted was my old life back.

So, as I sat there, snuffing out the candles on the homemade monstrosity that didn't even nearly resemble Belle from Beauty and the Beast the way my mother had intended it to, I made a wish that my dad would appear and take me into his arms.

Of course, he didn't though. He didn't even send a birthday card.

Later that night, I sprawled out on the second-hand couch Mum had bought in a local garage sale, an episode of ER playing out on our small screen TV. I don't remember a lot about that episode. Only that there was a young emotional boy that needed the help of a counsellor.

"Hey Mum, what's a counsellor?" I had asked.

My mother's face fell, her expression overcome with sadness. I didn't know why at the time. Looking back on it, maybe she was wondering whether a counsellor would benefit me, and the fact that we were in no position to afford one upset her.

Still, she'd answered my question. "A counsellor is someone who helps people when they're going through a sad time. Like a therapist."

Her eyes had brimmed with tears when I'd asked, "Do you need to see a counsellor, Mum?"

Mum was tough and she hid her pain well behind a polished facade, but I still heard her tears at night.

She didn't deserve the way my father had treated her. She'd given him the best years of her life only to be discarded like garbage for a twenty-something blonde tramp in a mini skirt. I'd vowed then and there that I would become someone who could help people through their emotional pain.

Hence the reason I sit here in this darkened auditorium listening to Caldwell's monotonous drawl about social psychology and cognition.

I don't regret my decision, despite making it at the tender age of eight. Although I have to admit that some days, I feel stretched, pulled in a million different directions.

Currently my time is split between university and working shifts at the Haven café to pay for at least some of the fees upfront, and it can be exhausting. But I get through it by reminding myself that I'm on the home stretch. There's only one year left in my post grad degree, and then I hope to score an internship as a qualified psychologist.

That's the dream anyway.

A few more minutes pass before Caldwell snaps her textbook shut and barks out instructions for a homework exercise that will apparently help with the final assessment for this module. I blow out a breath, closing my laptop gently and sliding it into my satchel.

"Hey, Kristen."

I turn at the sound of Chase's gravelly voice.

"Oh, hey, Chase," I reply. "Did you happen to catch any of that? I'm so drained I don't think I absorbed any of it."

He gives a half-hearted laugh and then hoists his backpack over his shoulder.

I met Chase at the beginning of this semester when we'd had to partner up for an exercise. We've been comparing notes to help each other through the course ever since. I enjoy his company and it doesn't hurt that he's ridiculously smart and always has the answers to questions I've missed.

Chase ticks all the boxes for the quintessential nice guy.

Sweet. Check.

Shy. Check.

Has a standing dinner date with his grandma every Thursday night. Check.

"I made a few notes, but yeah, I know what you mean. I think Caldwell's voice could put an ADHD kid in a deep sleep," he says with a grunt.

I laugh at his joke. As shy as he can be, he's actually kind of hilarious.

We're halfway to the fountain in the courtyard before he speaks again. "So, listen, I wanted to talk to you about something."

"Oh, okay," I stop, turning to face him, watching as the corners of his lips curl up in a small smile. "What's up?"

"I got a placement for work experience," he replies, combing a hand through his thick, dark hair.

"You did? That's awesome!"

Chase had mentioned to me that he'd put his name down at a few places to gain experience in the mental health field. Something that I really need to do myself, considering it's a requirement for the course this year.

"Where is it?" I ask.

"Cliff Haven Helpline," he answers.

"There's a helpline in Cliff Haven? I had no idea."

"Yeah. They've only just got it up and running so it's fairly new, but my sister is really good friends with the woman that's coordinating it all," he explains. "It's right in the middle of town, across from the beach."

"That sounds perfect! Congratulations, Chase."

"Thanks," he says, his face splitting into an even bigger smile. "It's a relief to find something so close by. I was afraid I'd have to travel into Milton again."

Milton is the closest city to Cliff Haven, and it takes over an hour to get there. It was the pits having to travel so far for work experience last time. I was hoping to avoid going long distance next time too, but there aren't many options locally.

"I know what you mean." I say. "I'm so happy for you! Jealous, even." I throw a playful punch into his bicep.

He nudges me back gently with his elbow. "Well, that's actually the reason I wanted to talk to you." His face lights up the way it does when he's passionate about something. "Volunteer positions are filling up fast, but they do have one more available. I told them I know someone who might be interested."

"You did?" I feel my eyes go wide in anticipation.

"Yeah. It's so hard to get work placement in our field, especially in town. So, when they mentioned they were looking for someone else, I kind of told them about you. I hope that's okay." He pulls a silver coin out of his pocket and flips it into the fountain, a gesture he does literally every time we pass it.

"Okay? Are you kidding? That's amazing!" I squeal excitedly. "Chase, you're an angel."

I'm so ecstatic I can't help but throw my arms around his neck. The blush that colours his cheeks as I pull away doesn't go unnoticed.

A position in Cliff Haven would be an absolute dream. The benefit of being able to complete my workplace training just around the corner from where I work meant that travelling fifteen minutes to my classes here at the university would be the furthest I'd ever have to go. Cutting down my travel time would be huge benefit considering how many hours I spend either working or studying.

Still, between the café, studying and now the helpline, I worry I might be spreading myself too thin. Chase must notice the change in my expression as I calculate in my head what little free time I'll have left.

"What's wrong?" he asks.

"I just realised that if I volunteer at the helpline, I'm going to have literally no energy left for anything. But I know how rare these opportunities are and there's no way I'm going to pass on it." I choose to let my worries go and beam up at Chase. "Where do I sign up?"

Chapter 4

HENLEY

I lay back on the large flat rock, one arm curled behind my head, the other resting on its cool, smooth surface. We had our first kiss here. Right on this slab of stone. Barely seventeen years old. I didn't know a thing about love, but I think some part of me knew, even then, that my life was about to change forever.

I watch as a seagull perches on the jetty, a steady stream of water flowing beneath its rickety wooden beams. We had our first real fight on that jetty. I don't remember what it was about. Something irrelevant probably. Or at least that's how I choose to see it now.

And that tyre swing over there? I'd wound up in the emergency room after attempting to do a backflip off of it, desperate to impress Kristen, only to end up with twelve stitches in my forehead.

This place upon the riverbank with its overgrown weeds and the giant oak tree that bends overhead, sheltering us from the hot summer sun.

It's ours.

It will always be ours.

Kristen sits cross-legged beside me, a textbook in hand. She's always had her head in a book, her thirst for knowledge a force to be reckoned with. We're polar opposites in that way. She curls her bottom lip between her teeth, and I swear it's the sexiest thing I've ever seen.

My eyes have trailed their way all over Kristen, committed every inch of her to memory, but right now it's as though I'm seeing her for the first time.

Her skin glowing in the sunshine, a scattering of tiny freckles barely visible across her nose and cheeks. The way the light hits her long, dark hair drawing red highlights from the strands like fiery embers.

She looks up from her book, catches me staring. I suck in a quick breath as her hazel eyes give me whiplash, tones of amber, chestnut, and green framed by dark lashes. Her eyebrows knit together and the left side of her mouth twitches in curiosity.

"What's up with you?" she asks me. "What are you thinking about?"

I pull myself up into a sitting position and rest my elbows on my knees. Usually, it's annoying when girls ask that question. Like, you feel forced to tell them that you're thinking about them when you aren't.

But lately I'm always thinking about Kristen.

About how I want to give her everything. Give her more than I'm capable of giving.

This time, I'm thinking about how I don't want to spend my life without her. About how every fight we've ever had was just a waste of energy and how we'll never be able to get back that time. About what an idiot I was when I hooked up with Jenny Stevens while we were taking a break, because there's no way any other woman could ever live up to the likes of Kristen Riley.

And I wonder whether I'll ever be enough for this amazing human with her big dreams and crazy ambitions. I don't tell her all of this though. I simply say, "You."

"Yeah, right." She shakes her head disbelievingly and I topple sideways slightly as she shoves me in the shoulder.

That's the other thing about Kristen. She can't see how amazing she is. Could never believe that anyone's thoughts could be solely fixated on her alone. She fails to see her effortless beauty and the joy she brings to the lives of everyone around her. She's selfless, pure light.

I'm sure it probably has everything to do with the fact that our two best friends have decided to tie the knot, but it dawns on me right now that I'd happily spend my life trying to make her understand.

And it cuts me like a knife through the chest remembering that not so long ago I could have lost her. I hadn't been there the night of the fire, when she'd almost been taken from me forever. She senses the tension in my body, looks over at me with concern.

"What's wrong?"

I shake the thought away. "Nothing. I'm just happy to be here with you." I lean forward, my nose grazing along the soft curve of her jaw. She hums softly then leans into me, turning slightly until her lips softly brush mine. I bring my hand to the back of her neck, her hair sliding through my fingers like silk. I murmur into her mouth. "I don't want to lose you."

"You won't."

Her lips move over mine, slow and light, but I need more. Need her.

I pull her into my lap and wrap my other arm around her lower back, her sun-kissed skin warm on my palm. When I'm with Kristen the rest of the world doesn't matter. It's only us.

She kisses me again and then draws away, leaving her arms still laced around my neck. "Hey, guess what?"

"What?" I ask, combing a stray tendril behind her ear.

"I might have a volunteer position at the new Cliff Haven helpline," she grins.

"That's awesome, babe. How did you score that?"

I know how important her future career in psychology is to her. And the way she lights up when she speaks about the thing that she's most passionate about always has a way of putting a smile on my face too.

"Chase got a job there. He said they're looking for another volunteer." Her palms move down, resting on my chest. "He's going to put in a good word for me."

"Chase?" My jaw tenses involuntarily. I can't help it. It's how I'm wired.

"Yeah. You remember Chase, right?"

"Yeah," I say, forcing a smile.

I remember him alright. How could I forget about the one other guy that gets to see Kristen even more than I do? It doesn't help to know that if she gets this position, she'll be spending even more time with him. Just the thought of it drives me crazy, but I know she hates my jealous streak. It's gotten me into trouble more than once in the past, so for the sake of Kristen's happiness, I push my feelings way down.

"That's great, Kris. I'm happy for you."

"Well, it's not a done deal yet. But I'm pretty sure I'm in," she says as she begins tracing the lines of my collarbones with her fingertips.

"Of course, you are. They'd be crazy not to hire you." I tuck a stray dark tendril behind her ear as she leans into me, peppering kisses along my jawline.

There are some things in this life that terrify me, not that I'd ever admit to them out loud.

I hate flying.

I have a borderline irrational fear of sharks.

I get claustrophobic in tight spaces.

But nothing in this world scares me more than the thought of Kristen realising that she's way too good for me.

That one day she's going to take on the world and I'll never be enough for her.

Chapter 5

KRISTEN

"How was the interview?" Liv looks up from her laptop as I enter her apartment, a hopeful expression on her face.

The interview she refers to is the one I had this morning over the phone with a woman named Jules, who to my delight, had informed me that it would be a pleasure to offer me a volunteer position.

"It was a success!" I exclaim. "You're looking at Cliff Haven helpline's newest volunteer crisis counsellor."

"Yay!" Liv cheers and claps her hands in excitement. "See? I knew you'd get it. When do you start?"

"The day after your party," I answer.

Liv winces at my response, knowing all too well that I'm not always a morning person the day after a big event. "Oh, I hope not too early."

"No. I don't need to be there till five. So, I can party all night long with you guys. And the first shift is just the induction. Online training, safety. That kind of thing." I perch on the armchair beside her. "After that, there's more on-the-job training before I'll be taking calls myself. Then I'll be doing two shifts a week from six till eleven."

"Oh, that's so exciting!" she beams.

"Yeah, it is. I'm kind of nervous, but in a good way. And speaking of your party," I say, peering over her shoulder at the screen of her laptop. "Where are you at?"

Liv and EJ have set the date for their engagement party for two weeks from now and there's still so many preparations to be made. Last time I'd spoken to her they hadn't even decided on a venue. I was starting to freak out that they would run out of time, but Liv remained her usual chill self.

"Well, I'm sending out the invitations right… now." She makes a show of hitting the enter key on her laptop keyboard. "You should be receiving one in your inbox any moment."

"Awesome! Does that mean you guys decided on a venue?"

"We did," Liv replies happily. "Steve has offered to shut down the tavern for a few hours so we can have the party there."

"The tavern?" I question, hoping the cynicism doesn't show in my voice.

Money is no object for Liv. They could literally throw this party anywhere in the world, but she was choosing to have it in her fiancé's father's rundown bar in a tiny town in the middle of the coastline.

"I know what you're thinking. I know Steve's isn't the most elaborate place we could have chosen, but we have a lot of memories tied up in that place." She drops her hands into her lap and shrugs. "It's home, you know?"

"Yeah. I know," I agree.

And I get it. She's right. It's our place.

It's home.

"I've been to so many fancy events and parties and I always hated how forced everything was. The caterers, the people. I mean, the food wasn't even that great. Give me a nice juicy steak or a cheeseburger any day." She laughs as she opens a new tab on the laptop and begins a Google search.

"I can understand that," I say with a nod.

Liv came from a wealthy family and a complicated past. I can appreciate how she relates these elaborate events with a life she no longer wants to be a part of.

"But in saying that," she continues, "We're going to invest in some decorative additions to give the place a more romantic vibe. I'm thinking fairy lights…"

"Oh! And flowers!" I cut her off mid-sentence.

"Yes!" she agrees excitedly, then places a hand over her heart in mock delight. "You just get me. Look at these."

Liv gestures for me to lean in closer to the laptop screen where she has a Pinterest board displayed with rustic engagement party themes.

"Oh wow, this looks so pretty," I tell her, pointing to a picture of a wooden sign, complete with cursive font and framed by wildflowers.

"So pretty," Liv echoes. "I like the simplicity of it. I really want to keep things chill, you know?"

"Yeah." I smile at my friend, knowing there's about as much chance of her turning into Bridezilla as there is of seeing a cow on a surfboard.

"I'll go ahead and order a few things online, but I'm gonna need your help when it comes to decorating."

The way her eyes light up with joy has me feeling the deepest happiness for her. Anyone that knows Liv and what she's been through could easily understand why. I've never been more grateful that she came to this town and that EJ happened to be the guy that caught her attention.

"Of course. Anything you need," I say. "And what about the catering? Will Steve take care of all of it?"

"Yes." Liv pauses, resting her chin on her hand, suddenly deep in thought. "But I'll talk to Carla and see if I can order some desserts from her. And I need to see Jenna at the bakery about the cake."

"I can mention it to Carla if you like," I offer. "I'm working tomorrow morning."

"Thank you. That would be super helpful," she says as she walks over to the fridge. "You want a drink?"

"No thanks, I can't stay long."

I take a glance at my watch. Today is my only free day this week and as much as I love my best friend, there are a few other things I need to do today before a cram study session this afternoon.

"You hanging out with Henley tonight?" Liv asks as she cracks the ring pull on her can of lemonade.

"Uh," I hesitate. "I don't know. Maybe later."

Now that I think of it, I haven't heard from him today. But I guess he's just busy with work or maybe he went out to catch some waves.

Liv notices the way my focus slips and eyes me with a devilish grin, squinting in suspicion. "Speaking of Henley...he's been giving off a weird vibe lately."

I raise an eyebrow in interest. "It's not just me that's noticed that, huh?"

"Nope," Liv says with a shake of her head, then asks, "What do you think it means?"

"Honestly, I don't know. I mean, he's always been that way with me, I guess. Just not so publicly."

I think about the way I've caught him watching me lately, lost in his thoughts, and his reaction to Liv and EJ's engagement news. For a guy so insistent on never getting married himself, he had seemed pretty optimistic about it.

"Well, I can tell you what it looks like." Liv takes a long skull of her lemonade.

"What does it look like?" I ask, fighting the urge to eyeroll at what I know is going to be a ridiculous notion.

"Like he's in love." She sets her lemonade down on the counter with a clink as she makes a face. "Like, serious love."

I shake my head and lose the battle with the eyeroll. "Maybe he's just really happy for you guys."

Henley has been a part of my life for so long. It was obvious from the moment we met that there was a connection between us, but I'd fought it. Maybe we both had. I've never been one to let people all the way in, but over time he'd somehow burrowed his way inside my heart. He'd made a home between my ribs, immersing himself into the air in my lungs.

I've carried him with me ever since, a part of me almost certain that despite the many twists and turns we've taken, that no matter where our lives lead us, at some point we'll find our way back to each other. That even if we get lost somewhere along the way, we're destined to be found.

I know that Henley does love me in his own way. I also know he isn't the type to make serious commitments.

Liv shakes her head in disagreement. "There's something else there, I'm telling you."

"I guess we'll see." I shrug. It suddenly seems too overwhelming to think about. "I have to go. I'm going to drop by my mum's house. Feels like I haven't seen her in forever."

"Oh, cool. Tell her I said hi."

"Sure, will do." I stand, shoving my hands into the pockets of my jeans. "Anyway, let me know which decorations you order, and we can come up with a plan. We'll make sure this party is epic."

34

Mum is only just stepping out of the bathroom when I arrive at her house, her hair carefully wrapped in a fluffy pink towel.

"Little early for a shower isn't it, Mum?" I ask curiously, dropping my car keys down into the bowl on the hall table.

Ben snickers from where he's seated at the table, hiding a smirk behind his coffee cup. Mum places her hands firmly on her hips and glares at him, a sign she's clearly unimpressed.

"Um. What have I missed?" I question, not sure if I really want to get into the middle of whatever this is.

Ben hides a smirk behind his computer screen as my mum begins to scold him. "You be quiet over there. It's not funny!"

"Oh, Pam!" Ben rises to his feet and makes his way over to my mother, encasing her in his arms. "You know I'll always love you."

Ben has been my mum's long-term partner for three years now and I couldn't think of anyone better equipped to make her happy. Ben owns the fresh produce store in town, aptly named Ben's Harvest and he's a total sweetheart. He's the complete opposite of my father. After a long string of jerks, I'm thankful every day that Ben came along to sweep her off her feet.

"Will someone please explain to me what the hell is going on?" I say, my hands splayed out in front of me in frustration.

"Mrs. Wexler was baking bread at home and her dog somehow got into the dough before she'd put it in the oven. Clogged his stomach right up," Ben explains.

"You mean Bruno?" I feel my eyes narrow. "I'm still confused."

"Well, thankfully, Bruno also ate a half kilo of chocolate which caused him to regurgitate the whole thing," Mum says, and then with a sigh she adds, "All over me."

"Mrs. Wexler's dog is a Neapolitan mastiff. That thing is giant!" I exclaim. "Last year she brought it to the Cliff Haven annual carnival and let toddlers ride it like a pony."

My mum raises her eyebrows in annoyance and sarcastically quips, "You think?"

I curl my lips together, attempting to hold in a chuckle, but I can't help the snort that escapes me. When Ben's gaze meets mine, neither of us can contain our fits of laughter.

"Oh, you two are as bad as each other!" My mother waves a hand at us and heads over to boil the kettle. "You have no idea how long it took me to get all of that dough out of my hair."

"I think there might still be some in there," Ben mutters under his breath, but Mum hears him and aims a tea towel at his head.

This only serves to intensify our hysterics. "Oh, Mum," I say, more sympathetically this time. "It can't be as bad as helping Mr. Owen's cow give birth."

As a veterinarian, my mother has had to deal with a lot of gross things. And as freaked out as she seems over this incident, I know she loves her job. She has a kind heart and she's worked extremely hard for her career, enduring countless hours of research. She'd worked her way up from vet nurse to veterinarian as a single mother with very little support. Whenever I think about throwing in the towel with my own studies, I think of her.

She's my inspiration.

"I think it was worse," she replies. "But anyway, how was your day?"

"Great, actually," I answer, a grin making its way across my face. "I got a position at the Cliff Haven helpline. It's a volunteer thing, but it will count towards workplace training for my post-grad degree."

"Kristen, that's fabulous!" My mum spins around and pulls me into a hug.

"Good work, kiddo," Ben says as he gives me a pat on the shoulder.

"Thanks. I had a phone interview this morning and then I dropped in to see if Liv needed any help with the engagement party plans." I reach for the grapes sitting in the fruit bowl on the kitchen bench and pop one into my mouth. "By the way, you guys should have got an invite in your inboxes."

"Oh, that's lovely. I'm happy for those two kids," Mum replies. "That reminds me. I got a visit from Henley at the clinic today."

"You did?" I ask, genuinely curious. "Why?"

And why has the thought of Liv and EJ's engagement reminded her of it?

"I don't know. He said he came by to see how I was doing, but he seemed off." She reaches for a coffee cup on the top shelf of the kitchen cabinet.

"Off how?"

"I'm not sure. It was the weirdest thing. Maybe I'm imagining it, but it was like he was nervous about something," Mum answers, cutlery clashing noisily as she fumbles for a teaspoon in the top drawer.

"Nervous? Henley? I doubt it," I scoff.

In the whole time I'd known Henley, I'd never known him to be nervous about anything. He was confident, self-assured to the point of arrogance at times, completely stoic.

"Yeah. I'm sure it was nothing," she says with a wave of her hand. "The clinic was busy this morning so like I said, I could have been imagining it."

I feel my forehead crumple in a frown. When Liv had mentioned Henley giving off a weird vibe, I didn't want to admit there might be something there. But if my mother has noticed it too there's a high chance something is going on with him.

It wouldn't be the first time Henley has dropped by the clinic to see Mum, but it's not something he does often, and he usually has a specific reason when he does.

Maybe Liv isn't so far off the mark after all. Maybe, as confusing as it seems, his feelings have grown into something more.

But even more confusing to me is the way the thought of that has my lips upturned in a reflexive smile.

Chapter 6

HENLEY

We've been getting smashed this afternoon. People have been filing in through the tavern doors faster than we can pour drinks and fill plates. It hasn't helped that Corey called in sick this morning and I'm stuck out the front on bar service with the new guy, Dylan.

Dylan has only been working at the tavern for a week and he seems nice enough. He keeps to himself, so I don't know his story or where he came from. But he keeps his head down and does his job which is all that really matters to me.

"Can I get a Heineken?"

I look up from where I'm standing behind the bar. That gruff voice is all too familiar to me. It seems Old Tommy is starting early today. The guy comes in every single day without fail, drinks himself into a stupor and ends up being forced to leave.

I know it isn't any of my business, but it infuriates me how anyone could choose to live their life this way.

I sigh, not bothering to look at him as I reach for a glass and pour him a beer. I silently slide it across the bar in his direction, my eyes on the glass instead of him, my jaw ticking in distaste.

"Thanks, kid."

Something about the tone of his voice draws my attention and I lift my gaze to his. I see a flicker of sadness in his eyes, quickly masked by a forced smile. Then he adjusts his stare into the beer in front of him.

Not for the first time, I wonder what could have happened in this man's life to turn him into this shell of a human. Did he take a sharp wrong turn somewhere that led him on this path of destruction? Or did he always walk a fine line, needing only the slightest nudge to tip him over the edge?

Even without knowing, I'm acutely aware of how easy it could be for any of us to wind up where he is, and it terrifies me.

Because I don't want to be like him.

"Henley." Steve's voice pulls me from the dark hole I'd unintentionally dove into, approaching me with a heavy box of liquor wedged under his good arm. His other arm was taken from him in a shark attack which is probably the main reason for my fear of sharks. I retrieve the box and place it down behind the bar. "I'm gonna need your help with ordering some extra stock for the engagement party next week."

"No worries, boss," I say to him, thankful for the diversion. "You want me to talk to EJ about the menu?"

"Yeah, that's probably a good idea," he nods. "Actually, an even better idea would be to talk to Liv about it."

"Right. Of course," I say with a short laugh.

We both know that of the two of them, Liv would be better prepared to plan the catering. Or literally the entire event.

"And also, I told Liv that she can come into the bar after hours to set up, so you'll be seeing her later. She'll probably bring Kristen along with her."

"Sure. Okay," I say, then clear my throat.

"Henley?" Steve asks, turning to face me head on. "You alright? You seem distracted."

"What? No." I manage, knowing I'm doing a really shitty job of hiding this sudden onset of anxiety at the mention of Kristen's name. "I'm fine. Just busy."

"Okay. Good." Steve slaps me on the shoulder with his good arm and then heads to the tiny office in the back.

I *am* distracted, but I'm not about to share that with him or anyone else. The truth is, I've been restless ever since Liv and EJ announced their plans to marry. Nothing shakes you up like your best friend deciding it's time to get hitched.

It's made me question everything I am and everything I've done up until this point in my life, highlighting every one of my flaws and insecurities.

And while I'm being honest with myself, I've wasted a lot of time. I've partied and I've had fun, but I don't have much else to show for it. If these last few years have taught me anything, it's that I'm a quitter. I have a bunch of dead-end jobs I was fired from and a half-finished carpentry traineeship to prove it.

But the one thing I've never wanted to quit was Kristen.

Lately, I can't stop thinking about her. About us, and how far we've come from those two awkward teenagers that met at the river.

I think about how when she isn't with me, it feels as though I'm not a whole person. And how when I'm exhausted after working a long shift at the tavern, seeing a message or a missed call from her on my phone makes my heart feel lighter.

When I get home, she's the person I want to see curled up on the couch or lazing in the hammock on the front porch, waiting for me.

41

I went to see her mum at the veterinary clinic today. I don't even know why. I thought I had a purpose until I got there, and all sense of reasoning left me. Maybe it's because Kristen's mother is the most important person in her life and that makes her important to me too.

For so long, it had been just the two of them, their strong bond forged by the hardships they had faced in the aftermath of her father's leaving.

Kristen had told me things about her childhood. She'd told me that when they'd arrived in Cliff Haven, they had little more than the clothes on their backs. She'd spoken of her mother's sadness but also of her strength, a trait that Kristen no doubt inherited from her.

But it was the things she didn't say that I heard the loudest.

Her father's abandonment had left her broken, forever questioning her worth. She had her mum, but she desperately wanted a family that would love her the way her father didn't.

There are two things I know for sure.

One is that I love Kristen.

The other is that I've taken her for granted for way too long.

I've always known what she's wanted, even if she's been too scared to say it out loud.

I'm ready now.

I want to be that family that she craves.

The only question left is whether I'm worthy.

I look back over to Old Tommy. He's hasn't moved from his position, hunched over on the barstool, his stare still focused intently on his untouched beer.

Chapter 7

KRISTEN

Steve's Tavern has been utterly transformed. What was once a ramshackle, dimly lit space now resembling a rustic ballroom garnished with fairy lights, wildflowers, and candles.

Liv and I had spent the early hours of the morning for the past week here converting the tavern into something Liv and EJ would remember forever. We'd had a little help from Henley with hanging the fairy lights and a few other tasks that our lack of height prevented us from being able to do easily.

The four of us stand off to the side of the bar, awaiting the rest of the guests that are due to arrive any minute now to celebrate the engagement of Olivia Petersen and Emmett Jensen.

Liv unfurls herself from EJ's embrace, then leans into me, wrapping an arm around my shoulder. "I love what we've done with the place," she says with a grin.

I turn my head and nod in agreement. "We are pretty amazing, aren't we?"

"I'll second that." Henley comes to my other side and curls a long arm around us both. "This place is unrecognisable."

"Well, we couldn't have strung up all these lights without you, Alex. So, thank you," Liv says. "And Kristen, your eye for interior design is on point, that's for sure."

I wave away her compliment. "No way. It was all you. You did all the research. I just threw it all together."

"Liv, you should know better by now than to give Kristen compliments. She doesn't know how to take them." Henley gives me a cheeky wink before pressing his lips to my forehead.

I shove him in the chest playfully, but he catches my hand and pulls me into him, his eyes blue as the sky on a summers' day as they bore into mine. He flashes a mischievous grin and I'm amazed how even after all this time it still sends my stomach into a flutter.

"Liv," I hear EJ say. "People are starting to show up. I think your dad's here."

Liv and EJ head toward the side door where people are starting to flow in. Victor Petersen is entering the tavern, my mother and Ben filing in closely behind him.

"Are you nervous?" Henley says in a low voice.

"Why?" I respond, pulling back from him in surprise.

If I'm being honest, there is something different about the butterflies that churn in my gut and I'm suddenly not sure what he's talking about. Is he asking me whether I'm nervous about our friends getting engaged? Or is there a reason beyond that, that he thinks might warrant a heightened state of anxiety?

"About tomorrow," he replies. "Your first shift at the helpline. Remember?"

"Oh," I breathe. "Right. Yeah, I'm nervous. But it will mostly be the induction and training stuff tomorrow."

"Well, I'm proud of you, Kris. I know you're gonna be great at it."

The way he smiles from ear to ear is proof of his genuine happiness for me. If there's one thing I can count on in this life, it's for Henley to be on my side.

"I hope so," I say, wishing I had as much confidence in myself as he does.

"And seeing as you're not working tomorrow, maybe we can sleep in. I can make us breakfast." His eyes drift over my face, over my neck, his gaze pensive.

"Yeah," I say, my head angled to the side in wonder.

I don't know what surprises me more. The fact that he's memorised my schedule or him offering to make me breakfast. It's usually me that does the cooking, or we make a trip to the Haven.

Henley has always been the outgoing one of the group.

The louder one.

The rule-breaker.

The drummer of the band.

Whenever there's a party, you can count on him being the guy handing out the beer. Sure, he has his quiet moments, the ones that usually come after one of our ridiculous arguments. But for the most part, he's the guy that does his best to make everybody laugh.

EJ is the sensible one and Henley, the wild one.

That's just how it is.

But tonight, he doesn't seem himself. He's being extra attentive, which I won't complain about, but as well as that he seems oddly quiet, detached... settled.

"Are you okay?" I ask him.

He nods once, then his hand moves up to my face, his thumb brushing over my bottom lip. "I love you, you know?"

I can't help the smile that spreads across my face or the heat that warms me from the inside. "I know. I love you too."

He suddenly pulls his gaze away from mine, releasing me from his embrace. "I better go and see if they need any help in the kitchen."

"Okay."

I feel my eyebrows knit together, not because I disapprove but because I'm taken aback by this new-found sense of responsibility. In the eight years that I've known him, he's never been the one behind the scenes of a party and I feel like I'm witnessing the transformation of a boy into a man.

I wander over to a table where Carla now sits and pull out a chair to join her.

"Kristen! Well don't you look gorgeous as always," she exclaims, gesturing to the black long-sleeved mini dress that adorns my frame.

"You're looking pretty hot there yourself, boss lady," I say with a wink.

Carla and I have worked together for so long, we're more like friends than employer and employee. As much as I sometimes loathe my early morning starts at the Haven, not to mention washing dishes and dirty floors, I know I'm going to miss the time spent there when I leave it one day.

A bright pink cocktail is placed down on the table in front of me and I turn at the sound of Henley's voice.

"Hey Carla. Can I get you a drink?"

"Sure. That would be lovely, Alex. I'll take one of those." She points to the rosy liquid in front of me, garnished with pineapple and a maraschino cherry.

Henley nods and once he's drifted back to the bar, Carla's eyebrows shoot up. "That's a real gentleman you've got yourself there."

"He's being weird though, right?" I say, my eyes following Henley as he disappears behind the bar.

"If by weird you mean that he's serving party guests fancy cocktails instead of doing a keg stand on top of the bar, then yes. But give him time. The night is still young."

I suppress a laugh at her depiction of my crazy, wild turned considerate, hospitable boyfriend. "You're probably right."

But as the night progressed, Henley didn't jump on top of a keg or do a beer bong or any other outrageous Henley-type act. In fact, he barely let a drop of alcohol touch his lips all night.

After dinner was served, Steve and Maggie delighted the crowd with a heart-warming speech, welcoming Liv into the family and embarrassing EJ with stories of his youth.

With a lot of persuasion from both EJ's parents and Liv, they were able to coax EJ up onto the stage to perform an acoustic version of his latest single. He protested when Liv begged him to play one more song, but his pleas were no match for her sad puppy dog eyes. He ended up playing an extra two songs and promising to perform a special song written just for her on their wedding day.

I catch myself gushing at the two of them as Liv laces her arms around EJ's neck. He smiles at her like she's the only one in the room and I feel their contentment like an ache in my bones.

"Hello, everyone." Victor Petersen's voice booms across the loudspeaker, demanding the attention of the room. "I hope it's okay with all of you if I say a few words."

The rest of us whoop and cheer in response. This big-city surgeon may not blend in with the rest of the folk in the small town of Cliff Haven, but we've grown to love him all the same.

He lets out a laugh at the crowd's response. "Liv, I just wanted you to know how proud I am of you. How proud your mother would have been too. I've watched you grow into a successful, beautiful, patient and caring young woman."

I glance at Liv, and seeing her eyes fill with tears has my own eyes stinging too. I watch as EJ's arm curls affectionately around the small of her back.

"And EJ, what can I say? I know you've both had to overcome great obstacles, in your lives and in your relationship. But you've done it together. And there isn't another soul in this universe that I wish to be standing by my daughter's side. Liv, I love you. EJ, welcome to the family."

The crowd applauses as Liv lunges forward, wrapping her arms around her father's neck. He smiles at something she says to him and then pulls her in closer.

As I swipe a stray tear from my cheek, I feel Henley's arms enveloping me from behind.

He drops his chin to my left shoulder and whispers into my ear. "You okay?"

I shake off my insecurities and force a smile, spinning around to throw my arms around him. "Of course. Why wouldn't I be?" I'm acutely aware of the unrealistically chipper tone that laces my voice.

Henley tilts his head to the side, his eyes searching mine.

"Come on, Kris. You don't have to be tough with me."

Sometimes I hate the way he can see right through me. To anyone else, I appear to be just another girl, overwhelmed by the delivery of a father's tearjerking speech to his daughter.

But Henley sees the damage.

How incomplete I am without the love of a father.

I've tried not to let it affect me. To keep this insecure version of myself tucked away underneath a hard exterior.

"It's fine. Really."

I turn my attention back to the rest of the room and regret it immediately. A slow song cuts through the tavern, echoing off its rafters, a slow bass beat reverberating through the floorboards.

Victor leans in to say something to EJ, who then steps away from Liv with a proud smile. Liv reaches for her Dad, her hands resting high on his shoulders as he holds her in a paternal embrace, swaying in time with the music.

It serves as a cruel reminder that I'll never have a father-daughter dance of my own.

I need to get out of this room.

I pull away from Henley, but his hand catches my arm.

"I need air," I tell him, unable to meet his eyes.

"I'll come with you."

"No," I say, shaking my head. "I just need a minute."

He knows better than to follow me when I need space.

Chapter 8

HENLEY

Kristen doesn't return until the cutting of the cake and when she does, it's obvious she's been crying.

At least, it is to me.

She isn't the type to put her feelings on display. She likes to think she has the world fooled, but I see through this bubbly, cheerful facade.

She wanders over to me, lacing her arms around my waist as EJ smears a fistful of cake in Liv's face. She laughs and even though there's a darkness inside of her, it lights up the room.

God, she's so beautiful and she doesn't even know it.

I'm observing her so intently I don't notice when Steve comes to stand on my other side.

"Kristen, you don't mind if I borrow your man for a second, do you?"

My head swivels in Steve's direction and Kristen loosens her arms from around me.

"Sure. If you promise to return him to me," she replies.

I aim a grin at her and then Steve gestures for me to follow him to the side exit, presumably opting for a quiet place to talk. Once we're outside, he grips my shoulder firmly with his one good hand.

"Alex," he says, rolling his lips together to form a thin line.

It's not often he calls me by my first name. His formal manner has me worried.

"Is everything okay, Steve?"

"Yeah. Yeah, it is." He nods and then a slow grin transforms his expression to one of contentment. "In fact, I'd say things are better than they've been for a long while."

"I'm glad to hear it," I tell him.

If anyone deserves happiness, it's this man standing right in front of me. He continues to give so much of himself, even after all he's been through. God knows he's gotten me out of some tough situations. Let me crash at his place when my parents fighting became too much. Offered me a job when I'd needed it.

"I have a proposal for you," he states bluntly.

I eye him suspiciously. "What are you talking about, man? What kind of proposal?"

I'm starting to wonder if Steve has had one too many drinks, but his eyes don't falter from mine. "I want you to run my bar."

"What?" I look for a sign that he's messing with me, that he's playing some kind of practical joke, but his expression is one of the most serious I've seen on him.

"I want you to manage it."

"Wh-what? But EJ…" I begin.

"EJ has his music career now," he says, cutting me off. "He doesn't have the time."

It was true that EJ's music career meant that he was often out of town, either recording or off touring somewhere. He still did the odd shift at the tavern here and there but only when we were in a bind.

I started filling in for EJ at Steve's Tavern when he'd needed to leave Cliff Haven not long after he and Liv had met. I'd just been fired from my job as a surf instructor at the Surf Shack after I'd failed, repeatedly I admit, to show up on time to give lessons.

I'd often wondered what lead Steve to take a chance on a screw-up kid like me. I figured he was just desperate to find a replacement for EJ in the bar. But here he was, taking an even bigger leap of faith.

"Wow. Steve, I don't know what to say. I don't know if..."

He brings a palm up between us. "Before you start giving me some spiel about how you don't think you're capable or that you're the wrong guy for the job or some other bullshit, know this." He looks me square in the eyes. "I'm not taking no for an answer. You've been working for me for two and a half years and you've come a long way. I know you won't let me down."

I shake my head in disbelief. "I don't get it. Why now? Are you retiring or something?"

"Pretty much," he says, a giant belly laugh erupting from him. "Maggie and I have always wanted to see the world. Now that EJ is settling down, we've decided to take a road trip around the country. Bought a campervan and all."

My incredulity turns into amazement. I'm sincerely happy to hear this. After enduring such pain and heartache, Maggie and Steve deserve this. They've spent their entire lives putting everyone else first, even in the aftermath of tragedy. It's time for them to have an adventure for themselves.

"That's fantastic! I'm so stoked for you guys." I pull him into a hug, and he slaps me firmly on the back.

"So, what do you say?" he asks as he pulls away. "Let me hand the bar over to you. I'll still own it obviously, but it will be yours to manage."

I hesitate, a frown pulling my features down. I've never had someone put all of their faith in me before. Steve's bar is his livelihood. It's everything he's worked so hard for and I'm afraid I'll fuck it up like everything else I've ever touched.

Then again, maybe this is the change I need. An opportunity to force me to get my shit together. To build a stable life with direction.

I run my hand over my head nervously. "You really believe I won't run it into the ground?"

"I think you're gonna do just fine."

His confidence in me is evident in the way his voice never wanes, in the way his eyes don't leave mine. And just like that, he's instilled in me a sense of self-worth. This is my chance to be successful at something.

To be the person Kristen needs me to be.

I blow out a long breath. "Okay," I say. "I'm in."

"That's my boy," he says. He pats me on the back as we re-enter the tavern. "Now go find that girl of yours before she gives me grief for keeping you away for too long."

I find Kristen on the dancefloor with Liv and my heart jolts at the sight of her. This is the woman I want to spend my life with.

I'm sure of it now.

Her eyes find mine across the crowded room and she beams, baring a flash of perfect white teeth. In seconds she's sidling up to me.

"Hey, you," she says flirtatiously.

"Hey, yourself," I smile down at her, and she traces the tattoos up and down my arm. When she sways in place, it becomes obvious that she's downed a couple of drinks while I was outside with Steve. Kristen has my heart on any given day, but tipsy Kristen is irresistible, a force to be reckoned with. "You having fun?"

"Yeah," she sighs. "But is it bad that I just wanna get out of here and go to your place?"

Her hands come up to smooth over my chest, her arms snaking their way around the back of my neck. I feel her body sag into mine as I pull her close, my fingertips tracing circles on her lower back.

"Sounds like the perfect plan, if you ask me." I lean into her, and she hums as I scatter light kisses along her jawline. She drives me crazy in the very best way.

"Okay. Take me home," she murmurs.

Kristen has her own apartment, but I know when she says 'home' she's referring to my house, and I love it. It fills me with a sense of pride that she feels that she belongs there.

That she belongs with me.

We mingle through the crowd, saying our goodbyes to everyone. Then we begin the short walk home to my place.

The house I rent isn't far from the esplanade that runs the length of town. I've lived there for almost three years now.

It's funny how even when I first moved in, still an idiot kid barely out of my teens, I always pictured Kristen living in it with me one day.

"Let's walk by the water," Kristen suggests, a flirtatious smirk forming on her lips. "You know I love the river at night."

"Oh, I'm very well aware. Just promise you won't drag me into it naked this time. It's too cold tonight," I tease, as we make our way down the sandy path through the trees until we reach the bank.

She giggles. "You loved it."

"I did. Until I realised we were being eaten alive by sandflies." I swing an arm around her as a laugh bursts from her, echoing across the canal. "It's not funny. I was itchy in weird places for a week."

She lets out another chuckle. "There's a story for us to tell our grandchildren."

In the past, this sentence would have freaked me the fuck out. It's no secret that I've never been big on commitment. My parents had fought for most of my life before they finally did what would have been best for everyone all along and called it quits.

But as those hazel eyes gaze up at me in the moonlight melting holes into my soul, I'm the complete opposite of freaked out.

I've never been less freaked out.

"Hey, come sit for a second." I motion for her to follow me to the park bench up ahead. She follows my lead and collapses down next to me.

"I freaked you out, didn't I." It's a statement not a question. "I didn't mean anything by…"

"No." I cut her off, combing a strand of hair behind her ear, my hand lingering on her cheek. "You didn't."

"Then, what's wrong? Why are you looking at me like that? You look so serious." She pouts playfully as she says the word 'serious' which causes a smirk to break out across my face.

"There's nothing wrong. In fact, everything is the opposite of wrong."

She squints at me in confusion, so I continue.

"Steve and Maggie are travelling the country in a campervan. Steve wants me to manage the tavern."

Kristen's eyes widen in surprise. "That's amazing!"

She stands and then throws herself into my lap, straddling me, her hands firm on my chest.

"Yeah. I'm scared as hell. But it feels like everything is falling into place for us. I mean, you getting the position at the helpline is a huge step for your career and now I've been given this awesome opportunity."

"Yeah. Look at us. Taking on the world and shit," Kristen says with a grin. I look down at her hands, place my own over them and release a deep breath. She feels the air leave my lungs, senses my apprehension. "Hey, what's going on?"

"I don't wanna fuck this up."

"You won't," she says as she traces my jawline with her fingertips. "This is a huge break for you. You're gonna do great."

"That's not what I meant," I say.

Although I'm shit scared about running the tavern there's something that terrifies me even more.

"What do you mean then?" Her eyes search mine for answers she won't find.

"You."

My heart hammers so hard in my chest there's no way she can't feel it underneath her palms.

"Stop worrying about me. I'm fine," she says, looking down at her hands.

"I know you say that. But it killed me to see you upset tonight."

We both know that I'm referring to the reason she had to escape the party earlier. She's been haunted by her father's abandonment ever since the day that low life scum walked out on her and her mother all those years ago. I want to be there for her in all the ways he hasn't been. My biggest fear is that I'm not up to the task.

She sighs, leaning forward until her forehead rests on mine. "I'm okay, Alex."

"Kristen," I tuck my finger under her chin and tilt her head until her eyes meet mine. "Enough with the tough girl routine. It's me."

"I mean it. I've survived the last sixteen years without him in my life. I can survive another sixteen. It doesn't bother me anymore." The way she says this is almost convincing.

"Is that why you write to him?"

Defeat fills her expression. "Alex…" she begins.

"I wasn't snooping," I say defensively. "I saw an envelope peeking out from under a pile of study notes on your desk. I didn't read it or anything. I wouldn't do that."

I don't mention that I've also seen another stack of letters addressed to her father in the top drawer of her desk.

"I know you wouldn't." She brushes a strand of hair from my forehead.

"Are you going to send it?" I ask.

She shakes her head. "No. I write him a letter every year on my birthday. I have since I was eight," she confesses. "But I've never sent a single one of them."

Her admission causes my heart to ache. Despite my parents having their differences with each other, they've always been there for me.

"Oh, Kristen," I exhale.

"Stop," she warns me. "Look, I'll admit it sucks that my father has never made an effort to be in my life. And it does hurt me. Because I can't understand why he wouldn't want to know me. Why he couldn't love me." My jaw tenses when I see the pain behind her eyes. "But my mother raised me well and she's worked hard to give me everything I've ever needed. I'm lucky."

"I think I'm the lucky one here," I whisper, setting one hand on her hip and the other at the small of her back. "I hate him for making you doubt yourself. You deserve to be loved. You deserve everything. And I know I've hurt you in the past too. But I'm done messing around. All I want is to be with you. I'm all in."

"Then we want the same thing," she whispers.

She smiles down at me, her nose grazing my cheek as her hands climb to the back of my neck. Her lips caress mine gently at first, and then with more force. My hand slides up her back and into hair, tugging at it gently before she pulls away from me.

"Alex," she gasps.

"Yeah," I reply breathlessly.

"I really need you to take me home now."

I huff out a laugh and then I stand, still holding her in my arms, her legs wrapped around my hips. I give her one more kiss before lowering her until her feet find the ground, then I take her hand in mine. "Let's go. I've got some of your favourite ice cream in the freezer."

"Mmm. Caramel honey macadamia?" she asks.

"Of course," I reply.

She rests her head on my shoulder as we continue to walk the rest of the way to my place.

Our place.

"You must really love me," she says as she grins up at me.

My response is automatic. "I can't not love you, K. Not even if I try."

Chapter 9

KRISTEN

I wake, wrapped in Henley's sheets, to the chirping of birds and a steady stream of sunlight beaming through the gap in the heavy curtains. If it wasn't for the dried drool that cakes the side of my face and the crumpled mess of hair that envelops me, I might be mistaken for a regular Disney princess.

I smile at the memory of last night. Of us fumbling through the front door, our hands exploring each other as we stumbled down the hallway and into the bedroom.

Then last night's conversation replays in my mind. Henley had said he was ready to tame his wild ways and focus on the future.

Our future.

And I took his newly disciplined behaviour and gentler personality to be a testament to that. I believe that he's truly ready to make things work between us. For real this time. And I feel happy.

Stupidly, blissfully happy.

I throw my arm lazily over to his side of the bed but instead of finding Henley's firm naked abdomen, my hand meets cool cotton sheets. My forehead crumples in a frown as I lift my head, brushing away the mess of waves that cloud my vision.

He isn't here.

A smooth, white piece of paper lies in the place where his head should be. I swipe it from the pillow and blink until my eyes adjust to the light.

K,

I have something important I need to take care of. I'll be back later tonight. Sorry for skipping out on breakfast. I'll make it up to you.

Alex

PS: I think you should move in with me.

I smile at the last line. It was true that I spent more time in this house than my own apartment. It would make complete sense, but even though we've known each other for what seems like forever, it still feels like a massive commitment. Then again, after last night's conversation, it's not so hard to believe that it's one we're both ready for.

I wish he was here, his arms encasing me, his breath in my hair. What could have been so important that he had to leave before I woke?

I reach for my phone on the bedside table and hit call on his name in my contacts. It rings for few beats, but I hang up when I'm sent to voicemail. If he said he had something important to do then I trust him, but I know I'm going to be wondering about it all day until his return.

I decide to view his absence today as a positive. At least this way I can get some undistracted study time in before I start my induction at the Cliff Haven helpline tonight.

But first, I need coffee. And breakfast.

I take a quick shower and dress in a simple white tee and pair of light wash denim jeans I'd left in one of Henley's drawers and head for the Haven, knowing I'll be in a much better frame of mind for studying once I've eaten.

I walk briskly, taking in the sights of the river as newly orange leaves float lazily to the ground. I pass the park bench Henley and I sat on just last night, when he had told me he was all in. Pieces of what we talked about resurface from my memory.

I know I've hurt you in the past. But I'm done messing around.

It is no secret that our relationship has been a long and complicated one. But the heartache had never been one sided. If we were being honest with ourselves, we'd both done our fair share of the hurting.

And reflecting on that, it's now obvious to me that every single one of those times had something to do with our insecurities. I've always had this almost paralysing fear of abandonment. He's never believed that he's good enough.

When I reach the Haven, it's blatantly obvious that Carla had a little too much fun last night. She hunches over the coffee machine, looking a little worse for wear, dark half-moons underlining her blue eyes.

"Hey Carla. Big night last night, huh?" I tease.

"Ugh," she grimaces. "I'm getting too old for this stuff."

"How late were you out?" I ask as I begin tidying a stack of napkins on the counter in front of me. Force of habit.

"I fell into bed about one in the morning, I think." Her mouth stretches in a yawn as if by way of proving her fatigue.

"Wow! That is late for you. Look at you go, girl." I hold up my open palm comically awaiting a high five which she reciprocates with an unamused look.

"It was an amazing party though," she admits. "And what you guys did with the place? Stunning. It was so beautiful." She grabs a takeaway cup from the back bench and takes a long sip. "You know, if you guys hadn't already found your calling, I'd tell you to get into event planning and interior decorating."

Her comment makes me laugh. "Well, thank you. I'll keep that in mind if psychology doesn't work out. Speaking of which, I have a big cram session planned."

"Sounds riveting," Carla says sarcastically. "You want your usual?"

"Yeah, thanks. I'll get it to go, please."

"Can you make a large cappuccino for Kristen please?" she calls to Harper, our most recently employed trainee.

Harper begins fussing over the coffee machine and fumbling with the takeaway cups. I haven't gotten to know much about Harper yet. She seems super shy. She's worked here for a week and in that time, the only thing I've learned about her is that she's nineteen and has a boyfriend named Ryan.

"Actually, can I get a bacon and egg roll too?" I ask.

"Sure."

"Add cheese, please."

"Going all out today, huh?" Carla jokes.

"I'm actually starving," I say.

My stomach growls in agreement. Henley and I never did make it to the freezer for that ice-cream last night.

"Big night for you too then, was it?" Carla stands with her hands on her hips, her eyebrows arched in question.

One side of my mouth twists up in a smirk as I think about the events that transpired after we arrived at Henley's house.

"Don't think it escaped my attention that you and Alex slipped away from the party early."

I nod sheepishly. "What time did everyone else leave? I've been wondering how Liv and EJ are feeling this morning."

"Nice deflection," she replies with a knowing smile, and then dipping her head toward the café doors she adds, "Why don't you ask her yourself?"

I turn in time to see Liv stepping through the entrance, her frame adorned with a gorgeous sky-blue sundress, her dark hair twisted on top of her head in a messy bun. Liv doesn't drink so it doesn't surprise me that she isn't hungover and looks a million bucks. She's halfway across the room before she spies me at the counter.

"Kris! How are you?" She beams as she pulls me in for a long hug.

"I'm awesome," I say. "Best party ever."

"It was, wasn't it?" She smiles, then her eyes begin searching the café. "Where's Henley?".

"He's … I don't know actually."

"Uh-oh," Liv eyes me with curious suspicion.

I can tell what's going through her mind. With the amount of times Henley and I have "taken a break" I don't blame her. But this time his unknown whereabouts isn't due to the volatility of our relationship.

"No. It's not like that," I correct her. "He said he had an important errand to run. I have no idea what or where, but he said he'd be back tonight."

"Oh ok, that's…secretive," she replies.

"Yeah. It's definitely a little strange." I pull my phone from my back pocket, subconsciously checking it for missed calls or texts. There are none. "But you know how he can be. I trust him."

"Okay. Then, so do I," she replies. "Hey, I wanted to thank you again for all your help with the party. It was such a fun night. We had the best time."

63

"Hey what are best friends for? I had fun too. I think it was a sufficient warm-up for the wedding," I say. "Speaking of which, do you have a venue in mind yet?"

"Not really. Considering how great the tavern scrubbed up, we could use it again, but I think we want the ceremony to be on the beach."

"Nice. I can totally picture that for you guys. How's EJ doing this morning?"

"He's great! He's out for a surf so I thought I'd surprise him with his favourite breakfast once he's finished." A grin appears on her face at the mention of EJ's name.

"You guys are adorable. I really am happy for you."

Liv and EJ have been living in the apartment Liv bought, located above her music studio next door to the Haven. Although they now could afford to buy something much bigger, they love their cosy space.

"I know you are. Thank you," she says. "Speaking of cute, you and Henley were pretty cosy last night. Did you find out why he was acting so weird?"

"I think you were right. He does want something more serious," I tell her.

I don't mention anything about Henley's promotion in case Steve hasn't had a chance to talk to EJ about it.

"I knew it!" Liv says with the click of her fingers.

"Kristen, your order's up," Carla interrupts, handing me my cappuccino and bacon and egg roll. "Hey, Liv. How are you doing this morning? What can I get you?"

Liv begins to answer, but I'm distracted by the bell above the door as Chase enters the café. He spots me immediately and bounds up to me with more liveliness than anyone should have this early on a Sunday morning.

"Hey, Kristen," he says excitedly. "You ready for tonight?"

"Hi, Chase," I reply. "Yeah. I'm nervous though."

I catch Liv side-eyeing us in my peripheral.

"Nah, don't be. Everyone there is really easy-going." He waves a hand, dismissing my self-doubt. "I've had a few shifts there now and it's been great. It can be tough but it's also rewarding."

"Well, I guess that's why we chose this career." I take a swig of my cappuccino and relish in the taste of the warm liquid as it heats me from the inside out. "Have you studied for the exam tomorrow?"

"Yeah. I'm confident but I'll go over my notes again later today." Chase's self-assurance is not surprising to me. The guy is ranking at the top of our class in pretty much everything he does. "Call me if you get stuck on anything. I'd be happy to help."

"Thanks."

Harper leans over the counter to take Chase's order. He purchases a banana muffin and a bottle of water, which she swiftly hands over to him.

"I'll see you tomorrow," he says with a friendly grin, then he makes his way back outside.

I nod just as Liv's voice breaks through the air beside me.

"Um, who the hell is that?"

"That's Chase," I tell her matter-of-factly. "From uni. I told you about him."

"*That's* Chase?" she questions, her mouth agape.

"Yeah. Why are you being weird?"

"Oh, you poor naïve thing," she says in a mock-condescending tone. "That boy has a thing for you. Like, a major thing."

"He does not!" I protest, swatting a hand in her direction.

"Really? *Call me if you need help with anything*." Liv mimics Chase's deep voice. "And how does Henley feel about you and Mr. Biceps hanging out and working together?"

"He's never met him," I say with a shrug.

Liv's eyebrows shoot upward. "If I were you, I'd keep it that way."

Before last night I would have agreed with her. Henley has a jealous streak a mile long that has resulted in multiple fist fights and verbal arguments. But after what he said last night, and from the context of the note he left this morning, I believe he's ready to put that all behind him.

I shrug off Liv's assumptions. "Chase is an attractive guy. So what? I'm unavailable."

"Does Chase know that?"

"Stop!" Her blueberry muffin almost slips from her grasp as I playfully slap her arm. "He knows I'm with Henley."

"Okay, okay." Liv holds her free arm up in surrender. "What are your plans for today, anyway?"

"Studying. And then I start at the helpline tonight."

"Oh, that's right. I forgot it was tonight!" Liv exclaims. "Goodluck with it. I'm sure you'll be great."

"Thanks. I hope so. I'll catch up with you guys later." I spin around and throw a wave in Carla's direction. "See you tomorrow, Carla. Bye, Harper."

In minutes I'm sliding the key into the front door of my apartment, juggling my coffee cup in hand. The place hasn't been lived in for days, so it comes as no surprise to me that the air is thick and musty. I open all of the windows and throw in a small load of laundry before opening my textbook and going over some of my notes.

As hard as I try, my brain won't absorb the information. I'm too focused on one particular external factor.

Henley.

I try his phone again, but there's no answer. For the millionth time this morning I find myself wondering what this secret errand might be related to.

I consider that it might have something to do with the tavern and Steve's proposition. Without a second thought, I pull up Steve's personal mobile number and hit the call button.

He answers on the third ring. "Hey Kristen, what's up?"

"Hi Steve. You wouldn't happen to know where Henley is, would you?" I try to keep the apprehension out of my voice.

"I haven't heard from him today, no. Is everything alright?" he asks.

I feel my forehead wrinkle in concern. "Yeah," I say. *At least I hope it is.* "I'm sure he's fine. I just haven't been able to reach him."

"You know Alex. He's probably gone for a surf and left his phone on the beach or something."

"Yeah," I say, shaking off my doubts. "Yeah. You're probably right. Thanks Steve."

Except he would have told me if he was just going surfing. I'm sure of it.

"If I see him, I'll tell him to give you a call," he offers. "Oh, and if you see him first, tell him I need some help taking these fairy lights back down."

I manage a small laugh. "Okay. Will do."

I end the call. God, I sound like some kind of needy stage-five clinger. Henley said he'd be back this afternoon and here I am ready to send out a search party at 11am. It's entirely possible that he has no phone service wherever he is.

I slam the phone down on the table beside my books and burying my head in them, knowing there's no chance I'm going to retain any of this information when my mind keeps going back to him.

I contemplate calling Chase. Maybe he could draw my attention back to the task at hand, but then what Liv said this morning enters my mind, raising a giant red flag.

I seriously doubt that her assumptions about Chase are correct. Obviously, if he ever showed interest in me, it would be purely one-sided. But now I can't help thinking that calling him to come to my apartment and help me with exam preparations could be considered presumptuous.

Another hour passes before my phone dings with the notification of a text message. I reach for it hastily, taking in the words on the screen.

> Sorry babe, bad service here.
> I'll be home tonight.

Okay. So, he's alive.

And I was right in thinking he had no service. I breathe a sigh of relief. I can stop freaking out now.

But where is 'here'?

And what is he doing?

I try to call him again and yet again, there's no answer. This time I do leave a message.

"Hey, babe." I say to his voicemail. "Where exactly are you? I've been trying to call all day. Hope everything's alright. I'll probably be getting ready to start my shift at the helpline when you get home and I'll be there till eleven, so I guess I'll see you after that. Love you."

I hang up. An overwhelming sense of relief floods through me knowing that he's okay, but I can't shake this feeling that everything isn't as it seems.

Chapter 10

KRISTEN

The air is fresh, a cool wind encircling me as I make my way down the esplanade. I'm thankful that I opted to throw on my suede biker jacket before hurrying out the door. The sky is darkening up ahead and I wonder briefly whether I should turn around and collect my umbrella, but I brush the thought aside, happy to chance it.

The helpline is located two blocks down from the Haven, around the corner in one of the ocean front buildings that line the beach.

When I enter through the door on the street and climb the stairs to the second floor, I'm greeted by a familiar woman who looks to be in her mid-thirties. She wears a knitted sweater and track pants, her hair piled on top of her head in an unruly bun. Her tone is chipper, despite the bags under her eyes that imply a lack of sleep.

"Hi, you must be Kristen," she says cheerfully. "Chase has told us so much about you."

"I sure am. Thank you so much for having me here," I say with more confidence than I thought possible. "I'm really excited to get to work."

"That's what we like to hear. I'm Jules." She extends her hand out to me in welcome. "I work most nights here at the helpline, but by day I'm usually at the medical centre part-time as a receptionist."

"Oh, cool." I realise that must be where I've seen her face before, although her casual outfit tonight differs vastly from the polished attire I've seen her wearing in the doctor's surgery. "I think I may have served you at the café before. The Haven? Just around the corner?"

"Oh, yes!" she replies. "I thought I recognised your face from somewhere. Small towns, huh? Everyone seems to know everyone around here." She says this as an observation and not a complaint.

"That's for sure," I agree. "You must be busy. It's so nice that you dedicate so much of your time here."

"Well, to be honest with you, I'm on maternity leave right now and I have a baby that doesn't sleep. So, I'm currently not working during the day. That's freed up some of my time though to help get this place up and running."

That explains where the dark circles under her eyes have stemmed from, but despite how insanely busy this woman must be, there's an air of calm surrounding her.

"That's understandable. How old is your baby?" I ask.

"Paige is already five months old now," she says with pride. "Time goes by so fast."

"I can imagine," I say.

"I'm due back at the medical centre in a couple of months. That's when I'll really know what busy feels like," she laughs. "I'm going to miss her every day that I'm away from her."

"I bet you will," I say. "I'm so glad we finally have a facility like this right here in Cliff Haven though."

"Yeah, me too," she agrees. "I used to work at a crisis centre in Milton but it's just so far away. There's no way I could travel that far now that I have Paige. And we need as much support for people in need as we can get."

"Of course," I say.

"Well, why don't I show you to a desk and get you started on the online induction training."

"Okay." I inhale a nervous breath and survey the rest of the room. It isn't a large space but from what I can see there are about a dozen small office cubicles scattered throughout. "How many people do you usually have working each shift?"

"Well, the helpline is still new," she explains. "And we are one of the smaller offices, so we only have roughly ten to twelve people working at any one time. And because most are volunteers, we can sometimes have less."

I follow Jules to a desk in the front corner of the room that looks directly out the window to the dark choppy sea below. The sky has darkened further, a storm appearing to be brewing off the ocean.

"Honestly, we'd love to take on more volunteers, but funding is low, and we just don't have the resources or the space at the moment," Jules says as she pulls out the padded office chair for me to take a seat. "This will be your desk for tonight."

"Okay." I sit down, taking in the outdated laptop and phone in front of me.

"We try to keep things pretty routine around here, but you'll have your own personal login if you need to use a different desk next time. The first part of the induction training is completed online but you are required to do one hundred and sixty hours of mandatory workplace training before you'll be considered ready to take calls alone. I know you've been studying psychology for a while now though so I'm sure you'll breeze through it considering your credentials."

"Thank you," I say, nodding nervously. "I just hope I can be of help to our callers."

"Don't worry. You'll be fine." Jules waves a hand as she continues. "You will get the odd phone call where emergency services may need to be notified, but most of the time all people really need is a non-judgmental listener. Some people will prefer to contact us via online chat, but a lot actually benefit from the intimacy that comes with hearing a friendly voice." She retrieves a small piece of paper from what I assume is her own desk and hands it to me. "These are your login details."

She instructs me to enter my username and password and helps me find the induction course online. I thank her and then I begin the training which she informs me should take around three hours.

Jules is right. I do breeze through it, and I'm finished in just over two and a half hours. After I've completed the induction, she tells me to take a quick break and then she'll let me sit in on a few of her phone calls.

I descend the stair well, stepping outside onto the cold, dark street, a sprinkling of rain droplets dancing subtly across my skin. I use the time to eat a granola bar and attempt to call Henley one more time. He doesn't answer.

Where the hell could he be at eight-thirty at night?

He should be back by now.

I tell myself that he's fine.

That maybe he got called to work a shift at the tavern and can't hear his phone. Or maybe he's taking a shower.

When I return to the office, a man around the same age as me is closing his laptop. "Sorry again for leaving early, Jules. I'll try to stay back a bit later next time," I hear him say.

"No need to be sorry," she replies. "We need to take care of ourselves too."

He nods at her and then gives me a small wave on his way out.

Jules turns to me. "That's James. He thinks he might be coming down with something. He didn't look too great when he arrived if I'm being honest."

"Oh," I say. "Hope he's alright."

"I'm sure he'll be okay. Hopefully it's just one of those twenty-four-hour things. We had a few volunteers call in sick earlier. Luckily, the phones are a bit slower tonight."

I guess that explains why there aren't many people in the office tonight. Maybe next time there'll be some more occupied seats.

The phone on Jules's desk begins to ring and she pats the seat next to her, gesturing for me to join her. She picks up the receiver, then puts the caller on speaker so I can hear too.

"Cliff Haven helpline. You're speaking with Jules."

There's nothing but silence from the other end of the line.

"Hi, this is Jules. Would you like to start by telling me your name?"

More silence followed by a shallow breath.

And then the line goes dead.

Jules sighs. "Another hang-up."

"Another?" I ask.

"Yeah, that's my third one tonight," she sighs, tapping the laptop keyboard.

"Oh." I feel my eyebrows dart upward in response.

"It's way more common than you might think. There isn't anything we can do. We can only hope that they find the courage to call us back. Unfortunately, though, in my experience, they're generally the ones that are most troubled."

I nod sadly as Jules stands up from her desk. "I'm just going to step outside for my break," she continues. "Make a quick call to hubby and make sure he's holding down the fort back home. There's some useful information in this manual for you to read. I won't be long."

She reaches across the desk, retrieving a thick folder which she places in front of me.

"Okay." I nod again.

I sit at Jules's desk staring out the window at the dark ocean, the night outside a black expanse broken up only by the streetlight on the esplanade below. The room is relatively silent, apart from the mild chatter that comes from the far side of the room. I flip the folder open, then I pull my phone from my jacket pocket.

Still nothing from Henley.

I rest my elbows on the desk and put my head in my hands. Today has been one of the longest days I've ever lived through. At least, that's how it feels right now.

I blow out a breath, allowing my eyes to rest for the briefest of seconds when I'm startled into the upright position by the shrill sound of an incoming phone call.

I react without thinking, picking up the receiver and clumsily planting it on the side of my head. I realise too late that I was supposed to wait for Jules. That I'm not trained to take calls yet.

"Hi… uh." I fumble for the right words. "You've reached Cliff Haven helpline. You're speaking with Kristen."

The response to my lame attempt at a cheerful greeting is a breathy sigh. Then there's a slight pause before the line goes dead and I'm left with the dial tone ringing through my ear.

If what Jules said about the number of hang-ups she receives is anything to go by, this is something I'm going to have to get used to.

I click the receiver back into place but it's on the hook for no more than a few seconds before it rings again. I know I should be waiting for Jules to come back, but the thought of a call going unanswered invokes an anxiety within me I can't explain. I collect the receiver and once again place it to my ear.

"Hello, Cliff Haven helpline. You're speaking with…" My voice trails off when I hear a small sob come through the line. "Don't… don't hang up," I whisper cautiously.

The caller blows out a shaky breath and then another sob escapes through the phone. I can tell now that the voice is female.

"Are you okay? Do you need police?" I ask her, my mind working overtime to recall the induction training from mere hours ago.

"No." Her voice is small, scared, her breathing uneven. "I mean, I don't need police."

"What's your name?" I ask her, in an effort to distract her from whatever has her worked up.

She doesn't reply. The line falls silent, and I begin to think she's no longer there.

"Are you still there?" I ask gently.

"Yeah. Um. It's… Em," she replies with a sniffle. "My name is Em."

"Em, do you want to talk to me about what has you so upset?"

I feel the tension even through the phone line. I can sense her uncertainty, her fear. I want nothing more right now than to fix this girl, a complete stranger to me.

"I can't," she chokes out, another sob escaping her.

I open my mouth to ask her why. Why can't she talk to me?

But then the line falls dead again.

She's gone.

She doesn't call back.

Chapter 11

KRISTEN

I'm exhausted by the time I get back to Henley's.

Not to mention thoroughly drenched through. The light drizzle of rain that had blanketed the town for most of the evening transformed into a heavy downpour just after I'd left the helpline. Not grabbing my umbrella on the way out the door had turned out to be a serious error in judgement.

I stumble up the porch steps, digging for my spare key in my saturated bag. I call out to Henley as I enter, hopeful he's somewhere inside.

But it hasn't escaped my attention that his car is still missing, and the house is in complete darkness.

I glance at the time on my phone, before sliding the key into the lock. It's almost eleven thirty. Surely, he'll be home any minute. Maybe the rain has slowed his journey home.

I kick off my boots, ignoring the puddle of water they leave at the front door and rake my hands through my soaking wet hair. I dump my bag on the small dining table, then wander over to the fridge, opening it for no real reason other than habit. I swing the door shut and then open the freezer. There are six tubs of caramel honey macadamia ice-cream staring back at me, all lined up in a row and despite my anxiety over Henley's whereabouts it makes me smile.

I take out a tub, collecting a spoon from the top drawer and carve out a scoop, eating it straight from the container. I ignore the brain freeze it gives me and take another few mouthfuls before shoving the tub back in the freezer.

Too exhausted to shower, I change out of my wet clothes and into one of Henley's favourite t-shirts. A tour shirt of one of the indie bands we've been to see together a few times.

I curl up on the couch with the remote and flick through the channels, though nothing on tv can distract me from the fact that he isn't here.

I picture him walking through the door at any moment, scooping me up in his strong arms and carrying me to his bed.

At some point I must drift off into unconsciousness.

Suddenly, an unrelenting, shrill sound wakes me from my slumber and I'm sitting upright before I'm even aware that I'm awake.

My phone glows from the floor next to the couch, its vibration causing an unpleasant sound against the hardwood.

Henley's face stares back at me from the screen, his eyes crystal blue against his golden skin, a stark contrast to the red baseball cap set backwards on his head. I'd taken that photo about a year ago, though I remember it like it was yesterday.

It had been a good day. A perfect day spent laying on the beach together enjoying each other's company. I'd been stressed out with uni, fearing that I'd done badly in an exam, and Henley had whisked me off for a day of fun.

He's always been the ying to my yang in that way. Him, a wild dreamer with his head in the clouds, and me, the voice of reason that keeps his feet firmly planted on the ground.

We'd swam in the ocean and lazed on the sand. At one point Henley had joined in on a game of beach volleyball with a bunch of other guys he'd known from his time working at the Surf Shack. I was more than happy to lie back and watch, drinking in the sun's rays.

Later, when the sky had turned from bright blue to a deep violet, streaked with every shade of pink, we'd grabbed some fish and chips from Larry's Takeaway and taken it to the river.

Sitting there, the only sounds coming from the water lapping at the banks and the occasional caw of a seagull, I'd asked him if he thought we were endgame.

He'd turned to me, that red cap hooding his features and said, "Of course we are. No matter what happens, we're always gonna find our way back to each other."

"How do you know that?" I'd questioned.

"Because I love you." His eyes had shone, the deepening colours of the sunset reflecting in them. "And because I can't not love you."

I believed him.

And when I'd spun that red cap around on his head and kissed him, I'd never felt happier than I did in that moment.

The phone rings again and I snap out of it, remembering how I'd set my volume to maximum so I wouldn't miss his call if I fell asleep. I scramble forward, grasping at it desperately.

"Henley?" My voice comes out muffled with sleep. For a few beats I hear nothing. "Henley? Are you there?"

"Yeah. Yeah, Kristen. I'm here." He sounds so far away.

Disconnected.

"What's going on? Where are you? It's…" I pull the phone away from my ear to glance at it momentarily. "Two in the morning."

"I'm sorry," he offers, but his tone falls flat.

"It's okay, babe," I say, brushing messy strands of hair out of my face. "Just hurry home. I miss you."

The silence from his end is deafening, carving an abyss between us.

"I'm not coming home." His voice is cold, void of emotion.

I huff out a disbelieving laugh. "Wh- what? What are you talking about?"

"I fucked everything up." This time his voice cracks with the words. "I can't come back."

I'm wide awake now, his words ringing in my ears. "Alex, what are you saying?"

"You deserve better than me, Kristen. You always have."

He sounds hollow, empty.

"You're not making sense." I scramble off the couch, suddenly wide awake and unable to sit still. I begin to pace the length of the living room, the TV still glowing from the corner, its volume muted. "Alex, this is insane. You can't just leave. What about your home, your job?"

"I'll take care of it."

"What about me?" I whimper.

"I'm not good for you."

Henley's words from last night echo through my head.

It feels like everything is falling into place for us. I don't wanna fuck this up.

This isn't the first time I've heard him say that. He's been fighting a war within himself his entire life. I don't know where this constant doubt that he isn't good enough has stemmed from, but I don't have time for it right now. I want him to be here.

I *need* him to be here.

"You're doing it again. You're running scared." I feel hot tears burning behind my eyes, but they aren't sad tears. They're tears of fury. "If you do this Alex, it's for good. I can't keep waiting for you to be the person I need you to be."

There's a long pause before he answers. "I know."

"You know? That's all you're going to say?" I scream into the phone.

He doesn't reply.

"Is there someone else?" I ask, my voice lower now.

I find my answer in his silence.

"What about the note you left? The things you said?" My chest starts to heave in panic, my anger transforming into despair.

None of this makes any sense.

None of it.

I must still be asleep. Stuck in some sort of twisted nightmare. How could the man that professed his love for me a mere twenty-four hours ago be telling me that there's no longer room for me in his life?

I hear him inhale before he expels a long, drawn-out breath. Then he confirms my fears with four simple words.

"That was a mistake."

"Where the hell are you?" I manage to whisper.

"It doesn't matter."

"Yeah," I say, the fire suddenly leaving me, the blood in my veins turning to ice. "You're right. It doesn't."

"Kristen…" he begins, almost pleading. "I want to explain, but right now…"

"Don't bother."

We both go quiet for a moment. I hear him swallow, take in another shaky breath, but he doesn't try to say anything else.

There are a million things I should probably be saying, endless questions that need to be asked. But I don't have the energy to persuade someone to come back to me when they're clearly intent on running.

My voice comes out cold, hard as stone. "Fuck you, Alex."

I end the call and throw the phone with all the energy I can muster. It slams into the overhead kitchen cabinet, falling to the ground in pieces. I can't help reacting with violence. I'm hardwired to lash out in upsetting situations. A trait Henley and I apparently have in common.

I'm still pacing the room when my stare comes to rest on the drum kit in the corner. I take one of the dining chairs and lift it way above my head, then launch it forward. It hits the snare drum with a loud clang and falls onto the bass drum, forging a crack through the centre of the head. I pick up another chair and repeat the process, then turn back into the kitchen.

The spoon I used to scoop the ice cream lies next to the sink, reminding me again of how considerate Henley had been last night.

How could he be so convincingly excited for our future?

For his promotion at the tavern?

Why would he ask me to move in with him?

And why stock the freezer full of my favourite ice-cream?

He's programmed to self-sabotage, to run from things when they're at their best. Running from his promotion at the tavern was one thing. But to run from me? The one constant in his life?

I slide down onto the hard, tiled floor, curling in on myself, the whiplash agonising. I've fallen from the highest high to the lowest of lows.

Our world, a perfectly stacked set of dominoes all lined in a row, crashing to the ground in one swift move.

We were meant to be endgame.

No matter what happens, we're always gonna find our way back to each other.

I'd believed him that day.

What a fool I had been.

Six
Months
Later...

Chapter 12

KRISTEN

"Em, is that you?"

She exhales softly from the other end of the line.

I've come to know when it's her. Become familiar with the ebbing of her sighs, the anxious tremors in her breath and the silences in between them.

"What are your parents like?" Her voice comes out a whisper, as it so often does.

I know I'm not meant to entertain questions from callers and I'm not sure at which point these phone calls with Em started to become about me, but like most people that contact the helpline, all she craves is someone to talk to, someone who will listen.

I completed the induction and the counsellor training. There's even an entire subject unit in my psychology degree dedicated to the textbook dangers of getting attached to cases, but God, this girl is so lonely it pains me. No one should ever have to go through life feeling this isolated.

So, I answer her question.

Because maybe if I do, she'll realise that the rest of us don't actually have it all figured out either.

"My dad isn't around, but I'm pretty close to my mum. She did the best she could to raise me by herself."

There's a pause on her end, as though she's considering this information, before she finally speaks. "What happened to your dad?"

"He left us when I was young." I know better than to give her too many details, so I keep my answer vague.

"Do you ever think about him?"

Her question makes me uncomfortable, forces me to look inward to the darkest parts of myself. Of course, I think about him.

Even when I shouldn't.

"More than I care to admit." I feel like this is the most honest answer I can give her, without disclosing personal information.

"That's stupid. Doesn't sound like he's worth the time," she says boldly, her hesitance replaced with confidence.

"Maybe you're right. But I've still missed growing up without a father figure around. And I hate how hard it has been for my mother, having me rely on her for absolutely everything."

Flashes of Liv and her dad enter my mind, of them dancing at the engagement party under twinkling fairy lights, the way he held his hand out to her. Such a simple yet significant gesture.

Who will give me away on my wedding day, if that day should ever come? I push that thought down before it can overwhelm me with sadness.

Because if I allow myself to deep dive into my insecurities, I won't be able to stop thinking about the fact that my father is not the only one that abandoned me. Henley has also done a brilliant job of making me feel unwanted and inferior.

"Have you ever stopped to think that maybe he did you a favour?" Em asks. She speaks louder this time, a sarcastic, almost viciousness overtaking her demeanour.

I'm silent for a moment, unable to decipher the undertones in her remarks. I know her actions aren't really saying anything about me, but rather everything about the broken relationship she must have with her own father.

"Is there something you'd like to tell me about your dad, Em?" I ask gently.

I've learnt by now that being too direct with Em will earn me nothing but a few curse words and a dial tone.

She ignores my question, deflecting the conversation back onto me. "Maybe you're better off without him in your life."

"Why would you say that?"

I'm not offended by her question, just concerned about what has happened in her own life for her to so casually suggest that anyone's life could simply be better off without one of their parents in it.

"It doesn't matter." She huffs out a breath and even from where I'm sitting in this tiny room, God only knows how many miles from where she is, her hostility slices through me as she abruptly ends the call.

It's hard to end a shift after a phone call like that. To step back into your own life after you've been given an insight into the turmoil of someone else's.

But I need to. It's part of the job. No matter what kind of sensitive information has been disclosed, we pack it up and bind it tight. We bury it inside of us and we carry on.

Sometimes it bleeds into my subconscious, and I find myself upright in bed at all of hours of the night, a cold sweat beading along my clammy forehead.

But this is what we do. And people like Em are the reason we do it.

So, I gather my things as I do at the end of every shift and say goodbye to Jules before heading out the door.

The air is balmy when I step out onto the street, signalling that the end of spring is inevitable. Although the days are becoming longer, the nights seem darker in Cliff Haven now.

Or maybe it's me.

Maybe I just can't seem to run from the darkness intent on swallowing me, no matter how hard I try. I never used to be quite so bitter.

But I guess that's what happens when the one person you believed would stand beside you through life up and leaves you with nothing but a string of distant memories in their wake.

Chapter 13

HENLEY

I'm exhausted.

I've been driving non-stop for over three hours, the occasional oncoming headlamps and brake lights in front beginning to blur into a kaleidoscope of bright whites, yellows and reds. The digital clock on the dash blinks.

1:04am.

Fatigue eats at me, in both a mental and physical sense, and I know that if I don't pull over soon, I'm not going to make it another hour on the road.

I drive a few more kilometres before I see it. A large structure, its roof decorated with vivid neon signage. I've never been more grateful for twenty-four-hour truck stops than I am right now.

I pull into the parking lot and head inside. I'm suddenly ravenous at the sight of food, aware that my last meal had been breakfast.

That's if you could even call day old cereal with curdled milk a meal. Most people wouldn't.

As expected, this service station doesn't have anything to offer in the way of actual nutrition, but I'm starving and anything calorie-dense will suffice. I settle for a couple of packets of chips, then swipe a few cans of coke from the fridge for good measure before bringing them to the kiosk at the front.

"That everything?" A large, bearded guy sits behind the register, slowly scanning the cans one by one.

"These too," I reply, hastily adding a few random chocolate bars from the display in front of the counter.

He raises an eyebrow at me. "Long day?"

"You have no idea."

It's not the worst day I've endured in my life, but a sugar hit just feels necessary if I'm going to survive the journey home.

The guy rings up the items and I tap my debit card to pay. I tense, hoping I've got enough money in the account, then breathe a sigh of relief when the sale goes through.

I'm halfway to the car when my phone begins to ring from the back pocket of my jeans. Juggling my purchases in one arm, I pull it out and swipe the answer key.

"Hey, Dad."

"What's going on? Where are you?" My father's voice is filled with worry and impatience. That's my fault though. I told him I'd call him an hour ago.

"I'm still on the road," I tell him.

"The road to where?"

"Home, Dad," I sigh.

He says nothing, as though he's afraid I've changed course somewhere along the way. As though he's unsure of which place I consider home these days.

But I'm done running.

For his benefit I confirm, "I'm coming back to Cliff Haven."

"Good." He grunts, but I know my dad and this tone signals relief. His brusqueness indicates that he's satisfied with my response. "Be safe, okay? I just want you here in one piece." He pauses then asks, quieter this time, "How are you doing?"

"Yeah, I'm okay. At least, I will be." I'm not sure I believe the words that leave my mouth.

I want to believe them.

"I got a hold of Steve. He wants you to call him, but he's agreed to give you your job back and a place to stay. He said you can take the loft space above the tavern until you get back on your feet."

"Thanks, Dad."

My chest caves with relief but the heavy weight inside of it remains. Steve's graciousness crushes me with guilt. He's giving me a second chance I know I don't deserve.

"I'll see you when you get here." Dad sounds tired. I hate thinking about what I've put him through these last six months.

Of what I've put everyone through.

"Okay." I wince, preparing myself for what I'm about to ask him. "You didn't tell her, did you?"

"No, son," my father says, a hint of sadness within his tone. "But I think you need to."

"I know," I say, running my palm along the back of my neck. There's a knot in the muscle, made worse from travelling in the car. I know he's right. There are a lot of things I need to do, none of them easy. "I will. When the time is right."

He grunts again. "Drive safe."

"See you soon," I say, before I hang up the call.

I open the door to my truck, tossing the chips and chocolates on the dash before collapsing into the driver's seat. I throw my head back on the head rest, squeezing my tired eyes shut briefly.

These past six months have been gruelling. There's nothing I want more than to be back in Cliff Haven.

I've missed the cottage on the creek I once called home, my morning surfs in Little Bay. I've missed cold beers at the tavern and hot mochaccinos at the Haven.

And I miss her.

More than anything, I've missed her.

But I'm not an idiot. As much as I long for the familiar I'm aware that the town I left behind a little more than six months ago isn't going to welcome me back with open arms.

I know for sure that Kristen won't.

Still, that place is my home. It will always be home.

The clink of my keys in the ignition echoes in the quiet stillness of the night as I start the car and pull back out onto the highway.

She stirs beside me momentarily, her head still resting against the passenger door, before a hand comes up to brush the honey blonde waves from her face. A yawn escapes her as she sits upright, rubbing the sleep from her eyes. She spots the cherry ripe on the dash, then reaches out to tear open the wrapper. She knows I bought it for her because she knows I don't like them.

"Where are we?" she asks me, her voice still groggy with sleep.

"About an hour away from Cliff Haven."

I glance sideways at her, only just making out the way her eyebrows furrow in the dark, her nostrils flaring nervously as she inhales a shaky breath. I hear the distinct sound of a cherry ripe wrapper crinkling and I know her anxiety has hit a new level.

"Are you gonna tell her about me?" she asks softly.

"No. But I think you should."

God. I sound like my father.

Truthfully, I have no idea what I'm going to say to Kristen when I see her. I don't believe there are any words in the English language, or any other language for that matter, that could bridge the divide I've forged between us.

But one of us needs to find a way to explain the reason I skipped out on her six months ago with zero warning.

And why I'm showing up now with a girl she's never met.

Chapter 14

KRISTEN

"There you go. One double shot espresso and a blueberry muffin," I say half-heartedly as I place Liv's order on the counter, a slight frown pulling at the edges of my mouth.

"Are you okay?" She eyes me dubiously.

I sigh. "Yeah, but I'm kind of jealous. I could really use a coffee."

"Oh no." Liv laughs but her tone is sympathetic. "Late night last night, huh? What did you get up to?"

"I spent all night studying for an exam I have this afternoon," I answer, a feeling of dread forming in the pit of my stomach. It seems that no matter how many times I reread over the subject matter, my brain refuses to absorb any of it.

"Your exam is today? What are you doing here, then?" Liv asks.

"Harper called in sick and Carla was freaking out." I wave off her concern. "It's all good. I've just been here for a few hours but I'm clocking off soon."

"Oh, I see," Liv says knowingly.

Lately Harper seemed to be off sick a lot and although we would never participate in idle gossip, we have our suspicions that she might be pregnant to her long-term boyfriend.

Presumptuous of us, I know. But the constant throwing up and gradually expanding midsection are kind of telling.

"Anyway, what's been happening with you?" I ask, changing the subject in an effort to distract myself from my pre-exam anxiety.

"I'm keeping busy," she smiles. "We still haven't found a venue for the wedding."

I feel my face fall at the mention of Liv and EJ's upcoming nuptials. It's not that I'm not immensely happy for my two best friends, because I am. Nothing in this world could compare to the love I have for them. But I'd be lying to myself if I didn't admit that it's been hard. The day Liv asked me to go wedding dress shopping I'd forced a smile so big that by the end of the day my face hurt.

Henley's absence has left me empty inside and I haven't been able to find anything to fill that void. I sometimes wonder if I ever will.

And it's not like I even wanted to get married myself. Just the promise of a future together.

I've done my best to carry on with life. I've tried new things. I took a painting class with my mum and as it turns out I'm not half bad at it, although I can't say the same for Mum. My surfing instructor labelled me a liability after I repeatedly got caught in a rip on my first lesson. I've been on a couple of dates, but none of them have measured up.

Liv, obviously sensing the sadness that's begun overtaking me, swiftly switches to a new topic. "Oh my god, you should see this adorable little boy I have for piano lessons. He's so freaking cute! And not to mention, a total musical genius."

"Oh really?" I perk up. "He does sound cute. You love teaching music, don't you?"

It's evident in the way Liv gushes about her students that she's found her life's calling.

"Yeah," she says, a smile breaking out across her face. "I really do."

I'd hate for her to feel that she can't talk to me about EJ and the wedding. I don't want to be that miserable friend, so I ask, "And what about EJ? How's he doing?"

Her grin grows even wider, and it makes me think about what the two of them have been through and their indestructible bond. If those two can make it work, there's surely hope for the rest of us.

"He's great," she beams, taking a sip of her coffee. "He's spending a lot of time in the studio. I think he's stressing out with the deadline for his next album release getting closer, but you know EJ."

"Yeah. That boy is determined."

"That's an understatement." Although her eyes roll subtly with this remark, her smile doesn't falter. I try to force a grin back at her, but nothing gets past Liv. "You still think about him, don't you."

It's more of a statement than a question.

I blow out a long breath. "Yeah. But I'm moving on. I gave up on waiting for him to be the person I wanted him to be a long time ago. Some people never change, I guess."

Liv nods, offering a sympathetic smile, but then her attention is drawn to the far corner of the café. "Um, don't look now, but do you know that girl sitting by the window?"

I wait a few seconds, then subtly turn my gaze to table sixteen where a young woman, probably in her late teens or early twenties, sits alone. Her long, golden blonde waves drape loosely around her shoulders as she scours the menu in front of her. Suddenly, her focus leaves the laminated card, her eyes shooting directly to mine.

I quickly glance back to Liv. "No. I don't think I've ever seen her before. Why?"

Cliff Haven is a smalltown, and although we do get the occasional drifters and tourists, most of our day-to-day customers frequent the café on a regular basis.

Liv raises an eyebrow. "Could be nothing, but she was watching us pretty intently a second ago. She didn't look happy. Wonder what her deal is."

"Who knows?" I shrug, then joke, "She might be pissed off about the poor service around here." A sarcastic laugh escapes me, but I know full well that I won't be laughing if this girl puts in a complaint about me. "I guess I better go see if she needs anything."

Liv winces. "Good luck. I better make a move. I've gotta down this coffee and get to my next lesson in…" She glimpses down at her watch and raises an eyebrow. "Three minutes."

"Damn. Well, I guess I'll see you later."

Liv drags her blueberry muffin from the counter and scurries out the door. I swipe my notepad and a pen, then head in the direction of the blonde girl. I silently pray that I'm not going to cop an insult for taking so long to serve her.

"Hi. I'm sorry about the wait," I say to her in the friendliest voice I can muster. "What can I get you?"

She looks up at me and I'm taken aback when her hazel eyes meet mine. Up close I can see the pallor of her skin, the heavy dark bags that underline her eyes. She stares at me a moment, just long enough to make me uncomfortable. There's something hostile about the way she surveys me. I guess I did piss her off with my lack of hospitality.

"Um. Are you okay?" I ask hesitantly.

"Yeah," she replies. "Can I just get some tap water?"

"Uh, sure."

I frown at her request. It's not intentional, but the way she's watching me has made me uneasy, as though she's trying to read my every thought. I turn toward the kitchen and return to her table with a pitcher of iced water and a glass.

"Would you like anything else?" I ask.

"No," she replies impassively.

I nod once, clasping my hands together awkwardly. Something doesn't seem to add up here. She's definitely acting unfriendly toward me, and I'd initially thought it was because I'd taken my time getting around to take her order. But all she has requested is free table water. Unless this girl is dying of thirst it just doesn't make sense.

I smooth out my skirt and turn to walk back to the kitchen when I hear her call out again.

"Hey."

I spin back around, wondering what she needs now. Her expression is unreadable.

"Yeah."

"How long have you worked here?" she asks.

Her question seems strange. Too personal.

"A while, I guess," I answer, blinking at her as I do the sums in my head. "Since I was seventeen. I'm almost twenty-five now, so I guess almost eight years."

She looks almost sad when I tell her this and I can't for the life of me understand why she should be.

"And you live around here?" she asks, waving a hand in a circular motion.

"Yeah." I don't mean to, but I draw the word out, an undercurrent of apprehension in my tone.

If her questions had been coupled with a friendly demeanour, I'd be happy to answer them, but her attitude is almost accusatory.

I expect her to come back with a new question, but she simply replies, "Cool."

"What about you?" I ask. "I don't think I've seen you around before."

If she's going to be interrogating me, I'm at least going to try and find out something about her too.

"Wow," she replies, her tone defensive. "So that's how small this town is, huh?"

"You could say that. Pretty much everyone knows everyone around here," I say. "I'm guessing you've come from out of town?"

"You've guessed right." There's that sarcasm again. "I'm staying with a friend right now."

"Oh. Anyone I might know?" I know it isn't my business, but she's probed me for enough information I feel it only fair to ask.

She looks away from me, scanning the street outside. "Just a friend."

"Okay. Well, I'll leave you to… drink your water."

I spin on my heel and return to my place behind the counter. Mr. Henderson is patiently waiting for his usual. A slice of pear and raspberry bread with a bottle of sparkling mineral water. I shuffle around the small space, fetching the items before handing them over to him. When I glance back at the girl by the window her eyes are on mine again.

I never used to consider myself a cynical person, but recent events have taught me not to trust people easily. Because the truth is, you can be as close or as intimate with somebody as humanly possible and still never really know them. I learnt that the hard way.

Working at the helpline hasn't helped deter me from raising suspicions about everyone I meet these days. A chance meeting with a strange, blonde girl in a café is no exception.

She doesn't trust me, but she has no reason to either. Nor does she have to answer my questions, even though I answered hers. The way she watches me from the corner, her secretiveness about the 'friend' she's staying with, the hostile attitude. It all screams cry for help to me. I can't stop my brain from digging up possible reasons for why this girl might have come here.

Maybe there is no 'friend' at all.

Why has she come into the café to simply sip on free water?

Is it the only thing she can afford?

God, why am I like this?

Why am I always searching for ways to help people that probably don't even need saving?

A quick peek at the clock on the register tells me my shift ended five minutes ago. I shake the questions from my mind. It's time for me to focus. I need to get back to studying. My exam is in less than two hours.

I untie my apron and toss it into the laundry hamper, snatching my satchel bag from the locker out the back. When I return to the front, the girl is still there, but this time she's staring out the window lost in thought.

I take a few pastries and a sandwich out of the refrigerated cabinet, using tongs to arrange them on a small plate.

"Carla, I want to pay for these," I say throwing down a twenty on the counter. Carla eyes me thoughtfully, so in a low voice I say, "It's for the girl at table sixteen. I think she might be homeless or something."

Carla sighs, but a small smile appears on her face. "You can't save everyone, you know?"

I nod. "I know."

"Three dollars change," she says as she places the gold coins in my palm.

"Thanks. I'll see you tomorrow afternoon."

I head for table sixteen, placing the plate down in front of the young woman. She eyes me warily.

"They're complimentary," I tell her.

"I'm not hungry," she counters rudely.

"Take them home for your friend then." I shrug, then continue on my way out the door and onto the street.

I cross the road and look back to where the young woman is seated behind the café window, just in time to see her pick up the sandwich and take a large, voracious bite.

Chapter 15

HENLEY

"It's good seeing you back here."

I jump, agitated by the voice behind me. When I turn abruptly, I'm suddenly face to face with my father. His smile is sad, but the weight in my chest lifts slightly when I see the relief he wears in his expression.

There are two entrances to the loft above Steve's Tavern. One from the inside, behind the tiny office down the hall from the bar, and the other an external staircase than can be accessed from around the back. Given the tavern hasn't yet opened for the day, I assume he must have taken the back route and that I must have been stuck too deep in my own head to hear his footsteps coming.

"Dad," I manage to choke through the overwhelming emotion.

He reaches out to draw me in for a hug and I can't help that my initial reaction is to flinch. I'm on edge all the time these days.

"Hey, you alright?" Dad asks, sensing my discomfort.

"Yeah. Just getting used to everything." I step away from him, my fingers raking through my messy hair. "You know. Being back here."

It's nine in the morning. I've literally been back for less than six hours. We'd arrived at my dad's place just after three and crashed in the loungeroom, leaving before he woke. I'm operating on about two hours sleep but coming into Steve's before opening was on the top of my priority list for one reason only.

I wanted to arrive when it was empty. To avoid the judgements, the stares. To allow myself a chance to prepare for all that would surely come at me within the next few hours.

"I understand." Dad nods. I hate the helplessness that mars his face. I hate that he pities me. "But if you're ever not alright, you know I'm always here. If you need to talk."

Talking is the last thing I want to do right now but I know he means well, so I nod regardless and then turn my attention back to the broom in my hands.

"Where's the girl?" he asks.

"She went to get us some cleaning products from the grocery store." I'm relieved she isn't here right now. That I get to have this moment alone with my dad.

"She okay?" he asks. He plants his hands on his hips and surveys the dimly lit space.

"Yeah. She's tough. I think she's probably doing better than I am." I manage a small smile, but it doesn't meet my eyes.

Dad huffs out a short laugh. "So, you think this place will be okay for a while?"

I scan the empty loft, its boarded-up windows and exposed brick, the half an inch of dust coating the storage boxes that seem to stretch on for miles. Steve only ever used the loft to store old junk, although with a little love, it could be an amazing studio apartment.

"It's fine," I tell him. "Just needs a bit of work. Nothing I can't handle."

It's not like I have much choice. When I disappeared, so did the lease on the house I was renting. Until I get back on my feet financially, I don't have much chance of finding another rental.

"Have you spoken to your mother?" he asks, widening his stance, his hand coming up to scratch the back of his neck.

"I tried calling but it went to voicemail." I don't even bother mentioning that the same thing happened when I tried to call Katie. I can't blame them for wanting to avoid me.

"She'll come around." There's only the slightest hint of optimism in his voice, which tells me that he has little faith in his own words.

"I doubt it," I mutter. I dump a large box on the ground, coughing as dust particles release from its surface.

My parents married young, and since their separation, my mum has spent most of her time travelling to various exotic locations as though she's trying to make up for her lost youth. I honestly don't even know which time zone she's in at the present moment.

"You know there's always a spare bed at my place if you need it," he offers.

"I know. Thanks, Dad."

I'm grateful for his hospitality, but there's a reason why I moved out of home the first chance I got. My father and I have never seen eye to eye, although things have been much better between us since my parents' divorce. Less tension and all that. Ironically, it was my mother that began to keep her distance from me. Though after everything that's happened, I can't say I blame her now.

I know I could just as easily take up residence at my dad's house, but there's another reason I choose to be here at the tavern. Turning my back on everything and everyone meant turning my back on Steve and Maggie too.

I realise how big of a chance Steve is taking, hiring me after I left him in the lurch all those months ago. I hate myself for disappointing him. The least I can do is stay close by and keep an eye on it until they're back in town.

Steve's Tavern has always been like a second home to me and now it literally is my home. Temporarily anyway. It might seem like a weird thing to say about a pub, but it has always been *our* place.

A place for us to gather knowing that no matter what was going on in our lives, we could leave it happier than when we entered.

When my dad called Steve to explain where I'd been for the last six months, I should have known he'd be gracious. It's in his nature to give people more than they deserve.

"I'll bring your bed by in the truck this afternoon," Dad offers. "Should only take a couple of loads to cart over what you need."

Dad has all my belongings in his spare room. I'll be forever grateful to him for rescuing all my stuff from the house I was evicted from.

"It's fine, Dad. I can manage. I'll come get it."

I pick the broom up from the floor and begin sweeping more dust into the corner. It's not that I don't appreciate the offer. It's the opposite. I've put him through enough and I'm sick to death of being a burden to him.

"It's really no problem. I'll just put it in…."

"I said it's fine!" Something takes over me and I snap, my father recoiling as though I've just slapped him. I'm revolted by my reaction, yet it doesn't stop me throwing the broom across the room and kicking one of the boxes, leaving a shoe sized hole in it. I crouch down to the floor and blow out a long breath into my hands. "I'm sorry."

"It's okay, son." My dad crosses the room, his hand coming to gently rest on my shoulder.

"It's not. Everything is such a mess right now." My eyes burn with the threat of tears, but I force them back down.

"I know," he sighs. "But none of this is your fault. You know that right? Sometimes shit happens."

"So eloquently put," I sigh.

"You know what I mean," he says.

I do know what he means, but he's wrong.

"It's all my fault. None of this would have happened if I didn't do what I did."

"That's true," he admits. "But there's a lot of good that never would have happened either."

He might be right, but it doesn't make me feel any better.

Chapter 16

KRISTEN

"Em, Em? Are you there?"

There's a crackling coming through the phone line followed by some staticky clicking. A sense of unease sits in my gut. Even before she speaks, I know something isn't right.

"Yeah, I'm here," she whispers softly.

"Why are you whispering?" I ask, my own voice low and quiet.

Her breathing is staggered, her demeanour different.

Frightened.

It's all the evidence I need to conclude that she's in some kind of threatening circumstance.

"I can't let them hear me?" She sniffles, a sure sign that she's been crying.

Maybe she still is.

"Who, Em?" I ask. "Who's there with you?"

I want to offer her some form of comfort, but I need to know what kind of situation she's found herself in. I'm worried she's in danger. When she doesn't answer right away it sends my heart into a flutter of nervous palpitations.

"He's coming," she croaks.

"Who?" I ask again, leaning forward on the edge of my seat. The pitch of my voice has crept up an octave, my nerves beginning to get the better of me. I fight to keep my breathing steady, to keep my voice calm.

I ask her again. "Em. Is there someone there with you?"

There's a long pause and I start to think she's no longer there. Then she finally murmurs her answer into the phone.

"Yes."

I breathe a sigh of relief hearing her speak again, but the urgency of this situation is still very real. It's obvious that whoever is there with her is someone she doesn't feel safe with.

"Are you in trouble? Do you need me to call the police?" I ready myself to go straight into emergency protocol at her instruction. If I knew where she was, I would have already.

She doesn't answer and then I hear a separate voice.

A male voice.

"What are you doing?" he asks impatiently. I'm assuming he's talking to Em. "Come on. We need to go," he adds, louder, angrier.

"Em, who is that? Where are you?" I plead with her. "Please tell me what's going on!"

There's interference on the other end of the line and then a clunk, as though she may have dropped the phone. I can't hear her anymore.

I jolt in my seat when I hear the male voice shout aggressively at her. "Who the fuck are you talking to?!"

"No one," I hear her reply timidly.

"Get up!" he shouts.

"Please. Don't!" She screams and then a sob escapes her.

A sickening thud turns the contents of my stomach over.

The dial tone is piercing.

My lungs are suddenly empty of air, my cheeks wet with tears.

And then I'm sitting upright in my bed, wiping beads of sweat from my cold, clammy forehead.

I've had this nightmare before.

This terrifying, recurring memory of that awful phone call with Em a few months ago lives rent free in my head. A reminder that my job will never be easy and that I can only help someone as much as they're willing to let me help them.

That no matter how strong I think I am, I can be rendered powerless in an instant. Sometimes, as much as I want to believe I can save someone, my best will never be enough.

I've felt inadequate ever since that day. I desperately wanted to call the police for her. To have them swoop in and carry her away from this life she doesn't feel is her own.

But we all know real life isn't that simple.

And rarely are problems solved with a simple phone call.

Chapter 17

HENLEY

My chest heaves, a gasp of air leaving me as I spring bolt upright on the couch. This isn't new to me. Awakening in the middle of the night in a complete state of panic. I'd hoped that the bad dreams would stop, that things would be different now that I'm back in Cliff Haven. That it would bring me a sense of peace to be back in familiar surroundings.

But this nightmare was as vivid as all the ones that have come before it.

I stretch my neck out to see if I've disturbed Mackenzie, but she lies motionless on my bed, one foot sticking out from under the covers, her hair a blonde tangled mess. The digital clock on my bedside glows. 4:37am.

There's no chance I'm getting back to sleep anytime soon. Apart from the fact that my body is way too big for this lumpy couch, I know that as soon as I close my eyes again, I'm going to be reminded of the worst day of my life.

Careful not to wake Mackenzie, I slide my phone into my pocket and slip out of the loft, padding quietly down the wooden staircase.

A soft glow illuminates the bar, throwing specks of light onto the bottles stacked neatly above it. I pace the length of the room, coming to a stop at the far back wall.

I wonder where I'd be now if it wasn't for missed opportunities. If I'd had the chance to take on the manager position at the tavern, would I have lived up to my potential?

Or would I have screwed it up the same way I've screwed up everything else I've ever touched.

I lean back, resting my head against the wall. It's then I see something that I'd forgotten all about. On one side of me is the stage, a small platform that I've played on countless times, back when EJ and I were in a band. How I wish we could go back to those days.

When everything was simple.

On my other side stands a tall mahogany cabinet, possibly an antique, a door frame barely visible from above its dusty shelves.

When I'd first started working for Steve, he had often talked about the old, abandoned room here at the tavern and his dreams of getting it fixed one day.

Not long before my family had moved into town, there had been a cyclone that ripped Cliff Haven to shreds. Many of the surrounding shops had needed rebuilding, but for the most part, the tavern had remained relatively unharmed. Except for the back end of it.

The tavern hadn't been doing all that well leading up to the storm and unfortunately, after it occurred, Steve and Maggie had been told there was a problem with their insurance policy.

As it turned out, after they'd changed insurers the previous year, the policy wasn't set for autorenewal and it had lapsed, meaning all the repairs had to be undertaken at their own cost.

The community had rallied together to help. They managed to fix the main area and get the bar up and running again, but the damage done to the back room of the tavern was a little more extensive and they couldn't afford the extra cost to repair it. They regretfully made the decision to board it up, hoping they would be able to repair it in years to come.

A couple of years after that, they lost their only daughter in a tragic accident, and I guess repairing that long lost room became the least of their worries.

For all the times I'd heard Steve talk about it, I'd never once set foot inside it myself. Now that I'm standing here in front of the door, I can't contain my curiosity.

I attempt to push the cabinet aside. It barely budges, it's weight greater than what I'd expected. I position myself so that I can focus all my strength and drive into it with everything I have. The cabinet slides inch by inch until I can access the door handle. I turn the knob.

It's locked.

Of course, its locked.

Who in their right mind would leave a hidden door open?

I sigh, ready to admit to defeat and return the cabinet to its original position, when a thought enters my head. Steve kept a set of keys in the top drawer of the office desk. Maybe one of them would work.

I go to the office and rummage through the top drawer until I find them, then return to the door. The fourth key I try works, an audible click letting me know that my attempt has been successful. I twist the knob and push. The door swings wide open, revealing a black hole.

I look back over my shoulder at the tavern behind me. The sun is only just starting to rise, a soft, blue light beginning to infiltrate the tavern's windows. But this room in front of me is shrouded in obscurity.

I reach for my phone and turn on the flashlight, then I cautiously enter. It's hard to see but the space appears to be large and mostly empty. The light catches movement on the floor in front and I jump back in surprise.

"Get a grip, Alex," I mumble to myself. "It's just a mouse."

As my eyes adjust to the darkness, I notice there are small beams of light entering the back wall. Daylight trying to pry its way through tiny cracks. I shuffle closer, holding my phone up to it. It's another door, a set of double French doors in fact, with glass missing in parts, though they've been boarded up from the outside. I've seen these boards from the beach, I realise.

I set the phone down, then using two hands I push through one of the broken pieces at a narrow plank of timber until it falls to the ground below, allowing a stream of light to penetrate the room.

I step up to the gap and peer through it. I see the sun rising above the horizon, the ocean misty in the morning light.

I retreat from the door and now that one of the boards is missing, I can see another large bay window on my left. It's broken too, shards of glass scattered on the window seat below it.

There are several cracks in the drywall in multiple places, the ground once pristine polished floorboards now littered with leaves and dirt. It's a complete mess. The cyclone sure did a number on this place.

It's sad to think a room that once held so much beauty has been left here to rot in ruins.

I pause as frantic footsteps fall on the floorboards above. My phone begins to ring, its high-pitched tone startling in the silence.

"Shit," I mutter to myself. I quickly swipe the answer key. "Hey."

"Alex, where the hell are you?!" Mackenzie's panicked voice fills my ears, her words rushing out all at once. "It's barely past five in the morning!"

"It's okay." I reassure her, exiting the room and heaving the cabinet back over the door. "I'm downstairs. I couldn't sleep, but I haven't left the building. I'm coming up right now."

A frustrated sigh echoes through the phone before she ends the call. When I arrive at the top of the stairs she's standing in the doorway, her face pale and troubled.

"I'm sorry," I say apologetically.

"I freaked out," she says softly, her shoulders slumping with relief.

"It's okay," I tell her again, as I wrap my arms around her shoulders. "It's going to be alright."

Chapter 18

KRISTEN

Another night, another conversation with a troubled teen.

This time it had been with a seventeen-year-old boy who wants to run away from home to avoid his parents' abusive relationship. Our conversation had lasted almost an hour, him confiding in me of the guilt he experiences over their arguments, me trying to convince him that sometimes relationships fall apart and it's never the fault of children.

Talking to him had stirred up so many memories of my own teenage years. Of Henley mostly, and how he would row his dad's canoe down the river to the small house I lived in with my mother on the edge of the water. He'd climb into my bedroom window Dawson's creek style and spend hours with me, sometimes the entire night. My bedroom became a safe haven for him, an escape from the rage his parents' so often directed at each other.

My chest heaves as I remember the warmth of his torso on my back, the way his big arms would enclose me. I was more than happy to absorb his pain. I'd have given anything to be able to take it away, and I wish with everything that I am that this boy has a window that he too can crawl into.

I wander down the esplanade on my way home from the helpline, checking off a mental to-do list in my head. Although it's late, there's so much for me to focus on right now. I have another assessment due at the end of the week, an early shift at the Haven tomorrow and some notes to go over that Chase had emailed me because I'd missed a class last Friday when I'd come down with a migraine.

The street is quiet, the night still. Maybe that's why my attention is drawn to a soft yellow glow coming from the upstairs windows of the tavern. They're partially covered with curtains but the light flickers with movement behind them. I squint, trying to see what or who could be up there. I've never seen lights on in the space above the tavern. At least not for many years.

It's five minutes past midnight. Closing time for Steve's. I cross the road, curiosity getting the better of me. I stroll to the entrance, pressing my hand up against the cold metal of the door handle. To my surprise it opens with a gentle shove.

I ponder the possibility that Steve could be back in town, but that wouldn't line up with what EJ had said earlier today about his parents driving their caravan up the north coast only yesterday.

I shove the door open further and make my way inside. It doesn't even occur to me that what I'm doing might be dangerous. That anyone could be waiting for me on the inside.

This place has always been an anchorage to me. To all of us. A place to go when there was nowhere else. A safe harbour when we had trouble navigating the turbulence of our lives.

The tavern has never changed. The same old rustic wooden floor creaks beneath my feet, the same dim glow emanating from the bar's overhead lights. Some things in this life are just better off staying the same and Steve's Tavern is one of them. So many memories are tied up within these walls, a rich sense of nostalgia echoing through its open rafters.

"Kristen!" Dylan gasps, his head popping up from behind the bar, his eyes as wide as a deer's caught in the headlights. "Jesus Christ. You scared me. Did I not lock that door?"

"Nope," I answer, with a slight shake of my head.

I toss my satchel bag onto the bar and take a seat.

"We're closed." He rubs his palm along the back of his neck, the detachment conveyed in those two words baffling. Dylan is usually friendly toward me, playful. But tonight, he seems oddly distant.

Uninviting.

"Yeah, I know," I tell him, cocking my head to the side. "Just saw the light was on and thought I'd stop by."

I realise how silly the words sound as they leave my mouth. The truth is I don't know what lead me here. So, the light is on upstairs? How is that any of my business? I guess my mind is more messed up from tonight's difficult conversations with strangers than I originally thought.

"Right," he replies, curtly. "It's just that I'm beat, and I still have a lot to do here."

I nod, unsure of where this newfound attitude has stemmed from. I frown as a loud thump resonates from overhead, followed by a scuffing sound, as though someone is sliding something along the floor above.

Dylan's eyes dart to the ceiling, then back to mine. "You should go," he says. "You know, so I can pack up and get home. It's been a long night."

"What's going on?" I ask. "Who's upstairs?"

"No one," he lies.

I roll my eyes. "Spare me the crap, Dylan. I saw the light on."

He sighs, a deep and raspy breath leaving him as his chest deflates. He doesn't say anything else. He doesn't have to.

Somehow, I know.

I haven't set foot in the loft since I got caught playing hide and seek with EJ up there as a ten-year-old wild child, but I still remember where the stairs are.

I vaguely hear Dylan's protests as I race to the back, climbing them without a second thought, my boots pounding heavily with every step.

I stop dead when I reach the top, unbelieving of what I see before me.

I've thought about the possibility of this moment for the past six months, never really believing it would happen. Even if I'd been certain that I was going to see him again one day, nothing could have prepared me for it.

That didn't stop my mind from playing out every possible scenario of this long-awaited reunion though. There was the one where I said nothing and let my fist do the talking. The one where I had nothing to say and simply walked away. Then there was the one where I confronted him, ripping him to shreds with my words, six months of carefully rehearsed insults pouring out of me like word vomit.

But when I see him there, bent over a large cardboard box, everything I've ever wanted to say vanishes from memory. Something squeezes in my chest, an iron fist around my heart, crushing, reminding me that no matter how much anger fills my veins, the hurt will always win out.

His body goes rigid. He hasn't looked at me yet, but he knows I'm here. There's no way he didn't hear my feet pounding up the steps and Dylan's pleas for me to stay downstairs.

He places the box down, straightening to his full height and it jolts me. His form is different. He's still tall obviously, but there's more definition in his back muscles, his t-shirt stretching over broader shoulders than I remember.

A defeated sigh escapes him as he pushes blonde strands of hair out of his eyes. He's grown out the short, neat cut he once had. He looks good, though I don't want to admit it to myself.

"Kris." I can hear the pain in the hoarseness of his voice and strangely, it makes me want to comfort *him*.

To go running into his arms and forget any of the last six months ever happened.

But then something snaps inside of me, like a rubber band reaching its threshold. This man abandoned me. My insides should be burning with fury. There shouldn't be this gravitational pull between us.

I've spent every day for the last six months pretending that Alex Henley doesn't have any effect on me. That his name doesn't echo through my thought process at least a hundred times a day. For so many reasons I want to let go, but the connection between Henley and I runs deeper than any ocean.

"What are you doing here?" My voice reverberates off the rafters, filling the silence between us.

"I live here now."

"You live here now." I echo his words, my eyes darting back and forth around the room.

There are moving boxes stacked up in the corner, his unmade bed set up on the far wall, the couch from his old house in the corner. The same couch I cried my eyes out on after he called to tell me he wasn't coming back. It all looks out of place here in this dusty, shabby loft.

"Steve gave me my job back. He's allowing me to live in his loft until I get a new place."

Suddenly, I'm angry at Steve. Why the hell would he help him after everything? I feel my nostrils flare, my teeth grinding together in frustration. I narrow my eyes at him.

"You think you can just walk back into town like you never left it?"

"God, Kristen. No. That's not what…" His voice cracks and then he trails off, averting his gaze as though he's too ashamed to look at me. Good. He should be. His eyebrows knit together, hooding those baby blues. "That's fair," he concedes.

He squeezes his eyes shut tightly and when they open, I see something in them that I've rarely seen before.

Remorse.

He drops his gaze to the floor, but he doesn't say anything.

"I don't want to see you," I say in a low voice. I pause, knowing the scathing impact the next words I say will have. And then I say them anyway. "I wish you never came back."

For maybe the first time ever, he doesn't try to argue with me, but when I see his jaw tick, it's obvious I've hit a nerve.

His shoulders hunch over uneasily. He sighs as he looks away and then when his gaze returns to mine it's like an electric shock to my heart. I'd almost forgotten how potent Alex Henley's stare could be. How his eyes could cut right through to my core and make me feel completely exposed.

Almost.

I've hurt him, but the satisfaction I thought I'd gain from it doesn't come.

I turn, readying myself to walk away once and for all. This is my chance to leave *him* behind.

"Kristen." The tremor in his voice holds me in place, my hand coming to rest on the door frame. I swivel back to him slowly, shocked to see the glassiness in his glare. "I'm sorry."

The sincerity in his apology almost breaks me. It's not like Henley to apologise. I've rarely seen him back down from a fight. In the earlier years of our relationship, we'd spend countless hours spitting retaliations back and forth, though our arguments always ended in us wrapped around each other, an entanglement of limbs.

Teenage Henley was stubborn and headstrong, but this version staring back at me is not the same one that left town six months ago.

And I hate that there are questions left unanswered. That I really don't know why he decided I wasn't good enough to be the one he settled down and built a life with. But even if he were to answer them now, there's no way I could trust him to tell the truth anyway.

"Yeah, well. Too little, too late."

I turn for the stairs, and I run.

Chapter 19

HENLEY

"Wake up, sleepyhead."

There's a thud as something soft pelts my shoulder. I groan, still so exhausted I'm unable to open my eyes immediately.

"What do you want?" I try to say, although I'm sure it comes out less than coherent.

My shoulders ache and there's a stiffness in my back that I know I'm too young to be experiencing as regularly as I am lately. I roll over clumsily on the couch, my long legs hanging over the end of it.

"You're shift starts in ten."

My eyes snap open. "Are you kidding?"

"No. It's almost eleven." Mackenzie hovers over me, her blonde waves draping around her face. "By the way, your bed is lumpy as hell. My back is killing me."

I rub a hand over my face and roll my eyes at her. "Sorry about that, princess. You're welcome to take the couch tonight."

She scrunches her nose up in disapproval. "Nah, I'll be okay." Her voice streams into my subconscious as my eyes drift closed again. "And watch it with the princess shit."

Fair call. There's not a soul on this planet that would agree with that nickname.

"Henley!" she shouts. "You said not to let you be late for work."

"Okay." My eyes flutter open again and I pull myself into an upright position. "I'm awake."

I can already sense that today is going to be a long day. The last time I'd checked my phone it had said 3am. In all honesty, I could blame my sleepless night on the fact that I was curled up like a pretzel on a couch half my size, but the truth is it had a lot more to do with Kristen barging into the loft last night.

I expected her to hate me but the way she had looked at me, the loathing in her stare, it had hurt me more than I could ever have fathomed. I'd lain awake for most of the night, tossing and turning, the pained look in Kristen's hazel eyes staring back at me in the darkness.

God, what have I done?

Mackenzie's voice snaps me back to the present. "So, can I?"

"Can you what?" I ask dazed.

She sighs. "I need some money."

"What you need is a job." I retaliate.

"I literally just got here, dude," she scoffs. "Where the hell am I supposed to find a job around here? This town is so tiny."

"As opposed to the small backward town you came from?" I tease.

"Yeah. Okay. Fair enough," she resigns. "I'll start looking today."

I stand up, stretching out my aching muscles as I stumble into the tiny kitchenette. "There's always the café across the street," I suggest.

"The Haven?" she asks, looking at me like I've just suggested she shave her head. "Yeah, right. Maybe when hell freezes over."

"Why not?" I sigh.

"You know why." She stares me down, her eyes narrow and cold.

"You have to talk to her sooner or later." I reach for a mug in the overhead cabinet and begin to pour myself a coffee from the percolator.

"Yeah well, later is preferable," she answers. "Besides, you're one to talk."

My lips form a thin line. I'll spare Mackenzie the details of mine and Kristen's reunion last night. It's probably the last thing she needs to hear right now.

"Whatever. I need to shower. There's a twenty in my pocket over there." I wave an arm in the direction of my denim jacket thrown over one of the dining chairs as I pull the coffee mug to my lips. The lukewarm liquid hits my tongue leaving a bitter, awful taste. I spit it out into the sink. "Oh, God! What did you do? That's terrible."

She throws a snarky look in my direction. "Too bad. I hear they make a mean mochaccino across the road."

"Ha ha," I say, unsmiling. "Real funny."

Even without knowing about last night's events, Mackenzie understands all too well that there's not a chance in hell I'm setting foot in the Haven anytime in the near future. But damn, a good cup of coffee would go down real nicely right now. I'll have to settle for one from the machine at the bar.

Mackenzie smirks at me as she lunges for my jacket. She pulls out the twenty I promised her, holding it up between two fingers. "Thanks. And maybe you could put in a good word for me with your boss?"

"Dylan? Why?"

"Maybe I could work with you," she says optimistically.

"That's a bad idea."

The last thing I need is Mackenzie working at the bar. Although I can't deny that her sarcastic attitude would come in handy warding off unruly customers and dealing with Old Tommy.

"You need an RSA to work behind a bar anyway," I tell her.

"Whatever." She scoffs at me, her tone thick with attitude. "I'm going out."

"Where are you going?"

"To get my RSA," she deadpans.

I shake my head as the door slams behind her. That girl is a force.

When I finally make it downstairs, I'm ten minutes late to my shift. This earns me a majorly dirty look from Dylan and it's clear that this is not the time for me to be asking him for favours, so I keep Mackenzie's proposal to myself.

Not that I want her working in the bar anyway. It would absolutely complicate things between us and Kristen.

I hold up a hand when I see him open his mouth to speak. "Sorry, Dylan. I know I'm late. It won't happen again."

"I hope not." He looks as though he wants to say more, but instead huffs out a frustrated breath.

I aim a single nod in his direction. It's hard to explain how shitty it feels having a boss that's three years younger than me frown upon me like the disappointment that I am.

"I'll start stocking the fridges," I offer, hoping that taking some initiative will help me get back into his good graces.

"Yeah, that'd be great." He places some chairs behind a table and then comes around to meet me on the other side of the bar. "And hey, listen. The Cliff Haven carnival is coming up in a few weeks and we need to make sure we can cater to a whole lot more people."

"Right. On it." I heave a carton of beer over my shoulder and walk it to the bar fridge.

"We'll need to double our stock and …"

"Yeah. I know. I got it," I tell him.

This ain't my first rodeo, kid, is what I really want to say.

The Cliff Haven carnival is an annual event, bringing customers from all around the region. It's always the busiest day of the year for the tavern and Steve usually pulls in every one of his staff to help out. For the second time in a matter of five minutes, Dylan looks at me like he wants to say something else but then thinks better of it.

I turn and begin the arduous task of shuffling a hundred boxes of alcoholic beverages into different areas of the tavern.

Just what I need. More time to think.

"Hey, stranger." I turn at the sound of a familiar voice floating through the tavern. Its usual easiness is missing, replaced with a gravelly edge.

I tense, knowing from his tone that my return to town hasn't been received well by my best friend.

"EJ," I say, not daring to meet his gaze. "Hey." I place a box in front of the fridge and move on to picking up the next.

"Hey? That's all you've got to say?" he says quietly, but there's an understated anger in the way he speaks.

I shrug. Not because I don't care, but because I honestly don't know what I can say at this point to preserve what remains of our friendship.

"I wasn't sure you were ever going to come back. For what it's worth, it's good to see you."

"I don't think there's a single other person in town that shares that sentiment," I say sarcastically.

This guy right here is my best friend in the world, but I've never felt so disconnected from him.

"Well, what do you expect? You left without a word, no real explanation." EJ's voice rises in volume as he moves in front of me. "You stopped answering your phone. You wouldn't reply to texts. How could you do that to Kristen?"

I stiffen at the mention of her name, remembering the hurt in her eyes, the anger I'd seen in them last night. I look up, realising we've caught the attention of a couple of customers, my nostrils flaring in defiance.

EJ takes another step nearer. "Where the hell have you been? She was a mess after you left."

"You think I don't know that?" I shout. "You think I didn't think about her every goddamned day?"

He shifts backward, seemingly intimidated by the weight of the glare I aim at him, but I move forward, encroaching on his personal space.

He holds up his hands in surrender and takes two steps back. I'm shaking, overcome with rage, my hands balling into fists at my sides. It takes a moment for me to remember we have an audience and in an instant, I snap out of it, retreating as quickly as I'd sprung.

EJ shakes his head.

In disgust, in disapproval, I can't tell.

Probably both.

"What happened to you, man?" he mutters.

I let out a shaky breath. There's no good way to answer that question, so I keep my mouth shut, lowering my glare to the floor.

"You're lucky my dad even let you come back here," he says quietly, before turning and heading out the door.

I'm still standing there moments after the door swings shut behind him.

"Show's over," I snap at a group of people sitting nearby, collecting a couple of dirty plates and a water jug from the closest table.

I storm into the kitchen, throwing them too aggressively in the sink causing them to shatter into pieces.

"That's coming out of your paycheck," I hear Dylan say as I continue through the back and up the stairs to the loft.

Fuck this day.

Fuck it all.

Chapter 20

KRISTEN

"Is it true?" Liv barges into my living room, incredulously waving her phone around in her hand. "EJ just called me and said he dropped by the tavern to check on things and Henley was back!"

I sigh before confirming. "Yeah, it's true. He's apparently living in the loft."

Word sure does travel fast in small towns.

"Oh my god!" she exclaims, eyes wide. "Are you okay? Have you talked to him yet?"

"Briefly. It didn't go so well," I answer. I'm mentally exhausted from replaying the conversation in my head. "Although, I don't really know what I was expecting. I guess I was expecting to never see him again. And then, all of a sudden, there he was."

"Did he at least give you a proper explanation about what he's been doing this whole time?" she asks.

"Not exactly," I answer.

But then I hadn't really asked, had I?

His presence alone had been too much for me to comprehend, let alone the words expressed between us.

"Yeah. That must have been crazy. Are you okay?" she asks again, softer this time. The couch cushion dips beside me as she slumps down into it.

I contemplate telling her that I'm fine. That seeing Henley last night has had little effect on my existence.

But that would be a big fat lie.

"Not really. I called in sick to work today. The idea of being right there in the building across the street from where he is just felt like too much." I don't want to admit that I'm running away from my problems, but today that's exactly what I'm doing.

Liv offers a sympathetic frown. "That sucks."

One of the things I love about Liv is that she's real. She's always telling it like it is. Sometimes there's no use trying to put a positive spin on something. And she's right. It does suck.

"Yeah," I agree.

"You want to hang out and watch TV or something? I'm meant to be meeting my dad for lunch in Little Bay, but I can take a raincheck. Or…" Hope crosses her expression as she tilts her head to the side. "You could come with me?"

I force a smile, but it comes off as weak. I appreciate that she's offering me a distraction but sitting with my sadness feels necessary. "You're the best. You really are. But I think I kind of need some time alone to process this."

She nods. Another thing I love about Liv is that she knows when not to push. She wraps an arm around my shoulder.

"He doesn't deserve you."

I stifle a sob. "Thanks for coming by."

"Of course. I'm around if you need me."

"Okay." I force another sad smile in her direction that I know she sees straight through.

With a gentle rub of my shoulder, she rises from the couch and exits my apartment, leaving me alone in a sea of thoughts.

When I close my eyes, I see Henley's glassy, ice blue stare. I wonder, for the millionth time why he left. Where he's been spending this time and who he might have possibly spent it with.

And I wonder what has led him back here.

I last another ten minutes on the couch before the walls of the apartment begin to close in on me, the atmosphere stifling. I slip on a pair of slides, desperate to overcome this sudden onset of claustrophobia. I start to walk, not really knowing where I'm going, and if I'm honest, not really caring where I end up.

An indistinct period of time passes before I find myself at the secluded inlet on the river, my bare feet sinking into its sandy banks. My internal compass still leads me here sometimes. Even after everything, I can't leave it behind.

I climb up onto the large flat rock and perch upon its smooth surface. This giant piece of stone we had once called ours. The tyre swing still hangs from the old elm tree, its rope frayed in places from years of use. That tree will stand tall until long after we're gone, a lifetime of memories held in its trunk.

Even though it's the last thing I want to remember right now, my mind takes me back to the first time I ever came here. I was sixteen and we were in the middle of one of the most scorching heatwaves this town has ever seen. The temperature had reached more than forty degrees Celsius for the fourth day in a row, meaning school had been suspended.

After almost a week at home, I'd become a bored and restless teen in need of an outlet, which coupled with the heat, had probably been the reason I'd had a fight with my mum about something stupid. We didn't often argue, and I couldn't for the life of me remember what we had fought about, but I must have done something bad because she had grounded me. A rare occurrence for sure.

Mum wasn't the best with discipline. In fairness to her, I rarely needed to be reprimanded, but in this instance, she'd felt the need to banish me to my room, completely overlooking the fact that I still had my phone. One of my high school besties, Leah, had suggested a trip to the river over text and I defiantly, and uncharacteristically, climbed out of my open bedroom window and joined her and four other girlfriends in cooling off in the still waters.

Leah's boyfriend, Matt and a bunch of other guys from school had the same plan. That was the appeal, I guess, even if we didn't care to admit it at the time. When we'd arrived, scantily clad in our favourite bikinis, to find that there was an additional member in the boys' group, not one of us could keep our eyes off the new guy. Not even Leah, much to Matt's disappointment. But I knew that it wasn't in my imagination that his attention was focused squarely on me.

I'd been standing waist deep in the river when he'd waded through the shallows to me, oozing confidence and charisma. He'd greeted me with a handshake, an act I'd thought oddly mature for a sixteen-year-old boy. Still, when he'd held out his hand and said, "I'm Alex," it wasn't just the summer heat that had me melting.

I'd taken his hand silently, an unintentionally flirty smirk playing on my lips as I met his gaze. I could never forget the affect his stare had on me from that very first day. His eyes a bright crystal blue that burned like the hottest of flames, tarnished with rebellion and all the broken hearts he's surely left in his wake.

I knew better than to give into a guy with a perfect pair of baby blues though. My mother had raised me better than that.

She'd drilled into me from a young age that a man needed to show his worth. *Make him earn it*, she would say.

So, without bothering to tell him my own name, I flashed him a wicked grin, then placed my hands on his chest. His smooth tanned skin formed goosebumps under my fingertips, despite the heat of the day, as I shoved him backwards into the river. I paddled away, only glancing back once I reached the shore. If his eyes hadn't turned my legs to jelly, the grin that he aimed at me had surely finished the job.

I could say those days were simple, but nothing between Henley and I has ever been simple.

I hear the rustling of leaves and the crunching of small twigs behind me, and a sense of nostalgia washes over me. I don't need to turn around. I know it's him.

He steps up onto the rock, then I feel the familiar warmth of his body next to mine as he sits down beside me.

"You still come here." It isn't a question.

"Sometimes," I admit quietly.

"There are so many memories here," he says, running a hand through his hair. I feel his gaze on me, but I don't dare look at him. "Good ones."

"And not so good ones," I counter.

I see him give a subtle nod in my periphery. He knows just as well as I do that of all the moments we've shared in this very spot, not all of them have been happy. Sometimes with passion came volatility. We've had hard times, although none of those moments had ever come close to being as difficult as the one we've found ourselves in right now.

"I prefer to focus on the good ones." He slides his palms down his thighs and pulls his knees into his chest, closing himself off to me.

I turn to him and something in the way he looks at me makes it easy to want to remember only those good moments, to block out all of the bad. I'm shaken by how much I long to wrap my arms around him, to have him hold me back.

Then I remember what got us into this mess and I'm struck with the urge to punch him.

"Why did you leave me, Alex?" I whisper, my eyebrows pulling down in a frown.

His chest rises with a heavy breath. "It's complicated."

His response only fuels my anger. "So uncomplicate it," I shout, throwing my arms up in frustration, my voice carrying across the river.

I really do want to understand why he decided to leave me, even though knowing could kill me.

I inhale, hoping to calm myself down and then I add, softer this time, "There has to be a reason you left me right after asking me to move in with you."

He raises his gaze to mine, and I'm met with eyes full of sorrow, a kaleidoscope of blue. "Kristen, I never meant to hurt you. If I could take it all back, I would."

"You haven't answered my question."

He sighs and then draws his knees in closer to his chest, like a little boy being scolded by a school teacher. He's withdrawing himself from this conversation.

From me.

I lose my last shred of patience.

"You know, after my dad left us and I saw how distraught my mother was, I made a vow to myself that I would never let a guy break my heart. Sure, maybe it would bleed a little. Get a few cracks. But I'd never let anyone tear it wide open."

He searches my face, his breath quickening as my eyes begin to well. I blink and a lone tear breaks free, tracking its way down my cheek.

I swallow, swiftly wiping it away as I push my emotions down. "But you did it, Alex. You broke my heart."

Chapter 21

HENLEY

Kristen and I were never inseparable in the beginning. But though our love was chaotic, it was also unwavering. We'd ended things more times than I could count. We'd seen other people, but we always wound up right back in each other's arms. I don't know how to love anybody else the way I know I love Kristen Riley.

And that kills me because I know now without any doubt in my mind that I can't fix this.

It's been three days since I saw her at the river.

Three days since I'd witnessed firsthand the pain that I inflicted upon her.

Three days since the last flicker of hope I held onto faded to black.

Deep down, I've known it's been over between us for good since the day I left. I know what a fool I've been for even entertaining the possibility that we could ever move past this. That there was ever a chance in hell that she'd forgive me for the biggest mistake I've ever made.

Because I am a mess.

I'm the product of all of my mistakes and regrets. I've confirmed everything I've ever believed about myself to be true. That I'll never be worthy of the love of a successful, intelligent woman like Kristen. That there's nothing I could ever do to redeem myself. Nothing I could ever do to deserve her.

That hasn't stopped me from sitting here on the couch, hopelessly spaced out, replaying our conversation at the river in my mind. I've contemplated every alternate scenario, imagined every parallel universe, tortured myself with the 'what if's and 'if only's.

I'd wanted to explain everything, but my lungs had begun to burn, my heart caught in my chest like a ticking time bomb, rendering me speechless the same way it always does. I can't talk about that day. My mind won't let me.

Mackenzie's footsteps fall on the stairs to the loft and then she wanders into the apartment, her shoulders seemingly slumped in defeat as she shrugs off her cardigan and slings it over the back of one of the dining chairs. I track her as she walks to the kitchenette and silently pours herself a coffee from the percolator.

She gets like this sometimes. Stuck in her own head. And I know if I don't drag her outside of herself, she'll spiral into her own negativity.

I put my issues with Kristen on the backburner. They'll have to wait until I sort whatever is going on with Mackenzie out.

"How's the job hunting going?" I ask, my tone so cheerfully fake it's a wonder she doesn't call me on my bullshit right here and now.

She startles, as though she's just realised I've been sitting here this whole time.

"Not great," she says as she moves toward me.

She flops down on the couch next to me, almost spilling the giant mug of coffee she's nursing. She pulls it to her lips and takes a long draw from it.

"I honestly don't know how you drink that stuff," I say to her, light-heartedly. "It's fucking terrible."

She narrows her eyes at me, a compelling death stare if I've ever seen one, but she remains quiet. Mackenzie has this tough girl vibe going for her. She's a lot like Kristen in that way. She's seemed happier since we left Coledale, as though a weight has been lifted from her shoulders.

But not today.

Today she wears a frown, much like the one I'd seen when we met.

"What's going on with you?" I drape my arm around the back of the couch, giving her shoulder a gentle nudge in the process.

"What do you mean?" She's expressionless as she stares into the muddy brown liquid in the cup nestled in her lap.

"You're chewing on your bottom lip. It's a dead giveaway," I say.

Kristen does that too.

She sighs and then looks up at the roof. Her phone vibrates from the arm of the couch, and she snaps it up instantly.

"Who is that?"

She doesn't answer. She purses her lips and drops her gaze to the floor.

"It's him. Isn't it?" It's not really a question. It's obvious to me from her reaction who's texting her. I'm sure now that it's also the reason for the sullen mood she's in. "Please tell me you haven't replied."

"Of course not." The look she throws my way is one of offence. "I'm not a complete moron."

"Let me see your phone." I hold out my hand and she reluctantly slaps the phone into my palm.

I immediately drop it into her half full coffee mug. Some of the liquid splashes onto her lap, leaving tiny brown splotches.

"Are you kidding me?" she yells.

"It had to be done," I say, my tone serious. "You know what could happen if he finds us."

"I know. I get it, okay?" She sighs, running a hand through her long blonde waves. "But you owe me a new phone."

I breathe a deep sigh. It was wrong of me to question Mackenzie's judgement. Obviously, she knows the full extent of the situation we've found ourselves in and now I feel guilty for destroying her phone. I realise that a replacement is going to seriously cut into my savings, but I can't stand to see her upset. Not after all she's been through. Besides, she needs a way to contact me. I pull myself from the sofa and grab my keys from the small, round dining table.

"Where are you going?" she demands.

"To get you a phone."

Normally there's nothing I loathe more than visiting the mall, but I welcome the distraction. Getting out might help clear my head.

"You're infuriating." She groans and her eyes roll so far back in her head I can only see the whites for a split second.

"Maybe I am. But it's only because I care," I say sincerely.

She looks up at me, her glare softening. "Yeah, I know," she resigns.

"You want to come with me?"

"No, thanks," she replies. "I'm beat. Going to see what's new on Netflix."

"Suit yourself," I say.

I'm inwardly relieved that Mackenzie has chosen not to take me up on my offer. The town is surely swirling with rumours of my return by now and the last thing I need is to be seen in public with the new girl.

Mackenzie flicks the remote and the television screen comes to life. I shake my head, a slight grin forming on my lips when I notice she's created her own profile on my Netflix account.

"Be careful," she calls over her shoulder. "Looks like a storm's about to roll in."

Chapter 22

KRISTEN

"Hello. Earth to Kristen." Chase's voice permeates my thoughts and I look up at him, aware now that he's been trying to get my attention. "What's going on?"

"Huh?" I mumble. "Sorry. What were you saying?"

"I said that what Mr. Abbott said was really interesting in that last seminar. It kind of makes you think about the relationship between dissociative identity disorder and people with borderline personality…" I look up again when I hear him trail off. "Seriously. What is going on with you?"

"Nothing. I'm fine."

"Really?" Chase arches an eyebrow. There's no use in trying to disguise my mood from Chase. He's always been able to read me. "Well, you've been pushing those salad leaves around with your fork for the last ten minutes without taking a bite. To be honest, I'm kind of offended that you find your leafy greens more exciting than the conversation I'm trying to have with you, but you know, whatever. I'll save my tears for my pillow tonight."

I manage a laugh at his witty attempt to humour me.

In all honesty, I hadn't heard much of Mr. Abbott's lecture. Mentally, I was still stuck on that rock by the river with Henley. Since then, I've been navigating my life on autopilot, unable to get him out of my head.

"I'm sorry," I say apologetically. "I've got a lot on my mind, I guess."

"Like…" Chase prompts me.

I sigh, combing a tendril of hair behind my ear. "I saw Henley."

"Where?" he asks, confusion passing over his face.

"At the river. Well, I saw him at the tavern first. He's living there." I continue to absentmindedly stir my salad around in the plastic takeout container.

"He's living in a bar?" Chase has lowered his burger to the table now, completely intrigued by what I'm telling him.

"No," I say. "Well, yeah. I mean, there's an apartment above the bar and he's living there."

"Wow." He pauses, allowing what I'm telling him to sink in. "So, he's back, huh?"

I nod, letting out a breath. "Looks like it."

"How do you feel about it?" he asks.

"Look, we don't have to talk about this. If it's weird for you…" I begin.

"Kristen, no." Chase cuts me off with the wave of his hand. "It's not weird. You don't have to feel like you can't talk about him with me."

"Okay," I say.

"Look, I know things didn't work out between us. But I'm always going to care about you."

The 'things' Chase is referring to happen to be our failed attempt at a relationship. A couple of months after Henley had left, Chase declared his feelings for me. Turns out Liv wasn't that far off the mark when she called it after seeing him at the Haven that day.

We'd gone on a few dates, which lead to a make-out session at his place. However, it lacked in heat, and we realised that we were ultimately better off as friends. It probably didn't help that Henley was always there, in the back of my mind.

"I'm not going back to him," I say, my tone defiant.

I don't miss the way his shoulders slump with relief as I say this, as though all the tension in him depended on this confirmation.

"What you do is your choice," he says, softly, his eyes kind. "I just don't want to see you get hurt again."

"I know," I tell him, my lips curving upwards in a small smile. "You're a good friend, Chase. But honestly, I'm not even sure that I'm the reason he came back."

"He'd be crazy not to want you back. But if you ask me, he doesn't deserve you."

"Yeah," I agree. He doesn't have to tell me twice. I know my worth. A huge part of me wants nothing to do with Henley, but I'd be lying if I said there wasn't another part of me that's drawn to him. A piece of my heart that will always belong to him. "I think I'm gonna skip the next lecture. My brain doesn't seem to be cooperating a whole lot today."

"That's understandable," Chase says sympathetically. "I can email you the cliff notes."

"You're the best, Chase. I'll see you tomorrow."

I force a smile as I stand up, taking the remnants of my salad and throwing them into the trash can on the way to my car. I slump down into the driver's seat and slide the key into the ignition.

When I attempt to start the car, it turns over repeatedly. I try again. And then again, but still the car won't start.

Damnit. What else could go wrong?

"This fucking car!" I shout, slamming my hands onto the steering wheel.

This little 1994 Mazda has gotten me from A to B for the last six years. I was really hoping it would survive to get me through my degree, but lately it's been showing signs of intense wear and tear. Ben had been warning me for the last month that something didn't sound right under the hood. I really should have taken his advice more seriously.

I blow out a frustrated sigh and squeeze my eyes shut. "Please start," I whisper, knowing how insane I am for pleading with a heap of metal. "Please, please, please."

The key clicks in the ignition and I wait with bated breath until I finally hear the engine turn over. "Oh, thank God."

I'm so grateful for the purring of the engine, I'm only mildly put off by the subtle tinkering undertones. All I really want to do is put on a pair of cosy pyjamas and crawl into bed with a good book.

I make it halfway home before I hear a clunk and a rattling sound coming from under the bonnet. A few seconds later torrents of steam spew upward from the hood, clouding my view of the road. I veer off to the side, coming to a dead stop.

God damn this car. It's bad enough that the air con gave out on me last week. Now it's rendered me stranded roughly ten kilometres from town on a dirt road in the middle of nowhere. I regret not taking Chase up on his offer to carpool with him to the university today. I could have avoided this situation entirely. Or at least prolonged it.

I exit the vehicle, stepping out into the heat. Somehow, it's even hotter outside of the car, the humidity clinging to my skin. The sky has begun to darken overhead, a distant rumble of thunder warning of an imminent storm.

I lift the hood on this heap of junk that's even older than I am, then circling the car I go to the boot and retrieve the old rag I keep for this very situation. I can't wait till I can afford a reliable car. How much simpler life would be. I twist open the radiator cap.

No coolant.

I might not have had a father to teach me how to navigate these kinds of situations, but I picked up plenty of mechanical skills over the years from Steve and, more recently, Ben. This old bomb has a history of overheating. I know the drill.

I swipe the sweat off my brow with my forearm and bend over the bonnet. The car needs to cool off before I can replace the coolant. I guess I have no choice but to wait it out, which wouldn't be a problem if it weren't for the increasing thunder.

Lightning strikes somewhere in the east. I reach through the unwound window into the passenger seat and retrieve my phone, hoping Ben might answer my call. No such luck. He'd probably be too busy at work to pick me up right now anyway.

I've been leaning on the passenger door for no more than five minutes when a familiar black, Ford ranger approaches. It slows down and I let out a groan when I see its hazard lights begin to blink, a burning orange against the grey backdrop of the blackening sky.

I swear this day couldn't get any worse.

He pulls over behind my car, then steps out onto the road, a cloud of dust pluming around his sneakers. I look away when I see him, gritting my teeth so hard it's a wonder my jaw doesn't become locked in position.

"Are you okay?" he asks.

"I was fine until you showed up." I know my reaction is childish. I've never had the finest defence mechanisms.

He ignores me, walking around to the front end of the car to survey the damage. I dare a glance at him and regret it instantly. He rests both hands on the raised hood of the car, his t-shirt riding up to reveal hard, toned abs. My mind fills in all the blanks involuntarily, reminding me of what's underneath that white fabric. The large tattoo that winds its way up the side of his rib cage, spanning one side of his broad chest before wrapping around the muscles in his left arm. He's wearing his favourite red baseball cap backwards, strands of blonde flicking out from underneath.

"Coolant is empty."

"No shit, Sherlock," I reply, bitterly. Frustrated, I fold my arms across my chest. "I've got some in the back. I've got it covered. You can leave now."

I know even as I say this that Henley isn't going to leave me out here all alone, no matter how much I wish he would. He may have left me six months ago, but my instincts are telling me that he hasn't completely lost his heart.

"I hate to tell you this, but I think you might have bigger problems."

"Oh yeah?" I question sarcastically. "Like what? My one true love rolling back into town after ruining my life? Yeah, I'd say you're right."

I watch as he takes in an uneven breath, a sadness filling his eyes. My words have hurt him but so they should. I want him to fall apart the way that I did when he walked out on me.

"Your radiator's completely shot." His voice is low as he turns his attention back to the car. "Possibly the whole engine."

"Great," I mutter.

I desperately want him to be wrong, but I can't deny that Henley knows his way around a car. The guy has multiple unfinished apprenticeships under his belt and although he could never seem to see any of them through to completion, it kind of made him a bit of a jack of all trades.

"Look, I'm heading back into town. I can give you a ride," he offers. There's no emotion in the way he speaks, his actions conveying nothing. "We can call for a tow truck when we get there."

I bark out a laugh. "*We?* No. *We* aren't doing anything. I'm not going anywhere with you."

"Suit yourself. But there's a nasty storm on the way."

"I'd rather be hit by lightning than spend a second in that car with you." I throw the hood down and grab my bag from inside. Then I storm off in the direction of Cliff Haven. Thunder roars overhead as heavy drops of rain begin to fall, speckling my tank top with wet streaks.

"Kristen." Henley pleads from behind me. "Let's just go."

"I told you I'm fine," I say boldly.

"Look, you've made your point." He pauses to rearrange his cap the right way around on his head. "You're an independent strong woman that doesn't need saving."

"That's your only takeaway from all of this?" I shout over the increasing rainfall.

"No. I get it. You hate me," Henley cries out. "But I'm not leaving you out here!"

"You've never had an issue with leaving me before," I call back over my shoulder, and then he's standing in front of me, his hand on my left bicep.

I stare at his fingers wrapped around my arm and when he removes them the heat remains, as though his fingerprints have been etched into my skin. My chest heaves as I raise my gaze to his.

Big mistake.

His irises are more potent than I remember, clearer than the bluest of oceans. He frowns and I see a sincerity within them that shakes me, an unexpected honesty.

I see the old Henley. Somehow, somewhere underneath all this bravado he's still in there. His shoulders hunch as he sighs. "Please, Kris. Get in the car."

We're both drenched, the rain falling faster and harder now, but I'm too stubborn to back down from this fight. Maybe we both are. Because as I try to push past him, he bends, throwing his arms around my thighs and hoisting me over his shoulder.

"Put me down!" I yell, although I know that at this point it's useless.

He strides toward his car, pulls open the passenger door, then gently lowers me to the ground. He holds his arms out around me, one resting on the open door, the other on the back passenger door to block me in. His eyebrows are raised in defiance. He has me trapped and he knows it.

I groan and then surrender, climbing into the passenger seat. I consider jumping out as he rounds the back of the car, but I know my efforts would be futile. There's no way he'll leave me out here and, although I'd never admit it to him, I'm relieved that he came along.

And that relief has everything to do with the fact that I'm no longer caught in a rainstorm ten kilometres out of town and nothing to do with the heat that radiates from him as he climbs into the driver's seat. Nor does it have anything to do with the familiar scent that fills his car or the way his eyes travel from my dripping wet hair to the water that clings in beads to my chest.

His car is cleaner than I remember it, apart from a couple of cherry ripe wrappers scrunched up on the floor. A brand-new iPhone sits on the dash, still in its box.

Henley leans forward, stuffing the key in the ignition. He pauses, leaning back into the seat. A long sigh escapes him, and I dare a sideward glance. I've never seen him look so worn, so defeated.

I no longer see the fun-loving party boy I fell in love with all those years ago. I see a man exhausted, tired from carrying a load that's too much for him to bear.

Where have you been, Alex?

I tell myself I don't care. That whatever has happened to him is a result of a poor choice that he made. But still, a large part of me is curious about what has swallowed his light.

"Are you going to drive?" I say impatiently. "I don't want to be in this car any longer than necessary."

He looks over at me. For a second, I think he's going to come back with something witty like he would have done in the past, but his eyes go back to the road. He's hollow. He doesn't even have a comeback left in him. He turns the key. The engine roars to life.

We drive in silence, his gaze steady on the road in front and mine on the rain-soaked passenger window, a blur of green grass and grey skies flying past.

When we reach my apartment building, he pulls over on the curb, gently shutting off the ignition. I pause and turn to look at him, my hand firm on the door handle.

"Why can't you just tell me where you went?" I don't really expect an answer, though I ask anyway.

He still can't look at me. Can't or won't, it doesn't matter.

A loud clap of thunder roars from the sky and he flinches, his shoulders lifting, eyes shut tight. It's so unexpected and out of character for him, it has my forehead crumpling in confusion.

He inhales a sharp breath and turns to me, his eyes travelling over my face. "I'm sorry," he says in a low voice.

I'm reminded of the conversation I had with Chase earlier.

I'm not even sure I'm the reason he came back.

But now, I am sure.

Disappointment seeps into my veins, pushing away every trace of hope as I come to the realisation that although he has returned to Cliff Haven, Henley never had any intention of returning to me.

I've pictured the moment I'd see him again so many times and there isn't a scenario where I haven't imagined him grovelling at my feet. Begging me for another chance. But he made the decision to give up on us.

He's here and he isn't fighting for me.

There's no fight left in him at all.

Chapter 23

HENLEY

Kristen slams the car door and stalks off to her apartment, her hair thoroughly soaked and clinging to her damp shoulders. The way she hugs herself with her head bowed to the ground breaks me. All I want to do is scoop her up into my arms and tell her she's everything to me.

But she isn't mine anymore and that reality hits me like a kick to the gut.

She isn't the same anymore either. Another thing I wear the blame for. This bitter, scorned version of her, filled with angst, is one of my own creation.

Life has a way of fucking people over, but I can't blame my problems on circumstance. It's easy to believe that our fate is in the hands of someone else, but at some point, we need to stand up and take some responsibility.

Turns out I'm pretty good at screwing myself over too, because as she sat there right in this very seat next to me, waiting for me to say something that could erase all the pain I've put her through, whatever the hell that might be, I stayed silent and watched the hope in her eyes turn to hatred.

There's no worse sensation in this world than feeling worthless and that's exactly what I am now.

I'm both a helpless, inferior speck of nothing and a colossal waste of space.

Overwhelmed with emotion, I let the tears fall, my shoulders shaking as I sit hunched over the steering wheel.

This impenetrable shield I've built around myself has to go. I know that now. I know that if it stays, I'll be surrendering myself to a life of solitude.

And I don't want to be helpless.

I don't want to be a waste of space.

I want to fix everything. To cut out all the bad parts and paste the good ones back together again, constructing a perfect map of a happy life.

I know there's no easy solution to this mess, but I've been given a second chance and I have to take it. I owe it to Kristen to be better.

I owe it to myself.

And I owe it to Steve and Maggie.

I need Kristen in my life, because after knowing what it feels like to be loved by her, I know that life isn't worth living without her in it. Our relationship is going to take more than apologies to mend. Right now, I know she needs space so that's exactly what I'm going to give her.

In the meantime, I need a distraction. Something to keep me busy when all I want to do is go to her.

An idea begins to take shape in my mind. There may be no quick fix for me and Kristen, but there is a way that I can repay Maggie and Steve for their generosity. Or begin to at least.

I step on the accelerator and swing the car around. I need to make an extra stop at Bill's Hardware.

Chapter 24

KRISTEN

I enter the helpline office, forcing a smile at Jules before finding my desk. I seem to be doing that a lot lately. Forcing smiles. Faking pleasantries. Not that things were great before Henley showed back up in town, but I was starting to get used to existing without him. As unbearable as that notion felt to me, I was moving on.

I power on the computer and gaze out at the dark ocean below as I wait for it to load. I've been seated for close to ten minutes when the phone finally rings. I stare at it a moment, giving myself a chance to get out of my own head, to enter a mindset that will better equip me to help people that are potentially going through worse things than I could ever imagine.

That's the one thing I'm constantly reminding myself of these days. That whatever life has thrown at me, there are others that have been dealt a lesser hand.

"Cliff Haven helpline. You're speaking with Kristen." I wait, listening intently for a reply to come through from the other end.

"Finally," comes a sarcastic response. "I was beginning to think the place had shut down."

"Em." I smile at her cynicism. "I'm really glad you called."

It's been weeks since I've had her on the phone. I'm still disturbed by our previous chat, been haunted by all the things she didn't say.

"It's that boring at the helpline, huh?"

I'm so relieved to be speaking to her I can only laugh at her attempt at dry humour.

"No, I've been concerned about you," I say, honestly. "I feel like our last conversation took a dark turn."

"Welcome to my life," she mutters.

"We talked a lot about me last time. About my parents," I say gently. "I thought that maybe this time you could tell me about yours."

I hear her scoff. "My parents aren't worth talking about."

"Why do you say that?" I ask, careful not to press too hard.

"I don't even know my mother." Her casual tone is unnerving.

"So, you were raised by your father then?"

"If you can call it that." Her answer saddens me. Or maybe it's that I can sympathise with her.

"I take it he's played a bit of an absent role."

"I mean, physically he's there, but yeah. He's not really there." I pause, waiting for her to elaborate. She finally takes another breath before she blurts out, "He's drinks. A lot."

"I see."

"No. You don't."

"What?" I'm stunned by her blatant response.

"You have no idea what it's like." Her voice increases in volume. "Let's not do this whole thing where you pretend to understand what it's like to grow up with an alcoholic father."

"I'm sorry, Em. I didn't mean to upset you."

I realise now that I've made a serious error in telling Em personal details about my life. Regardless of the fact that I

153

broke protocol by doing so, I've given her fuel to use against me.

"You're lucky he left you," she spits. "It gave your mother the chance to meet a stand-up guy."

I'm speechless and it takes me a moment to realise she's referring to my own father's abandonment. Her words are as vicious as a slap in the face. I suddenly want out of this conversation. My reflexes take over and I slam the phone down in frustration.

"Kristen." I jump in my seat, realising Jules is standing close by, peering over my shoulder. "Everything okay?"

"Uh, yeah," I stammer. "Prank call."

"Ugh," she groans. "People can be so inconsiderate. Tying up the phone lines when other people are desperate to get through."

"Um, yeah," I agree. "It's a whole new level of selfishness, that's for sure."

I feel bad for the lie, but something about the conversation I'd just had with Em isn't sitting right with me at all and the last thing I want to do is admit to Jules that I've shared things I shouldn't have with this girl.

Jules drags a chair over from the space underneath the window and flops down onto it with the appropriate lack of energy a mother of a one-year-old should have.

"I wanted to talk to you real quick while things are quiet around here. James is going to take your incoming calls for the next couple of minutes."

"Oh. Okay." I say hesitantly, fearing that I'm in trouble. This is it. She knows I've broken protocol with Em. "Is… is everything okay?"

"Yeah, of course," she replies, looking up to where Chase sits on the far side of the room. "Chase, do you think you could come over here a moment?"

Chase gives a nod and then wheels another chair over from a nearby desk to the position beside me. Our schedules don't often allow us to share the same shifts, but tonight is an exception.

"Uh oh. Are we in trouble?" he jokes.

I know he's only kidding but the possibility makes me nervous anyway.

"No, of course not." Jules gives Chase a playful shove in the shoulder, and he grins. "The opposite actually! You guys have been doing a great job and I wanted to say that all the hours you've both been putting in are really appreciated."

I breathe a sigh of relief. "That's what we're here for. And of course, your efforts are appreciated too, Jules. We'd be lost without you."

"Thanks, Kristen." Jules gushes. "Just don't forget to let me know if it gets too much. This job can be really stressful, and I know everyone here has other commitments outside of this."

We both nod. "Of course," Chase says.

"Now, as you guys are probably aware," Jules continues, "the annual Cliff Haven carnival is coming up soon and this year the helpline will be holding a stall of its own to raise funds for new equipment."

"Wow, that's cool," I say.

"It's very cool. We're talking new desks, a few extra chairs and most importantly, headsets."

"Ooh, fancy." Chase wiggles an eyebrow up and down and gives me a wink.

"Exactly," Jules agrees with a chuckle. "We'll no longer have to use these phones that look like they come from the stone age. And it also means we might be able to take on more volunteers and therefore, help more people."

"That's great, Jules!" I'm genuinely excited to see the helpline get an upgrade. It's become a cause close to my heart. "If there's anything I can do, I'd love to be involved."

"Yeah, me too." Chase pipes up from beside me.

"Good, because that's exactly what I wanted to talk to you about," Jules says, a sense of relief washing over her features. "The thing is, I'm having trouble coming up with ideas on how we can raise the money. James suggested a car wash, but we don't really have easy access to water on site. It has to be something fairly simple."

I chew on my bottom lip, mulling over some ideas in my head. "Well, what about a bake sale?" I offer. "I work at the Haven café and I'm sure my boss would be happy to donate some baked sweets. I bet she'd even let me use the commercial ovens after hours to make a few things. Muffins, cakes, that sort of thing."

"Sounds perfect," Chase approves. "And we could maybe run a raffle. See if a few local businesses will donate a couple of prizes."

"Yes! I bet Ben would donate some vouchers for Ben's Harvest. He's always been big on donating to charity," I suggest.

"I knew you guys would be good at this," Jules says, rubbing her hands together with glee. "I just have one more favour to ask."

"What is it?" we both ask in unison.

"James and I can run the stall in the morning, but neither of us are available to run it from the late afternoon into the night. Is there any chance you guys might be able to help us out?"

"Not a problem," I say. "I can do it."

"Yeah," Chase shifts in his chair beside me. "I can be there too."

"Okay. That's awesome. James and I can run the stall from say, nine to three? And then you guys can take over from there. I think it ends around ten."

"No problem at all," Chase says.

"The other thing I wanted to mention is that as of next week the helpline is going to serve as a collection point for food and essential items for the homeless. We'll be liaising with the homeless shelter in Little Bay to get items to the people who really need them."

"That's awesome," I comment.

I remember back to the time when my mother and I had fled our hometown with little but the clothing on our backs to start our new life in Cliff Haven. We were better off than a lot of others, but we still spent a few nights sleeping in the car and even had a few hot meals in the women's shelter in Little Bay before Mum found us a house to rent.

"It's a great initiative," Jules agrees. "But it means more work for us. Compiling things into hampers, transporting the items over there, it will all be quite time-consuming. So, I'll be putting out the feelers for a few extra volunteers to assist but I might need you guys to be prepared to help sort things."

"No worries. Sounds like a plan," Chase says.

"Anyway, that's all I needed to tell you. Great work, team. I'll let you get back to it."

After Jules and Chase both wander back to their desks, I sit and think of all the recipes I can make to earn money for the helpline.

I'm grateful for the distraction this new task has given me. Maybe I'll be able to keep Henley out of my head for more than a few seconds.

I form a list of baked items in my head. Strawberry danish, almond friands and passionfruit slice. Banana muffins are always a hit at the café and people love my chocolate brownies.

Henley loved my chocolate brownies.

Damnit.

I couldn't go more than ten seconds without him intruding on my thoughts.

And still, the conversation I had with Em is playing on my mind. Whenever I think I'm making progress with that girl we end up taking three steps backward.

But this time was different than all the others. The viciousness in her tone, the accusatory nature of her dialogue. I've been unable to put my finger on why it has me so rattled.

And then it hits me.

You're lucky he left you. It gave your mother a chance to meet a stand-up guy.

What she said isn't untrue.

But I never once mentioned to her that my mother had met another man.

Chapter 25

HENLEY

Fuck. I wish this loft apartment didn't have a direct view into the Haven.

I awoke at four this morning, which is better than yesterday's 2:30am. I used my insomnia to my advantage though, spending hours lugging the paint cans, screws and nails, cleaning supplies and random tools I'd purchased from Bill's hardware yesterday into the abandoned room downstairs.

I sat for another hour, formulating a plan to repair the damaged drywall and locating phone numbers on Google for a good local window repairer. I began cleaning up some of the broken glass and debris but left the room before Dylan began his shift.

I think it's safe to say he doesn't have a high opinion of me. I'm pretty sure he wouldn't approve of my extra-curricular activities, although he probably doesn't even know that room exists. Nevertheless, I figured it's best to keep my plans a secret.

Today is my day off and I'm restless to say the least. Since returning to the loft, I've spent the better part of the morning sitting by the window watching as Kristen greets customers with her perfect smile, probably asking them about their day and making them feel like a million bucks because that's what Kristen does.

She makes people happy. She gives them a sense of worth. At least, that's what she'd always done for me, even when it was the last thing I deserved.

My phone echoes from somewhere on the other side of the room. When I finally find it smothered in my unmade bed sheets, I see that it's Katie calling. My sister has been ignoring my calls since I returned to town so there's something unsettling about seeing her number displayed on the screen. I swipe the answer key and hold the phone to my ear.

"Hey, Katie."

"Hi," she says, her voice clipped.

"I've been trying to call you," I say. "I guess Dad told you I'm back in town. I'm living in the…"

"Yeah, that's great, Alex," she says, cutting me off. "Look, I'm only calling to tell you to back off, okay?"

"Back off?" I ask, genuinely confused. "What do you mean 'back off'?"

"Please don't take this the wrong way. It's just that word has started to circulate about you being back in town and I can't have it affecting my business."

"Your business," I parrot dumbly.

"Yeah," she sighs. "I'm kind of a high-profile real estate agent now and I can't be drawing negative attention."

I slump back down into the chair by the window, running a hand down my face. "I see."

"I'm really glad that you're okay. It's just that…"

"You're worried I'll make you look bad." It's my turn to cut her off.

"Alex."

"No, I get it. Don't worry. I won't bother you anymore."

I abruptly end the call and peg the phone across the room, watching as it bounces off the dresser in the corner.

I don't know why I'm surprised. This is what happens when you bring shame upon your family.

Now I'm both reckless and pissed off. I know I can't really blame Katie for not wanting to interact with me. Thousands in her position would do the same.

I look back out the window at Kristen again. At the way she beams at Mr. Henderson and his dog. I keep watching her, hoping that if I stare at her long enough, the smile she wears will replace the vision of the scowl she'd aimed at me in the car. Since our encounter yesterday, it's all I can see. The resignation in her eyes expressing the words she couldn't say.

That she's completely given up on me.

With nothing to keep my hands busy I feel like I'm going insane. I don't want to sit still. My fingers tap the edge of the windowsill, a habit I formed the moment I decided to learn the drums. I shift slightly, my eyes landing on the drum kit in the corner of the loft.

I need to play.

I know Dylan will be pissed at me if it bothers the handful of customers downstairs, but the sweet release I know it will give me to play outweighs the risk. I need to hit something and better it be this instrument than anything else. I'm full of pent-up aggression and this is the safest way to get it out of me.

I collect a pair of sticks from the top drawer of my dresser and take a seat on the stool. I stare at the kit in front of me, knowing full well it's going to sound like shit, and not just because Kristen attacked the bass drum with her boot, but because it's been over six months since I've played. But this instrument has always been an escape for me, a way to

161

transport my mind somewhere else, and in this moment, I crave it.

I tap the drums randomly, getting a feel for their sound again. Then I form a beat. It's slightly out of time at first, but I soon get a feel for the rhythm again as the tempo builds.

Drumming provides the perfect distraction, filling my head with a myriad of things all at once. A drummer's mind is always ahead. Always thinking about where the next fill or roll needs to be, which beat and which drums need to be played. When I'm drumming my mind is never in the present moment and that's exactly what I need right now.

I allow the beat to take over me as sweat begins to bead on my forehead. I smile at the familiar ache that burns through my arms and close my eyes, letting the world fall away.

I become so immersed that at first, I don't hear the shouting. My eyes snap open. And then I see her, waving her arms around, an expression of hostility marring her beautiful features. I lose my grip on the sticks, and they fall to the ground with a clatter.

"What the hell are you doing, Alex?" Kristen stands in front of the drum kit, her hands on her hips. A stance I'm familiar with. She'd always held this position when she was mad at me for something. "You're scaring away customers from the café. It's senior's day, for Christ's sake! Not to mention, Dylan's pissed about the noise too."

Unexpectedly, my lips twitch up in a smirk. I can't help it. She's cute when she's angry and I've missed it.

"Sorry," I manage. "I'll stop."

"Good," she mutters, running a hand through her long, dark hair. "Sounded like shit anyway."

"Really?" I scoff. "Might have something to do with the fact that you kicked the crap out of the bass drum."

"I didn't," she argues, her eyebrows raised in defiance.

"No?" I question, my grin widening.

"I threw a chair at it," she deadpans.

"Oh, I see." I nod, my gaze meeting hers. The glimmer of a smile twists her lips ever so slightly. "And you enjoyed that, didn't you?"

"I did," she admits smugly.

I nod again. "Okay. I deserve that."

"Oh, you deserve a whole lot more." She storms toward me, full of fiery anger, until her face is mere inches from mine.

My grin fades when I see the hostility she aims at me. "You don't have to worry. I've already paid the ultimate price."

She takes a step back, her gaze falling to the floor.

"Okay. I'll bite. What would that be?" she asks, not meeting my eyes.

I move closer to her, noticing the way her chest heaves as I close the space between us. "You."

"You still haven't told me where you've been." Her nostrils flare, her jaw jutting out in anger.

I've been to hell and back, I want to tell her. I've been to places you couldn't even imagine.

Instead, I simply shrug. "It doesn't matter."

"It matters to me," she says through gritted teeth.

I sigh, combing a hand through my hair as I turn and step toward the kitchenette. "I was in a place. A town. About four hours' drive from here."

"And what did you find there that was worth giving up your entire life?" Kristen glares at me, her arms crossed over her chest.

"I told you. It's complicated."

She shakes her head, clearly fed up with my lack of transparency and then starts for the stairs. I reach for her wrist. She pauses at my touch, spinning slowly back around. I know I should let her go, but I don't want to.

"Give me a chance," I plead softly. "I'll try to explain."

And in that moment, I actually believe that I can.

That I'll be able to get the words out before the panic sets in. Before my chest begins to burn, my lungs collapsing in on themselves as though they're allergic to air.

My hands instinctively reach behind me to grab at the counter, a desperate effort to keep me from hitting the floor too hard. The colour leaves Kristen's face as I slide down onto the tiles, the kitchen cabinet behind me bearing the full brunt of my weight. I pull my knees into my chest, burying my head between them, and I try to remember how to breathe.

"Henley?" Kristen is kneeling in front of me now. I'm aware of her hands on my shoulders, her fingers in my hair, although I can only vaguely feel her touch. "What's happening?"

I squeeze my eyes shut, unable to respond.

"Just breathe," she encourages.

I'm not sure how many moments pass before the darkness clears.

"I'm sorry," I say, breathlessly. "I'm sorry. I'm sorry. I'm so sorry for everything."

She takes my head in her hands, her palms soft as they stroke my face. "Henley, what just happened?" she whispers. "Are you okay?"

No. Not at all.

"Yeah." My voice comes out raspy as she wipes a tear from the corner of my eye that I didn't realise I'd shed.

"Does this happen often?" Her hazel eyes are greener in the sunlight that streams through the open window.

"Sometimes," I admit.

I know how helpless I must look to her right now, how unworthy of her attention. Which is why I'm so confused by what happens next.

Her palm, still resting on my jaw, moves downward to my chest, coming to rest in place over my heart The warmth of her touch calms me in ways nothing else can.

She leans in, her breath dancing on my cheek. When her lips graze mine, it's so good it hurts, because I fear the emptiness when she finally pulls away.

But she doesn't pull away.

She presses her lips to mine, her fingers weaving through my hair as my hands find their way to her hips. I pull her onto my lap and she crushes her body against mine, the kiss becoming deeper and more urgent.

I don't deserve this. I know that. But I can't stop myself from taking what isn't mine. What I've longed for all this time. My hand slides to the nape of her neck, my mouth trailing downward greedily, the billowing scent of her shampoo intoxicating.

We're so lost within each other that we don't hear the footsteps that climb the staircase into the loft.

"Alex, I got milk like you asked and …" a familiar female voice begins. "Oh."

Kristen looks up in time to see Mackenzie standing in the doorway, a set of keys in one hand, a carton of milk in the other. She slowly rises to her feet, realisation dawning in her expression as she takes in her surroundings. It doesn't take a psychic to understand what she must be thinking.

She surveys the loft, the assortment of hair ties on the dresser in the corner, the women's cardigan draped over one of the dining chairs, before her line of sight finally falls on the far wall, where the only bed in the apartment is situated. Her hand flies to her forehead. "God. I'm such an idiot."

"Kristen," I say breathlessly. "This isn't what you think."

"I can't do this." She shakes her head in anguish.

And then she turns and bolts for the stairs, leaving me cold and empty, a pathetic mess on the kitchenette floor.

Chapter 26

KRISTEN

There's someone else. There's always been someone else. There's *still* someone else.

Of course, it makes perfect sense. As much as I'd tried not to, over these past six months, I'd allowed myself to imagine what Henley was doing, and who he might be doing it with. But seeing him playing house with some other woman in the loft yesterday had torn open a wound I've been struggling to heal for so long now.

To say I was blindsided by what happened with Henley would be an understatement. I'm not even sure what did actually happen. I know that Professor Abbott would call it a textbook panic attack.

All the signs were there. The trembling of his hands, the way he struggled for breath, the rapid pounding of his heart under my palm.

I've never known Henley to be an anxious person. If anything, he was the opposite. Always the strong one, stubborn, independent.

I didn't storm into Henley's loft yesterday intent on making out with him but the way he crumpled to the ground in his tiny kitchen, so helpless and afraid, conjured up a fear

I never knew existed within me. And I'd caved in a moment of weakness, lured by the warmth of his skin under my touch.

What alarms me even more is knowing that this has become a regular occurrence for him, and I can't help being curious about why. As frustrated as I am with him for his indiscretion about his new girlfriend, I can't deny the way my own heartrate increased at the sight of his suffering.

I keep trying to push my feelings down, to remind myself that whatever mess he got himself into is no longer my problem, but I can't help that Alex Henley is ingrained within every fibre of my being. Caring for him is second nature to me and, unfortunately, a strange blonde woman isn't going to change that. Apparently, him leaving me for someone else in a town four hours away isn't either.

Call me a glutton for punishment.

I've seen her before, I realise. The woman from the loft. I couldn't put my finger on it at first. But those wild, blonde waves had captured my attention the day I saw her at the Haven. And like an idiot, I'd given her that plate of pastries. I'd foolishly thought she was someone that needed help and here she was hooking up with my ex.

My phone purrs from underneath the couch cushion. I'd stuffed it under there this morning after what must have been Henley's sixty-seventh attempt to contact me. His calls and texts have been coming for the better part of last night and this morning. Though I hate to admit it, they're getting harder to ignore with every second.

I tap my pen anxiously on the crisp, white pages of the textbook in my lap. I've been sitting here on the couch for over an hour now, though I've long given up on absorbing any of its information. There's no point when my mind is elsewhere.

The phone stops ringing.

I stop tapping the pen.

The phone starts ringing again.

It's obvious he isn't going to quit, at least not until I shut him down for good. A defeated sigh escapes me, and I toss the textbook aside. I reach one arm underneath the couch cushion, digging until I retrieve my phone.

"What do you want, Henley?"

"Kristen." He sounds breathless as he says my name and it takes me back to that moment in his kitchen, his chest rising and falling as he fought to get air into his lungs. "I need to see you. I'm at our spot by the river. Will you meet me?"

I don't answer him right away and his anxiety reaches a new level. "Please, Kris."

Something heavy rolls over in my gut. Maybe it's the psychologist-in-training in me. Maybe it's the history we share, but I can't ignore his pleas.

"Fine. "I'll be there in twenty minutes."

I spend the next twenty minutes cursing myself for giving into him. I consider turning back around a few times, but something propels me forward, an intuitive voice, urgent and pleading, telling me that none of this makes sense.

Henley's panic attack came on yesterday after I'd asked him where he'd been. Why would he react to my question with such fear?

And how did he become this obscure version of himself?

I zig zag through the trees down the winding path that leads to the river until I reach the clearing.

At first, I don't see him but as I inch toward the water, his large form comes into view. He sits in an old canoe that lies on the bank, head down, shoulders hunched, his elbows resting on his knees. We used to row out onto the river in this thing, but it's looking worse for wear now, a giant gaping split in its side.

The sun sits high in the sky, its light pouring down through the old elm tree, speckling the ground with the shadows of its leaves. A piece of bark crunches under my foot and Henley's head snaps upward at the sound. He watches me as I cautiously step forward, a mixture of apology and hurt in his eyes. He pats the canoe seat across from him, beckoning for me to join him.

My bottom lip curls under my teeth as I give a slight shake of my head. I'm scared, I realise, to be in such close proximity to him. Because I don't know if I can handle seeing him as fragile as he was yesterday. And because I'm not sure if I can be trusted to keep my hands to myself.

"Come on, Kris," he begs, his eyebrows pulling down in a frown.

I'm taken aback by the emotion in his voice. I surrender and climb into the canoe, but not without gritted teeth and a heavy heart. As much as I care about him, and as concerned as I am about whatever it is that's causing his anxiety, I'm really not looking forward to having a heart to heart about his girlfriend. He looks up at me, trouble brewing in those baby blues.

"Yesterday wasn't... This isn't what you think. It's not what it looks like." His jaw clenches as he swallows.

"Really?" I squint in mock thought. "Because it looks like you brought some girl back from wherever the hell you've been and invited her to live with you."

He blows out a long breath. "Well, yeah. I guess that part's true." I sigh and begin to stand but he reaches forward, his touch like fire on my forearm. "But she's a friend. She's just a friend."

"Whatever you say. It's not really my business. We aren't together anymore." I feign disinterest and ready myself to step out of the canoe.

Something in his eyes stops me, an unexpected anguish that's only surface deep. I try to remind myself that this is what he wanted.

He made this choice.

He gazes down at the canoe, running his hands along its worn sides.

"Remember when we used to take this thing out? Spend all day just rowing down the river." I don't say anything, but he continues anyway. "Remember that day we had that crazy fight and you threatened to jump out and swim to shore? I never thought you actually would. And then you started screaming because an eel wrapped itself around your leg." He smiles at the memory and the corners of my mouth twitch upward involuntarily.

"Yeah. And you thought you were such a big man coming to my rescue." I sit back down opposite him, mentally exhausted from this exchange.

I remember that day as clear as anything. Henley had come to my aid, pulling me up into the canoe. I'd been furious at him for laughing at me, but when he'd wrapped his arms around me and kissed me anyway, I'd allowed myself to fall into him, his hard chest warm and comforting.

Like home.

Henley shakes his head with a tight grin. "What were we fighting about anyway?"

"I caught you flirting with Sheree Clayton in fifth period."

The smile fades from his lips. "I was a stupid kid."

"Yeah. What's your excuse now?" He looks at me like I've stabbed a spear through his heart. "Who is she?"

His jaw ticks again before answering. "Mackenzie. She needed a place to stay. She had nowhere else to go."

"So, what?" I question. "You just picked this girl up off the side of the road because she needed a place to stay."

"That's actually a pretty accurate way of putting it, yeah."

"There's only one bed in the loft."

I search his face, looking for signs that he's being dishonest. Henley tends to look to the left when he lies, sometimes scratching at a spot in his eyebrow. He doesn't do either of those things this time.

"Yeah. Tell me about it." He manages a half laugh. "I've been sleeping on the couch since we got here. I think I need to see a chiropractor."

My head tilts to the side in suspicion. "Since when are you the type to take in random blonde strays?"

"This is different. You don't understand." He shakes his head, dropping his stare to his feet.

"How can I possibly understand!?" I cry. I'm angry now. His statement has me seething. "You're not telling me anything! You turn up here after six goddamn months like you're a different person, with a new girl staying at your place."

"I'm sorry. There are things I can't say, no matter how much I want to tell you. Mackenzie has her own stuff going on and it's not my place to tell her story." He sighs again, defeated. His eyes are glassy. "Look, I know I've messed up. I don't expect you to ever forgive me for what I did. But I need you to believe that I'm not the heartless jerk you think I am."

"Guess I'll have to take your word for it." While it annoys me that he won't be more transparent with me, I can respect him for maintaining Mackenzie's privacy. "Can you at least tell me what happened yesterday?"

He opens his mouth to speak, but when he closes it again, I know I've pushed too far. Whatever is causing his anxiety is still too raw for him to revisit.

"I can't talk about that either," he rasps.

Something about the way he says it tells me it's not his choice to keep it a secret.

I nod, climbing out of the canoe. "If you ever feel like you can, you know where to find me."

I walk back the way I came, only daring to glance back once. He hasn't moved from his position in the canoe. He's still hunched over himself, his head held up by his hands, the sun casting him in silhouette.

The picture of a broken man.

Chapter 27

HENLEY

It's just after three in the afternoon. That quiet moment in between the lunch rush and happy hour. I used to find this part of the day boring, having to do mundane tasks like washing glassware and dishes and mopping tables down.

Now, I welcome it like a breath of fresh air. It's when I'm able to take a break from the masses of people that flock into the bar on the regular, a respite from the rumbling of voices and clatter of boots on the hardwood floors. I never use to be so sensitive to crowds and noise.

Things change, I guess.

Kristen wants answers. I get that. But she can't see what I see. A violent hurricane of memories that swirls through my head, raw and crippling. She doesn't know what it's like to feel like you're stuck in a life that isn't your own.

How the hell am I supposed to explain to her that most days I'm not really living?

That I'm barely surviving?

A group of women leave the table by the window, and I wander over to clear their plates. I glance outside, suddenly distracted by the vibrant shine of honey blonde hair in the sunlight.

Mackenzie crosses the road toward the tavern, her face crumpled with sadness. She lifts a hand to her cheek, presumably wiping at tears, and drops her gaze down to the ground. Seeing her upset always puts me on edge and lately it's happening all too often. I push through the tavern's door and race in her direction.

"Mackenzie!" I call.

She doesn't turn around. Her footsteps quicken on the pavement but I'm faster. I reach her, stepping into her path and blocking her from running away from me.

"Mackenzie, what's going on?" I ask, steadying her by the shoulders.

She shakes her head in frustration as more tears stream from her eyes. A ball of dread forms in the pit of my stomach when I see the brand-new iPhone she cradles in her hand. My mind goes to the worst possible scenario.

"He didn't call you, did he?" I ask her.

Logically, I know it would be impossible. She has a new number now. But that's the thing about anxiety.

It's never rational.

"No," she sobs, swiping at her cheeks.

"Then what is it? Please tell me what's going on," I plead with her, my hands still gripping her shoulders.

I hate seeing her so distraught. My insides are hollow knowing there's nothing I can do to make things better for her right now. Nothing I can do to ease her worries.

"Nothing." She shakes her head in frustration.

"Okay," I say, taking a few steps back from her.

I don't believe her, but I don't want to push her too hard for answers. I've done that in the past and it only ended in her storming away and both of us feeling even worse.

"I don't know how much longer I can live like this. I'm just so scared," she cries. "I'm scared all the time and I hate it."

"I know. It's okay," I reassure her. "It won't be like this forever, okay?"

"But how do you really know that?" Mackenzie usually guards her heart, never letting her true emotions show, but right now she exudes a ferocity that no one I know has ever displayed.

No one except Kristen.

I'm not sure what else I can say to her to take her fears away because the truth is I don't really know. Neither of us can predict the future.

"Did something happen, Mackenzie?" I ask, softer this time.

"I was down at the pier, and I saw this guy," she snivels. "I thought it was him."

An ice-cold shiver runs down my spine. "But it wasn't, right?"

Every molecule of my being depends on her confirmation of this.

"No. It was just some guy with the same haircut. But it scared me." A fresh tear rolls down her cheek and I reach out and brush it away. "And it just sucks. I mean, is this the way I'm going to have to live my life now? Always watching over my shoulder?"

"I know how hard this is but there are people in this town that will have your back," I say. "If you let them."

She gives me a knowing look, aware of exactly who I'm referring to. "What if they come looking for me? What if he already knows where I am?"

I sigh, knowing that I'm the only one that can offer her any form of comfort. I'm literally all she has right now.

I reach out for her, pulling her in close. She buries her face in my chest as I wrap my arms around her, resting my chin on her head.

"It's okay. I'm here," I tell her. "They have to get through me first."

I've never felt more protective of anyone in my entire life.

I've also never been more terrified.

Chapter 28

KRISTEN

Chase's cherry red jeep wrangler pulls up on the curb outside the Haven. This morning's course session had been a gruelling one on the fundamentals of neuroscience and behaviour. My mind feels completely blown and the only thing I want to be doing is taking a hot bath and falling into bed for a long nap. But Carla had called asking if I could fill in for a couple of hours this afternoon because Harper – who as it turns out, is well and truly pregnant – had a midwife appointment to go to.

"Thanks for the lift, Chase. I don't know what I'd do without you."

"No problem. Same time tomorrow?" Chase throws the car in park and loops an arm around the passenger seat headrest.

"Yeah." I wince. I had really hoped my car would be fixed by now but unfortunately Henley was right. The whole engine is shot and for the cost to replace it, I may as well buy a new car. "Sorry. I know I'm a pain."

"Oh, you're the worst," he deadpans before breaking out into laughter. "Kidding. It's fine. It's not even out of my way."

"I know. I just don't want to be a burden," I say.

"Are you kidding?" His brown eyes are sincere. "You could never be a burden to me, Kristen."

I know he means what he says but I hate having to rely on other people for anything. I've always wanted to be completely independent, strong in the same way my mother is. Even as a single mum with a few hundred dollars to her name, she'd been able to build a life for us from next to nothing.

"Well, thank you. I really appreciate it." I pause, my hand on the passenger door handle.

"Are you okay?" he asks. "You still haven't seemed like yourself these past few days."

"Yeah," I say. "It's just stuff with…"

"Henley," he finishes.

I purse my lips and nod. It's been almost a week since our last encounter but even though we haven't spoken, I've caught glimpses of him disappearing into the tavern, his eyes finding mine across the street.

"Something is going on with him. I just can't figure out what it is. And I know it's not my place to even care anymore but…"

"But you do." Chase finishes my sentence again.

"Yeah." I sigh.

"You can't help that. It's who you are," he says. "Just be careful."

"I will," I nod then open the door. "I'll see you tomorrow."

He holds a hand up in salute as I climb out of the car. "Oh, and hey, we need to finalise arrangements for the fundraiser."

"Sure. We can talk about it tomorrow in between seminars," I suggest.

"Sounds like a plan."

I shut the car door, then give a wave as Chase drives off down the esplanade. I spare a glance across the street and find Henley watching from outside the tavern.

Even from here, I can see his jaw ticking. A sure sign that he doesn't like what he's seeing. He's never been Chase's biggest fan. I guess I can't blame him considering Chase asked me out mere weeks after his disappearance.

The Haven is packed full of customers when I enter, and I instantly understand where the desperation in Carla's voice came from when she phoned asking me to work today. I round the counter, pulling an apron from the pile on the shelf underneath.

"Hey, Kristen." Carla whizzes past me, her arms laden with plates. "Table eighteen has been waiting for a while," she calls back to me over her shoulder.

"On it," I reassure her as I finish tying the apron around my waist.

I turn my attention to table eighteen and cringe inwardly when I see who occupies it.

Mackenzie sits by the window, chewing on her bottom lip nervously. She sees me notice her and drops her focus back to the phone in her hands. I know nothing about this girl that Henley has opened up his home to. And though we aren't even together anymore, and he swears there's nothing romantic between them, I'm jealous.

Plain and simply.

And that notion has me more confused than any of the things that Henley isn't telling me.

There's something oddly mystifying about Mackenzie, something about the way she closes herself off to the world. I can see why Henley would be drawn to helping her, because in a lot of ways he is the same.

And I'd be lying if I said I didn't lie in bed tossing and turning last night, dreaming up as many innocent possibilities for why Henley was hugging her outside the tavern yesterday. I'm sure neither of them were aware that I could see their interaction from inside the cafe. Watching him take her into his strong tattooed arms, her cheek pressed against his chest.

It had ruined me.

The only thought running through my mind after seeing them together was who the hell is this girl that has stepped into my place? Because I used to be the only one enclosed in Henley's arms.

I equip myself with a notepad and pen and move toward Mackenzie's table.

"Mackenzie," I say, probably a little too sternly. "What brings you here?"

"Hi, Kristen." Hearing her address me by name throws me off guard. There's something eerily familiar about the way she pronounces it, the way the 'K' seemed to get stuck in her throat. "Could I just get a caramel latte?"

"Sure. Anything else?" I say robotically.

"Um, yeah. I just wanted to say how sorry I am about last week. I didn't mean to interrupt you guys. I honestly had no idea you were there." She rushes through her words, barely taking a breath. "Believe me if I'd known I would have stayed away."

Her hand gestures and the sarcasm in her tone indicate a level of disgust, as though seeing Henley making out with someone is the last thing she'd want to see.

"Why are you staying with Henley?" I ask, my eyes narrowing as I cross my arms over my chest.

She hesitates, twirling a blonde curl between her fingers. Her eyes wander away from mine, and I realise I've done a sufficient job of intimidating her. "I'm not really in the best place right now. He was kind enough to offer."

"You're saying that you are essentially homeless," I state.

"Yeah," she whispers.

She looks down at her phone again and I realise that I've seen it before. Brand new and still in the box on Henley's dash the day my car broke down.

She looks back up apologetically. "Sorry, I'm just waiting on a call. Had a job interview yesterday."

I feel sick at myself. I could argue that my words were based on general curiosity, but I know deep down that they were cruel. I wanted to make her feel less.

Less than me.

Less than Henley.

And I have.

"Did he buy you that phone?" I ask her.

She nods. "He's a good guy."

"I really want to agree with you on that, but I've had a different experience."

"He speaks really highly of you, Kristen." She looks up at me earnestly, waiting for my response. I'm afraid I can't give her the one she's hoping for.

"I'll get that caramel latte for you." I turn on my heel and head back to the kitchen.

It kills me that this girl seems to know more about Henley's current situation than I do. Like the two of them share some kind of secret that I'm not privy to. An entire world existing between them that I'm not a part of.

But none of this is her fault, I realise.

She's homeless for Christ's sake. And I've let my bitterness make me ugly, treating her as though she doesn't matter just because I'm uncomfortable with their closeness.

When I return to her table with her hot drink, she's staring aimlessly out the window. Not unlike the first time I met her, she seems stuck in her head. She emanates resilience and determination, but her insecurities are not hidden as deep as she'd like to think.

"How is it?" I ask her, attempting to redeem myself for the harshness I'd bestowed upon her no more than five minutes ago. "Living in the loft, I mean."

"Okay, I guess." She laughs nervously, almost weirded out at my effort to be friendly.

"He told me he sleeps on the couch," I muse.

"He does," she replies. "He's too much of a gentleman to let me take it."

There aren't many people that would describe Henley as a gentleman. He used to reserve his manners, his tenderness, for me. Jealousy rears its ugly head again at the thought of her sleeping where he once did. Where *I* once did. But I push it back down and swallow my pride.

"Look, I know things must be pretty cramped over there. I mean, does that place even have a decent bathroom."

She eyes me warily, unsure of where I'm going with the conversation. She stutters a short, "Uh, okay?" But she doesn't answer my question.

I take a breath, giving myself the chance to back out of what I'm about to do. Her eyes search my face. She can't read me.

"I live alone. In an apartment not far from here," I begin. Her eyes narrow. She gives a slight shake of her head, clueless as to why I'm telling her this. "If you'd like, you could stay with me instead."

Once the words are out of my mouth, I can't take them back, so I continue. "I have a spare bed. It's only a single but the mattress is decent."

Her brow knits in confusion. "You'd really let me stay with you when you know nothing about me?"

Why am I doing this again? I could say that it makes sense for her to live with another female, but the main reason I offer is to distance her from my ex-boyfriend. "If Henley can trust you, then I guess I can too."

She's seemingly uninterested in my offer, her gaze drifting out through the window to the tavern across the street. Trouble brews behind her eyes and I realise she's as wary of me as I was of her no more than five minutes ago.

"It was just a thought," I begin, ready to retract my proposal.

She turns back to me, her lips twisting upward ever so slightly. "Well, the bathroom situation is pretty dismal up there."

"Then it's settled," I say. "Just don't make me regret it."

Chapter 29

HENLEY

I can't wait for this shift to end. Every muscle in my body is fatigued and I literally feel as though I'm hauling ass around this bar, every minute that passes longer than the one before it.

Mackenzie moved in with Kristen yesterday. I'm happy that fate has given the two of them the opportunity to become closer. I've always thought it would be good for them to connect, but damn this loft is quiet without her. I almost miss her sarcastic complaints and the sound of her tone-deaf voice echoing from the shower.

I have a feeling my nights will be even more sleepless than before. I'm sure Mackenzie had thought of me as her security but honestly her presence had made things more bearable for me too. Last night, I'd tossed and turned for hours before I finally gave up and crept downstairs to the old, abandoned room.

I'd spent a few more hours there, cleaning and filling holes in the dry wall. I'm amazed at the progress I've made with it in such a short time.

After removing all the debris and dust from the timber flooring, I was surprised to find it in better condition than that of the rest of the place. I'd replaced some of the skirting that had been ruined with water damage and moved a couple of old, damaged pieces of furniture out of the way.

Of course, there's still so much work left to do. There are chunks of drywall missing that need to be replaced completely, but I'm hopeful that I'll be able to make another visit to Bill's Hardware when my next pay check comes in.

I'm running out of cash fast. I had some money put away in an account that I'd saved before I left, but between groceries, my hardware purchases and supporting Mackenzie, there isn't a lot left.

I'm wiping down the bar when Mick and Jay Nelson approach, otherwise known as the Nelson brothers. Mick slaps a hand down on the counter.

"See, Jay! I told you he was back!" he exclaims loudly.

"Henley!" Jay yells. "Where the hell have you been, man?"

"Hey guys," I respond in a low voice, not wanting to draw any further attention to myself. "What's up?"

"It's good to see you, dude," Mick reaches across the bar and slaps me on the shoulder.

"Yeah, you too," I say. "Can I get you something?"

"We'll take two beers. Whatever's cold." Jay slumps down on a stool while I pour Heineken from the tap.

"You guys been busy?" I ask, hoping to distract them from their first question.

"We got slammed over the winter, but things have slowed down a bit. Which is shit for business, but it keeps the old man off our backs."

I manage a laugh as I slide their glasses along the bar.

I worked with the Nelson brothers for a while, not long after we finished high school. Their father owns Nelson and Sons Glass Repairs and he had always hoped that his two boys would take over the family business one day. And maybe if they laid off the pot, they might actually be successful with it. With the bloodshot stares they aim at me coupled with their chill demeanour I'm guessing that day hasn't come.

An idea forms in my head and I glance behind me to make sure Dylan isn't within earshot. "Hey," I say, leaning across the bar. "I'll be needing some work done soon if you're interested in doing a quick job for cash."

"Sure, man. Whatever you need," Jay replies, taking a long draw from his beer.

"Cool. Just need to keep it on the downlow."

"Oh, it's like that, huh?" Mick gives me a conspiratorial wink.

"Nah, mate. Nothing dodgy," I assure him. If these guys have been involved in dishonest dealings, I don't want to know about it. "Just need some windows replaced. I'm working on a project, but it's kind of a surprise."

"No worries. Let us know when you need it done and we'll be there." Jay tips his beer in my direction. Mick gives me a nod. Then they both stroll over to a table along the far side of the tavern to join a group of tradies eating lunch.

My shoulders sag in relief, knowing I've dodged the major question about where I've been for half a year.

Then my hackles rise when the door swings open. I breathe a heavy sigh as EJ appears and I'm reminded of the last interaction I had with my best friend in this very spot. I shudder to think what he might want from me now. He'd already made it clear that I ruined Kristen's life and that I don't deserve the help his father has offered me.

I move to the other end of the bar to serve Old Tommy. He requests his fourth bourbon and coke for the day. It's only one thirty in the afternoon. Normally I'd tell him impolitely that he's had enough, but today I hand it over willingly, thankful that his being here has helped me evade EJ. But when I'm done serving, EJ hasn't moved from his place.

"Can we talk?" he says, a veil of seriousness falling over his features.

My jaw tenses. I glance at Dylan, who gives a small nod of approval. I don't think I'm ready for anything else he has to say to me, but nonetheless I nod my head in the direction of the side door and wait for EJ to follow me out into the courtyard.

When we reach the open space, I move to lean on the far wall, unable to hide my discomfort. "What's up?"

"I came here to apologise." There's a sincerity in his eyes as he moves toward me.

"No need." I rub the back of my neck uneasily and ready myself to return to the bar, but he steps in front of me.

"Look, man. I talked to my dad," he explains.

My breath hitches in my throat. "He told you."

He told you what he knows of it, at least.

"Yeah. But don't worry," he replies. "I haven't said a word to anyone."

This may very well be true, but if EJ knows, it's only a matter of time before the truth makes its way around the tiny community of Cliff Haven one way or another.

Even if it's only half of the story.

"Do you hate me?" I ask him.

It doesn't hit me until this moment how terrified I've been of the possibility of losing my best friend for good.

"Dude, I could never hate you." EJ's eyes meet mine and there's so much emotion in them I have to look away. "Look, I was pissed at you for leaving. But that was before I understood."

I squeeze my eyes shut as they begin to sting. I inhale a shaky breath and push the tears down.

I remind myself that he doesn't really understand.

EJ throws a sympathetic look my way. His pity is torturous, like a knife slicing through an open wound. "I take it you haven't talked to her?"

It doesn't take a genius to know he's referring to Kristen. "Not about that."

"How are things going with you guys?" he asks.

I shake my head hopelessly. "I think it's safe to say she hates me."

"Only because she doesn't know the whole story," EJ argues. "You have to see it from her point of view. We all thought you wanted nothing to do with us."

"I can't tell her."

EJ doesn't know the whole story either. He only knows what my dad told Steve on the phone that night.

"But you do still love her."

It's not a question. EJ knows how I feel about Kristen. I think he knew even before I did that she would always have an impact on my life.

"It doesn't matter. She deserves better." I run a hand down my face and turn and pace the courtyard.

"So *be* better," he says earnestly. "She deserves to know the truth."

He's right. Kristen does deserve to know the truth and I wish I *could* tell her. My chest starts to heave, my eyes beginning to burn, reminding me yet again that my body is physically incapable of allowing me to speak the words.

"I can't," I manage to choke out.

I turn my back to him again, but he doesn't let it go. "But if you…"

"I said I can't tell her, okay?" My voice comes out much louder than intended. Fiercer. Meaner.

EJ takes a step back away from me, his arms held up in surrender, but instead of aiming a look of disgust my way as he'd done last week, he looks at me with pity. "Okay, man. But I think you're making a mistake. Maybe you just need a little more time."

"Maybe. Look, just promise me you won't tell her," I plead with him.

When and if Kristen finds out about the past, she needs to hear it from me.

And she needs to hear the full story.

"I won't," he says, walking toward me. "I'm sorry man. I didn't come here to upset you."

"I know. I'm sorry too. I didn't mean to be an asshole," I say. And I mean it. I'm honestly glad to have my friend back. "It's just really intense being back here and everything. It feels like I've been gone a lifetime. Everything's different."

"Yeah. I get that," EJ says, resting his shoulder up against the wall. "Look, I just wanted you to know there's no bad blood between us."

I nod. "Thanks."

"You still drumming?" he asks. "Music helps, you know?"

EJ has always been a major advocate for music cleansing the soul and all that. I don't disagree with him.

"It's hard to play when the entire street can hear me from up there," I say, gesturing to the loft above. "Besides, there's not much left of my drum kit. Kristen kind of gave it a beating after I left."

"Ah yes," EJ says with a single nod. "She might have mentioned that."

"She did, huh?"

"Well, bragged is probably a better word for it."

This earns a laugh from me. And not one of those forced, fake ones I've been displaying of late.

"Feel free to come by the studio and jam with me some time," EJ offers. "Got a brand new Tama seven piece just last week."

"Nice," I say, impressed. "I'm not sure Liv would like it if I started coming by though."

"Let me handle Liv. She'll come around."

"She doesn't know though, right?" I ask. "I mean, you haven't told her?"

"No." EJ sighs and I can tell I'm asking too much of him to keep such a huge secret from his wife-to-be.

"Thanks, man. I'm sorry," I tell him. "I'll figure my shit out soon, okay?"

My secret is bigger than me. It's bigger than me and Kristen. It's now affecting my best friend's relationship too, spilling over into other facets of my life like rain through a floodgate that I can't seem to keep shut.

Chapter 30

KRISTEN

It didn't take Mackenzie too long to get settled into my spare room. Unsurprisingly, considering the only belongings she had on her fit neatly into a small duffle bag. Now that she's here, I want to know more about her. I want to know her story and where she comes from.

But the standoffish vibes she's been throwing my way tell me I'm going to have to be patient. She's only been here since last night and so far, the only things I've gotten to learn about her is that she likes pepperoni pizza and watching Outer Banks on Netflix.

Still, I'm hopeful that if I let her be for a few days I can start to chip away at her bit by bit. It's only fair that I should know at least a few things about this stranger I've allowed into my home.

That's if she ever resurfaces from the spare bedroom. I've been patiently waiting in the living room, pretending to read the giant textbook on cognitive psychology that's been spread across my lap for the past hour waiting for her to wake up.

Another ten minutes pass before she finally emerges, dressed in a pair of denim cut-offs and a crochet tank top.

She eyes me warily, sidestepping around the couch and into the kitchen.

"Is everything okay?" I ask. She throws me a dubious look. "With the room, I mean."

"Oh," she says. "Yeah, it's fine."

That bedroom has water views and an actual dresser she can put her things in. Compared to Henley's loft, it's a castle. But if 'it's fine' is all she's willing to say, then I'll take it.

My apartment is basically one large room consisting of the kitchen, living and dining with two bedrooms coming off it. It's pretty self-explanatory, but that doesn't stop me from getting up and wandering around, pointing everything out like some sort of robotic idiot.

"Well, this is the dining area. I normally just eat breakfast here and eat dinner on the couch over there. And the fridge is right there. Help yourself to the coffee machine." I point to the small Nespresso machine Mum bought me for my birthday a couple of years ago.

Mackenzie doesn't say anything. Just surveys the room with caution and eyes me awkwardly.

I realise I'm trying too hard to please right now. I need to reel it in a little, so I decide to lay down some ground rules. "I don't mind if you stay here but I'd like it if you helped me out with groceries."

"Okay." Her face falls and I slap my forehead comically remembering she doesn't have a job.

"I'm sorry," I say quickly. "I forgot that you're not working yet. Do you have any money with you at all?"

"Not a lot," she admits. "Henley has been helping me out, but I feel bad to ask him for anything else."

"Henley has been supporting you all this time?" I ask.

"Since we got here. Yeah." Her gaze wanders over to the far window where a hint of blue ocean can be seen peeking above the buildings further down on the esplanade.

I don't know why my eyebrows shoot up in surprise. I'd managed to put enough facts together to know that Henley has been helping Mackenzie considerably where finances are concerned. He'd bought her a new phone after all. It doesn't take a genius to know that wherever this girl may have sprung from, she didn't bring a truck ton of money with her. She's barely scraped together enough items of clothing to accommodate each season.

Henley *is* a good guy.

I might not know everything about him anymore, but I do know that to be true. I know without a doubt that he would help anyone in need. But the level of responsibility it takes to care for another human being? That sort of has me stumped. It's not that I've never believed him capable of it. I've always had faith in him. But I have to admit I'm suspicious of the reasons behind it.

This girl obviously holds a special place in his heart, but why?

"I can cover groceries for now," I tell her. I'm not even sure how long Mackenzie will be staying with me, but I think at least a few weeks is a fair assumption. "Mackenzie, I don't mean to pry. But what exactly are your plans for the future?"

She stares at me long and hard, her face a mixture of anxiety and anger. It's obvious she doesn't have an answer to my question.

I really didn't think this through. Maybe I'm going about this all wrong. Maybe Henley is better equipped to take in strays than me after all.

A brisk knock on the door startles us both and saves her from my unintentional interrogation. I'm perplexed as I wasn't expecting anyone today. When I pull open the door my mother practically flies through it.

"Mum!" I stagger backwards, stunned.

"Hey, baby," she says, throwing her arms around me.

The first thing I notice is the sweat band stretched around her forehead. The next is the black and aqua activewear set that adorns her curvy frame. Mackenzie watches on in astonishment, no doubt perturbed by this outgoing, flamboyant woman that's crashed our serious conversation.

"Mum, what are you doing here?" I ask, my eyes wide. I haven't even had a chance to tell her about my new roommate.

"I was in the neighbourhood," she says breathlessly.

"You were?" I ask.

My mother's house is a good three kilometres away from my apartment and not really nearby any of the places she frequents.

"Yeah. I need to use your bathroom," she explains. "I decided to take up jogging, but I didn't realise the toll it would take on my bladder. This body is not what it used to be."

"Oh," I say with a small smile. "Okay, Mum. You know where it is."

I look over at Mackenzie who is leaning on the door frame of her new room, a suspicious expression on her face. "Sorry. That's just my mother. She can be a little crazy sometimes."

She nods at me once, folding her arms across her chest.

Another thirty seconds or so pass before Mum appears from the bathroom, dabbing at her cheeks with a tissue.

"Wow. I did *not* realise how hard it would be to take up exercise in your forties."

"Mum, you're not that far away from fifty."

She lets out a loud and dramatic gasp. "That's blasphemy, my child!"

I roll my eyes, but I can't stifle the giggle that escapes. This is why I love my mother. Pamela Riley does not do things in halves. She gets these crazy ideas and then dives headfirst into new things without stopping to give them any real thought first.

Mum swings around, following my line of sight to where Mackenzie stands, realising only now that there is another person in the room.

"Oh," she gasps. "I didn't realise you had company!"

"Mum, this is Mackenzie. She's going to be staying with me for a little while."

"Hi, Mackenzie!" Mum says in a lively tone. "I'm so sorry! I didn't even see you there. It's nice to meet you."

"Hi." Mackenzie offers a short reply. Her smile is friendly but there's an edge to her voice.

Mum glances down at her watch. "I'm sorry girls. I can't stay long. I really need to get back to Ben. He's taking me out to lunch today and then we're going into Little Bay to see that new Sandra Bullock movie."

"Oh, cool," I say. "You guys have fun. That movie is meant to be amazing."

When I see the gushy smile that spreads across my mum's face, I'm once again grateful that she found Ben. Finally, after a string of morons, a guy that will take her for a nice day out every once in a while and treat her like a lady.

Mum lunges at me, smothering me in a hug. When she waves a hand in Mackenzie's direction, I don't miss the grimace that Mackenzie quickly masks with a smile.

"I'll catch up with you soon girls."

When she leaves, I shut the door behind her and turn to Mackenzie. "Sorry about that. She can be quite the whirlwind."

"It's fine," she replies, bleakly. "She seems cool."

She says this with a negative tone, as though it's not cool that my mum is cool.

"Yeah. She can be a lot sometimes. But she has a heart of gold," I offer. "She's the local vet here in Cliff Haven. Massive animal lover."

"Of course, she is," she replies, her tone laced with bitter sarcasm.

"Is everything okay?" I ask.

I'm not sure where this cynicism is coming from, but I've decided I don't like it. This is my mother she's talking about.

"Yeah. Fine."

I wonder if she'll extend her vocabulary much further than these two words today.

"So anyway," I continue. "I'm meeting up with my friend Chase today to discuss some things we need to sort out for the carnival, so he'll be picking me up soon. He's kind of helping me out since my car died."

"Okay," she replies timidly.

"What are you going to do today? Do you have plans?"

"Not really," she replies. "I was just going to go down to the library and see if I can use the computers there to print off a proper resume."

"Oh," I say. "You don't have to go to the library for that. You can use my laptop. I don't have a printer, but my mum does so we can go over there and print as many copies as you need."

Mackenzie looks reluctant. "I don't know. Are you sure your mum wouldn't mind?"

"Of course not. I print things out at her place all the time. She lives over the other side of the bridge by the river." I glance at my watch. Chase will be here any minute. I throw back the last of my coffee and walk the cup to the sink, rinsing it quickly under the tap. "If you pull out the top drawer of that desk over there, my laptop should be inside."

She wanders over to the desk. The top drawer creaks as she slides it out and lifts the computer from it. Something must catch her eye because she stalls, her focus on something beneath it. I watch as she pulls out a small photograph with dog-eared corners.

"Is this you?" she asks.

I pull my hands from the water, wiping them with the dish towel and hastily move to where she hovers above the desk. I peer over her shoulder at the photograph she holds delicately between her fingers, at the image of me, a chubby four-year-old in a navy and white sailor dress. My father, dressed in an expensive white, linen shirt wraps his arms lovingly around my waist, holding me up against a backdrop of crystal-clear Mediterranean Sea, a perfect white smile lighting up his tanned face. It depicts another time.

Another life.

"You used to be blonde," Mackenzie states.

"When I was little, yeah."

"And this is your dad." A crease forms between her brows, but her eyes don't leave the photograph. I'm not sure if I'm imagining the way her stare becomes glassy.

"Yeah. No," I stutter. "I mean, biologically. He was my dad, but he hasn't been a father to me for a really long time."

I take the photo from her hands and toss it back into the drawer. Mackenzie's gaze lingers on the stack of letters I keep inside of it.

One written for every birthday I've ever spent without my father.

All of them addressed to him. None of them ever to be sent.

Her nostrils flare temporarily, a gesture so small I almost miss it.

Chase's horn beeps somewhere outside on the curb, shaking us both out of the moment. I abruptly slam the drawer shut, securing the photo and letters inside.

"I need to get going. The charger for the laptop is over there by the wall. The password is July20, capital J," I explain.

I don't mention this is Henley's birthday and I have no idea if she knows him well enough to know that.

I rush out of the apartment and down the stairs, unsure of whether the intensity I'd felt in the room as Mackenzie's stare had locked upon that photo was merely a fabrication in my mind, or if there is something else I'm missing. I make a mental note to ask her about her own family when I get home tonight.

Not that I think she will give me a straight answer.

Chapter 31

HENLEY

After a long deliberation, I decided to take EJ up on his offer to go and vent my frustration out on the new drum kit he and Liv bought for the music studio.

I regret it instantly when my presence is met with an arctic reception from Liv. I can't blame her. Kristen is her best friend, and I blew it enormously. I'd expect nothing less from her than the ice-cold death stare she aims in my direction and the insults she mutters under her breath to EJ as I enter the room.

"Hey, Liv," I say, uncomfortably scratching at my eyebrow.

"Hey," is the only word that leaves her mouth before she heads out the back to the staircase that leads to their apartment upstairs.

"Sorry, man," EJ winces.

"It's fine," I say. "At least I know I can trust that you haven't told her anything."

As I say this I realise if she knew what EJ knew, she may very well still choose not to give me the benefit of the doubt. It's highly probable that she would still hate me.

"Yeah," EJ frowns sympathetically. "But honestly, I don't know how long I can keep that up. It's getting really hard to keep lying to my future wife."

"I know," I say, hanging my head in shame. "I'm sorry."

"Forget about it." He waves my apology away. "We're here to jam. Forget all the bullshit."

I nod. "Sounds like a plan."

That's all I really want to do right now. Work out all the tension I've been carrying and jam with my best mate. Maybe try to pretend for a few short hours that things could ever be as simple as they were when we were younger, playing in a garage band on weekends and performing at Steve's every Friday night.

We play a couple of our old songs, but it isn't the same without Cayden. It's not the same for a lot of reasons. So much has happened since those carefree days that they almost feel like they happened in another life.

Still, I feel good today.

EJ's theory about music being better than therapy is one hundred percent accurate. It's liberating to finally be able to play again. On a drum kit that isn't damaged, without the confines of the tavern and its unapproving customers. Thank God for soundproof studios.

I stop for a break, wishing I'd bothered to bring a spare t-shirt. I'm betting I could just about wring the sweat out of this one.

I'm wiping the moisture from my brow and stretching my tired, burning biceps when Levi enters the studio. I look up in time to see him unhook a shiny black bass guitar from the far wall, slinging it around his neck in one swift movement.

"What's up guys?" he asks enthusiastically. "Good to see you, Henley."

"Thanks. You too," I reply, curious about his arrival.

EJ didn't tell me we'd have company here today. I don't know Levi that well, but we've jammed in the past, both of us having laid down backing tracks for EJ's first album.

"I hope you don't mind, H," EJ says, adjusting the dials on the amp his Gibson is connected to. "I asked Levi to swing by and help me practice a few songs for a gig I have coming up."

"Dude!" Levi scoffs. "Don't tell me you haven't asked him yet."

EJ bites his lip, squeezes his eyes shut, then removes the guitar from around his neck.

"Ask me what?" I say, my attention darting back and forth between the two of them.

EJ throws an annoyed look at Levi, then his eyes shoot back to me. "Are you going to the carnival next weekend?"

I hadn't forgotten about the annual Cliff Haven carnival. How could I possibly forget when Dylan has been breathing down my neck about stock levels all week?

"Pretty sure I'm gonna be stuck working the whole time if Dylan has any say in it. He's freaking out about how packed the tavern will get."

"Well, you're in luck." EJ says, rubbing his hands together conspiratorially. "I might be able to get you out of there for a few hours if you help me out with something. No pressure though."

"Oh yeah? What's that?" The idea of getting some relief from the bar does sound appealing.

"I'm doing a gig there. Probably five or six songs," he explains. "I need a drummer. Thought I'd ask you. See if you wanted to do it. For old times' sake."

"Come on, EJ," I complain. I realise now that he had a motive for offering me a jam session in the studio today. "You roped me in here under false pretences?"

"Well, when you put it like that you make me sound evil or something," EJ says light-heartedly. "Please. Help me out. Damon was meant to drum but something came up and he can't do it."

"Oh yeah? What's his excuse?" I mutter.

"His wife's due to have a baby."

I raise one eyebrow, twirling a drumstick between my fingers. "Fair enough."

"So…what do you say?" EJ holds his hands up in mock prayer. "I don't have a show without you."

"You sure you want to share the stage with the town pariah?" I'm not just asking EJ but Levi too.

Levi shrugs. EJ persists. "Come on, dude. People will come around."

I let out a heavy sigh. "I'll think about it."

I can't deny it. I'm tempted. Playing with EJ today has made me feel alive again. Performing on stage would make me feel human again.

"Cool. Like I said, no pressure." EJ picks his guitar back up and hangs it around his neck. Then he holds up a finger to the air. "Also, a little bit of pressure. It's for charity."

"It's for charity?" I groan.

"All proceeds go to the Cliff Haven Helpline," he explains. "Now there's one way to get back into Kristen's good books."

I shake my head at this attempt to convince me. I know it's going to take a lot more than performing at a charity gig to get back into Kristen's good graces.

With EJ knowing half my secret, it's only a matter of time before everyone does.

I used to fear irrational things.

Like flying, getting eaten by sharks and being caught in claustrophobic spaces.

Now I fear the day that Kristen discovers the darkest parts of me.

Chapter 32

KRISTEN

"You got plans for today?" Mackenzie asks as she swallows the last mouthful of toast from her plate.

She still sounds mopey, but I can appreciate her attempt at small talk after how sullen and angsty she's been since she first moved in. It's been almost a week since she took up residence in my apartment and I haven't really had much of a chance to talk to her, thanks to my busy schedule at the Haven and the extra shift I pulled at the helpline last night. It's left me feeling guilty but unfortunately, I don't have time to work on our bond today either.

"I do," I answer, regretfully. "Chase is picking me up in about ten minutes."

"You spend a lot of time with Chase. Is he your boyfriend?" she asks inquisitively.

I laugh. "No. He isn't."

"But you *want* him to be your boyfriend."

I turn my attention to her, my eyes narrow with curiosity.

"No," I say bluntly. "He's just a really good friend."

"Huh," she muses, a frown overtaking her brow. "You guys just seemed extra friendly when he came to pick you up for uni yesterday."

"Well, we are friendly. Because we're friends," I say matter-of-factly. Her eyes follow me as I wander over to the kitchen sink, my coffee cup in hand. The suspicion in her gaze makes me feel as though I need to offer her some form of an explanation. "Look, you're right. It isn't your business. But Chase and I went on a couple of dates a few months ago. He was into me, and I guess I didn't see the harm in us hanging out. But we realised we were better as friends. And that's all we've been ever since."

"Cool story," she says sarcastically, as if she didn't probe me for the answer I've given.

And we're back to square one.

"What about you?" I ask, taking her plate from the table.

"What about me?"

"Do you have a boyfriend? Did you leave some poor guy lost and heartbroken when you came to Cliff Haven?"

"Hardly," she scoffs, averting her focus out the window.

I've noticed she does this whenever I ask her a question. She gives me vague answers, never letting me all the way in.

"Where is Chase taking you today anyway?" she asks. "I thought you said you didn't have a class today."

"He's taking me over to Ben's Harvest. I need to collect the ingredients for all the things I'm making for the bake sale for the carnival tomorrow."

"You're actually working at the carnival tomorrow? Do you even know how to have fun?"

My eyebrows pinch in a frown and this time it's me that has to look away because her words have hit a nerve.

Because I *have* forgotten how to have fun.

Henley's spontaneity had once kept my life exciting but when he left, I'd thrown myself into my studies and my work. I took on more than I needed to because that way I didn't have time to stop and wonder where he was and what he was doing.

I turn back to Mackenzie. She's chewing on her bottom lip, an air of regret seemingly surrounding her.

"Sorry," she says. "That was rude."

"It's okay," I tell her, shaking off her insult.

"No," she disagrees. "It isn't. I know I haven't been the greatest house guest." She stands, fumbling with the hem of her t-shirt. "Henley told me you were the kindest person he's ever known. He said so many great things about you that I thought for sure he was making half of them up. But I see it now. You really are a good person."

"I'm not perfect," I say, remembering the way I'd spoken to her in the café. Before I'd offered her a place to stay, I'd belittled her, made her feel inferior.

"Maybe not. But according to him, you're the closest thing to it."

I frown at her words. Half of the problems between Henley and I had arisen from the pedestal he'd constantly put me on. And though everything has changed, he's still singing my praises. It doesn't make sense.

The distinct sound of Chase's horn signals his arrival and to my relief, breaks the tension between us.

"Uh, I should go," I say. "See you this afternoon?"

"Sure," she nods.

I exit the apartment and wander down the stairs, Mackenzie's words still running through my head. When I launch myself inside Chase's jeep, I slam the door shut a little too hard.

"Whoa. You okay," he asks.

"Yeah, fine," I say, combing my hair behind my ear. "Why?"

"You seem flustered." His face pulls downward in a frown.

"Ah, yeah. I'm okay," I say, shaking my head as though nothing is okay. "There was just this weird moment with Mackenzie. But it's fine. I don't want to talk about it."

"Okay then. To Ben's Harvest?"

"To Ben's Harvest," I agree.

I'm grateful that Chase has the good sense to let things go when I need him to. He puts the car in gear, and we set off in the direction of the largest produce store in the area.

Ben is loading boxes into the home delivery truck when we arrive, so we give him a quick wave and move through the store straight to the section where the baking needs are kept. I know I'll find most of what I need there.

"What's first on the list?" Chase asks.

"Flour," I answer, my eyes skimming over the various types in stock.

Chase reaches for two extra-large bags of self-raising flour from the bottom shelf, lifting one over each shoulder as though they weigh nothing. "How many of these do you need?"

"Whoa! Settle down," I laugh. "Those are ten kilograms each. We're feeding the town not the entire country."

He gives me a look that lets me know this information is irrelevant to him. "So… just one then?"

I tilt my head to the side contemplating how many muffins, slices and brownies I'll be able to get out of one bag. Surely way more than I could possibly have time to bake.

"Yeah. Okay. I'll take one. It's better value anyway."

A lot of the baked goods I'm making are made at the café from time to time. They're mostly things I've had a lot of experience with, so the ingredients and steps are etched into my memory.

We move through the store picking out the items I've written down in a list on my phone. Sugar, vegetable oil, butter, vanilla beans, eggs, pears and some fresh green apples for my mum's apple pie recipe. We take them to the front and place the items that fit next to the register on the counter. Chase props the extra-large bags of flour and sugar up against it on the floor.

"Did you find everything okay?" Ben asks with a friendly smile.

"I think so," I say, double checking the list. "Thank you again for donating these items to our bake sale. We couldn't do this without you."

"Well, I'm always willing to support a worthy cause."

"Oh, actually," I say, holding up a hand. "I need to get some raspberries for the raspberry and white chocolate muffins, but I couldn't seem to find any over there."

A wave of sadness suddenly washes over me at the memory of the last time I'd made those muffins. It had been in Henley's kitchen, not all that long before he disappeared. I remember his arms around my waist, the way he'd nuzzled into my neck from behind as I'd gently folded the flour through the buttermilk and eggs.

It seems like a lifetime ago now.

"No problem," Ben's voice snaps me back to reality. "I just got a delivery this morning from Peacock Farms. I'll go and fetch some for you out back." He disappears through a door behind the register in pursuit of the raspberries.

"You okay?" Chase asks. "You kinda spaced out just then."

"Yeah." I nod and force a smile, knowing full well that he sees through it.

He doesn't push the issue though, instead grabbing a gigantic bag of grapes from beside the counter.

"I'm taking these," he says with a smirk, to which I grin.

He plucks one from the bunch and tosses it into the air catching it in his mouth proudly.

I raise my eyebrows, impressed. "Nice! Now do me," I say, opening wide for him to aim a grape in my mouth. He tries but I stumble, and it ends up hitting me in the forehead and bouncing behind the counter. "Oh, good one. Chase! Now we're going to have an occupational health and safety incident on our conscience later today."

"So dramatic," he teases with a chuckle.

He tosses another grape my way which bounces off my nose. "You're so bad at this game."

"I know!" I say, laughing even harder, grateful that he's successfully been able to pull me from the flashback I was having only seconds ago.

Chase laughs too, but then his amusement falls short, his gaze dropping to the ground as footsteps fall on the floor behind me. I don't really need to turn around to know who it is, but still I do. Henley moves closer, the room suddenly smaller as his form fills the space, the tension in the air palpable.

He doesn't look at me.

Only at Chase.

His jaw grinds, the tell-tale vein protruding from his neck the only sign I need to know he's furious seeing Chase and I together. Jealousy has always been a problem for Henley, and I tense, remembering the few times in the past when he'd tried to solve his issues with physical violence.

"Hi," I say nervously, my voice small.

"Hey," he replies, still not looking at me. "What's wrong, Chase? Don't you have the guts to look at me?"

Chase looks up reluctantly. "Hey, Henley."

Henley pushes past me, sizing Chase up. He stands over him, attempting and succeeding in intimidating him. I watch as Chase swallows, giving a slight shake of his head.

"Walk away, Henley," he mutters uneasily. "It's what you're good at, isn't it?"

Henley's jaw clicks again. "Why? So you can take advantage of my girl as soon as I turn my back?" He grabs Chase by the shirt collar, his face reddening in anger.

"Alex," I bark. "Don't."

I lay my hand on Henley's forearm, attempting to diffuse his anger. Just as I'd hoped, he hesitates, his grip on Chase's shirt weakening. He drops his gaze to the ground, his nostrils flaring with the deep inhale he takes. Then he releases Chase, taking a step backward.

"Sorry," he mumbles before shoving past me and exiting the store.

I expel the breath I've been holding as Ben returns from the back door with several punnets of raspberries.

"Found them," he says, oblivious to the recent commotion. "Sorry, I wasn't sure how many you needed so I…" His voice trails off as he examines the deep frowns on both of our faces. "Are you guys okay?"

"Yeah," I say.

"Hurricane Henley just blew in." Chase is still visibly shaken.

"I'm sorry." I sigh. "I just need a minute."

I burst through the door, desperately sucking the air into my lungs. I'm embarrassed and upset for the way that Henley has treated my friend.

I'm also a little impressed with his self-control if I care to admit it, because the old Henley wouldn't have thought twice about pounding Chase's face to a pulp.

Henley's truck is parked on the curb down the road. I watch as he kicks the gutter with his shoe and then leans back onto the back passenger door, folding his arms across his broad chest. My feet carry me there before my mind has had a chance to catch up.

He holds up a hand when he sees me. "Don't Kris. I already hate myself."

"What were you thinking?" I cry, my nostrils flaring in defiance.

"I was thinking… I don't know what I was thinking." He pulls off his cap and runs a hand through his hair before repositioning it. "I was jealous. I'm jealous, okay?"

His admission sends a jolt through me, and it stops me in my tracks. I shouldn't be surprised that he still has some residual feelings for me deep down. We've been ingrained into each other's souls for the better part of the last decade, but to hear him confess it out loud fills me with the hope that maybe I was wrong.

Maybe he does still care about me.

But all of this is irrelevant, I tell myself. Because if he had loved me, he wouldn't have left me. The shock dissolves, leaving me with the rage that had propelled me out here in the first place.

"You are the most goddamned selfish man I've ever known, you know that?" I shout. "You only care about one thing and that's yourself."

His eyes snap to mine, his glare cold. His jaw hardens in anger, then he opens his mouth like he's about to say something but closes it again. The fury in his stare vanishes just as quickly as it appeared.

"You have no right to be jealous," I continue. "You don't have ownership over me. You left me."

Henley cringes at my words, or maybe because he's just now realising how ridiculous it was for him to call me 'his' girl mere moments ago.

"I know," he says softly. "I know I'm being an asshole, okay?"

"Well at least we can both agree on one thing."

I turn and head back to the store, leaving him to wallow in his regret.

Chapter 33

HENLEY

I'd spent the entire afternoon rehearsing with EJ and the band for the gig at the carnival tomorrow. After the eventful morning I'd had at the produce store, I'd hoped it would help relieve some of the tension that had built up inside of me. I'd smashed those skins with everything that I had but no amount of musical therapy could erase the way I'd acted today.

And nothing could make me forget the hurt in Kristen's eyes.

Dylan had sent me to Ben's Harvest this morning to pick up extra supplies for the expected rush of customers that will surely come during tomorrow's inaugural Cliff Haven carnival. The last thing I expected to find there was Kristen laughing and joking around with Chase the way she used to with me. It's an awful thing knowing that you are replaceable.

Guilt and stupidity don't feel too great either.

I'm not proud of my reaction. But seeing them so soon after Mackenzie had texted me to tell me that the two of them had once dated, I guess poor timing had a lot to do with it.

It hadn't mattered that Mackenzie's sole reason for texting me had been to inform me that they were only friends. That although they went out a few times, they hadn't worked out as a couple. Seeing how comfortable they had been in each other's company had caused me to see red and all logic had flown out the window.

Being around noise all day in the bar and then the studio was a stark contrast to the quiet of the loft. Once the tavern closed and the rumble of people had dispersed onto the street, I was left with nothing but eery silence and the negative thoughts that constantly fight their way through to the forefront of my mind.

I glance over at my phone on the nightstand, which tells me that its ten past one in the morning. I've been tossing and turning in this bed for close to an hour.

Frustrated, I haul myself over to the large window that overlooks the esplanade. A heavy cloak of darkness has fallen upon the town, the only light emitted from the streetlights that hover overhead and, to my surprise, a soft glow that comes from within the Haven.

This strikes me as odd because they don't normally leave lights on in the Haven. There's usually a blue haze radiating from the refrigerators, but other than that the café is generally dark. Tonight, someone has definitely left a light on.

I don't have Carla's number, so I consider calling Kristen, but she'd probably just hang up on me anyway, especially at this hour and after how psychotic I acted this morning. I pull a plain white t-shirt over my head and slip into my sneakers. I'll go check it out myself.

A balmy breeze sweeps through the street as I cross the road to the café. I try the door. It's locked, which I guess is a good sign. It looks like somebody has just left a light on in the kitchen. I cup my hands around my face and peer inside the glass.

Everything looks normal enough. The chairs are perched upon the tables, a soft fluorescent glow emanating from the fridge in the corner. I pull back from the window, readying myself to return to the loft.

But then I see her, as she wanders behind the counter, reaching for something in the draw underneath. Her eyes shoot to the window, widening in fear as she sees me standing there. Then anger overtakes her expression as she realises that the mysteriously creepy looking stranger lurking at the window is actually her irredeemable disappointment of an ex.

She rushes to the door, then there's a series of audible clicks as she unlocks it and drags me forcibly by the arm until I'm inside with her.

"Alex! What the hell are you doing? You scared me half to death!"

"I'm sorry. I saw the light on," I stutter.

She sighs and then turns her back to me. I follow her past the serving counter and through to the kitchen.

From the state it's in, I can tell she's been busy back here. There are dirty mixing bowls piled up in the sink. The island bench is covered with baking tins, all lined up in a row. Some are filled with muffin batter, others have already been baked. There are several trays of what looks like caramel slice and a giant bowl of chocolatey batter sitting beside them.

The sugary scent of baked goods fills the room, and it takes me back to a better time, when Kristen would get the urge to whip up something delicious in my old kitchen. She's always been an amazing cook.

"Wow," I say. "What's all this?"

"It's for the carnival," she huffs out, clearly still agitated with me. I can't say I blame her. "The helpline is running a bake sale to raise funds. I offered to make a few things."

I smile when she says 'a few things.' She's obviously going above and beyond here but it's so like Kristen to remain modest about her efforts. "It looks amazing."

"Yeah, well I still have a long way to go, and I've lost a batch of brownies already because I had the oven set wrong." She brings a hand up to her forehead the way she does when she's stressed.

"It'll be okay," I reassure her. "The raspberry muffins have always been my favourite." I move to snatch a muffin from the plate at the end of the bench.

"Hey!" she lunges forward, gripping my hand. Her eyes meet mine, her delicate fingers still wrapped around my arm. Her voice drops in volume when she adds, "I don't think I have enough of these as it is."

"Sorry," I say as she turns back to place two extra muffin trays in the oven. "And I'm sorry about today. I was a dick."

"Yes. You were," she chides, her attention focused only on the mixing bowl in front of her as she aggressively whips its contents.

She's clearly not thrilled by my presence back here, but she hasn't kicked me out yet either. I decide to take that as a win.

"How are things going with Mackenzie?" I ask.

"She's a mess. Leaves her stuff all over my apartment."

A soft chuckle escapes me. She has no idea how typical that sounds. "Yeah. She'll do that."

"She's okay though. I tried to get her a job here, but Carla isn't hiring right now. There will be a maternity leave position coming up but not for a few months yet."

"It's nice of you to ask anyway." I don't tell her that Mackenzie wanted to work in the bar with me. I'm still not sure I want that for her but at the end of the day it's going to be her decision. Mackenzie isn't one to listen to what other people think is best for her. "How's everything going at the helpline?"

"Good. Stressful, but good." She moves to the island bench and begins absent-mindedly stirring the bowl of brownie batter. She continues, almost as though she's forgotten who she's talking to. As though the last six months never happened. "It can be tough hearing some of the things these people are going through. But I think I'm making progress with this one girl. She calls me regularly. At least, I hope I'm getting somewhere with her." She looks up, disturbing this newfound ease between us. "Sorry. I'm rambling."

"Don't be sorry," I say, stepping closer to her. If she only knew how badly I've longed to hear her voice. "I love listening to you talk. I've missed this."

She turns to me and we're standing only inches apart now. For a moment, neither of us makes another move, although I'm certain we can both feel the heat radiating between us. A pulling, as though an invisible tether is drawing us together.

I place a finger through her belt loop and tug her nearer. I can't help it. This is second nature to me. She sighs, my chest filling with warmth where she comes to rest her forehead on it.

"Alex," she breathes into me.

I wrap my other arm around her waist and pull her flush against me and then she's looking up at me with glassy eyes.

Eyes that have a way of communicating to my soul.

They tell me how much she wishes things were different, how she wishes they had stayed the same.

They show me all the ways I've disappointed her.

I feel her fingers tugging at my t-shirt as she looks away and then back again. She's fighting an internal war with herself, wanting what she shouldn't want. Her hand travels upward, skimming my abdomen and chest before coming to rest on my face. Her fingers delicately trace my jaw before she laces both of her hands around my neck.

"I missed you," she whispers, her voice pained.

Those words take all the air out of my lungs. "I missed you too." I manage to choke out. "Every day."

Then her lips are on mine, kissing me hungrily. She leaps upward, wrapping her legs around me and in one swift movement I swing her around, lifting her up onto the bench behind us. Her hands claw at my t-shirt and mine find their way up her thighs.

She pauses only to raise my shirt up and over my head. Then she's kissing me again with urgency, as though this could end at any moment.

Maybe it could.

My hands slide upward underneath her t-shirt, skimming her rib cage as her fingers skim the waistband of my grey trackpants. All I can think about is how much I've wanted this and for a moment I can almost forget every lonely night I've spent these last six months.

Almost.

Then that voice of self-doubt finds me.

It always finds me.

And reminds me that I'm not worthy of any of it.

The shrill screeching of tyres on the street outside stops me dead and I pull away from her, slamming into the island bench behind me. There's a pounding in my chest, my heart as it hammers against my rib cage.

The world goes dark.

The only sound my own breath, rapid and irregular.

Then I hear her, her voice soothing. A light in the darkness.

"Henley, what's wrong?"

I want to reply but my mouth can't form the words. It takes me a second to realise I'm sitting on the tiled floor, my back hard up against the kitchen cupboards, my knees curled into my bare chest.

"Henley," she says. There's only the slightest hint of panic in her voice and I find that reassuring in a way. "What happened? God, you're shaking."

"That noise," I manage through gasps of air. "The car."

Kristen shakes her head, confusion flooding her features. "It was just some idiot teenagers doing a burnout in the street."

I nod, taking more air into my lungs. "Okay."

"Just breathe, baby. It's okay. I'm here."

I become aware that she's kneeling beside me now, her hands making light circles on my bare shoulder blades. The world slowly becomes lighter as the blackness fades.

Suddenly, Kristen pauses, her hands coming to stop over a section of my back. I tense, my body immediately going rigid when I realise what has caught her attention. The jagged scar that runs across the length of my left shoulder blade down to the centre of my back.

"What is this?" she demands, her eyebrows pulling down in a frown.

"Nothing." My voice is cold as I scramble forward, reaching for my t-shirt on the ground in front.

"Alex, that is not nothing." Her voice is husky, a mere whisper.

I feel my nostrils flare with the sudden intake of breath as I pull the fabric over my head, desperate to cover myself.

"It's fine."

"No, it's not. Why won't you open up to me about this? Why won't you tell me what happened?" She reaches for me, a tortured look in her eyes, but I pull away before she gets close enough.

"Because you wouldn't want to know. It's for the best. I never should have come here. This shouldn't have happened. It was a mistake."

Her glare cuts me straight through the heart. I know how unfair I'm being. I've come over here and taken what wasn't mine to take and it kills me that I've hurt her again.

"Alex, we should talk about this." Her voice is soft, sympathetic.

A reminder of how much better of a human being she is than me.

"We don't need to do that. I'm not one of your callers at the helpline."

She tilts her head and watches me in pity. It's more than I can stand. I turn my back, bursting through the Haven's doors and out onto the street, feeling even more miserable and reckless than I had before.

Chapter 34

KRISTEN

I have no self-control when it comes to Alex Henley, that much is clear. Even despite his behaviour toward Chase yesterday I still couldn't keep my hands to myself.

More than that, I'm worried about him. I once knew everything there was to know about Henley, but he's become a puzzle I'm not sure I'll ever figure out. And even more baffling to me is the fact that even after everything, I still care.

There's only one thing I need more than coffee right now and that's my best friend, which is why after gathering my phone and throwing on a t-shirt and denim shorts, I'd found myself standing in Liv and EJ's apartment watching Liv bang the top of her coffee machine violently with the palm of her hand.

"Stupid freaking thing!" she cries.

"Hey! Hey! Be kind to that freaking thing," I interrupt. "I need it to make me a giant cup of caffeine."

She pivots around at the sound of my voice. "The only thing this thing is going to make you is insane," she replies. "Certifiably insane."

"Aww." I shoot a sympathetic look her way. "What's wrong with it?"

"It's just not very user friendly. It's too fancy for its own good." She rolls her eyes and then slumps onto the couch in the corner of the living room. "It was an engagement present from Dad. I have no idea why he chose to buy us a coffee machine when we live above a café. Nice gesture though."

I smile, following her to the couch. "Where's EJ?"

"He's getting us coffee from downstairs."

I laugh at the irony, but it comes out half-hearted. Liv eyes me curiously. It's obvious she's sensed the strange mood I'm in. "What's up with you today?"

I fill her in on recent events. The showdown with Chase, the make out session in the kitchen, the huge scar on Henley's back. And the way he freaked out over the screeching tyres in the street.

"Maybe there's a whole lot more to the story than we realise," Liv says, resting her chin on her hand, her eyes narrowing in deep thought.

"Yeah," I scoff. "Like maybe he was abducted by aliens or kidnapped by the mafia."

Liv laughs but then a seriousness takes over her face. "I'm not kidding though. None of this sounds normal."

"Whose side are you on?" I swat at her knee as we sit on opposite sides of the couch.

"No ones," Liv says bluntly. This earns a glare from me. "I mean yours. Obviously, yours. Always. All I'm saying is what if things aren't exactly as they seem?"

"What do you mean?" I feel my brow crease.

"I don't know. EJ went to talk to Henley the other day and the next thing I know, he's practising in the studio on the new Tama and joining the band for their gig at the carnival," Liv explains.

"That is weird," I agree.

Henley hadn't mentioned he would be playing at the carnival, but I guess we didn't really do all that much talking last night.

"I just don't get it. Something is definitely going on." Liv reaches for her bagel and takes a small bite.

"You think EJ is keeping something from you?" I ask.

"Yeah, I do," she says earnestly.

"That's crazy," I wave off her apprehension. "No way."

That doesn't sound like EJ at all. He's transparent. He doesn't keep secrets. If he's keeping one now, then he must believe it's one that's worth protecting.

"Yes way," Liv continues. "Only just last week he went to give Henley a piece of his mind. He was so angry at him for what he had done to you. And himself as well. I mean, they were best friends and he left EJ without warning too."

I nod compassionately. "Yeah, he was a jerk. The worst kind of jerk."

"Yeah. But that's just it. A few days later EJ had a completely different attitude towards him. He seems to have forgiven him."

"Wait. What are you saying?" I ask. "You think he might know why Henley is having these panic attacks?"

"I'm saying EJ knows something. Something he isn't telling. You know. Bro code and all that." At that moment, EJ bursts through the door carrying a tray containing three large takeaway coffee cups. "Oh, thank God! Gimme all the coffee."

EJ laughs as he hands over a cup to Liv. Then he reaches for the second and hands it to me. "Double shot cappuccino with extra chocolate on top."

"For me?" I ask, taking the cup from his hands.

"I saw you out the window walking past the stair well. Figured you might need one because you're... well... you."

"Thank you," I say, eyeing him curiously. "Do you know something that you aren't telling me?"

"Like what?" He takes a long draw from his own cup then comically slaps his forehead as he lowers it. "Oh, shit. Yes. I forgot to ask for soy milk."

"Not about the coffee, you goof." I roll my eyes. "I'm talking about Henley."

"What about him?" he asks. His poker face sucks.

"Cut the crap, EJ. I know you know something. You were so fired up when Henley came back to town and the next minute, you're offering him a place in your band? What gives?"

EJ sighs. "Look, it really isn't my place to say. I don't think I even know the full story."

"What story?" Liv pipes up, lifting her head from the coffee cup.

"Henley didn't just leave town. Something happened and he couldn't come back," EJ explains.

"What the hell could possibly have happened to make him have to stay away from me? After all the things he'd said to me before he left. It doesn't make sense." I shake my head in denial.

"Exactly. He told me he wanted all in with you. That's why I was so pissed when he left."

"Come on, EJ. He just ran away. He ran scared like he always does." I want to believe that it's as simple as this, though deep down I know Henley's panic attacks must stem from somewhere.

We all know that Henley has had commitment issues that stem from way back to his childhood. His parent's constant arguing and lack of affection for each other affected him more deeply than he'd ever care to admit. I've believed for six months that he left town because he freaked out about us.

225

That he found someone else to move on with. That's the story I've told myself this entire time, but what if it isn't true.

Because I'm questioning it now.

I'm questioning all the things that don't add up. All the ways that my theory doesn't make sense.

"He didn't, Kristen. Think about it. He isn't even the same guy anymore." EJ's green eyes meet mine. "He's jumpy all the time. It's like he's always watching his back."

"You noticed it too."

"Yeah." EJ drops his gaze to the floor, running a hand through his messy, brown hair. He sighs as though he's at war with himself. He wants to tell me something. He just doesn't know if he should.

"EJ, what are you not saying?"

He flops down onto the other couch opposite me and Liv. He takes in a long breath before he begins to speak again. "I called my dad because I couldn't believe he would offer Henley a place to live and his old job back when he'd just walked out on us all like that. I was angry."

"And?" Liv asks.

"And he told me that I shouldn't be so hard on him. That there were things I didn't know about," he answers.

"Like what?" Liv and I both say in unison.

EJ groans, throwing his head back onto the headrest of the couch. He pauses, as though he's deciding whether to keep this secret for his best friend or reveal it to his oldest friend.

"It's not my place to tell you," he resigns. "If you want answers, you're gonna have to get them from Henley himself."

I think about all the ways in which Henley has changed.

The way he flinches at loud noises and screeching car tyres. The way he forgets how to breathe.

I need to believe that he just simply left me. It's easier to think him a complete jerk that just decided to up and leave town with no real reason at all.

Because the alternative, that something life-changing, something unimaginable happened, is too heavy to comprehend.

Chapter 35

HENLEY

It's just after 4pm when I pull up at the showground with EJ's seven-piece Tama in tow. In the distance Levi and EJ pace along the mainstage, a couple of soundcheck guys swarming around them carrying cords and equipment. We play at seven and I have to admit, I'm nervous as hell about it.

I've got three hours to kill so I text Mackenzie to see if she wants to hang out at the carnival for a while. I can see that she's received the message but in true Mackenzie style, she waits four hours to reply. Okay, maybe not four hours. More like ten minutes. I can't help but smirk when her reply finally comes through.

Mackenzie
> Sounds lame...

> It's totally bussin'. Get your butt down here.

Mackenzie
You're using that word wrong

> Please. There are hotdogs and nutella funnel cakes.

Mackenzie

Is that code for "I'm a loser that has no friends and I need you to come and make me look good?"

> Guilty

Mackenzie

You're lucky there's nothing on TV. See you in ten.

I lean against the brick wall of the surf club while I wait for her. After a quick scan of the showground, I spot the Cliff Haven helpline tent set up to the far left of the carnival. Chase crosses the field, two bottles of water in hand and I cringe inwardly at the memory of how I'd treated him in the produce store the other day.

It killed me to learn that Chase had dated Kristen. I'd always sensed that he wanted more from her than friendship and when Mackenzie confirmed it, I got pissed.

But I had no right to demean him after my part in all of this. My accusations were unwarranted. If anything, I should be thanking him for looking out for Kristen in my absence. Be grateful to him for standing by her side.

I barely know who I am anymore. I'd set out on a journey not so long ago to find a better version of myself but somewhere along the way I got hopelessly lost. There are many things weighing on my conscience right now. I'm not sure how much more guilt I can carry but I do know of one way that I can lighten the load.

"Chase!" I call out as I begin to jog across the field. Chase stalls when he sees me and I raise my hands in a show of peace. "I'm not here to fight."

"What do you want?" Chase asks. He doesn't seem annoyed, just genuinely curious.

"To apologise."

Chase sighs. "It's not me you should be apologising to."

"You know what I mean. I shouldn't have treated you that way and I'm sorry."

"Don't worry about it," he says as he turns to walk away.

"How is she?" I call out. He swings back around slowly. "I mean, how was she after…"

"After you left?"

"Yeah." I know I'm not going to like his answer, but I deserve nothing less than the ache it will bring me.

He shakes his head. I follow his line of sight to the bake sale booth where Kristen manoeuvres around the front of the table to serve a box of baked treats to an elderly customer.

"Devastated. Lost. Broken," he lists each word and I wince at every one of them. "She tried to hide it, but I could see through it. Still can."

I nod hopelessly. "Thank you. For being there when I wasn't."

His mouth pulls in a grim line. "It's never been me she's needed."

He turns and I watch as he jogs back to Kristen. I don't think I could hate myself any more than I do right now.

"You okay?" Mackenzie's voice comes from somewhere behind me.

"Not really," I reply honestly.

"You wanna talk about it?"

I shake my head.

"Come on," she says, linking her arm through mine. "I know something that might help cheer you up."

"I doubt it," I say, but I let her lead me across the showground until we're standing directly in front of the petting zoo.

She points to the animal that has caught her eye. "Isn't that the most freaking adorable thing you've ever seen in your life?" Mackenzie asks, gripping my arm tighter. "I mean, look at it!"

She squeals. Like, literally squeals. It's the most un-Mackenzie thing I've ever heard, I have to do a double take to make sure this tiny blonde hanging from my arm is the same girl that spent months torturing me with sarcastic remarks and more recently, bullying me for snoring.

But no, it's definitely Mackenzie that's gone completely gaga for a three-foot-tall baby alpaca, who according to the sign on the gate, is named Lola.

"Look at her eyelashes!" she gushes.

When she smiles, I can't help but think that this is the first time I've actually seen her happy and that has me smiling too.

"Yep, those eyelashes are something," I agree.

"She's beautiful! And you're smiling. See? I knew I could cheer you up."

I shake my head at her, although I am grateful for this distraction. "You know, these things spit when they're angry."

"They do not," she insists, reaching out to pat the alpaca. "You're making that up."

"I'm really not."

And just to prove my point, Lola rears her head back and hisses at her. Mackenzie jumps backward in fright, clinging onto me for dear life and I can't help the laughter that bursts from me.

"You weren't kidding," she says, her eyes still wide.

"No. I really wasn't." I fold my arms across my chest as Mackenzie gives me a playful shove.

"Mackenzie!" A familiar voice says. "It's nice to see you here."

"Uh, hi, Pamela." Mackenzie's smile falters.

Pamela Riley stands inside the small fence that contains the animals. I should have known better than to let Mackenzie drag me over here. Kristen's mother runs the petting zoo every year. When her eyes find mine, I wonder what she sees in them.

Failure, probably.

But if she hates me for what I've done to her daughter she doesn't let on.

"Oh. Hi, Alex," she says. "Good to see you back in town."

"Thanks. It's good to be back." I can't think of anything else to say so I stand there awkwardly.

Great. The first time I'm seeing Kristen's mum in over six months and it's here, at a petting zoo she's running. With Mackenzie literally hanging off my arm.

God, this is not what I need right now.

Mackenzie has the good sense to break the tension. I make a mental note to thank her for it later. "So, Pamela. How old are these little goats? They look so tiny."

"These ones are nearly eight weeks old," Pam replies. "They're getting a little impatient because it's their feeding time. Would you like to come in and help me out?"

"Oh, I... I don't know about that," she begins.

"Come on, it's easy. I'll show you what to do." Pam opens the gate for her to enter. She looks to me for what seems like approval, and I give her a nod, urging her on.

"Okay, I guess it couldn't hurt," she agrees.

Pam ushers Mackenzie inside as the baby cow pushes toward the gate. "Hold up, Daisy! Sorry, you'll have to excuse her. She's had enough of being contained and wants to escape."

Mackenzie laughs lightly, giving Daisy a pat on the head. I watch as Pam instructs her to feed the goat. I don't miss the way Mackenzie's face lights up as the goat begins to greedily nurse from the bottle.

"That's it. Look! You're a natural," Pam says to her.

And she's right. Mackenzie looks completely at ease with the goats as they all herd around her.

She giggles as Daisy nuzzles her hair and a chicken pecks at her shoe. "Yeah, this is actually pretty cool."

"So… not lame then?" I question, one eyebrow raised, my arms still folded across my chest.

She rolls her eyes and tries to hide the smile that creeps across her face.

"Would you mind if I took a picture for the clinic's Instagram page?" Pam asks.

"Sure," Mackenzie replies.

After Pam takes a few photos, I help Mackenzie back through the gate.

"Thanks Pamela," Mackenzie says. "That was so awesome, but we need to get going."

"You're welcome anytime, Mackenzie." Pam smiles and then her voice takes on a sternness. "Oh, and Alex? Whatever it is you're looking for? I hope you find it soon."

And just when I'd thought I'd dodged any kind of judgement from Pamela Riley, there it is.

The pity.

The disappointment.

She let me off easy though. Because I deserve a lot worse.

Chapter 86

KRISTEN

The Cliff Haven carnival is in full swing, and it seems there's an even bigger turnout this year than last. When I'd arrived at the showground just before 3pm, the sun had been high in the sky, the heat still scorching. But it's now just after six and the light is slowly but surely being swallowed by the horizon, the air still balmy.

The bake sale has proved to be a complete success. Along with the carload of baked goods I supplied, Jules had been able to get some other volunteers to donate both sweet and savoury treats. The community has been more than enthusiastic in helping our cause, buying them up in droves. In fact, we're down to our last tray of muffins with only a few random cookies, scones and brownies left. Chase's raffle tickets were sold out hours ago too.

"Hey, look." I elbow Chase in the arm where he's seated beside me in a folding chair. "Here comes Mrs. Mayfield. I bet you twenty bucks she buys up the last dozen muffins."

"What? A whole dozen?" Chase eyes me sceptically. "No way she's gonna buy that many. You're on."

I hold out my hand with a wink and Chase shakes it firmly.

"Hope you brought some cash with you," I smirk.

"Hope *you* did. Easiest twenty bucks I'll ever make."

Mrs. Mayfield has been a regular at the Haven since before I'd even begun working there. Besides knowing all about her pet chihuahua and her love of cryptic crosswords, I've learnt that she has a standing regular order. Black coffee and a banana muffin.

"Hey, Mrs. Mayfield," Chase says in greeting as she approaches the table.

"Hello, Chase," she replies in a soft British accent. "What's all this?"

"We're here to raise money for the Cliff Haven helpline," I explain.

"Oh, how lovely!" she says, delighted. She eyes the cardboard tray of muffins beneath the thin film of plastic wrap. "Are these banana?"

"They sure are, Mrs. Mayfield," I say with a smile. "Would you like one? They're three dollars each."

"Hmm," she muses, her pointer finger coming to rest on her chin. "How much for the lot?"

"It's thirty dollars for the whole dozen," Chase answers, shooting a quick dubious glance in my direction.

"I'll take them all," she says. She reaches into her tan, leather purse and plucks three ten-dollar notes. I throw Chase a conspiratorial grin as she passes them over the table.

Chase takes the money and tucks it safely into the cash box while I hand over the tray of muffins. "Thank you so much for your support, Mrs. Mayfield. You enjoy those!"

I grin as she walks away in the direction of the Ferris wheel.

"How the hell did you predict that?" Chase asks.

"Are you kidding? Everyone knows Mrs. Mayfield has a weakness for banana muffins."

"Oh, everyone does, huh?" he jokes, giving me a light, playful nudge in the ribs.

I giggle and attempt to shove him back, but he blocks my hand with his own. I squirm as he playfully pokes me in the ribs. "Stop!" I say in between laughs.

A moment later we're interrupted by a couple, who purchase a random selection of scones and brownies. Then a group of teenagers approach the stall to buy up the rest of what's left on the table. Chase and I can't help noticing their laid-back demeanours and bloodshot eyes. We snicker to each other as they turn and meander toward the beach scoffing down their goods with urgency.

"Looks like we're sold out of food *and* raffle tickets now," Chase says. "I'll give Jules a call and see what she wants us to do."

Chase pulls his phone from his back pocket and a moment later I hear him greet Jules. I don't hear much of anything else though, because my attention is drawn to the man standing across the field. A man I used to know so well who now seems like a complete stranger.

Henley runs a hand through his unkempt, blonde hair, turning as a woman steps into view behind him.

Mackenzie.

She laces her arms around his neck, and he bends, leaning into the hug. From here it appears an intimate gesture, although they say they are nothing more than friends. Still, something eats at me, refusing to add up in my mind. They may not be dating, but there's an obvious connection between the two of them.

Something has united them, but what?

"Hey." Chase moves up to stand beside me, his voice pulling my attention away from them.

"Yeah. What's up?" I turn to him, attempting to seem unbothered by the display I've just witnessed.

"I said we can pack up now."

Clearly, I had been too distracted to hear him.

"Oh, really?" I ask. "So we're all done?"

"Yeah. Jules said to pack up the tables and boxes and we're free to enjoy the carnival." His eyes scan over the opposite side of the field and I know he can see what had piqued my interest while he'd been on the phone. His gaze drifts back to mine, the crease between his brow deepening. "Are you okay?"

"Mmhmm," I say, knowing he can see right through me.

He tilts his head to the side, his eyes searching my face for the words I'm not saying. "You still love him, don't you."

I breathe out a heavy sigh. "I don't want to."

"But you do."

I nod reluctantly, my bottom lip between my teeth. Because it's true. Even after everything he's put me through, with all that he's done, it's like I'm hardwired to love him anyway. I don't realise a tear has escaped, tracking its way down my cheek, until Chase reaches out and swipes it away with his thumb.

"Sorry. This is stupid." I sniffle.

Chase shakes his head. "Your feelings aren't stupid, Kristen."

I let out a bitter laugh. "But they are though. It's like I'm a glutton for punishment or something."

"Maybe you guys will work things out. You never know." He shrugs.

"I doubt it. Unless he reveals whatever mammoth sized secret he's keeping from me." I swipe at my wet cheeks and lower my gaze to the ground. "And apologises to you for being a complete asshole."

"Well, he's done half of those things so those aren't bad odds."

My head shoots up. "What? He spoke to you?"

"Yeah. When I went to get us drinks earlier. For what it's worth, I don't think he's such a bad guy. I mean, he's broody as fuck." His eyebrows shoot up and I manage a laugh. "But he's not all bad. He obviously still cares about you. I think he has a lot of regrets."

I glance back over at Henley. Mackenzie is saying something to him, but his stare is focused squarely on me.

"Just give it some time. Maybe he'll come around," Chase says, rubbing my upper arm.

"What am I supposed to do while I wait for that day to happen?"

"Well, you've got me." He pulls me in for a hug, gives my shoulders a squeeze and then adds, "First we're gonna pack up all of this stuff and then we're gonna ride the big zipper till we puke."

I grin up at him through my tears. "Sounds like a plan."

Chapter 37

HENLEY

We like to think we're irreplaceable, that it would be impossible for anyone else to just waltz in and fill our shoes. And I never expected her to wait for me, but it kills me to see her with someone else, even if that someone else is not actually dating her anymore. He still gets to spend all of his free time with her.

I watch as he pulls her in close, the way she tilts her head to meet his gaze and something heavy turns over in my chest. I lean back onto the brick wall behind me, thankful it's there to support my weight. I can't take this torture anymore.

"Stop tormenting yourself. You know they're just friends." I catch Mackenzie watching me in my peripheral, but my stare doesn't waver.

"So they say. But it doesn't look that way," I mutter.

"Well, it is that way. She told me so."

"It's not like it matters. She hates me." I force myself to look away from Chase and Kristen.

"She doesn't hate you. She just doesn't know the truth. And that's my fault." Guilt mars Mackenzie's features, but she isn't the one to blame.

"It's not your fault. I just want to protect you." I don't mean for my voice to increase in volume, but frustration is getting the better of me.

"I know you do, but this is getting ridiculous," she retaliates. "I mean, back there at the petting zoo? That was awkward as fuck."

"Yeah," I agree. Running into Pamela Riley had not been pleasant.

"I heard what she said to you when we were leaving. It's not right."

"I know, Mackenzie. But what am I supposed to do?" I ask her. "If I tell the truth, it affects you too."

Mackenzie lets out a frustrated sigh. She doesn't like what I'm telling her, but she knows I'm right. Our truths depend on each other.

If I go down, she goes down with me.

"I'll tell her," she says in a voice so quiet I almost miss it. "Soon. I'll tell her what I need to tell her. Then maybe you can stop using me as an excuse."

"You know that isn't what I'm doing," I say. "I care about you. But we have to come clean sooner or later."

"Yeah."

I suck in a breath, running a hand through my hair. "You'll really tell her?"

"I will," Mackenzie says defiantly. "Soon."

"Okay."

"All is not lost my friend," she says, slapping her palm on my shoulder then reaching around to give me a quick hug. "I'm gonna get out of here. Might go enjoy having the TV to myself before Kristen gets home. You gonna be alright?"

I smile at her concern for me. Even with the weight of the world on her back she still has time to worry about me.

"Yeah. EJ's set starts in half hour so I need to go find the band."

"Okay," she replies. "I'll talk to you later. We'll figure this out."

"Be safe," I tell her.

She gives me a knowing look. "You too."

I observe Mackenzie walking back to the esplanade until finally, she begins to blend with the crowd, becoming lost in a sea of people. Then I turn and make my way in the direction of the main stage.

I stride through the sideshow alley, passing the dodgem cars on my right and the carousel on my left. That's when I see them again and it's as though I've been hit at full force in the chest. It's almost impossible to bear the gut-wrenching pain that gnaws at me seeing them both stagger out of the gates of the big zipper, Chase laughing as he hooks an arm around Kristen's neck.

I try to push down the memories that resurface. Of me and Kristen doing the same thing years ago, stumbling our way behind Madame Zelda's fortune-telling tent where we'd made out for an unknown amount of time, our heads dizzy from spending too much time on the big zipper. It's hard to believe that not so long ago we were inseparable, unable to keep our hands to ourselves.

I can't be thinking about this. In less than twenty minutes I'll be on stage, and I need to be focused on the music and nothing else.

I haven't played live with EJ since before he hit the big time. He draws way bigger crowds now than the ones I was used to performing for in our little garage band. It's going to be hard enough to face the masses of people that will surely swarm the stage without Kristen interrupting my every thought.

I can do this. I have to do this.

I force my head to the ground and keep walking.

When I reach the main stage, EJ is waiting for me with the rest of the band. "Hey, man." He slaps my palm with a solid handshake. "You good to go?"

"As ready as I'll ever be," I say, hoping I sound more confident than I feel while pulling three pairs of drum sticks out of my back pocket. Spares in case I break a couple. I've broken more than usual lately.

There's a young girl on stage playing a keyboard and singing, a slight country twang to her voice. Liv watches her from the corner of the stage, clapping her hands and cheering her on. If I had to guess, I'd say she's one of her students at the Music Box.

When she launches into her final song my nerves start to get the better of me. I've played for EJ so many times on stage, not to mention in the studio when I'd laid down the drum tracks for most of the songs on his first album. But that feels like a lifetime ago. In so many aspects of my life, I'm no longer enough.

I'm not enough for Kristen.

I hope I'm still enough for this.

"Okay. We're on," EJ says. "Same set list we practiced. Five songs. Then we go get beers."

"Hell yeah," Levi hollers. "Best pep talk you've given yet, EJ."

I don't look up at either one of them. Instead, I find my place on the stage behind the shiny silver and black drum kit, my palms already slick with sweat.

The entire crowd goes wild when EJ makes his way to the microphone, his turquoise fender slung around his neck. "What's up Cliff Haven? You all having a great night?"

The response to this is more roaring and cheering which only gets louder when he announces the first song. There's no denying that performing was what EJ was born to do. I'm proud of my friend and how far he's come.

Normally, I'd feed off the energy of the crowd. Tonight, I do my best to drown it out. I tilt my head to the side, working out a kink in my neck and pull my shoulders back to stretch out the tension in my back and arms. Then I lift the sticks and count us in.

I don't break any sticks in the first song. Instead, I forget where I am, and I forget this life I'm living that doesn't resemble anything like the one I thought I'd have. I melt into the song, letting it be my escape from the spiralling mess that I've become. I find irony in the fact that in life I am lost, but up here I'm the leader, the steady driving beat that guides everyone else through.

I glance at the crowd and instantly regret it. Because the first thing I see is her, and she reminds me of everything.

She takes me back to nights at Steve's Tavern when she would cheer me on from the table near the stage. And yeah, where sometimes I'd see her scowling at me because we'd had some stupid fight but knew we were going to make up before the night was over.

Only now she doesn't look at me in either of those ways. She observes me like I'm a stranger, and I guess that's what I am to her now. She doesn't know this version of me, and I'll never be able to go back to the way I was. I've been forever changed, shaped by circumstance. I know that in my core.

But despite the way this realisation fills me with despair, it ignites something from within. A tiny fire that had long ago lost its spark. I'm not sure I've ever believed I'm worthy of someone like her. And maybe I'm not. Maybe I'll never be, but I want to be. I've never wanted it more.

I break two sticks in the fourth song. EJ's material is softer than the stuff we used to play in the band together, but that doesn't stop me from giving it everything.

Sweat beads on my forehead. I smile at the ache in my arms. I know my entire torso will be stiff tomorrow, but I welcome it. Drumming has always provided me with a way to release stress. It's always made me feel alive, and tonight, even with everything that's been happening and all the thoughts running through my mind, it's no different.

I'm blissfully ignorant of what else is going on around me.

Until the last song anyway.

We get a quarter of the way through the final track and that's when I fall apart. I dare a glance up at the crowd and it takes the breath out of me. My heart hammers against my ribs.

This can't be happening.

Not now.

But I'm certain of what I've seen. Or at least I think I am. A tall long-haired guy whose face rises above the rest, a grimace adorning his face in the darkness.

He's found me.

He's found *us*.

I stand suddenly, the drumsticks falling to the ground either side of me, the stool crashing to the back of the stage.

Mackenzie is the only thing going through my thought process. Then I see Kristen's head angle to the side, a crease between her brows.

"Henley, what's up?" EJ turns to me, his guitar still hung around his neck. He doesn't look mad, just confused by my behaviour. "You okay?"

"I have to go." The words leave my mouth, but I hear them as though someone else is saying them.

The whole band has stopped playing now, the only sound a low rumble from the crowd. I can't see him anymore, blinded by the stage lights. I start to second guess myself.

Did I imagine him standing there?

Have I finally gone insane?

Either way, I've stuffed up the set and I need to get out of here. If my eyes haven't failed me there is too much at stake. I jump off the back of the stage, reaching for the phone in my back pocket.

"Henley!" I hear EJ call.

I don't have time to answer or explain. I need to find Mackenzie.

She picks up on the third ring. "Hey, what's up?"

I exhale a long sigh of relief at the sound of her chipper voice. "Mackenzie," I breathe.

"Yeah?" she answers. "Geez, what happened to you? You sound like you've run a marathon. You might need to get on the treadmill every once in a while if this is what drumming does to you, old man."

I manage to choke out a laugh at her attempt to tease me. I've never been happier to hear an insult in all my life. "I'll keep that in mind. Is everything okay there?"

"Yeah. Just watching tv and eating snacks so I'd say everything is perfect."

I hear the crunching sound of potato chips echo through the phone. "Okay." I say. "Good."

"Everything okay there?" she asks curiously, no doubt sensing the stress in my voice.

I pause, contemplating if I should say more. I decide against it. There's no point in upsetting Mackenzie for no reason. For all I know this is all in my head. It wouldn't be the first time my mind has played tricks on me.

"Yeah," I say. "Yeah, everything's fine.

"Okay. In that case, I'm gonna get back to my Doritos and chocolate."

"If those are Kristen's Doritos, you know she'll kill you," I warn.

"I'm willing to take that chance," she mumbles through a mouthful of food.

I let out a relieved chuckle as she hangs up the call.

Then a new wave of panic hits me as I feel the weight of a hand on my shoulder. I spin around bracing myself for impact, my left fist raised high. I'm met with EJ's wide green eyes as he holds both palms up in the air.

"Henley! Dude! What the hell?"

I press my palm to my forehead as embarrassment rushes through me. "God, EJ. I'm so sorry."

"It's fine. What the hell happened back there?" He still doesn't seem angry, just genuinely anxious.

"I wish I could explain it. I'm so sorry. I fucked up the set. I shouldn't …"

"Forget the set. I finished the last song as an acoustic." EJ cuts me off. "Are you alright?"

EJ has every right to be pissed at me, but I should have known he would only be concerned for my well-being. He's always put friends and family first. Before work, before music. Before anything else. Sometimes I hate how understanding my best friend can be. I don't deserve his loyalty.

I suck in a breath and nod. "Yeah. I think so."

"I'm worried about you. Kristen told Liv you've been skittish lately." He places a hand on my shoulder, and I flinch, only proving his point.

Great. I know Kristen talking about me to Liv only comes from a place of concern, but it makes me mad regardless. I can't have the entire town thinking I'm a head case, even if I'm resembling one more and more with every passing day.

"Look, it's understandable given what you've been through. Have you ever talked to someone about it?" EJ asks. "You know you can always talk to me if you need to."

"I don't want to talk about it," I say, my voice low. "I can't."

"For what it's worth, I really think you should." EJ sighs, knowing he isn't going to get a further response from me on the subject. "But for now, you wanna drink about it?"

I'm not entirely sure it's a great idea to go back to the tavern right now. The way Dylan has been riding me lately, I'm probably more likely to wind up behind it than throwing back beers at a table.

But then again, I live there. What choice do I really have?

"Yeah. Let's go."

Chapter 38

KRISTEN

Watching Henley on stage had sparked an old flame from somewhere within me, that for just a moment had burned brighter than the wildfire of rage I'd felt in his absence.

I'm not ready to forgive him for his blatant lack of consideration for me all those months ago, whether what EJ had alluded to is true or not. I want to stay mad at him but seeing him thrash that drum kit, the way he'd fed from the crowd's energy, it had reminded me of our carefree days.

I'd caught a glimpse of that fun-loving guy that had always been the life of the party. I want to believe that he's still in there somewhere, that this imposter has him buried just below the surface.

It's almost midnight now. The noise from the carnival died down a little while ago. The only people left wandering the streets are the teenagers not old enough to buy a drink at the tavern, most likely debating where the after party should be.

I'd said goodbye to Chase after declining his offer to drive me back to my apartment. The night is still, the air warm. This is the perfect time to wander along the river.

I follow the winding path toward the water, the trees bent over, their branches like limbs reaching for each other in the darkness. I pause when I see a figure draped across the park bench up ahead, contemplating whether it's safe to continue further.

But then an arm flings out sideways revealing a familiar pattern of tattoos. I sigh, then push forward, knowing this version of Henley I'm about to meet isn't going to be my favourite.

He's lying on his back on the park bench, his knees up, one arm serving as a pillow behind his head, the other flailing out to the side. He doesn't move when he sees me standing above him. Even in the dim light of the moon his eyes are ice blue.

"What are you doing out here, Henley?" I ask him, not really expecting an answer.

"Wanted to see the stars," he answers, his gaze still on the sky overhead. There's a slight slur in his voice that lets me know he's been drinking. "There were no stars where I was."

"What do you mean?" I ask, unsure if I should even try to decipher his drunken babble.

He breathes a heavy sigh. "I thought about you every day. When I couldn't see the stars, I thought of you then, too."

"Henley, you aren't making any sense."

"Yeah," he agrees with a half-laugh. "Nothing makes sense anymore."

His eyes close, his head rolling to the side. If he passes out on this bench, he'll have to stay here. There's no way I could carry him back to the loft.

"You need water," I say to him. Then I reach into the small bag I'm carrying and pull out the still almost full bottle of water Chase had purchased for me at the carnival.

He doesn't respond when I tell him to drink it. He's well on his way to passed out cold. I unscrew the cap off the bottle and pour a stream of water over his face.

His body shoots upright into a sitting position and he almost topples from the bench. "What the hell?"

"Well, you wouldn't drink it." I stand in front of him, my arms folded across my chest.

"You enjoyed that, didn't you?"

There's a hint of a smile on his lips. His words are still slurred but I don't think we're in danger of him passing out again any time soon. He lifts the hem of his shirt up to wipe the water from his face and I try to pretend that his abs are doing absolutely nothing for me.

I sigh and then flop down on the bench next to him. I can't help but think about the very different experience I had with him on this bench a little more than six months ago.

"Contrary to what you may think, it's not my only life's mission to get revenge on you," I tell him.

"Why not? I hurt you. I deserve it."

"Something tells me you're already in enough pain." I don't feel right taking advantage of his drunken state, but I feel like this is my one opportunity to get some information out of him. "How did you get that scar?"

"What? This one?" He points a thumb over his shoulder to where I'd seen that silvery pink, jagged line running from one side to the other. "Got shanked with a toothbrush."

I sigh, my eyes rolling back in my head. "I should have known I wouldn't get a serious answer from you while you're this drunk."

He shrugs his shoulders and shakes his head, the trace of a smile disappearing.

"Are you ever going to tell me what happened?"

"I don't want you to be disappointed in me." He doesn't look at me when he speaks.

"You think I would be?"

"You already are." He leans forward and puts his head in his hands. "I wish I could be more for you, Kristen. But I'll never be enough." He straightens himself and then turns to me, his eyes a turbulent ocean of blue. "I can't take any of it back."

A loud boom fills the air, and a series of coloured sparks rips through the sky. Midnight fireworks. The sound sends Henley cowering behind his fingers again, his head slumped toward the ground. It's not until he feels the weight of my hand on his shoulder that he looks up.

"You're shaking," I whisper.

"I don't do well with loud noises. In case that isn't obvious," he mutters.

I don't need to tell him I've noticed. He reacted the same way that night in the Haven when the car tyres screeched on the street outside.

"Pretty ironic for a drummer," I joke.

He laughs and it's a real laugh. For a second, I see the old Henley, relaxed and fun. Then a shadow falls over his face and he's replaced with this sullen version.

"What happened tonight? On stage," I ask, my curiosity getting the better of me.

He shakes his head. "It was nothing. I thought I saw something. The stage lights were in my eyes."

I nod, although I don't believe him. I know that this is the only explanation I'm going to get right now. I've known Henley long enough to know when to push and when to let things go and if I push right now, he's going to lose his patience with me. And regardless of how hurt I am by the way he's treated me, I don't want to leave him out here by the river all alone.

"I think we should go. It's late," I tell him.

"I'm okay here," he argues.

"I'm not okay with leaving you here," I say. "Come on. Let's go."

He groans as I stand up, extending my arm out to him. He stares at my hand a moment before he finally reaches for it, and I use all of my strength to pull him up. He staggers a little, so I tell him to lean on my shoulder. He's too strong though and I stumble under his weight, but with great difficulty I manage to guide him to the esplanade. EJ spots us when we reach the front doors of the tavern, rushing to our aid.

"Henley, what happened?" EJ asks, slightly panicked.

Henley doesn't appear to be in any condition to answer. His eyelids flutter as he loses his balance again. The short walk hasn't seemed to sober him up in the slightest.

"I found him by the river," I tell EJ. "He was almost passed out on the park bench."

"Shit. We were having drinks, then he started doing shots behind the bar. Next thing I knew he'd disappeared." EJ says to me, then to Henley he asks, "Are you good, man?"

Henley offers a nod, blinking slowly.

"Help me get him upstairs," I say to EJ.

EJ goes to Henley's other side and together we lead him up to the loft. Thankfully the loft isn't a huge space, and we don't have to struggle far to get him to the bed. When he reaches the mattress, he falls down onto it in a heap.

"Thanks, EJ."

"No worries. I'm sorry you had to find him like this, Kristen. I should have kept a better eye on him." EJ frowns, a hint of guilt in his expression.

"It's okay. You aren't his keeper," I reply. "You weren't to know."

"Yeah, I guess. I still feel a little responsible," he sighs.

Henley stirs on the bed behind me.

"He's a grown man, EJ. He should know better."

"Don't be too hard on him. He's fighting some pretty badass demons." EJ looks at me like he wants to say something he shouldn't, but then he turns on his heel and descends the loft stairs two at a time.

I turn my attention back to Henley, watching as he drifts in and out of consciousness. I circle the end of the bed. I pull his shoes off one at a time and drop them to the floor, then I perch beside him on the edge of the mattress. His arm is splayed out beside me, painted in swirls of black and coloured ink. I trace the lines with the tip of my finger, something I'd always done when we were together. If he feels it, he doesn't let on.

I brush a strand of hair from his forehead. He looks so peaceful as he lays here. So innocent. He doesn't look like someone capable of breaking a heart into thousands of tiny pieces.

Of crushing dreams of a happy future into dust.

He looks like someone who could love me.

Someone I could love back.

"Stay," he murmurs, his eyes opening slowly to reveal arctic irises. "Everything is calmer when you're around. Better." His eyelids flutter closed again, an exhausted sigh escaping him as his head rolls to the other side. "You quiet the noise."

"Careful, Alex," I whisper. "It sounds like you still love me."

I don't expect a response. Especially not the one he gives me.

"I can't not love you."

It comes out so low, I'm sure I've imagined it at first, but there's no mistaking the words I've heard him say so many times before.

His breathing slows and when I'm certain he's asleep, I sit in the quiet as another minute passes.

"Yeah. I know what you mean," I whisper as I stand and tiptoe down the stairs and back out into the night.

Stay.

That one word plays over and over in my head for the entire journey home. Is it bad that after everything we've been through I still wanted to? To lay down next to him, curling myself into the space between his outstretched arm and bury my head into his chest?

I arrive back at the apartment sometime after one in the morning to find Mackenzie on the couch, one of my fluffy blankets tucked over her legs. Her phone reflects blue light onto her flawless skin, letting me know she's still awake.

"Oh, hey," I say.

"Hey," she replies. "How was the carnival? How did the bake sale go?"

"The bake sale was a success," I tell her.

"Why do you look upset? Did something happen?"

"No. Well, just some stuff that happened afterwards, I guess. Let's just say it was…eventful."

"Eventful good or eventful bad?" she asks, lowering her phone to her lap.

"I'm not really sure. I don't really want to talk about it." I flop down onto the armchair adjacent to the couch noticing the empty packet of Doritos lying next to her. "Are those my Doritos?"

She winces. "Uh, yeah. Sorry. I'll replace them first thing in the morning."

"It's fine." I wave off her apology. "You're up late."

"Couldn't really sleep," she replies. "So I thought I'd just spend the time deleting emails. I got another rejection letter today. Didn't get the job at the post office."

"Damn. I'm sure something will come up eventually."

"Yeah, I'm trying to stay positive about it, you know?" she says. "Dum spiro spero and all that."

My head snaps up in time to see her eyes roll before her attention is focused back to her phone. "What did you just say?"

"Oh...Um... nothing," she says as she resumes scrolling through her phone. "Actually, I'm pretty tired after all. I might head off to bed."

My eyes track Mackenzie as she stands and walks into her room leaving me sitting there bewildered, the memory of the last time I'd heard those words spoken now in the forefront of my mind.

Everything is beginning to make sense and yet nothing really adds up.

When I finally fall into bed, I lay awake for hours, the conversation I'd had with Em almost six months ago playing repeatedly in my head. Though it was so long ago, I remember it like it was yesterday. I still recall the shakiness in her voice, the uncertainty in her words.

"I was wondering when you were going to call me again," I had said, genuinely relieved to hear from her.

The last time we'd spoken had been when we were interrupted by an abusive male voice. The conversation I still have nightmares about to this day.

"Sorry. I haven't had the chance," Em had replied. I remember how distant she sounded, the gut feeling I'd had that something had happened.

Something that wasn't good.

"Why is that?" I'd asked her.

She'd answered my question with a question, as she so often did, her voice low and miserable. "Why do you care?"

"I care about what happens to you, Em," I'd said with a sigh. "I'm worried about you. I'm worried you don't have someone looking out for you."

"I do," she had said.

"I hope you don't mean the guy I heard last time you called."

I didn't know everything about Em or what went on in her life. But I did know that guy was bad news.

"No," she'd replied quietly.

"Who was that guy?" I didn't expect her to give me an honest answer, so I was surprised when she told me exactly what I had already assumed.

"He's my boyfriend."

"No offence, but he didn't sound like he was being a good boyfriend."

I didn't want to overstep but I needed her to know that she could do better. That the way she was being treated was not normal.

"I know," she had struck back. Louder. Angrier. Then her tone softened as she'd added, "I'm leaving him."

"When?" I knew better than to push her too hard, but I couldn't bear the thought of her spending another second with that waste of space.

"When I can, okay?" she retaliated.

"What does that mean?" I asked. "Em, does he have something over you?"

I remember wondering what her leaving this guy could possibly be dependent on. But she didn't answer me, instead withdrawing from the conversation, my ears filled with nothing but her shaky breath as it left her lungs in tremors.

"Does he hurt you?" I had dared to ask.

"Sometimes," she had admitted.

My heart had ached hearing her confession. I was rendered helpless, unable to be her saviour, knowing that unless she spoke up about his abuse it was going to keep happening. "You need to call the police."

"It's not that simple," she had argued.

"It can be."

"I have nowhere to go." Her sobs had broken me.

"But you do have someone looking out for you?" I asked, remembering what she had said earlier.

"I did," she whimpered.

"You did?" I'd asked, echoing her words.

"I did. But he's gone."

"Where did he go?" I demanded, my knuckles turning white with the strong grip I had on the phone receiver.

"I can't say."

"Okay," I sigh.

I had come to know when I could push and when I needed to leave well enough alone. I knew that if I pushed too hard, she'd hang up and I potentially wouldn't hear from her for another few weeks. I needed to be the person she could trust. The one that always had her back.

"He's coming back for me though. I know he is." Her voice had risen an octave, an indication of the belief she still had in this person that she'd put all of her faith in.

"How do you know?"

"Dum spiro spero, remember?"

"Yeah, I remember," I'd said, the hint of a smile touching my lips as I recalled one of our earlier conversations. Of when she'd asked me how I got through my darkest days.

While I breath, I hope.

She believed that this person was coming back to save her. For her sake, I'd hoped she was right.

And now as I lay here in the darkness, I try not to believe what I know in my heart to be true.

I'd taught Em the meaning of the words *Dum spiro spero* and she'd later used them in conversation.

Mackenzie had used the same saying tonight.

Em had made an unwarranted comment about my mum moving on with a 'stand-up guy' when she was never previously informed about Ben.

But it's possible that Mackenzie did know about Ben at the time.

I've only heard from Em once since Mackenzie showed up here in town.

Maybe it's the sleep deprivation. Maybe I'm becoming paranoid. But the more I turn this information over in my brain, the more convinced I become.

That Mackenzie is Em.

M for Mackenzie.

Chapter 39

HENLEY

I've been awake for hours, but I haven't been able to bring myself to leave this bed. Not even to close the gap in the curtains where a steady stream of bright sunlight pierces through the otherwise dark room directly into my bloodshot eyes.

I don't remember much of last night. I remember being at the carnival, the way my chest deflated seeing Kristen with Chase's arm draped around her neck as they left the gates of the big zipper. I remember being on stage and the paralysing fear that had gripped me when I thought Mackenzie might have been in danger. I have some vague memories of doing shots in the bar with EJ afterwards.

Or maybe it was just me doing the shots now that I come to think of it.

Kristen's face flashes into my mind, a backdrop of stars behind her, the glow of the moon like a halo around her long dark hair. She was there last night, somewhere along the banks of the river, but that's as far as my memory will take me. The rest is a blur.

A glance at the clock lets me know that my shift starts in thirty minutes. I drag myself into the shower, my head heavy as lead. Shit. How much did I drink last night? I try to scrub away the regret, but the sour taste of shame lingers.

Dylan sizes me up when I enter the tavern half an hour later. "You're gonna have to pay for that bottle you took from behind the bar last night."

"What bottle?" *Jesus, what did I do?*

He shakes his head, his bottom lip curling in annoyance. "Wild Turkey."

I nod once. That explains the hangover then. "Sure. Sorry about that."

"Don't make a habit out of it. I don't want to have to tell Steve that the guy he's taken a chance on is fucking things up. Again."

I grit my teeth. I want to say something to defend myself, but he has a point. I am fucking things up. So instead, I nod reluctantly. "I'll do better."

"I've heard that before," Dylan mutters under his breath as he saunters back to the kitchen.

I start clearing the tables along the window when I notice Old Tommy hunched over in the far corner. I pause, a stack of plates resting on my forearm. Another day that he's visiting the bar before it's barely hit midday means another night that I'll be kicking him out for intoxication. I'm hungover and I don't have time for this bullshit today.

I slam the stack of dirty plates down in front of him. "Back so soon?"

Old Tommy lifts his head slowly and then he does something unexpected. He snickers at me. "You've never really liked me too much, have you kid?"

A fair comment. I haven't really kept my disdain for Old Tommy a secret.

"I just don't understand you. Why are you always here?"

"This coming from the kid that can throw back Wild Turkey like it's fruit juice." He huffs out a laugh. His eyes crinkle at the corners and I realise Old Tommy is even older than I thought he was. "You didn't seem to mind me hanging around last night. Thanks for the shots by the way."

I squeeze my eyes shut, my headache suddenly severe. "What shots? I wouldn't buy you shots."

"I didn't say you paid for them," he snorts.

Fantastic. Yet another reason for Dylan to write me off. I'm starting to think that leaving town again isn't such a bad option. Maybe it would be best for me to find a place where I can start all over again.

"You didn't answer my question," I say, trying to redirect the attention back onto him. "Why are you always here?"

Old Tommy's face slackens, the smirk disappearing from his mouth. "I don't have anywhere better to be."

"That can't be true," I say.

"Sorry to disappoint you boy, but it is true. There's no one out there waiting for me." He takes a long sip of his beer, then sets it down again in front of him.

"You don't have a family? A wife?" My anger has dissipated now. I'm generally curious to hear his answer.

"I did. Once."

He sighs and his eyes fill with sadness. He pulls his wallet from his back pocket and pulls out a tattered old photograph, handing it to me between wrinkled fingers.

A woman beams back at me from the picture. She looks like she couldn't be more than thirty years old here. A toddler rests on her lap. A girl with big, bright blue eyes, cherry red lips and a mass of blonde curls.

"This is your family?"

"Was." Old Tommy doesn't look up from his beer.

"What happened?" I know it isn't my business, that after the way I've treated this old man I don't really deserve to know, but I hope he'll tell me anyway.

"They died. Car collided with a truck. It was my fault." His gaze drifts out the window to the sidewalk where a young mother has stopped to check on her baby, bending over the pram with an adoring smile on her face. "I was driving."

"How old were you?" I ask.

"Twenty-nine. My baby girl was barely three years old."

I pass the photograph back to him, noticing now the way his hand tremors as he collects it. "How was it your fault?"

His bottom lip quivers as his eyes mist over. "I was speeding. I was imprisoned for ten years."

I'm stunned into silence, my mouth gaping like a complete dumbass. I've given this man shit almost every day that he's come in here. I'd written him off as the town drunk, as someone who selfishly drinks himself into oblivion. I'd carelessly assumed that this man would rather down bourbon than pay attention to his family somewhere. Never in my wildest dreams would I have imagined he did it to escape a life of shame and suffering.

"I'm sorry."

"Not your fault, kid." He shakes his head and places his beer down with a clunk. "I'm more than happy to wear the full force of the blame."

"You're punishing yourself," I say.

Old Tommy shrugs. "I thought that if I could just move to a new town, find a place where nobody knew my name, maybe I could leave it all behind. But that's the thing about guilt. It stays with you."

"So you come here every day and you drink yourself stupid because you don't think you're worthy of anything else?"

"If you were in my shoes, wouldn't you?"

I can't answer that. I have no idea what it would be like to live with the guilt of taking the lives of the two most important people in my life. But everyone has their cross to bear, and I'm no exception.

"You made a stupid mistake a long time ago," I tell him. "I'm not saying it would be easy to forgive yourself. But while you're taking up space on this earth, shouldn't you find a way to make it count? Give yourself a chance to do something special with the time you have left?"

"Wise words, kid. Do you have the guts to take your own advice?" Old Tommy raises an eyebrow as his eyes meet mine. "What ever happened to that girl that was always here with you? Watching you play the drums and hanging on your every word."

"Hanging on my every word?" I question him dubiously. "I think you've got the wrong guy."

"No. I remember her." Old Tommy shakes his head. "The one who was always smitten with you. Long brown hair, killer curves. You know who I mean."

He's definitely talking about Kristen but where he got the idea that she was smitten with me, I have no idea. It was always the other way around in my eyes.

"We broke up." I realise this is putting it mildly. Went off the rails, collided with a Mack truck and burst into flames is probably a better description. "She's always been too good for me anyway."

"Geez, kid. You're even dumber than I thought you were."

"Sorry?" I can sympathise with Old Tommy's story but I'm not about to stand here and take his insults.

"You had a chance to be with a girl like that? And you let her slip through your fingers? You're crazy."

"You don't know what you're talking about." I want to argue further but instead I clamp my mouth shut.

"Maybe I don't. But I sure do know a thing or two about feeling sorry for yourself. Stop bitching and whingeing about how you're not enough for her and get out there and be enough." His voice is gruff as he slams a hand down on the table. "Do whatever you have to do to deserve her."

"It sounds good in theory," I tell him. "But I don't think anything is really that simple though."

He shrugs, placing his empty beer glass down. "Being happy is a choice, kid. Don't be like me."

He stands from his chair and shuffles back to the bar for round two, leaving me clueless as to what I should make of this conversation. The last thing I expected to be doing today was participating in a deep and meaningful with the town drunk but hearing Old Tommy's reasoning for the way he chooses to live his life has struck a chord with me.

Because I don't think that he should be punishing himself for something he did thirty years ago, although I can't say I wouldn't do the same in his position. If I can believe that Old Tommy deserves to move on with his life, then I should believe that I deserve to as well.

It's time to come clean. I know that without question. I need to tell Kristen everything.

But first, I need to talk to Mackenzie. This affects her too.

And as I look up and catch a blur of blonde hair exiting the Haven, I decide now is as good a time as any.

"I'll be back in five," I call across the room to Dylan and Corey.

I abandon the dirty stack of plates and burst through the tavern door onto the street, ignoring Dylan's pleas for me to come back.

"Mackenzie!" I call out as I cross the street.

She hears me and comes to a stop on the corner, juggling a grocery bag hung on each arm and a takeaway coffee cup in her left hand. "Whoa." She aims a suspicious glance at me when she sees the desperate expression on my face. "What's up?"

"We need to tell her. It can't wait any longer," I say breathlessly. "I have to tell her everything."

Mackenzie's shoulders slump in resignation. She knows just as well as I do that we can't keep going on the way we are.

"We talked about this yesterday, Henley. I said I would tell her what I need to tell her, but does it have to be right now?" she complains.

"Yeah. It does."

Mackenzie sighs. "Fine. But you need to let me speak to her first."

"Okay," I agree.

She sighs again. "You realise she's going to think I'm completely psychotic, right?"

"She isn't like that. She'll understand."

Mackenzie looks away, a strained look on her face. "She'll kick me out of her apartment. I'll have nowhere to go."

"She won't. Haven't you gotten to know her at all? You know that's not going to happen."

"And if it does?"

"I'll fire up the couch in the loft," I say. "It's all yours."

The left side of her mouth twitches. "You mean it's all *yours*."

"Fine," I agree.

"Okay. Just give me till tonight," she pleads, her eyebrows pulling together.

"Okay. Tonight."

I can work with that. I head back inside the tavern, ready to grovel for Dylan's forgiveness.

As much as I hate to admit it, Old Tommy has a point. I've been promising myself I'll become a better version of myself one day, but one day is already here. And I have nothing to show for it.

It's time I stopped talking and put a plan into action.

It's time to step up.

It's time to be better.

Chapter 40

KRISTEN

Mackenzie was gone before I stumbled out into the kitchen this morning, my eyes puffy after the restless night I'd had. I'd glanced inside her open bedroom door to find her bed made and no sign of her inside.

I'd tossed and turned all night, weighing up all of the theories that had swirled through my head, but in the end, I'd only been left with more questions than answers.

Are Mackenzie and Em the same person?

And if that is the case, then what role does Henley play in all of this?

Could he be the saviour she'd hoped would rescue her from a bad relationship?

Who the hell is this woman that I've allowed into my home? That I've supported financially for the last couple of weeks.

I anxiously pace the length of the kitchen. I'm so confused, my mind contemplating all the possible ways that I could confront her about this.

Do I get mad?

Should I be gentle?

Should I come out guns blazing, demanding to know what she's hiding, or do I take a more subtle approach by asking her twenty questions?

Or should I go straight to Henley?

I power on the Nespresso machine. Maybe my thoughts will be more logical after coffee. As I reach for a mug from the overhead kitchen cabinet, I hear a knock on the front door.

Mackenzie must be back. She probably forgot to take her key again. I'd hoped I'd have more time to figure this out without her being here. I inhale a nervous breath and swing open the door with no real plan or clue about what I'm going to say to her.

And then my breath hitches in my throat.

It isn't Mackenzie at all.

The face that stares back at me is familiar and yet also completely foreign. His skin marred with deep wrinkles, the whites of his eyes a sickly shade of pale yellow, his complexion an unhealthy grey. It's clear the years have not been kind to him.

But there is no mistaking who he is.

"Dad?" The word feels foreign as it leaves my mouth.

Biologically this man is my father, but he hasn't been my dad for many years.

"Kristen," he whispers, his bloodshot eyes brimming with tears. "You're beautiful. You've grown up."

"That happens," I say bitterly. He doesn't reply. "What are you doing here?"

"I know that I'm probably the last person you really want to see right now…"

"You're right. You are," I interrupt.

He nods, his gaze dropping to the ground. He's too ashamed to look at me.

So he should be.

"I'm sorry, Kristen," he begins. "I've made some terrible mistakes in my life. Leaving you behind is my biggest regret."

I swallow the lump that forms in my throat. I will not let this man reduce me to tears. I am stronger than that. "What happened to you?"

"I wouldn't know where to begin to answer that." He shakes his head and looks down at the carpet again. He doesn't offer me any other explanation.

"Well, it was lovely seeing you, Dad," I say cynically as I swing the door closed.

"I got your letters." His voice is muffled through the solid wooden door. The hinges moan and creak as I slowly reopen it.

"What letters?" I ask.

"The birthday letters."

He couldn't possibly be referring to the letters hidden in the top drawer of my desk. The sixteen letters I had written pouring my heart out, expressing the pain and loneliness I'd felt at his rejection.

The ones I had vowed never to send.

He reaches into his jacket pocket and pulls out a tattered bundle of papers. Sure enough, there they are.

Anger boils below the surface of my skin, twisting through my veins like poison. I don't appreciate this breach of privacy in the slightest. My brain ticks over, searching for someone to blame.

Henley had been the only person that knew those letters existed. Until Mackenzie went searching for my laptop in the drawer that day.

"I never intended for you to read those," I spit, feeling the blood rise in my cheeks. "I don't know how they were mailed out to you. They were meant to be private."

269

His gaze softens unexpectedly, his next words a complete surprise to me. "I'm glad I read them."

"You are? Why?"

Those letters were not kind. They were infused with my true thoughts and feelings. I'd held nothing back.

"This," he says, shaking the wad of letters in his palm, "was the wake-up call that I needed. It's no secret that I've wasted my life. I've done many things I'm not proud of but being a deadbeat father tops the list. I failed you."

My bottom lip disappears between my teeth. I'm not sure what he expects me to say right now. I'm not going to argue his point.

"I can't stay long," he continues. "I need to be on the eleven o'clock bus to Milton. I'm on my way to a facility there. I wanted to stop by and let you know I'm getting help. I'm an alcoholic and I'm going to rehab."

I didn't know my father had turned to alcohol. How could I, when both my mother and I had lost contact with him all those years ago? He'd never cared to look for us. Now here he is, trying to make amends, trying to save himself. And I have no idea what to make of it. No idea what to do.

He holds the letters out to me, and I notice now the way his hands quake. He's withdrawing, I realise.

"Keep them," I tell him with a shake of my head.

"Thank you." He pulls the letters in, clutching them to his chest and I can see that they mean more to him than they ever will to me. He turns slowly, readying himself to leave.

I don't know if there's a world in which I can forgive Greg Riley for his abandonment. I don't know if I can forget all the hours I've spent wondering why he didn't think I was worthy of a visit, a phone call, a birthday card. But I do know that I don't want this to be the last time I ever see him.

"Dad," I call out, my voice quivering. The word still leaves a bad taste in my mouth.

He swivels slightly, throwing a glance back at me over his shoulder.

"Let me know how it goes," I say. "The whole rehab thing, I mean."

His lips twitch upward in a sad smile, a tiny flicker of light glimmering in his eyes. "I will," he says before turning in the direction of the lift. "Oh, and Kristen," he calls back. "That guy you've got seems like a real keeper. Don't let him go."

I feel a deep crease form between my brows. "What guy?"

"Tall, blonde and handsome," he replies. "Alex someone or other. He seems worth hanging on to."

I watch as my father disappears into the elevator, then I enter the apartment, closing the door behind me, more confounded than ever.

How the hell does my father know who Alex Henley is?

I rake my hands through my hair, suddenly unable to keep still. Several moments pass and I start to think I'm going to wear a hole in the carpet the way I'm pacing back and forth, but I can't help it.

A hurricane of emotions swirl within me, threatening to expel the contents of my stomach. Confusion mostly, as to how my father knows my ex, and fury at Mackenzie, knowing it had to be her that posted those extremely personal letters.

What right did she think she had?

I stop in my tracks as the front door creaks open and Mackenzie shuffles in, her arms weighted by two grocery bags.

"Okay, I got bread, and I picked up some..." her voice trails off when she looks up and sees the enraged expression I don't even bother trying to disguise. "Ahhh, hey. What's going on?"

"I think it's time that we had a talk." Screw taking the gentle approach. I don't have the patience for that option anymore.

She blows out a breath as though she knows what's coming. "What do you want to talk about?"

"How about you tell me?"

"I don't know…"

"Cut the bullshit, Mackenzie." My voice is calm, yet I can't stop my hands from shaking. "When I offered you a place to stay, I thought it went without saying that you didn't mess with my stuff."

"If this is about the Doritos, I bought three huge bags and…"

"It's not about fucking corn chips, Mackenzie!" I shout, losing my cool. "Why did you post the letters?"

The grocery bags slip through her fingers, landing with a thud on the floor where she stands. She's trying to maintain her tough girl bravado, but her eyes give her away. She's intimidated by me.

"How did you know about that?"

"Because my father just showed up at the door waving them around." I flail my own hands about at the risk of looking like an insane person, but I don't care. I've had enough.

"He did?" Mackenzie asks, her eyes wide with shock. "He's here in Cliff Haven?"

"He was." I pace another lap of the room. "He said he was just passing through on his way to a rehab clinic."

"He's going to rehab?" Mackenzie is taking way too much interest in this aspect of my life, which leads me to the other reason I'm upset.

Mackenzie isn't who she says she is.

I don't really know how to broach the subject with her, so I decide to be upfront and ask. I boldly fold my arms across my chest. "Have you been calling me at the helpline?"

She takes a step back, her gaze dropping to the floor. The guilt is written all over her face.

"It was you, wasn't it?" I ask, my eyes wild with ferocity. "You're Em."

"Kristen, before you jump to conclusions you need to let me explain." She speaks surprisingly calmly given the accusation.

"Go ahead and explain then," I retaliate. "Explain to me how you've gone from calling me on the phone to living in my apartment. And while you're at it, maybe you can shed some light on how you've managed to get to know my ex-boyfriend so well."

"Okay. You're right," she admits. "I've been keeping something from you. But before I say anything, you need to know that Henley isn't to blame for any of this. He wanted me to tell you all along, but in case you haven't noticed, I'm not exactly quick to trust people. He told me you were one of the good guys, but I had to see for myself."

It troubles me further that Henley is already privy to whatever she's about to tell me. The idea that he is in on this deceptive charade hurts me more than I care to admit. I'm getting the sense that this is a whole lot bigger than anything I could have imagined.

"Okay," I say, bracing myself for what comes next.

"It's true. I knew about you before I came to Cliff Haven. I already knew who you were that day I met you in the café."

"I don't get it." A bitter laugh leaves me, echoing off the walls of the tiny apartment.

"I wanted to meet you." She sighs, then pinches the bridge of her nose, clearly stressed. "I know how this sounds."

"Do you?" I ask incredulously. "Because it's sounds like you're some kind of twisted stalker."

"Look, I only found out you existed six months ago, and I knew I had to meet you." She takes a step in my direction. "And yes, it's me that's been calling you at the helpline."

"Why?" I stagger backward, the full force of her words hitting me.

I'm shocked and hurt hearing her confirm what I'd already believed to be true. I think back over the many conversations we'd had on the phone.

Forget the fact that this situation is extremely unethical. That I could lose my position at the helpline over this. I liked this girl. I was sympathetic of her situation. I'd offered her a place to live. I'd allowed her into my life, and she has been deceiving me this whole time.

Mackenzie, seeing my reaction does her best to derail my obviously escalating thoughts. "You can still trust me, Kristen."

"I don't know what to believe anymore. I did trust you and now I find out you've been lying to me."

Not only am I struggling with the notion that this girl knew who I was even before she came to town, I'm desperately trying to put the pieces together in my head, to figure out what Henley has to do with all of this.

"Why should I trust another word out of your mouth?"

"Because I'm not your enemy, Kristen." Mackenzie takes a step closer to me and it's then I notice her eyes are wet with tears. Her chest heaves with the long breath she draws in. "I'm your sister."

I blink at her, dumbfounded, the words registering in my brain one syllable at a time. "What?"

"Our phone calls... The father I mentioned..." she trails off. "His name is Greg Riley."

"Greg Riley?" I echo. The world tips on its axis. "Greg Riley is your dad?"

She nods as more tears stream from her eyes. "I'm sorry. I should have told you sooner. I was scared."

"You're my sister?"

"Technically, your half-sister," she whispers. "I'm so sorry, Kristen. I didn't know how to tell you."

I stand frozen in place, not knowing whether to believe her. I do the sums in my head. Mackenzie is nineteen, which means she was born when I was five. My parents didn't separate until I was eight, but my mother had found out after their separation that my father had cheated on her many times before that.

Still, how could he have had a child we didn't know about?

A whole *life* we didn't know about.

But as I gaze into those hazel irises, swirls of chestnut and green, I'm struck with the memory of her in the Cliff Haven café. The attitude she exuded, the distrust of absolutely everything. And I know.

I know she is my sister.

"When did he start drinking?" I ask her.

"I don't remember a time where he didn't," she answers, swiping a fresh tear from her eye.

And I don't remember him as an alcoholic.

"When we first met at the cafe, I thought you hated me," I tell her. "You were so defensive."

"I didn't hate you. I envied you," she admits.

"You envied me?" I ask dubiously. "Our father abandoned me! He had another child he couldn't even be bothered to tell us about."

"I know. But living with our dad has been no picnic for me. He's a terrible father. You got the better version of him. You got him when he was making a steady income, when he could take care of you. When he loved you." She pauses. "I got the unemployed drunk."

Fragments of conversations with Em fight their way to the forefront of my mind.

Did you ever think you knew someone? Only to find out they're not at all the person you thought they were?

My whole life is a lie.

She'd been referring to Greg Riley. This man that had previously led a completely different life than the one she'd known.

Have you ever stopped to think that maybe he did you a favour?

It makes sense now.

The way she'd reacted toward me at first, the bitter looks she aimed at my mother, her sarcastic comments. We've both had two very different upbringings despite sharing the same father.

"What happened to him?"

"I think he's the only one that can really answer that. The way I understand it is that he went back to my mother after his divorce, but then not too long after that my mum left. A few months before my fourth birthday." Her bottom lip quivers as she continues. "I don't really remember her. She was young and too irresponsible to raise a child. But I think when she left...that was when things really went downhill."

I give her a sympathetic look. "I'm sorry. I wish I knew you existed."

"Me too," she smiles sadly. "I'm sorry I sent the letters. I wanted to punish him. I wanted him to know how much he hurt you." Another tear falls from her eye, her voice breaking when she asks, "Do you hate me?"

The letters are the least of my worries right now. I'll admit that when I'd first met this sarcastic grumpy teenager, I'd been suspicious of her motives. I'd been resentful of her, jealous even, of the relationship she has with Henley. But this new information has shed light on her situation.

"I hate the way you felt that you couldn't just come out and tell me. I hate that you've been raised by a shitty father. But I could never hate you." I take a step toward her and her shoulders sag with relief. "I have a little sister." It comes out as a whisper, but I feel my face brighten with the realisation.

I'm suddenly overcome with protectiveness and love for this young woman standing before me. As I throw my arms around her neck, she leans into me, her body trembling as she releases a heavy sob. I hold her and for a moment I forget about everything else, but then in a rush it all comes flooding back.

Henley.

Why would Henley keep something like this from me?

This is bigger than the reason he left. This is my own flesh and blood.

"How does our father know who Alex Henley is?" I pull back away from her, brushing a wild, blonde tendril from her face.

She sighs. "That's a question for Henley himself."

"I don't get why he wouldn't tell me. Why he would offer you a place to stay and kept this huge secret from me."

"It wasn't his place to say anything. I told him to keep my secret until I was ready."

I remember back to the day that I'd met him in the canoe by the river. I'd thought it honourable that he was willing to keep Mackenzie's secret.

"I guess that's fair enough."

"You've got to give him a break. He took me in and helped me when I had nothing," she pleads with me.

"He left me." I scoff. "Giving you a place to stay hardly redeems him of everything else he's done."

She bows her head. "There's so much you don't know."

More extracts of conversations with Em surface from the depths of my memory. There were the times she spoke about her father.

Our father.

Then there were the days where she barely spoke at all, and I was forced to read between the lines. The times when it was obvious that she was stuck in a violent relationship.

"You had an abusive boyfriend," I recall. "You were waiting for someone to save you. It was Henley, wasn't it?"

She looks up at me, her hazel eyes pooling with green. "Henley sacrificed everything to save me. I'm the reason he didn't return to Cliff Haven all those months ago. It was all my fault."

I draw away from her. I'm not sure I can handle another revelation right now. "What does that mean?"

"He isn't this terrible person you make him out to be." She sighs as she flops down onto the couch. "He's the one who told me about you. He told me you worked at the helpline. And he's the one who brought me to Cliff Haven. He rescued me from a really bad situation." She pauses for a moment, then lifts her gaze to mine, her hazel irises brimming with sadness. "I owe him everything, Kristen."

I hadn't stopped to wonder whether there might have been a specific reason that Mackenzie had ended up in Cliff Haven. I've spent the past week walking on eggshells around her. Never daring to ask too many questions for fear she'd shut me down. I'd never asked her where she came from, assuming Henley had just met her somewhere along the way.

I guess I assumed a lot of things.

I still have so many questions but there's no point in directing them at Mackenzie.

It's time to find Henley and get the truth from him once and for all.

Mackenzie, as if reading my mind, nods toward the door. "Go. Find him."

Chapter 41

KRISTEN

I hurry down the street and burst through the doors of the tavern, almost knocking Dylan over as he juggles a stack of plates and a drink tray. "Whoa! Where's the fire?" he exclaims.

"Sorry. Is Henley here?" I ask, breathless from running the last three blocks.

Dylan grunts at the mention of Henley's name and then mutters, "He was here, but he's taking his lunch break. He might be upstairs."

"Thanks." I race to the back of the bar and climb the stairs two at a time. I call for him when I reach the top but there's no answer. He's not here. I think of all the possible places he could be. His dad's place, the grocery store.

The park bench by the river.

I take the stairs back down even faster than I ascended them, whirling past Dylan once again. He curses as he almost drops yet another stack of plates. I yell out an apology on my way out the door and run down the cobblestone path toward the river.

I pass friends sipping coffee and children flying kites, running as fast as my feet will carry me. When I make it to the riverbank, the park bench is vacant. He isn't here either.

I slow down to catch my breath, walking a little further until I find myself at the entrance to the winding trail that leads to the most secluded part of the river.

I push through the undergrowth, stepping over large twigs and broken branches until I reach the clearing. Henley sits on our rock, his eyes steady on the river before him. I say his name out loud and he flinches, a reaction I've come to expect with this version of him.

"Thought I might find you here," I say.

"I come here to think." He picks up a small rock and skims it across the water's surface. It bounces a few times before sinking to its depths.

I nod. "I know."

"Why did you come?" he asks, his eyes still on the water ahead.

"I spoke to Mackenzie. We talked about a lot of things."

His head snaps up in my direction, a fearful look in his crystal baby blues. "You did?"

I nod again. "She told me we're sisters," I admit. "You already knew that though."

He frowns. "I'm sorry. I wanted to tell you, but it wasn't my place."

"I get that." I move closer to the rock, climbing up to take the space beside him. "But she said something else that didn't make a whole lot of sense to me."

"What did she say?"

"She said that you sacrificed everything to help her out of a bad situation. She said it's her fault that you didn't come home."

He shakes his head defiantly. "It was never her fault. I told her that."

"She also told me that I need to give you a chance to explain."

He looks away from me and I see his back muscles constricting and expanding with every breath he takes. I cup his cheek, turning his face toward mine. His nostrils are flared, his chest heaving in an effort to get air.

"Alex. I know something happened. There must be a reason you left the way you did."

"I want to tell you."

I've never seen Alex Henley helpless before but right now he's the most vulnerable I've ever seen him. He takes another deep breath, then his eyes, rimmed with dark circles, focus in on mine. I've been so focused on my own suffering but now I'm suddenly aware of the pain that hides behind them. How didn't I see it before?

"Please," I beckon. "Tell me."

His jaw clenches as he swallows, his voice gravelly when he finally utters one word. "Okay."

I don't miss the way his hand trembles when he reaches out and takes my palm in his.

Chapter 42

HENLEY – SIX MONTHS AGO

You can be anywhere when your world caves in. When it's changed forever in an instant. Your darkest moment could come in the brightest of places, a brilliant summer's day underneath the bluest of skies.

At least, that's how it happened for me.

I merge onto the highway, adrenaline coursing through my veins. Today will be the day that I finally act on something that has troubled me for years. I know what I need to do.

The memory of this morning is still fresh in my mind. Of Kristen lying next to me, her skin golden, bathed in shimmery light as it poured through the cracks in the bay window curtains in my bedroom. I'd always considered myself unbreakable, untouchable. Relatively unphased by anything.

But that was before.

Before I realised that I have everything to lose.

It's her. It's always been her.

The girl, who at sixteen, was able to see through the façade. Who, by eighteen, knew me better than anybody else on this planet. Who had seen me bleed, felt my heartbeat underneath her palms.

And the woman, who can now decipher even the most subtle of my gestures, who knows how to melt me even when I'm stone cold.

She's everything.

And I'm going to marry her.

But not before I see her father.

Not that Greg Riley deserves that title. I mean, what kind of father doesn't visit or call or send a simple birthday card?

Kristen puts up a front, but I know it makes her doubt herself and I hate him for that.

I know I'm granting him more than he deserves by informing him of my intentions, but that's simply all I'm doing. I'm not asking. I'm telling him. I want to marry his daughter and I want to lay into him for being the piece of shit that he is. I want him to know how much heartache he's caused her, but I also want him to know that despite his neglect, she turned out just fine.

More than fine, no thanks to him.

I glance at the speedometer and realise I'm doing twenty kilometres over the speed limit. I lift my foot, easing up on the accelerator, knowing I can't let my anger overtake me. My temper has led me to speeding fines in the past and I still have a few hours left of driving to do.

I've never met Greg Riley. I've seen an old photograph of him, but it had been taken so long ago I doubt I'd recognise him if I passed him on the street. But I know where he lives, thanks to the bundle of letters Kristen keeps in the top drawer of her desk. All of them addressed to him, though she's never been able to bring herself to send a single one.

I know that he lives in Coledale, a small inland town almost four hours from Cliff Haven. I don't care how far I have to drive. I'd drive all day and night for her.

I'm hungry and tired, but I don't stop until I see the weather-beaten 'Welcome to Coledale' sign appear, adorned with scribbles of graffiti. Someone has scrawled a giant H over the C, so it reads Holedale.

Clever. And also fitting.

I pull over to the side of a dirt road and scroll through the images on my phone until I find the photo I took of one of the envelopes. It's blurry, having been taken in a rush, but I can still read the address easily.

23 Woodville Road, Coledale.

I type the address into maps and wait for the app to find the best route. Phone service is practically non-existent in this town but after a long and painful two minutes, I finally get it to load. Apparently, I'm only four minutes away. I indicate and ready myself to pull out on to the road again when a black four-wheel drive hoons past, music blaring. A guy hollers out of the window swinging a bottle of amber coloured liquid.

Wanker.

Four minutes later I'm parked out the front of my destination.

23 Woodville Road is not what I expect. This decrepit house with its overgrown front lawn, littered with weeds and junk, is not where I pictured Greg Riley would end up. It's a far cry from the elaborate two storey mansion I've seen in the photographs Kristen has showed me of her early years. This has to be a mistake.

I blow out a breath as I make my way up the paved path, weeds weaving through its cracks, and knock firmly on the battered, old front door. There's no response, so I knock again, louder this time.

A deep bellow comes from behind the door and then it swings open, revealing a thin man with greying hair that seems to match his wrinkled complexion. The bitter scent of alcohol lingers in the air between us.

"What?" is all he says when he sees me.

"Are you Greg Riley?" I ask.

I expect him to say that I have the wrong address. There's no way this loser could be Kristen's dad.

"Depends on who's asking," he mutters.

I nod. It all suddenly makes sense to me now.

Why Kristen's mother was happy just to let Greg go. Why she was content to let her daughter have no relationship with her father. Why she didn't push for him to be a part of their lives. Greg Riley has nothing to offer them.

I can already see there isn't a point in trying to converse with him, but for Kristen's sake, I try anyway.

"My name is Alex. I'm Kristen's boyfriend."

"Who?" He slumps against the door frame, his hand coming up to scratch his forehead.

"Kristen. Your daughter." My voice remains calm but I'm fuming on the inside.

What kind of lowlife needs to be reminded of their only daughter's name?

"Right. What can I do for you?" He sounds bored. Or maybe he's frustrated that I'm keeping him from his next whiskey and coke.

"Nothing," I say through gritted teeth. "I just wanted to look into the eyes of the father that abandoned her before I ask her to marry me."

Greg's eyes darken. The door swivels open further, and he stumbles backward as though my words have physically assaulted him. It's then I see the half empty bottle of Jack Daniels in his other hand and the untidy living room littered with dirty dishes and glasses behind him. He stares me down and I expect him to lash out at me, hit me in the face. But he doesn't.

Instead, a guttural sob leaves his mouth as he turns away from me. He tosses the bottle, and it hits the carpet leaving a tawny-brown stain where the liquid trickles from it. I don't know what to do so I stand frozen in place.

"I know I fucked everything up," he says, turning back to me, his face twisted in anguish.

I can see that he does indeed know. That he's a broken man haunted by everything he once had.

"Good," I say to him.

His chest heaves rapidly, his eyes wandering around the room before they finally come to rest on mine, infused with desperation and shame.

"What is she like?" It's not so much a question but a plea.

"You don't deserve to know."

I spin around, turning my back on this sad excuse for a man, preparing myself for the four-hour drive home, but there's a heavy ball of lead weighing in my gut.

I wonder why he wants to know about her now, when knowing could be more torturous than not knowing. A small part of me has hope that if I tell him about how perfect Kristen is, he might actually change his ways. The rest of me knows there's about as much chance of that happening as hell freezing over.

But I turn back to him anyway, an impatient sigh leaving me as I allow myself to slump against the door frame. "She's amazing. She's smart and gorgeous and funny. She's brave too. Knows how to hold her own. Doesn't take my shit, that's for sure."

"Sounds just like her mother," he says, a weak smile twitching at the corners of his lips. "You seem like you care about her a lot. She's lucky to have you."

This comment annoys me. It only makes it clearer that he knows nothing about Kristen at all.

"No." I shake my head adamantly. "You've got it wrong. *I'm* the lucky one. And you would be too if you'd stuck around. Been a part of her life."

He draws in a deep breath, waving a hand back and forth between himself and the chaotic living room behind him, a helpless expression crossing his face. "I'm a mess."

"I can see that," I say. "But I'm not here to listen to your excuses. Only you have the power to change all of this. You made a choice. If you wanted to be in her life, then you would be."

"It's not that simple." His lips form a thin white line, his eyes narrowing into slits.

I don't care how angry I make him. I came here to tell him what I think and I'm not going to back down. "Actually, it is. It really is."

He doesn't answer. His forehead crumples in a frown as he collapses into a tattered armchair behind him, more pitiful sobs wracking his bony frame. This time when I turn, I do leave. I storm toward my truck, heave the driver's door open and lunge inside.

I'm angrier than I was before I decided to make this trip, if that's even possible. I'm disappointed for Kristen, having seen what a trainwreck her father has become, and sad that she'll never know what it means to have a father who is proud of her accomplishments and loves everything there is to love about her.

But it also fills me with purpose. I'm now more determined than ever to give her everything she deserves. I check my phone, finding a number of missed calls and texts from her and type out a quick reply.

I need to get home.

The only place I want to be right now is wrapped in her arms.

As I turn the key in the ignition something catches my attention in my peripheral vision. A young woman with long, honey blonde waves tumbles from the left side window of 23 Woodville Road.

She expertly lands on her feet in a crouching position with the stealth of a cat, clearly having done this before. She rises, scanning the area for anyone that may have seen her, as she brushes the grass from her baggy jeans and smoothes out the crocheted crop top that adorns her thin frame.

Then her sights are set on my truck. I watch as she races toward me, not hesitating to open the passenger side door and climbs right in beside me.

"Drive!" she shouts at me.

"Wh – what?" I stutter.

"Hurry! Go!" she yells again, waving her hands and motioning for me to power forward.

I'm stunned at the fact this young woman has the balls to both throw herself into a stranger's car and expect them to meet her demands, but still, I do as she says.

"Where do you want me to take you?" I finally say.

"Anywhere but here," she mutters. She sighs, leaning her elbow on the window, propping her head up with her hand.

"Seriously, though. You're gonna have to give me some direction. I'm not exactly from around here."

And there isn't much around here as far as I can see. Other than a tiny storefront I'm yet to see further signs of civilisation. When I glance out the window, I'm met with nothing more than a blur of blue and green.

"No shit. Like that's not half obvious." She laughs bitterly. "What exactly are you doing in Coledale?"

"Nothing. I'm on my way home."

I'm taken aback by her abruptness but I'm also too exhausted to call her on it. I see a roadside diner up ahead and realise I'm suddenly ravenous, having not eaten since last night.

"It didn't sound like nothing to me," she argues, shrugging her shoulders casually.

"Really? What about you? You have some kind of habit of breaking into people's houses and eavesdropping on their private conversations?" Now I can't hide my annoyance.

This makes her laugh out loud, which only exacerbates my mood further.

"I didn't break into anyone's house. At least not today." She shakes her head with a grin, then tilts her head in thought. "Not gonna deny the eavesdropping though."

"Then what the hell were you doing climbing out of Greg Riley's window?" I ask.

I pull the car into a parking space out the front of the roadside diner and pull up the handbrake. Her head spins in my direction, her blonde curls swishing around her like golden curtains.

"How do you know him?" she asks, eyeing me sceptically.

"I don't," I sigh. The answer to her question is too exhausting to comprehend let alone communicate. "What were you doing in that house then?"

"It's not really any of your business," she says slyly.

"Right. Says the girl that threw herself into my vehicle and demanded a ride," I deadpan.

She rolls her eyes at me dramatically. "Whatever. That was my bedroom window," she explains reluctantly. "Greg Riley is my father."

"You're kidding," I say, my voice expressionless.

"Why would anyone joke about that?" She glances out the passenger window briefly and then her eyes return to mine, swirled with flecks of amber and green.

"How old are you?" I ask.

"Nineteen," she says defensively. "What's it to you?"

I ignore her question, my mind working in overdrive to understand how this could be possible. I quickly do the sums in my head. There's a five-year age gap between Kristen and this girl but Greg didn't leave until Kristen was eight, which means that she had a sister she didn't know about three years before he left. I'm almost positive that Pamela has no idea this girl exists either. She wouldn't keep something like this from Kristen.

Was Greg Riley leading a double life long before they both realised?

"Where is your mother?" I ask.

"Ha. I wish I knew." Sarcasm drips from her tone. "Look, if you're gonna ask me twenty questions, can you at least buy me a burger first? I'm starving." She raises an eyebrow and nods ahead at the diner in front of us.

I drag my eyes away from hers, the shock of this realisation beginning to set in.

Kristen has a sister. And she has no idea.

"Sure," I agree.

I guess the two of us have a lot to talk about, although I'm not entirely sure it's my place to say anything. We both exit the vehicle, but as I'm slamming the driver's door shut, a black four wheel-drive screams around the bend, coming to a screeching halt right beside my car.

I hear the girl mutter profanities under her breath. Her hand comes to her forehead, brushing strands of hair away from her face. I notice a shift in her posture, the way her shoulders slump forward. As though she's trying to make herself appear smaller.

Four guys emerge from the SUV. There's a charge in the air, a noticeable tension in the atmosphere. They look like trouble, and I immediately dislike them.

The guy that stepped out of the driver's position runs a hand through his greasy, long black hair and then reaches for the young woman, gripping her tightly by the arm.

"Well, hey there, Mackenzie. Who's your little friend?" he taunts.

I've got at least a foot of height on him, so this comment makes me want to grab him by the neck. But I won't.

Because I'm not that guy anymore.

But I'm also not the kind of guy that will stand idly by while a woman is made to feel intimidated.

I watch as the girl, Mackenzie as he'd called her, shrinks away from his touch, obviously uncomfortable in his presence.

"He was just giving me a ride," she says softly, and I see this sarcastic overly confident girl I've just met melt into a puddle of insecurity.

"I'm Alex," I say assertively, extending my hand to him.

I don't actually want to shake this asshole's hand. I just want him to get his hands off her. Kristen is family to me and that means Mackenzie is too. I'm suddenly protective of her, ready to do whatever it takes to get these idiots away from her.

He doesn't accept my handshake, but he does let go of her. Instead, he snickers at me, an ugly grimace overtaking his features. His three sidekicks stand behind him, echoing his sentiment.

"Alex," he repeats, emphasising the 'x' with the click of his tongue. "Why don't you explain to me what you're doing here with my girl?"

"Your girl?" I ask, my left eyebrow shooting upward. "She doesn't really seem like your type."

The way Mackenzie's eyes widen in fear let me know that these are probably not the kind of guys I should be messing with. In all honesty, I don't know what I'm doing. All I know is that I'm getting a bad vibe from these guys and I need to get her away from them.

"Oh really?" As soon as the words leave his mouth, he's lunging toward me.

He shoves me in the chest. Hard.

I stumble backward toward the road. A truck horn sends panic through me as I realise how close I'd come to becoming roadkill. I manage to sidestep around him quickly so that I'm now facing the street, the girl swaying nervously on the spot beside me. All four of them snort at my reaction.

"Better watch yourself there, Alex," the leader snarls, once again accentuating the 'x' in my name.

"Mackenzie. Why don't you go inside and get us a table?" I say, gesturing to the diner behind us.

I can see her chest rising and falling with every laboured breath. She's terrified. Her eyes shift upward slowly until they meet mine, but only for a second, because then her attention is pulled back to the driver of the SUV, a look of horror taking over her face.

I turn to see what she's looking at, only realising my mistake as his fist meets my jaw. I stagger momentarily and then I'm diving at him. I punch him in the gut, winding him and he doubles over. At that point the three other guys move in on me too.

I hear Mackenzie scream as the next blow connects with my eye socket, the crunching sound of crushing bone filling the gaps between her screams. It hurts like hell.

But they don't stop there.

I lose count of how many times they hit me. The pain is excruciating, until suddenly it isn't. My body becomes numb, my vision blurred with my own blood. I can barely hear their laughter through the throbbing of my own pulse, echoing through my ears like the drumbeat in some up-tempo rock ballad.

I almost give in to unconsciousness, but then I remember the girl standing behind me. I hear her sobs carrying through the car park.

Mackenzie.

Kristen's sister.

I need to protect her. I can't let them win. I lift myself off the ground, my shoulders throbbing as they bear my upper body weight. I see their ringleader, hear his taunts. And then I charge.

My shoulder pummels into his chest and we fly through the air for a considerable distance before I fall forward onto the asphalt.

A second later I hear it.

The screeching of tyres, the thud of flesh and bone on metal, and the blood curdling scream that follows.

What happens after that is a blur.

I'm vaguely aware of the crowd of people that gather, of flashing lights of red and blue. Of someone lifting me into an ambulance, my face sticky with blood, probably not all of it mine.

I lean forward to empty the contents of my stomach. Mackenzie cries hysterically, screaming my name, seemingly paying more attention to me than her own boyfriend, whose limp body had been thrown onto a stretcher and carted to the nearest hospital.

A female police officer tries to restrain her, but she pushes her way toward me. Another officer drags me forward from the ambulance, ripping my aching arms behind my back where he bounds a pair of handcuffs tightly around my wrists.

"Alex Henley." The officer states my name. I don't even remember giving it to him.

"Yeah," I reply, my voice trembling.

"You're under arrest for assault occasioning grievous bodily harm. You have the right to remain silent. Anything you say can and will be used as evidence against you in a court of law."

This can't be happening.

My stomach turns, threatening to eject whatever else might be left in it. I've had run ins with the law before but never to this extent.

I was given a warning once for getting caught graffitiing a public toilet block when I was seventeen. When I first got my licence, I got done for running a red light. But this is completely foreign territory for me.

Grievous bodily harm.

"No!" Mackenzie cries from somewhere beside me.

I'm petrified, not only for myself but for her too. I have no idea what will happen next, but I know that if this is the kind of company this girl keeps, she's still in danger too.

I'm aware of what the police officer said about remaining silent, but I need to help Mackenzie. So, as I'm pulled toward the police car waiting on the curb, I say the only thing I can think of that might help her.

"You have a sister. She works at the helpline in Cliff Haven," I blurt, another wave of nausea washing over me. "Her name is Kristen."

She looks at me, stunned, as if she isn't sure whether she's heard me correctly.

"Cliff Haven helpline," I repeat urgently, before my head is shoved downwards, and I'm thrust inside the car.

The door slams shut, the car in motion seconds later. Mackenzie doesn't move from her place on the curb, her terrified face growing smaller in the window as I leave her behind.

We arrive at the Coledale police station where I'm thrown into a holding cell. It's cold and it stinks of piss but at least I don't have to share it with anyone. I'm in a state of utter disbelief at the events that have occurred this afternoon, my aching body still vibrating with shock. From the cell, I can hear two cops talking at a desk down the hall.

"Here. File this report," a woman's voice says. "Assault occasioning grievous bodily harm. Hopefully it doesn't turn into a murder charge. The victim's still alive for now."

"What a mess," I hear someone else reply.

"Tell me about it. That's not even the worst of it. The guy he put in the hospital? It's Ethan Davis."

"Shit. He's going away for a long time."

"No doubt about it."

I shove my head into my hands, the gauze the paramedics placed over a gash on my forehead slicking my fingertips with blood.

This can't be happening.

I was ready to start my life.

I was really ready. To take the promotion at the tavern. To commit to Kristen.

Oh god, Kristen.

What have I done?

My injuries may be serious, but in this moment it's my heart that aches. She must be going out of her mind right now, not knowing where I am. I wonder whether she's assuming the worst has happened, although I know that whatever she might be thinking could never be close to the truth.

I don't know how long a 'long time' is, but I know it's too long to expect Kristen to wait for me. I know that if I tell her where I am, she'll wait as long as it takes for me to be set free from prison. She would stand by my side through it all.

But I can't be that selfish, no matter how much I want to be. I know what I need to do.

I walk to the front of the cell. I wrap my fingers around the cold, hard metal bars. "Excuse me," I shout down the hall.

A short policewoman shuffles down the aisle, her blonde hair pulled back tight into a ponytail. She doesn't say anything, just raises her eyebrows at me.

"Do I get to make a phone call?"

I'm not sure if I imagine the slightest hint of sympathy that crosses her features. "Sure. You only get one. Make it count."

I call my father. I explain the whole situation and he drives four hours to post bail. When they release me at around roughly 2am, I'm instructed not to leave town.

They tell me someone will be in touch about my court hearing. My dad checks us both into a cheap motel and I try to prepare myself to make another dreaded phone call.

"Are you sure you want to do this right now?" Dad asks. "She'll be sleeping."

I shake my head stubbornly. "I have to do it now. It can't wait."

"Okay, son. I'll be right here when you're done." With a grim expression, he pats my shoulder and then turns and seats himself in the small tub chair in the corner of the motel.

I wander to a secluded park at the end of the road where I slump down into one of the swings. I pull my phone out and stare at it for several moments, trying to psyche myself up for what I need to say.

I know I'll have to be cruel.

Brutal.

I'm going to have to make her hate me.

But it's for her own good.

I find her in my contacts, the picture of her gorgeous face lighting up the screen. A face I have no idea if I will ever see again.

And I hit the call button.

Chapter 43

KRISTEN

I sit motionless on the rock, the silence stretching out between us. I've never been rendered so completely powerless as I have been in these last twenty-minutes, watching Henley relive the tragic events that occurred six months ago.

I've listened intently, observing the way his shoulder blades expand and contract, the tremors in his hands and the cold sweat that collects on his brow. He's fighting off another panic attack.

He's been fighting an internal battle I've known nothing about.

There's a dull ache in my bones, a burning between my ribs. A sadness I'm not sure will ever leave me after learning the truth. How could I not know? How could I put aside the obvious signs of trauma Henley has displayed?

Everything is beginning to make sense now. The sleeplessness he described, the panic attacks, the aversion to loud noises. The way he fell to the ground the night those tyres screeched outside the Haven. They're all obvious signs of PTSD that relate directly to this incident.

My mind churns over thoughts and memories of the night he left, selfishly trying to absolve me of the shame I deserve to feel.

"You wanted me to hate you," I say, turning to face him, my cheeks wet with tears. "You made me think you had a life with someone else."

"I'm sorry. It was the only way." He clenches his jaw, squeezing his eyes shut, then he buries his face in his palms.

"Why didn't you just tell me?" I cry. "You know I would have waited for you." I'm aware I'm only exacerbating his already guilty conscience, but my frustration has gotten the better of me.

"I know you would have, Kris. Because you're so good." He does meet my gaze now and I can see his blue eyes are shimmering with moisture. "I knew that if I told you, you would have driven four hours without another thought. You would have dropped everything to be there for me whenever I called."

"What's wrong with that?" I ask, wondering why he's making my loyalty to him sound like such a burden.

"They told me I could be in prison for up to fifteen years. Longer if the guy didn't make it," he admits. "Don't you see? I'd never want that life for you. The best gift I could give you was the chance to move on without me."

"Even if that meant me hating you," I whisper.

Understanding washes over me. I realise now that Henley had chosen to selflessly put my needs ahead of his own. He'd made the ultimate sacrifice, and I'd blamed him when I should have been comforting him. Accused him instead of thanking him.

This man, this incredible man, had put himself on the line for me, for my family, and I'd let him sink to the depths of the deepest, darkest ocean. I should have paid more attention.

To the way his breath hitched at the sound of thunder, the way his gaze darted to the ground at the sudden burst of fireworks after the carnival last night.

I ignored the signs, allowing my hurt and anger over his betrayal to override what I knew deep down all along. That there was something bigger brewing below the surface.

All this time I've been trying to pry from him the truth about why he'd left, belittling him for not being honest. Now I realise.

He didn't guard his story by choice.

He's been physically incapable of speaking the words. To offer what I'd assumed could only be a simple explanation but was in fact a recount of the severe unspeakable trauma he's experienced at the hands of fate.

My lungs collapse in on themselves, crippled by the heaviness of my own guilt and the magnitude of Henley's pain. I try not to envision Henley being brutally attacked by four men, but the images find their way into my head anyway. I'm crushed, physically pained by the thought of him being forced to sit in a jail cell for months on end, never knowing if he'd ever be able to gain his life back.

All of this lost time, stolen from us in an instant.

"Who is Ethan Davis?" I dare to ask.

"Mackenzie's ex." Henley expels a heavy breath before he continues. "He's a really bad guy, Kristen. He's involved in a drug ring. His father is the chief of police in Coledale. From what I heard, he's a dirty cop. I had no chance going up against him in court."

I shake my head in confusion. "But you're here. How did you get out?"

"My dad managed to get me one of the best lawyers in the country. He fought for an appeal. When a witness finally came forward and told the court that it was an accident, they had no choice but to drop all charges," he tells me. "Apparently there were a few customers inside the diner that had watched the scene play out, but nobody wanted to go up against Ethan Davis and his father. Thank God someone finally did."

"Mackenzie was with this guy?"

"Yeah. I don't know much about their relationship, but he seemed to be holding something over her. She contacted me a few times in prison." He pauses, his eyes darkening as he gazes back out to the river. "I told her to catch a bus to Cliff Haven. That she should go and find you. She wanted to, but Ethan's father threatened her. He said that if she ever left town, he'd find her."

"Poor Mackenzie," I whisper.

I think back to my very first shift at the helpline. The same night as the accident.

And the night I'd first spoken to Em.

Jules had taken so many hang-ups that night. Most likely all from Mackenzie. The sister I never knew I had who had known I was working there. She had been waiting for me to answer.

"She was terrified to defy them," Henley explains. "When I got out, I went back to her house. We left town in the middle of the night. We stayed in a few different places for a while, making sure they weren't on our trail, but we knew we had to come back to Cliff Haven. We needed to come home."

"Where is Ethan Davis now?" I ask.

"No idea," he answers, his jaw clenching. "Last I'd heard he was in physical therapy learning how to walk again. The injuries he sustained that night were pretty horrific. I don't remember the details, but he had a lot of broken bones, a severe head injury." He pauses, choking on his next words.

"He was in a coma. At first, they thought he'd be brain dead if he ever woke up. Luckily, he recovered."

He looks out across the river again, his eyes narrow, his posture tense. I'm losing him to that dark place inside his head.

"I can't believe it. Henley, you were in jail." I feel the full scale of these words as they leave my mouth. "How did you survive it?"

Even as I ask the question, I know that although he's here in front of me, he hasn't come out unscathed.

He turns to me, swallowing hard before he answers. "I thought of you, Kris. Sometimes it got so dark inside my head, but then I thought of you, and it kept me going. I can still picture that night so clearly, as though I'm reliving it all over again. I can't forget that sound. I can't unsee…" he trails off, unable to say anymore.

"I'm so sorry," I say, blinking away another tear before it trails down my cheek. He reaches out and swipes it away with his thumb.

"Not as sorry as I am." His icy blue eyes are intense, glassy like glaciers. "I almost killed someone, Kristen."

"But you didn't."

He shakes his head in despair. "I've messed up so many lives. I've ruined everything."

"None of this is your fault, Henley." I pause, remembering why he'd gone to see my father in the first place. He'd gone there for me. "You did it all for me," I say softly. "You wanted to marry me."

A crack rips through my chest knowing I've treated this man terribly. A man who would literally do anything for me.

His chest rises with a heavy breath, then he looks away from me back to the river. "I've had some bad days since then. Days where I just sat and thought about how you deserved to be with someone better. Someone like Chase. Not some screw up like me."

"Stop. Don't you dare say that," I plead with him. It's killing me to see him like this.

"It's true. I only ever wanted to be someone you could depend on. I still do. I want it more than anything. I know I'm not worthy of you, Kristen." A lone tear falls, trailing its way down his cheek. But I'm never going to stop trying to be."

I grab his face between my palms and force him to look me in the eyes. "Henley, this was a horrible accident. You saved my sister. You brought her to me. I love you for that." My hands move into his hair as I whisper. "I love *you*."

His ocean blue eyes stare back at mine as tears stream silently from each one. "I love you too, Kris. You know I always have."

And then I'm climbing into his lap, my arms wrapped firmly around him. At first, he doesn't move, his body rigid beneath me, but then his arms find their place around my waist, and he buries his face into my neck. I feel his breath warm on my cheek as he exhales, his body slumping as the tension leaves him. I hold onto him so tightly, as though if I squeeze him hard enough, I'll be able to mend all of his broken pieces back together.

"I wish you'd told me. I wish I could have been there for you." I tell him. "You have to let me be here for you."

"I didn't think I was ever going to see you again." His voice comes out muffled against my neck, each word piercing my heart.

"It's okay. I'm here. I'll always be here. We're gonna be okay."

I hold him tighter as his shoulders shake with the release of the pent-up emotion he's carried with him for the last six months.

And I don't stop holding him.

Not even when his tears stop flowing and the violent sobs that wrack his body finally cease.

Chapter 44

HENLEY

Kristen lies beside me, her head resting on my chest. Her fingertips trace the tattooed lines that run from my shoulder down to my bicep. This is something she always used to do, and I've missed it. I've missed all of it.

The way her dark chocolate hair splays out behind her on the pillow, the warmth of her breath on my shoulder as she sleeps.

After everything that's happened, I never imagined I'd get her alone up here in my loft, but here we are, having just shared the most intimate moments of our relationship. I've known Kristen for what feels like forever, but I've never felt closer to her than I do right now.

Having her back in my life is all I've ever wanted, but I know that her forgiveness doesn't mean anything unless I can learn to forgive myself. That road is going to be a long one, but I'm on my way.

She sniffles softly, nuzzling further into my torso and it's then I realise she's crying.

"Hey," I say, catching a tear with my forefinger. I tilt her face upward towards mine. "Those better be happy tears."

"I am happy." She offers me a weak smile that doesn't meet her eyes.

"But...?" I ask.

I need her to share her insecurities. In the past Kristen hasn't always been an open book. She's kept her feelings guarded, but we can't afford to be anything but completely transparent with each other now. Not after everything.

"I just can't help thinking about all the time we've lost." She gazes up at me, her hazel eyes spilling with sorrow. "The time that's been stolen from us. And all the time I've wasted hating you when you didn't deserve it."

"I know." I'm reminded of the conversation I had with Old Tommy in the bar this afternoon. So much has happened since then, it feels like a lifetime ago, but his words will forever be etched in my mind.

Do you have the guts to take your own advice?

I'm under no delusions that everything will be easy now that Kristen has accepted me back into her life. I know that moving on is going to have its challenges, no matter which path I choose to take. But I also know that I can get through anything with her by my side.

"I guess we need to try and put it in the past and focus on the time we have left. Make every day count."

"Like a fresh start?" she asks, entwining her fingers through mine.

"Yeah," I answer. "Like a fresh start."

"I like that," she says.

The corners of her mouth lift upward as she snuggles in closer to my chest again. She curls her arm over my shoulder but her hand stills when her fingers glide over the raised skin across my back. I feel her chest expand with air as she takes in an anxious breath, her eyebrows pinching together in a frown.

"It's okay," I reassure her, combing my fingers through her hair. "I'm okay."

"You weren't kidding," she states softly. "When you said you were shanked with a toothbrush."

I want to lie to her. Say anything to stop her eyes searching mine for all the things I haven't been able to say. But I won't do that. "No. I wasn't."

What I won't tell her though, is that I was targeted in prison. That Ethan Davis had paid off one of his subordinates to do his dirty work from the outside, attacking me in my sleep in the middle of the night.

I'll tell her eventually, but she's had enough for one day. I don't want to scare her, and honestly, I'm enjoying her company too much to bring it down with any more sad stories.

"I can't even begin to understand what you must have been through." She brushes loose strands of hair from my forehead, her fingertips tenderly grazing their way down the side of my face to my jawline.

"It's okay," I say again.

"It's not," she says sympathetically. "It's not fair. I wish I had of been there." She drags her hand downward, covering the place where my heart beats with her palm.

"You're here now. That's enough."

She nods and I wrap my arms tighter around her waist, pulling her body against mine. She kisses me like she's afraid to lose me again and I hold her as though this is my last day on earth.

Eventually, she drifts off to sleep and I stay awake as long as I can, watching her lie peacefully in my arms, grateful for second chances.

Sleep finally comes for me, but when I wake, I can tell that it's still dark outside by the lack of light coming in through the crack in the curtains. I reach for my phone on the nightstand, glancing at the time on the screen. I expect it to be somewhere around the middle of the night, but I'm surprised to find it's just after five in the morning. This is the longest I've slept consistently without waking up since I can remember. I smile to myself as Kristen stirs beside me.

"You alright?" she murmurs, her lips on my neck.

"Never been better," I whisper.

And I mean it.

This has been the first restful night I've had in over six months. The first without broken sleep. The first without cold sweats and panic attacks. I've woken with a sense of optimism. I realise now that I'm not what happens to me. I'm what I choose to become.

And I'm ready to be the man Kristen needs me to be.

I'm ready to be enough.

"Hey," I whisper, pressing my lips to her forehead. "I want to show you something."

"Now?" she asks, one eye fluttering open. Kristen has never been much of a morning person despite all the early shifts she's pulled at the Haven.

"Yeah. Right now."

I chuckle at the way her eyebrows crease as I rise from the bed, retrieving my t-shirt from the floor and pulling it over my head. She sits up reluctantly. Then I take her hand and pull her close.

"Okay," she grunts begrudgingly.

I guide her down the stairs and through the empty tavern. She gives me a strange look when I begin to lean all of my body weight into the bookshelf.

"You woke me up before sunrise to come down here and rearrange the furniture with you? Henley, that's criminal."

I straighten, raising my eyebrows at her choice of words, but a grin plays out on my mouth. "Really?"

"Oops." She winces. "Too soon?"

I shake my head at her, continuing to slide the bookshelf across the floor. Her eyes widen when she sees the closed door that leads to the abandoned room.

"I've been working on something down here."

She narrows her gaze in curiosity as I swing the door open. "What's in there?"

"Come see for yourself." I wave a hand, gesturing for her to go ahead of me.

Her hand touches on the handle as she enters the space, her fingers brushing over the new paint work. She spins around, confused. The sky is only just beginning to lighten outside, and the room is otherwise dark.

"What exactly am I looking at?" she asks.

I shuffle through the darkness to the far side of the room. A tinny echo fills the air as I accidentally kick over an empty paint can.

Kristen cries out from the doorway. "Alex! Are you okay?"

"Yeah," I mutter. "Sorry. I forgot that was there."

My hands fumble over the wall in search of the power switch. When I finally locate it, the room instantly brightens with the soft glow of a thousand fairy lights. She scans the space in wonder, marvelling the freshly painted bay windows, a stark white in contrast to the shades of purple and pink filling the sky behind them.

"Alex!" she gasps, bringing her hands to her mouth. "This is amazing. I had forgotten this room existed."

"I hope Liv won't mind that I made use of her fairy lights."

"No way. This is incredible. It must have taken you weeks. Have you told Steve?"

She hovers near the double French doors that open out onto the lawn, gazing out at the sand in the distance. The waves appear an icy grey-blue as they crash on the shore in the intensifying morning light.

"Not yet. Wanted to make sure I could pull it off first." I fold my arms across my chest, watching as she takes in the view from the bay window. Her palms smooth over the glossy woodwork, then she lowers herself onto the window seat below.

"It still needs to be re-upholstered," I say, waving a hand at the newly built bench she's sitting on. "I was going to do it myself, but I wanted to give Maggie and Steve the opportunity to choose the colours they like."

"You built these yourself?" Her eyes are wide with wonder.

I give a subtle nod and I can't deny the warmth that fills my chest when her face beams with pride.

"It's beautiful." She rises from the seat, wandering to the middle of the room, then gestures to the final piece of my project. "What's all of this?"

"I'm halfway through building a table. There were some old pieces of broken furniture dumped in here and I thought I could save some of the timber and repurpose it," I explain. "I was thinking it might look good there, on the paved area outside." I point to the small patio on the other side of the French doors, currently still overgrown with weeds and in need of a serious acid wash.

She moves to the doors, and I follow behind her, resting my hands on her hips. "It sounds perfect," she says.

"I thought it could make a great function room for the wedding reception," I offer. "For Liv and EJ."

"They're going to love it." She spins around, snaking her arms around my neck and I lean forward to place a kiss on her forehead. "Seriously. This is beyond amazing."

Just like Kristen, I'm not the best at taking compliments so I attempt to hide my unease with a lame joke. "Who knew I had it in me to create something out of nothing?"

Her eyes pierce mine, determined and all-consuming. "Me," she says. "I did, Alex."

Chapter 45

KRISTEN

"You have a sister?" Liv asks incredulously. "That you knew nothing about?"

"Uh huh," I say, swirling my straw around in the pink cocktail that Henley had ordered me. My favourite, though I don't really feel much in the mood for drinking.

I glance over at him where he rests an elbow on the bar. His eyes soften as they find mine and I catch a flicker of a smile, then EJ says something that draws his attention back away from me.

"I still can't believe what happened," Liv says, blowing out a breath.

"Me neither." I sigh. "He's been through so much. I honestly don't know if he'll ever heal completely from this."

"He'll get through it. He's strong," Liv says earnestly, reaching forward to grasp my hand. "And he has you."

I nod. "I know. I'm just glad he's back." I feel the threat of tears as my eyes begin to sting, but I push them down. I've spent too long letting this sadness overwhelm me. I want to focus on the present, the future. The second chance we've been given.

"Me too," she agrees with a warm smile. "I feel so guilty that I ever doubted him."

"You and me both," I say. "I get it now. Why EJ hadn't shared his secret. He's a good friend."

EJ appears, dropping down into the booth next to Liv. "You talking about me again?"

"Always," Liv replies sassily, pulling her hand back from mine. "I was just about to fill Kristen in on your suit fitting fiasco."

EJ shakes his head, his cheeks rosy with embarrassment. "Of course, you were."

"Wait. What?" I ask, confused, as Henley slides into the seat beside me. He tucks an arm around my waist, pulling me in against his side and I revel in the warmth of his body.

"Okay. I need to hear this story." Henley grins and it reminds me that the carefree, fun-loving version of him is still in there.

"Yeah. Me too," I say. "What happened?"

EJ pinches the bridge of his nose, then runs a hand through his hair as Liv begins regaling us with a mortifying tale.

"We had to go for EJ's suit fitting for the wedding last week in this fancy little boutique in the city. My dad kind of knows the staff because he's been going there forever, so he came along to help us get a good price."

Liv starts to chuckle as EJ groans. "Please stop," he begs his fiancé, knowing that she's having way too much fun at his expense.

"Long story short," she continues. "The saleswoman set up a change room for EJ with a bunch of suits. Except he went into the wrong one. He tried on this suit that was two sizes too small."

"It wasn't my fault she gave me the wrong suit!" EJ interrupts.

"Just as he emerged from the change room, barely able to move, this woman dropped her purse behind him by accident. Emmett here, ever the gentleman, crouched down to pick it up and the whole backside of his pants split open," she tells us through fits of giggles.

"Oh my god! No, EJ!" I can't help but join Liv, laughing at EJ's misfortune.

"That's not even the best part!" Liv cries.

"Best part?" EJ deadpans. "You mean the worst part."

"What do you mean?" Henley asks.

"He was wearing his bright green Scooby Doo briefs," Liv blurts.

Henley and I crack up at this as EJ hangs his head in mock shame.

"Thank god the sales assistant took pity on me and didn't make me pay for them," he mutters.

"You mean after she asked for your autograph?" Liv snickers. "You're lucky she was a fan of your music!"

EJ shrugs. "True."

In this moment everything feels just how it used to.

Like old times.

Like we're just a group of friends blowing off steam at our favourite bar, the air thick with nostalgia. Despite knowing that nothing will ever be the same again, especially for Henley, we've found a way to fall back into past patterns.

"Wow, dude," Henley says. "You flashed the saleswoman and your future father-in-law? That's brutal."

"Tell me about it," EJ says. "I think I need another drink."

"You want me to get another round?" Henley asks as he drains the rest of his beer.

"You gonna take it out of your paycheck this time too?"

"I think I'll have to." Henley gives a short half-laugh. "There's no way Dylan will let me get away with climbing over the bar."

"Dylan's a sweetie," I say. "But he does like to run things by the book."

"Where's Mackenzie tonight?" Liv asks.

"She's in introvert heaven. At home. Watching Netflix," I reply. We had invited Mackenzie along to have drinks with us, but she'd declined the offer, happy to stay in instead. "Oh, that reminds me," I say, glancing at my watch. "We promised her we'd bring her home a pizza. We should probably get going. Raincheck on the next round?"

"Yeah. We should go too. I have to be up early for a lesson in the morning and EJ's going into the studio." Liv slides her phone and keys from the tabletop and puts them in her pocket and we all make our way to the exit.

Outside, she pulls me into a warm hug. "If you need anything at all, just call, okay?"

"Thank you. I will." I'm so grateful for my friend. I don't know where I'd be without her.

We move in separate directions, Liv and EJ crossing the street to their apartment, and Henley and I continuing to the pizza shop down on the corner.

We pick up two pepperoni pizzas at Mackenzie's request and stroll through the quiet street to my apartment.

Henley's demeanour is calm, subdued, even more so now that we're alone. Not unlike that night six months ago at Liv and EJ's engagement party. I don't quite know how to interpret it. He hasn't said a word since we left the pizza shop and I'm beginning to take his silence for sadness.

"Are you okay?" I ask him.

He looks down at me, his eyes searching mine. For what, I'm not sure. "Yeah. Yeah, I am."

"You're being awfully quiet."

"I'm content, I guess." His shoulders jump in a small shrug as he stops and turns to me. "You have no idea how much I missed the simple things. The things I took for granted. Grabbing a drink with friends. Getting a pizza from the corner shop." He takes a step forward, leaning into me. His nose grazes my cheek as he whispers, "Kissing you on an empty street."

He tucks my hair behind my ear, caressing my jaw with his free hand while gripping the pizza boxes in the other. He lingers there long enough for me to drink in his scent, cedar and citrus, and the random tiny freckles spread across his nose.

He cups the back of my neck, placing a tender kiss on my cheek, then his lips hover near mine, savouring the moment. He's taking his time with me, something he can finally afford to do, but I'm impatient, having waited too long to have him back in my life.

I reach for him, fisting his shirt as I pull him closer, pressing my mouth to his. He kisses me slowly, deeply, with more restraint than he's ever showed before.

"What was that for?" I ask when he pulls away.

He shrugs again, then with a wink he says, "Because I can. And because you're mine."

I laugh softly as he links our fingers, swinging our joined hands as though we're two lovestruck teenagers without a care in the world. "You know what, Kris?"

"What?"

"I think we're gonna be okay."

I smile up at him and he beams back, throwing his arm around my shoulder. I lean into him as we walk the next block, thanking the universe for bringing this amazing man back to me.

A few minutes later, I swing open the apartment door, announcing our arrival to Mackenzie. "Hey, we're home."

My greeting is met with an eyeroll as she repositions herself on the couch, a tub of popcorn resting in her lap. "Thank God. I'm starving!"

"You're literally eating popcorn," Henley teases. "Good to see you haven't given up the dramatics."

He dumps the pizza boxes down on the coffee table. Flipping the lid, he takes a slice and slumps down beside her on the couch. She turns in time to see him bite off half the slice, cringing as pizza grease drips down his chin.

"Ew, dude. You eat like an ogre," she chides.

I laugh as Henley pulls a face, baring his teeth in a toothy grin despite the fact that his mouth is full of pizza.

"Hmm, nice," Mackenzie says sarcastically.

He gives her a gentle dig in the ribs with his elbow. "At least I don't make coffee fit for an ogre."

She throws a handful of popcorn at him, to which he laughs. I can't help but smile watching the way they interact. Knowing now how Mackenzie has come to be in our lives has given me a new insight into their friendship. Watching them bicker, almost like brother and sister, sends warmth through me, and my pride and respect for Henley has deepened knowing that he put his life on the line for my sister.

I take a slice of pizza from the box and nestle into the single armchair beside the couch, pulling the throw rug over my lap. "What are we watching, Mackenzie?"

"Outer Banks," she replies, taking a piece of pizza for herself. "Best show ever."

"Cool. You should come to the tavern with us next time."

"And give up my date with John B and Jay Jay?" she scoffs, holding one arm out toward the TV. "No thanks."

I'm not sure I'll ever understand this cynical young woman I can now call my sister, but I sure am glad she's here. And I have my amazing boyfriend to thank for that.

My gaze meet Henley's and I smile watching the corners of his lips turn upward in a grin, his eyes glimmering in the blue light reflecting from the TV.

And I start to think that maybe he's right. Maybe we are gonna be okay.

Chapter 46

KRISTEN

The first thing I see when my eyes flutter open is the silvery line that makes its way across Henley's shoulder blade. I don't know if I'll ever be able to look at it and not feel a punch to the gut. Whether this constant reminder of where he's been and what has happened to him in this half a year away from me will ever fade.

I lean into him, wrapping my arms around his torso, my hands moving over the hard muscle of his abdomen as I make small kisses along the scar.

He stirs, rolling over to face me, a smile forming on his lips. He cups the back of my head, his fingers threading through my hair as he plants a kiss on my mouth.

"I can't believe you're here in my bed," I whisper.

"You better get used to it," he grins, then he narrows his eyes in seriousness. "Because I'm not going anywhere."

He tucks a wild strand of hair behind my ear, then pulls me in closer, a soft groan escaping him as his hands explore their way up my back.

I'd long ago lost hope that Henley and I would ever share moments like this one again and now that he's here in my apartment, I never want to let him leave.

"I love you," I tell him as I move over him, my legs straddling his hips.

He pulls me down onto him and kisses me again, this time with more urgency, his fingers trailing their way upward to my breasts. Warmth shoots up my spine as he drags his lips over my collarbone, the heat between us escalating, as though we're both afraid that life could change in an instant.

We both know now how easily it can.

Henley's phone alarms from the bedside table. "Shit. I have to go."

"No. It's still early. Stay with me a little longer," I complain as I snuggle into his chest, my grip tightening around him. I wink at him cheekily. "I need a replay of last night."

Henley lets out a groan, as though he's in physical pain. "I wish I could, but we have a delivery arriving at the tavern in half hour and I told Dylan I'd handle it."

He pulls me in for one last embrace, his lips grazing my forehead.

"But it's your day off," I protest again.

He lets out a long sigh before launching out of bed, reaching for his light grey trackpants on the floor below. "I could hardly say no when I live there."

"Fair enough," I say, reluctantly tossing the covers back. "I need to get ready to go to the Haven anyway."

I'm thankful to only be working a quick four-hour shift today. Yesterday had been a busy one. I'd spent most of the day at uni, then worked the afternoon at the helpline. Today, I plan to get my responsibilities out of the way early so that Henley and I can continue making up for lost time.

"Meet me at the tavern after your shift?" he asks.

"Can't wait," I say.

He curls an arm around my waist and presses one last kiss to my mouth, leaving me standing there wondering how we both got so lucky to be given this second chance.

I shower and make a quick call to my mum. So much has happened since our last conversation. It feels like forever ago that we last spoke. The phone rings for so long I'm about to give up, but then my mother's breathless voice comes through the line.

"Hi, Kristen," she pants.

"Hey Mum," I reply. "Why are you out of breath? You still trying to be the next Usain Bolt?"

"Don't tease me," she pouts. "I'm injured. Took me forever to get to the phone."

"Injured? Mum, what happened?" I ask, now genuinely concerned.

"Oh, it's not too bad," she explains. "I sort of sprained my ankle the other day. That'll teach me for trying to sprint along the beach. Running on sand is really hard, you know?"

I stifle a giggle. "Yeah, Mum. I know. How are things at the clinic?"

"Not too bad. Luckily not too busy at the moment with this stupid ankle giving me grief," she complains. "What's happening with you? How are things going with your new roommate? Mackenzie, isn't it?"

"Uh, good," I say. "She's good."

I want to tell her everything. I need to tell her. About Mackenzie. About Henley. All of it. But this is not a conversation to be had over the phone. I have no idea how she is going to take the news that my father was leading a double life long before he left us. I need to see her in person.

"So, listen, Mum. Are you free around lunchtime? I thought we could go to that restaurant near Ben's Harvest and grab a bite."

Maybe I could even get Mackenzie to join us.

"Sure. Oh, wait. No, I can't do today. Mrs. Hillier is bringing her German Shepherd in, and I promised I'd take care of him myself. What about tomorrow?"

"Okay, sure," I agree. "Tomorrow it is."

By the time I finish talking to my mother I still have about forty minutes till my shift begins. I decide to take a walk along the esplanade then grab a quick coffee before I start work.

"Mackenzie," I call out across the apartment. "I'm going to the Haven. You want to come with me and grab a coffee?"

Mackenzie doesn't answer right away. Her door is slightly ajar, so I walk over and push it open the rest of the way. "Mackenzie?"

Her bed is empty but unmade. She must have gone out earlier while Henley and I were otherwise occupied. Sometimes she likes to go out for a morning jog, so I assume that's what she's doing. That, or she's already sitting at a table at the Haven waiting for me.

The air is crisp when I step out on to the street, but the sun shines low in a clear, blue sky. There isn't a cloud in sight. I never thought I'd be this happy again and although I know there's a long road ahead for us, I've chosen to remain positive about the future. I breathe in, never more ready to take on the day.

I want to believe that our darkest days are behind us, but my optimism is challenged when I round the corner onto the esplanade and the tavern comes into view.

You can be anywhere when your world caves in. When it's changed forever in an instant. Your darkest moment could come in the brightest of places, a brilliant summer's day underneath the bluest of skies.

You could be strolling down your favourite street in a town you've always called home. A town that becomes suddenly transformed into the foreign, most dangerous of places.

In one moment, you could be daydreaming about your one true love and in the next wishing with all of your heart that you held them closer. And that moment will take your breath away.

At least that's how it happened for me.

My vision blurs with flashes of red and blue and I know, with that sinking feeling churning in my gut, that nothing will ever be the same again.

The energy is abruptly sucked from me, my heart jackhammering against my ribs. Dylan stands on the corner outside Steve's Tavern, his hands cupped over his mouth as he paces back and forth. Even from here I can see the way his chest expands and contracts with every laboured breath.

My feet are frozen in place on the pavement, shock setting in as paramedics emerge from the tavern's doors pushing a stretcher bearing the weight of a lifeless body.

Suddenly I'm triggered, my feet awakening. I'm running now, faster than I thought I knew how to. I don't need to see the tattooed arm hanging limp from the side of the stretcher to know it's him. His skin normally tanned a golden brown is pale and grey, his white t-shirt now stained red in patches as a medic holds gauze to his side.

The air is gone from my lungs, and it takes me a second to regain my voice. "Henley!" I scream.

I've almost reached the ambulance when strong hands pull me back. "Kristen, let them do their job."

"Dylan, what the fuck is happening?" I cry. Dylan holds me close as more police cars screech around the corner. "Is he going to be okay?"

Dylan is silent.

"Dylan, he'll be okay. Right?" I wait for him to comfort me, to reassure me that everything is fine. Or better yet, wake me up from this nightmare. But when my eyes meet his, they only mirror the terror I know are in mine. "Why aren't you saying anything?" I lash out at him, my right-hand curling into a fist. I grit my teeth and hit him in the chest. "Dylan!"

Our eyes dart back and forth from each other to the ambulance as its doors swing shut and Henley is taken away, sirens blaring through the otherwise quiet street.

"I'm so sorry, Kristen," Dylan chokes, his breath ragged.

"What happened?" I demand.

Dylan's face is pale with shock. "He was unconscious when I got here. I found him behind the bar. He'd been stabbed."

I shake my head in denial. "That doesn't make any sense. Who would want to hurt Henley? No. It's impossible."

The name Ethan Davis comes to mind as I say the words out loud.

"Kristen." Dylan swallows the lump in his throat as his eyes fill with tears. "I saw him."

"He's going to be okay though." There's no question in my tone. "They'll fix him."

Dylan squeezes his eyes shut and turns away from me, his hand coming up to his forehead.

"Right?" I ask. *He has to be okay.*

He turns back to me, pain in his expression. "He lost a lot of blood, Kristen," he croaks.

"No," I say, stricken with panic. "He's going to be fine. I need to go to him. Where are they taking him?"

A police officer steps toward us and I become aware of the scene unfolding behind us. Several forensic investigators file into the tavern, armed with bags of equipment, another closing off its entry with police tape.

"Dylan Alcott?" the police officer says.

"Yes," Dylan replies.

"I was told you were the one that found Alex this morning." The officer rests one hand on his belt and uses the other to pull a notebook from his back pocket.

"That's right," he confirms with a nervous nod.

"I know you've been through a lot today but I'm afraid I'm going to need to bring you in for questioning."

"Sure. Whatever you need."

The officer turns to me, taking in my obvious state of distress. "I'm assuming you know the victim."

The victim.

I don't like the way he describes Henley.

I want to argue with him that Henley is not a victim. That he's strong, caring and protective. But in my helplessness, I can only offer three simple words. "He's my boyfriend."

"Okay. I'm sorry for what you're going through today. This is obviously quite a shocking situation to bear witness to," he offers. "They've taken Alex to Milton Hospital where he'll undergo surgery."

"Milton? Why wouldn't they take him to Palm Grove?"

Palm Grove is the closest hospital to Cliff Haven. It seemed like an obvious choice to take him there, instead of all the way into the city.

"Palm Grove isn't equipped to deal with the extent of the injuries that Alex has sustained. He'll be in safer hands in Milton."

I know that this information will only alarm me further if I let it, but I can't let my mind go there yet. I need to be strong. I need to be there for Henley.

"Kristen!" Liv's frantic voice echoes from across the street. I turn in time to see her running toward me, EJ in tow.

"What happened?" EJ asks, his eyes telling me he already suspects the worst.

"Henley was stabbed. They've taken him to Milton hospital," I say, the words rushing right out of me. "I need to get there."

"We'll take you," Liv says, her eyes wide in shock as she drapes an arm around my shoulder. "Come on."

I'm ushered across the road and EJ helps me into Liv's car. We don't speak on the way to the hospital. We all know there's nothing anyone can say to fix this.

Nothing to spark hope in the darkness.

Chapter 47

KRISTEN

When we finally arrive at the hospital, Henley is still in surgery. We're informed it could be several hours before he goes into recovery. EJ and I sit in the waiting room, getting as comfortable as we possibly can on the tiny plastic chairs that adorn the space along the window, while Liv goes to fetch us coffee. EJ gets up and paces the length of the room, a blur of city skyscrapers visible in the floor to ceiling windows behind him as he makes two calls. One to each of Henley's parents.

Once he's done talking, he makes his way back over to me and drops down once again into the chair beside me.

"His dad is on his way, but it will be ages before he gets here. He's interstate for work and needs to get a flight. His mum is in Hawaii so who knows when she'll show up."

"She's in Hawaii?" I ask.

"With a new lover," EJ confirms.

"I'll call Katie," I say.

"Already tried," EJ says. "There was no answer."

I try again anyway, but just as it had with EJ, the call goes to voicemail. I leave a message telling her to call me back urgently.

I'm upset that Henley's family won't be here when he wakes up.

If he wakes up.

No.

When.

I silence the voice of doubt in my head. He will get through this. We'll get through it together.

I try Mackenzie's number again. I'd tried to call her in the car on the way here, but she isn't picking up either. I sigh as it goes to voicemail again, then I leave a message for her too.

Liv storms back into the waiting room carrying three small coffee cups. She hands one to each of us. "Have you heard anything yet?" she asks.

The way she grips EJ's hand hurts my heart. What if Henley never gets to feel my hand in his again?

"No. He's still in surgery," EJ answers.

Another hour ticks by and I'm sure I'm not going to have any nails left by the end of the day the way I'm nervously biting them down.

Finally, a surgeon appears. We all stand, eagerly awaiting the news of Henley's condition. EJ places a gentle arm around my shoulder as he approaches.

"Are you relatives of Alex Henley?" the surgeon asks.

"Yes," I answer automatically, then realise I need to correct myself. I'm not a relative but I'm the closest thing he has to one right now. "I'm his girlfriend."

"Oh," the surgeon replies. "Does he have any family here?"

My shoulders slump. I've watched enough TV medical dramas to know they aren't going to tell me anything because we aren't blood related.

Liv speaks up as EJ's tries to comfort me. "His family couldn't be here. We're all that he has right now."

"I understand," he nods. "But I'm only supposed to give out information to family."

"Can't you tell us anything?" I throw my head into my hands in despair.

We've been waiting here for hours, and this jerk isn't even going to tell us whether he's okay.

"Dr. Harris," I hear a familiar voice boom from down the corridor. "This young lady is very important to Alex. Perhaps we could bend the rules given the circumstances."

I look up to find Victor Petersen standing over us, clipboard in hand, looking as authoritative as ever. I give the surgeon a hopeful look. I can't bear to hear bad news. "Please tell me he's okay."

The surgeon wears a grim expression. "As you know, Alex sustained two serious stab wounds to his right side. There was significant damage to his right kidney, part of the liver as well as the large and small bowel. We've done everything we can, but he has suffered extreme blood loss."

My heart races as the surgeon rattles off the extent of Henley's injuries, my anxiety escalating with every word.

"We were able to stop the bleeding, but he isn't out of the woods yet. The next twenty-four hours are crucial, and we'll know more after that."

"Can I see him?" I plead.

Dr. Harris turns to Victor as though asking for permission. Victor gives a quick nod.

"Okay, I'll allow it," the surgeon agrees. "But be aware, he isn't conscious, and it will be sometime before he wakes up."

"Okay," I nod, chewing nervously on my bottom lip.

He leads me down the corridor to the room that Henley occupies. I pause at the door, mentally preparing myself for what I might be about to witness. I take a deep breath as I round the door frame and step into the room.

My knees go out from under me when I see his motionless form draped across the hospital bed, his head propped up on the pillow. There's an oxygen mask strapped over his mouth and nose, his forehead and jawline adorned with purple blue bruising.

I move closer to the bed, my feet dragging with every step. I reach for his hand. There are scratches on his arms, some deeper than others, and a bandage over one that must have been more serious than the rest. He looks utterly helpless lying here, his skin still grey, his lips pale.

I collapse into the chair beside his bed and a loud sob bursts from me. Up until now I've been in too much shock to cry actual tears. But now they flow so freely I begin to wonder if they'll ever stop.

"Alex," I say, my voice a mere whisper. "What happened?" I sniffle and wipe at the tears streaming down my face, squeezing his hand in mine. Fragments of our last conversation flicker through my mind. "You said you weren't going anywhere. You're not meant to leave me again."

I wait for some kind of sign that he hears me. A twitching of his hand, a change in his breathing.

But it doesn't come.

I sit in silence for a few minutes longer, watching and waiting. When Officer Greenberg taps on the door, I jump in fright.

"Sorry to disturb you, Kristen." His expression is genuine, sympathetic. "I was wondering if I could ask you some questions."

"Okay," I say. I stand, turning to take one last look at Henley before meeting the officer on the other side of the door.

"How are you doing?" he asks me.

"I'm surviving," I tell him. I don't know any other way to describe how I'm feeling at this point.

"I'm sorry you're going through this, Kristen."

Officer Greenberg knows me on a first name basis after helping me on the night of the fire at Liv's house last year. I'd hoped we wouldn't need to meet again under such dire circumstances.

"We've got a list of suspects we think may have been involved." He pulls out a piece of paper and unfolds it. "Does the name Ethan Davis mean anything to you?"

"Yes. He was the guy that started the fight with Henley. He was hurt in the accident."

"Yes, that's correct," he confirms. "We believe that Ethan was out for revenge on Alex. He's apparently less than impressed that his prison sentence was cut short."

"So, this was all an act of vengeance?" I ask.

I've never met Ethan Davis, but I already hate him with every fibre of my being.

"There may be more to it than that," Officer Greenberg replies. "We were hoping you might be able to shed some more light on the situation."

"I'm sorry. Alex has been pretty tight lipped since he came back to town. He only recently told me about what he went through. I don't know anything about Ethan Davis that you wouldn't already know."

"That's okay. There is something else though." Officer Greenberg's expression softens, and I sense he's about to unveil more bad news. I pray that I'm wrong. I don't know how much more I can take today. "I spoke with your friends in the waiting room. They've brought to my attention that you've recently developed a close relationship with Mackenzie Riley."

Oh God.

Mackenzie.

The girl Henley rescued from an abusive relationship with Ethan Davis.

Mackenzie, who hasn't been answering her phone all morning.

"Yes." My heart begins to race as I explain to the officer how I've come to know Mackenzie. "I recently found out that she's my half-sister. Henley brought her to Cliff Haven. He helped her escape from Ethan." As I'm saying the words, the puzzle pieces click into place. I realise the serious error I've made in not reporting her absence. "Ethan wants revenge on Henley because he took Mackenzie away from him."

Officer Greenberg nods. "That's one of our theories. We don't think he's working alone. Dylan told us he saw three suspicious looking men on the street before he found Alex inside."

He looks at me, his expression grim. I get the feeling he has more to say, but I need to find Mackenzie.

"I need to call her again." I reach into my back pocket for my phone and scroll through my contacts, panic rising in my chest.

"Kristen." Officer Greenberg places a gentle hand on mine and then he confirms my worst fears. "We can't find Mackenzie. We think she's missing."

"Oh my god," I gasp. "She wasn't home when I woke up this morning. I thought she went out for a jog. I was out looking for her when I saw the ambulance outside the tavern. What if something has happened to her? What if he's hurt her?"

"We've got our team on it," he assures me. "We'll let you know if we find out anything at all."

He gives me an affectionate pat on the shoulder before continuing his way down the corridor.

I fall back against the wall, allowing it to take my weight. I can't lose the love of my life and my sister in one day.

I just can't.

I slide down the wall, crumpling into a ball on the floor. I hug my knees tight to my chest and sob. I don't know how long I sit there, letting the walls cave in on me, before a familiar voice momentarily brings me out of my despair.

"Kristen," I hear her say.

I lift my gaze to meet hers. "Mum."

Chapter 48

KRISTEN

It's been twelve hours since Henley came out of surgery and there hasn't been any change. A quick glance at the clock on the wall of his hospital room tells me it's just after 3am.

Liv and EJ had left at about eleven, after making me swear that I would call them if I needed anything or if Henley woke up. Mum stayed for a few hours. Then after begging me to go home and rest, she'd left shortly after, promising to bring me a fresh change of clothes in the morning.

I'd told her everything. About Henley being in prison. About how I didn't know how I would ever live without him. About how my father had shown up on my doorstep on his way to rehab.

And about Mackenzie.

As I'd suspected, Mum didn't know about Mackenzie's existence, although she was aware that my father had been unfaithful in the years prior to their relationship's demise. I'm not sure it came as much of a shock to her as it had to me.

Other than to say goodbye to the three of them, I haven't left this room and if any of the hospital staff have any intention of me leaving, they haven't made it known. There's absolutely no way in hell I'm walking out of this place.

Not without him.

I'm not only anxious about Henley's condition, but about Mackenzie's whereabouts. I still haven't heard from Officer Greenberg and the wait is killing me. I reach for Henley's hand and trace the trails of ink on his forearm.

"Come on, Alex." My whisper is barely audible over the beeping of the machines that monitor his steady but slow heartrate. "Come back to me."

I close my eyes fleetingly. I'm exhausted but I won't allow myself to sleep. I wrap my hand tighter around his.

"I know that you've always felt like I've never really needed you. That I'm this tough, independent strong woman. I hate to break it to you, Alex. But I need you just as much as you need me. We're in this life together. It's you and me."

More tears fall from my eyes. I've cried so much today I have to wonder how they're still falling at all. "I don't know what I'm gonna do if you don't wake up. Please wake up." I clutch his hand in mine. "I love you."

It's so small I think I must have imagined it. But I'm certain Henley just squeezed my hand. I wait for another sign that he's heard me, but the minutes drag on and still there's nothing. I begin to lose hope.

Maybe I did imagine it.

At some point, the rhythmic bleeping of the machines must lull me to sleep in the chair at his bedside. I wake sometime later to the sound of Officer Greenberg's voice. "Kristen."

I squint, adjusting to the harshness of the hospital lighting. "Officer, is there any news?"

"Yeah," he says, a small smile on his face. "We found her."

I jump up from the chair, unsteady on my feet. "You did? Is she okay?"

"Why don't you come out here and ask her yourself?"

My eyes widen in surprise. "Are you serious?"

He nods. "We were able to track her phone to a truck stop about two hours from here. We've taken all the suspects into custody. They won't be bothering any of you again."

I breathe a sigh of relief as I exit the room and turn the corner. Mackenzie stands in the hospital hallway. She looks exhausted. Her eyes bear dark circles around them and her blonde, tousled waves are a mess. There's bruising on her right arm that matches the shape of a handprint, but she's alive. She has survived. I lunge at her, wrapping my arms around her neck as I feel her body shudder with relief beneath mine.

"Thank God," I breathe. "What happened? Are you okay?"

"I'll be fine." She nods. "I went for an early morning walk on the beach and then when I reached the esplanade, Ethan and two of his friends jumped me and threw me into their car. I heard them bragging about how they'd finally given Henley what he deserved." Her face crumples in sadness. "Please tell me he's going to make it."

My face falls, my voice quivering as I explain. "We don't know much right now. They say he may have lost too much blood. That it may have affected his brain."

"Oh god," she cries. "This can't be happening."

I clutch her to me, and she clings onto me tighter than she ever has. I hate how cruel the universe can be. The possibility that it could unite me with Mackenzie but take Henley away.

Officer Greenberg shifts in place beside us. "I'm really sorry to interrupt but I just need to ask you a couple more questions, Mackenzie."

"Okay,' she says as she pulls away, then to me she says, "I'll just be a minute."

I watch her walk down the hall and back out to the waiting room with Officer Greenberg, then I retreat back to Henley's room. I slump down in the chair and grasp his hand again.

I definitely feel it this time, a twitching of his fingers in mine. I'm certain of it. I look up in time to see his head shift slightly in my direction. His eyelids flutter fleetingly before partially opening, revealing crystal blue irises.

My breath hitches in my throat as I watch his Adam's apple bob as he swallows.

"It's you and me," he rasps. "Forever."

Chapter 49

HENLEY

I grab the remote and begin flicking through the channels. There's nothing but reruns on and I'm bored. I've been stuck in this bed for four days and they say I'll be here awhile longer. It's nicer than prison though, so I guess I can't complain.

When I first woke up from the coma my pain was an eleven out of ten. At times it was so excruciating it made it hard to breathe. It's become tolerable these last couple of days though. Endone helps.

And Kristen.

She's been by my side since I arrived here, even sleeping in the chair next to my bed. But I finally convinced her to go home and take a shower and have a proper rest. She had refused to leave me alone, waiting until my dad had come to visit to make her exit.

I love her more than anything in this world.

I hate that I've put her through hell, and I'll never be able to take any of it back.

My legs are restless. I know I'm not supposed to be moving around without a nurse present but I'm feeling so agitated. I'm already propped up pretty high with pillows so sitting up isn't too much of a struggle, but when I swing my legs over the side of the bed there's a slight tearing in my abdomen. I wince with the pain as I attempt to reach for the pair of crutches leaning on the chair across from me.

"Should you really be going walk about on your own, Mr. Independent?"

That voice is one I know well, but one I haven't heard for a really long time.

"Katie," I say, surprised.

"Hey little brother," she says, her voice low. She wanders over to the chair, picks up the crutches and hands them to me. "You wanna go out to the courtyard?"

"Fuck yeah," I say. "My entire body is going numb from being in this bed." Probably a side effect from the Endone too, if I'm being honest.

A smile plays out on her lips, but it's marred with sadness. "What do you need me to do?"

"Just come over here and be ready to catch me if I fall," I say, knowing that there's not a chance in hell her tiny frame could bear my weight.

She shakes her head and, for a second, I think she's laughing at my lame joke. But she isn't. She's sobbing.

"Alex," she cries, her sandy blonde hair hanging in waves around her face.

"Hey," I say, falling back onto the bed. "It's okay."

"It's not," she argues. "I'm a horrible person. I disowned my own twin brother and he nearly died."

"Well, I can't argue with you there," I say, but the joke falls flat.

"Come on, Alex. Be serious," she whines. "How can you joke at a time like this?"

I feel my mouth lifting upward in a grin. Because it feels like forever since I *have* been able to joke like this.

"Because I'm alive," I answer simply.

"I'm so sorry," she cries. "Kristen explained everything. I never should have said those things to you. I never should have put my work ahead of you."

My smile fades remembering the phone call I'd had with Katie. When she'd made me feel as though I'd brought shame upon our family. Now that she's here, none of it seems relevant anymore.

"And I'm sorry," she continues. "If I've ever made you feel like you were less than enough. You're the best brother a girl could ask for."

"I forgive you."

"Just like that?" she asks.

"Yeah," I say. "Just like that.

Because I do forgive her. I forgive her with my whole heart.

"If there's one thing the last six months has taught me it's that life's too short to hold grudges," I say. "Even grudges against annoying big sisters."

Her mouth turns upward in a grin as she swipes at her wet cheeks. "You called me your big sister."

"Twenty-five minutes," I say holding up my forefinger.

She rolls her eyes and wraps her arms around my neck, and I let her even though the force of her hug sends pain rippling through my side.

"I love you, little brother," she whispers.

"I love you too. Now are you gonna help me break out of this place or what?"

"Yes," she says, pulling away from me. "To the courtyard."

"Just watch out for that nurse with the black hair at the reception desk. She'll kill me if she catches us," I tell her.

Katie giggles as she helps me stand and then she supports me in making my getaway to the courtyard.

We're halfway down the corridor when a throat clears distinctly behind us. We both freeze on the spot.

"Mr. Henley," says a petite but stern voice. "Just where do you think you're going?"

Katie throws a glance back over her shoulder.

"Is it her?" I ask. "Black hair?"

"Mmhmm," Katie confirms.

"Red lipstick?"

"Yep."

"Kinda hot?" I ask.

"That's her."

The nurse clears her throat again as she steps in front of us. "You know you aren't meant to leave your room without assistance, Mr. Henley. Your girlfriend is going to have me fired."

"Ahh, so Kristen is in on this?"

"Yes," she replies. "That feisty little thing has us watching you like a hawk. Told us you'd try to escape the second you were alone in that room."

"She knows you well," Katie muses.

"Yeah." I raise my eyebrows and tilt my head to the side. "I guess she does."

"We were just going to go to the courtyard for some air," Katie explains. "And technically he does have assistance. He has me."

"Hmm," the nurse grunts, then she nods in the direction of the courtyard. "Go quickly. Before she comes back and kicks my ass."

She returns to the nurses' station as we continue down the hallway and out of the large sliding doors that lead to the quad. It isn't much to look at, unless you love architecture, I guess. There's nothing but buildings for miles. Give me sandy beaches and waves any day of the week.

But I'm getting fresh air and I'm not confined to four walls, so I'll take this as a win.

"How are you feeling about all of this?" Katie asks me.

I blow out a long breath. "I don't even really know where to begin to answer that."

"Try."

"Since I got out of prison, I've been having these flashbacks. Of the accident. Of being attacked in prison. I see the scenes playing out so vividly in my head, it's like I'm right back there reliving it all over again. I can even hear the screams, the car tyres spinning out on the road." I hear Katie stifle a sob. "Sorry."

"Don't be," she says, her voice firm. "You have nothing to be sorry about, Alex."

"Yeah," I mutter. "I'm starting to see that. Kristen thinks I have PTSD. She wants me to see a therapist. I think I will."

"That could be good for you," she says. "How are things at the tavern?" she asks.

"Okay, I guess. I mean, I don't think Dylan thought much of me at first, but he came to visit me yesterday and we had a good talk. Besides, I can't blame him for being pissed at me. I've been doing a pretty shitty job."

A laugh burst from Katie, and it makes me laugh too. It's nice. Being able to laugh with her again. It almost feels like it did when we were young.

"You gonna keep living in the loft?"

"Well, I'm going to be staying with Kristen for a while when I get out of hospital. Her apartment has an elevator, and I don't think I can climb stairs just yet."

"Fair enough," Katie says.

"But I have been doing some thinking about the future these past few days."

"Uh huh," she replies. "You mean while you've been hopped up on oxy?"

"Shut up." I laugh, reaching out to slap her playfully on the knee. "I think I want to open up my own business. As a handyman. I mean, I'll need to finish up my qualifications and obviously I need to be able to cover start-up costs, so it isn't going to happen straight away. But it's something I'm ready to work towards."

Katie's eyes search mine and I can't decipher what she's thinking from her expression.

"You think I'm crazy, right?" I say, shaking my head. "It's a dumb idea. Too many painkillers obviously and ..."

"I think it's an amazing idea," she interrupts, her tone serious. "I mean it. I think you'd be great."

"Yeah?"

"Yeah," she smiles.

We both turn as the courtyard doors open and Kristen and Mackenzie walk through them.

"Uh oh," Katie says. "You're busted."

"You are in so much trouble!" Kristen points an accusing finger in my direction. When she reaches me, she gently ruffles my hair and kisses me on the forehead before taking a seat in the chair next to me. "Hey, Katie."

"I know. I know," I say, waving off her concern. "Katie, this is Kristen's sister, Mackenzie."

"Hey," Katie says. "Nice to meet you."

Mackenzie offers a small wave. "You too. How's it going?"

"Better now," Katie says, giving me a knowing look.

"Me too," I wink. "Got my three favourite women right here in the same space. What more could a guy need?"

"Coffee?" Mackenzie asks.

"Sure," I answer. "As long as you aren't making it."

Kristen laughs as Mackenzie scowls at me. "Come on Mackenzie. Let's go get some coffees."

"Before you do," I start, holding up a hand. "Do you think you could get the nurse for me. My painkillers are starting to wear off and if I'm not back in that bed in ten minutes, you're gonna have to scrape me off the floor."

"God, you're dramatic," Mackenzie teases and the three of them giggle.

"We'll get the nurse." Kristen laughs, but there's a hint of concern in her tone.

Katie and I watch as the two sisters walk through the doors to the nurse's station. I wonder for the millionth time how I got so blessed.

"You really love her, don't you? Katie asks.

"More than anything," I say. "I'm the luckiest guy in the world to have that woman by my side."

Katie smiles. "Something tells me she's pretty lucky to have you too."

Epilogue

KRISTEN

Liv looks gorgeous in a simplistic silk gown, her chocolate brown hair glossy under the glimmer of soft light. EJ, equally as gorgeous in a striking, grey tux twirls her around on the dance floor. She throws her head back and laughs as he whispers something in her ear. Something only for her.

It's hard to believe that our two best friends are finally married. Their wedding ceremony had been a simple but beautiful one down on the sand behind the tavern, with the waves crashing in the distance. And now that most of the reception formalities have been completed, everyone is enjoying all that the rest the night has to offer.

Victor Petersen is beaming with joy, the picture of a proud father. Maggie and Steve look relaxed and happy, having not long ago returned from their trip around the country. Carla looks as though she's working towards having an even bigger hangover tomorrow than the one she had after the engagement party. Even Mackenzie and Dylan seem to have hit it off over by the fire pit down on the beach. Or maybe they're arguing. It's hard to tell from here.

I feel warm, strong arms curl around my waist as Henley leans into me, his breath on my cheek. "They seem happy," he says, nodding to where Liv and EJ dance under the canopy of fairy lights.

"They do," I agree. "And so am I."

I spin around so I can lace my arms around his neck. His eyes glisten, sapphire under the moonlight. "Me too," he says.

And I believe him.

Henley has been seeing a therapist since leaving the hospital three months ago and the progress he's made with overcoming his demons is evident. He still has bad days. And maybe he always will. Sometimes his posture stiffens, his eyes glaze over and I know he's gone to his own personal hell. But most days are good days, his eyes shining a little brighter than they had the day before.

And on those bad days, when his light is suppressed by the shadows, he has me. I'll be there to reach in and pull him out of the darkness.

"Hello, you two!" Maggie's voice comes from beside us.

"Maggie!" I squeal. "How was your trip? You have to tell me all about it."

"It was wonderful," she says. "We had so many fantastic experiences along the way."

Steve wanders up behind her. "Maggie got to feed the dolphins up at Finnigan's Bay. Highlight of the trip."

"Oh wow!" I exclaim. "I've always wanted to do that."

"Well," Steve begins. "I'm sure Henley would love to take you there one day."

I smile up at Henley and then snake my arms around him. "I'm just happy to have him back."

"So are we," Maggie says, giving Henley a pat on the arm.

"I can't thank you enough for what you've done with the place," Steve says.

We all look back into the tavern from our position on the lawn, marvelling at the hand-built furniture, the stunning bay windows and the refurbished French doors. Henley was able to create a modern space, while still managing to keep the tavern's original features. And he was right. It has served as the perfect wedding venue.

"It was the least I could do after what you've both done for me." Henley outstretches his arms and takes them both in a group hug. "I really appreciate you guys."

"We've always believed in you, Alex," Maggies says, a tear forming in the corner of her eye.

"Thank you," Henley replies. "And I guess while I've got you here, I should probably tell you the news." He takes a deep breath and I squeeze his hand, urging him to continue. "I'm going to start my own handyman business. Building repairs and renovations, maybe even custom-built furniture."

"That's great news!" Steve exclaims.

"Obviously, I'll keep working at the tavern as long as you need me," Henley interjects. "There's still a lot for me to finalise before I can make it happen."

"Well, if you need any help with start-up costs, you just let me know." Steve reaches for Henley's hand, giving it a solid shake.

"Steve, I couldn't possibly accept anything else from you. You guys have already done so much."

"Nonsense. Call it a repayment for the work you've put into this place," Maggie offers.

"You guys are amazing," Henley says, his face splitting with a wide grin.

I love seeing him so happy, so excited about his future.

"Guys, quick!" Liv's voice rings out from the dancefloor. "I'm about to do the bridal bouquet toss!"

"I guess that's my cue," I say. I give Henley a peck on the cheek and turn to the bonfire on the beach. "Mackenzie! Let's go!"

I watch as Mackenzie bickers about something with Dylan, a scowl overtaking her features, before storming off in my direction.

"Are you okay?" I ask her when she reaches the dance floor.

"Yeah. Fine," she grumbles.

"What was all that about then?"

She doesn't have time to answer my question though. Because Liv's bridal bouquet is suddenly flying through the air, and she's directly in the line of fire. She splutters as it hits her head-on in the face, clutching at its petals with all the grace of a cat in a fishing net.

"What the hell!" she cries out, dropping the bunch of flowers faster than a hot potato. "Eww! I don't want it!"

I can't help but crack up, glancing over my shoulder at Henley who is now doubled over in a fit of laughter. I see Dylan snicker behind him. I'm not sure I want to know why.

But then something else grabs my attention. Katie is here, and she's speaking inconspicuously in Alex's ear. I watch as she drops something discreetly into the palm of his hand and then strolls back up to the street.

I don't have time to wonder though, because the next minute EJ is pulling me up onto the dance floor. "Come dance with me, Kristen!"

I laugh as he begins to perform some extremely eccentric moves on the dance floor and then Liv and I join in, imitating him until we've drawn a decent crowd. "I love you guys," I say, throwing my arms around the pair of them.

"We love you too," Liv says. "Which is why you need to trust us with what's about to happen."

"Huh." My eyes narrow in confusion. "What do you mean? What's about to happen?"

Liv giggles as EJ pulls a silky ribbon of material from his back pocket. It takes me a minute to recognise it. It's the tie he'd been wearing for the wedding ceremony. He stretches it out in his hands and loops it around my neck.

"Henley has a surprise for you," he says.

"He does?"

"He does," Liv confirms. "And because it's a surprise, you need to wear a blindfold."

"Um… kinky?"

Liv laughs. "No. Well, maybe. I don't know."

Henley is now walking over to us, a devilish smirk on his perfect face.

"Are we leaving now?" I ask.

"Yes," Liv replies. "And we will see you both for brunch at the Haven tomorrow morning. Thank you for all your help with the wedding preparations. Now go and have fun."

Liv gives me a tight hug and then EJ uses his tie to blindfold me. Henley moves his hands over my waist and leads me to his truck. I hear him open the door and then I squeal as he lifts me up and places me in the passenger seat.

"What are we doing? This is insane!"

"Do you trust me?" I hear his voice to my right.

"Always."

Then he slips the key in the ignition and the engine roars to life. We're only in the car for a few minutes before I feel it come to a complete stop.

He exits the car, then the passenger door is opening and he's lifting me out of it again. I gasp as my feet find the ground, tiny blades of grass pricking at my feet between the straps of my sandals. Henley guides me further forward for a few steps, then the ground becomes harder, pebbles crushing underneath my heels. Another ten steps or so and then he stills me in place.

"Are you ready?" he asks.

"Yes."

His fingers brush my neck as he loosens the blindfold. I blink, my eyes needing a chance to adjust to the night.

"Oh my God," I say in awe, my hands coming up to cup my mouth. "Is this..."

"Yep."

I stare in wonder at the small riverside cottage we've shared so many memories in. The back porch roof is still adorned with the same festoon lights, but the decking is larger, wider, a wicker loveseat now in place where our old wooden chairs once were.

"Come on." Henley holds out his hand to me and I allow him to lead me up the stairs.

"These stairs," I say. "They're different."

"Yeah," he replies. "Well, the old ones were falling apart."

"I don't understand. Did you build all of this yourself?"

He doesn't answer, just grins as he unlocks the back door and gestures for me to lead the way inside. I enter to find that the place is fully furnished too. Some of it new, some of it pieces that Henley must have brought back over from the loft.

"This is amazing. You got your house back? How?"

"I had a lot of help from Katie. She used her connections at the real estate," he explains. "When she found out it was up for rent again, she put in a good word for me to get it back. I had some help from our friends getting the furniture over here. Katie stocked the fridge with food today."

I smile, remembering how Katie pressed something into his hand tonight. It must have been the key.

"Wow," I breathe.

"You haven't even heard the best part."

"I haven't?"

"Nope," he answers. "The landlord is going to be putting it on the market next year. I told him I'm interested in buying it. Hence, the reason he allowed me to build a new back porch. I've been working on it for the past couple of weeks."

"Oh my god! Are you kidding?" I shriek. "Henley, you're going to buy a house!"

His eyes wander over my face, an edge of calm in them. "We're going to buy a house," he says. "Move in with me."

I can't help the smile that must light up my whole face. I crush my lips to his in answer and he scoops me up, carrying me down the hallway and into the bedroom.

Our bedroom.

When I awake the next morning from the most blissful sleep I think I've ever had, there's a note on his pillow in place where his head should be.

K,

Meet me on the back porch. I'm making breakfast.
Love you forever. I can't not.

Alex

I pluck the note from the pillow, a smile curling up the edges of my lips. Then I climb out of bed and wander down the hallway, the old floorboards creaking beneath my feet.

The air is balmy as I step through the back door and out onto the porch, the creek a vibrant blue to match the summer sky above.

Henley stands over a small weber barbeque, flipping bacon and eggs. He turns at the sound of my feet on the deck.

"Good morning, gorgeous," he says as he moves toward me, cupping my face in his hands and placing his lips on mine.

"Hey," I say. "What's all this?"

"Well, I promised you breakfast a while ago and I never came through." He rakes a hand through his hair and then draws me into a hug. "Thought it was time I made it up to you."

"Be careful," I warn him. "I could get used to this."

"I hope you do," he says, his voice serious. "Now go sit. I'll get your coffee."

I beam up at him then find a comfortable position on the wicker lounge. I stare out at the creek pensively, thinking about all that's happened to lead us to where we are right now.

I know our struggles are far from over, that there will always be mountains to climb. But there's no one else in this world that I'd rather climb them with than Alex Henley.

A few moments later, he returns, placing a steaming mug of coffee in my hands. I thank him and watch as he plates up two bacon and egg rolls, before joining me on the loveseat.

You can be anywhere when your life begins. The back porch of a house on a creek, a coffee cup in one hand, the love of your life's palm in the other.

You can be hopeful that your darkest days are far behind you. Always thankful. In love with every minute of your life.

I'm grateful for every second I get to spend with this man.

I'm grateful for our fresh start.

"Alex," I say, turning around to meet his gaze, a wistful smile twisting my lips ever so slightly.

"Yeah," he replies, his eyes sparkling as they search my face intently.

"Marry me."

The End

Playlist

◄ ► ►|

Only Place I Call Home
EVERY AVENUE

Jaded
MILEY CYRUS

About You
THE 1975

My Mind and Me
SELENA GOMEZ

Fall Apart
EVERY AVENUE

Polaris
JIMMY EAT WORLD

I Guess I'm In Love
CLINTON KANE

Crash
YOU ME AT SIX

Never Say Never
THE FRAY

Last Night
MORGAN WALLEN

I Won't Lie
GO RADIO

You'd Never Know
BLU EYES

I Can't Not Love You
EVERY AVENUE

About the Author

Eve Blakely writes contemporary romance novels with an edge. She currently resides in a small town south of Sydney, Australia with her husband and two crazy kids.

She's an avid daydreamer and a self-confessed chocoholic who ditched her city-based career to enjoy a simpler life. When she isn't writing, she's probably trying to get through her never-ending TBR pile, painting or rewatching One Tree Hill for the millionth time.

@eveblakelywrites

@eveblakelywrites

www.eveblakely.com

BOOKS BY EVE BLAKELY

-The Cliff Haven Series-

The Other Version
Versions of Us

COMING SOON

Book #3 in the Cliff Haven series.
Stay tuned for Mackenzie and Dylan's story,
coming in 2024…

*Have you read book #1 in the
Cliff Haven series?*

Read on for a sneak peek of
The Other Version…

The Other Version

eve blakely

Chapter 1

OLIVIA

The uber comes to an abrupt halt on the corner of Maine and Geraldton in Milton's central business district, exactly two blocks from the Salt Factory. God, why is it that there are absolutely zero uber drivers that can (a) actually drive and (b) get you to the exact location you ask? Like their jobs are that hard.

"Where did you tell your dad we were going?" Katerina asks as she scoots sideways out of the car.

"Library," I reply as I follow her lead.

"And he believed you? Dressed like that?" she asks incredulously, gesturing to the low-cut romper that adorns my petite frame.

It's a piece that had been given to my mother by some up-and-coming designer during fashion week. People are always giving her things. It's ironic really, how many free things rich people are given.

"Please," I scoff. "He barely glanced in my direction when I told him I was going out. I could have told him we were going to work the street corner and he wouldn't have bat an eyelid."

Maybe I'm exaggerating, but most of the time my father's head is buried in his laptop and his phone glued to either ear. He always puts his job ahead of me, of my mum. Ahead of everything really.

"Is it me or did you down a cup of instant bitch before we left?" Katerina smirks. "I'm getting some seriously negative vibes from you right now. I mean, you know, more than usual."

"Shut up." I roll my eyes and give her a playful shove. She laughs, rocking backwards on her Manolos before regaining her balance. "I guess I'm still pissed about Sean."

Sean is my boyfriend, though lately it seems like we barely ever speak. Actually, it doesn't just seem that way. It's exactly that way. When I'd told him I wished we could spend more time together he'd brushed it off, explaining to me instead how important it is for him to be studying right now so he can get in to medicine next year at Milton University. I get it. It's our last year of high school. Investing time into our futures is important.

Maybe I'm envious of the fact that he knows what he actually wants to do with his life. Maybe I just want to have fun before I have to grow up and adult. Either way, I didn't pressure him. There's no way I'm going to be portrayed as one of those nagging girlfriends that no guy wants hanging off their arm.

"Forget Sean." Katerina throws her bony arm around my neck as we near the Salt Factory. She raises an eyebrow suggestively with a wicked grin. "Guys suck. Let's get wasted."

Katerina is many things. To her friends, she's kind, caring, protective and nurturing, but if you get on her wrong side she will bring the wrath of hell down upon you. She is earth, wind, fire, and ice. And she's my best friend in the world.

The Salt Factory is an exclusive club, frequented by only a handful of kids from Hampton Ridge College, the local private school in our town. The select few of us have three things in common. Fake ID, social status and, of course, money. It's amazing what you can get away with when you're loaded.

I shadow Katerina toward the door of the club. Her long, auburn waves stretch behind her like flames, her sequinned cami glistening under the neon sign as we bypass the hopeful wannabes waiting in the queue and attempt to slink behind the velvet rope.

An arm shoots out in front of us, forcing us backward, then a strong hand wraps its way around my upper arm.

"ID," the bouncer insists sternly as he folds his arms over his chest, his dark eyes piercing into ours.

He's tall, built from lean muscle, but he can't be more than a few years older than we are. He seems completely unfazed by Katerina's resting bitch face, nor does he react to the bitter scowl I aim back at him.

"You must be new here," I state, my voice icy. "First of all, you touch me again and you'll be dealing with my lawyer. Secondly, we're regulars here. We keep you in business. Therefore, we keep your pathetic little pay checks coming."

He raises both eyebrows and takes a step back, then condescendingly says, "Well, sorry princess, but it's my job to check ID."

Katerina's eyes roll dramatically but she pulls out her counterfeit ID regardless, handing it over with a perfectly manicured hand. The bouncer takes it and folds it over several times in his palm.

He gives a half laugh. "I think you girls should head home. It's past your bed time, isn't it?

"Excuse me?" I say, disbelievingly. "Where's the other guy? The one that's normally here? We'd like to see him."

"Why?" he responds. "You think he can't tell a fake ID when he sees one, princess?"

Ugh. I shudder at his overuse of that word.

"You have no idea who I am, do you?" I smile mockingly at him, my hands resting confidently on my hips.

"Should I?" he asks, combing a hand through his dark, unkempt hair.

"There he is!" Katerina screeches, as she spots the usual door man lingering just inside the club. Then, turning to me, she asks, "What was his name again? Seth? Stan?"

The new bouncer follows our gaze. "That's Mitch," he says, looking at us as with distaste. So, we didn't remember the guy's name. Big deal. "His name is Mitch."

"Yeah. We get it." I hiss, not even attempting to hide my annoyance.

Katerina calls to Mitch, thrashing her arms about in a desperate attempt to get his attention. This no-hoper has severely underestimated who he's dealing with here. There is absolutely no way in hell that we won't get our way tonight.

We always get our way.

Mitch, finally seeing us, meanders over. "Is there a problem here?" he asks.

"Actually, yeah," the other bouncer says, handing him Katerina's fake ID. He folds his arms across his chest again, a stupid grin plastered across his face.

Mitch takes the ID, and without even so much as a glimpse at it, hands it back to Katerina. "It's all good."

Lifting the rope, he allows us inside and as we pass them I hear him say, "That's Victor Petersen's daughter."

I'm not sure if I heard the new guy correctly over the loud music, but it sounded as though he said, "Who?" I guess he isn't just new to the club. He must be new around here. Period.

We sashay through the crowd, absorbing the stares of pretty much everyone around us. Young hotshot business men trying to mark their place in the world and old, gross corporate washouts, well passed their expiry date. I ignore them, but Katerina enjoys it as usual.

I spot the bar manager, a tray of cocktails floating gracefully on his outstretched arm. "Enzo! Babe!" I call out over the reverberating bass beat.

Enzo immediately dumps the tray of drinks on the bar and ambles in our direction. "Olivia Petersen and Katerina Van Sant! To what do I owe the pleasure?" he greets us in his usual flamboyant manner, embracing us both with air kisses. "What can I get you?"

"Well, a private booth would be nice." I flash him my most persuasive smile, clasping my hands together as though in prayer. "Pretty please!"

"Oh, I'm all booked out tonight, babes." Enzo replies, waving his hand theatrically.

"Oh, no!" I pout. "I just really wish we had somewhere we could sit without these perverts staring at us all night."

"Maybe we should find somewhere else to go instead," Katerina adds.

We definitely have no intentions of doing so, but Katerina knew the thought of us leaving the club would make Enzo sweat.

"Look, we're totally booked, but I'll see what I can do." Enzo pulls an iPhone from his shirt pocket and saunters away, probably to somewhere quieter. Within minutes, he's back and leading us to a booth of our own.

We spend the next hour sipping back cosmopolitans from the white suede lounge in our private booth, gossiping about this week's scandalous events.

Katerina tells me that Jessica Lawrence and Matt Holden had the most epically embarrassing break-up in first period on Thursday and were back together by Friday lunch. I tell her about how Sheree Ackers had finally announced she was into chicks, much to the dismay of Brent Waterhouse who has been crushing on her since the third grade. And rumour has it that Brian Attfield's dad showed up in the school office demanding that his son's grades be changed or else he would stop his rather large donations coming. There was never a dull moment at Hampton Ridge College.

"Brian Attfield is so hot though," Katerina says as she plucks an olive from the complimentary canape platter and pops it between her teeth. "Cheater or not. Whatever that guy got up to this past summer has earned him some serious biceps!"

I laugh. It's obvious by her hooded eyelids that she's getting very tipsy, but then again, so am I. "You think so? I hadn't really noticed."

"Of course, you didn't! You've got total tunnel vision for Sean."

"Ugh! No. No talking about Sean. I was almost in a good mood," I reply.

"What do you mean? You love Sean, don't you?" she asks. A waiter places a jug of water and two glasses between us. A not-so-subtle hint if I've ever seen one.

"Yeah. I do." I answer.

I do, don't I? Sean and I have been together for over a year and I love spending time with him. It's just that lately he only wants to spend time with me when it's good for him.

"You guys are cute together. But I still think you should have made out with Jesse Bradman when you had the chance." Katerina is referring to the hot pool guy her mum employed over the summer, one half of the Bradman twins, who was apparently totally into me. His brother Taylor had been all over Katerina.

"Oh my god, girl! You must be totally trashed right now! You know I would never cheat on Sean."

I've done a ton of crappy things in my life, I'll admit it. I ridiculed Jeannie Purcell in the eighth grade when she finally got her period. I fat-shamed James Vardan when he tried out for the football team in tenth grade because he could barely run a quarter of the field without stopping. I can lie my way into any place and there are no lengths I won't go to when I want something. The truth is I've done a bunch of shit things and I'll probably continue to. I mean, who doesn't? But if there's one thing I definitely am not, it's a cheater.

"I'll be back in a sec. I have to go to the bathroom." I stand, smoothing out my romper as I make my way to the ladies' room, leaving Katerina chewing on her straw and bobbing her head along to the beat in an out of time fashion.

I enter the immaculately decked out restroom and perch on the edge of a crimson suede ottoman situated in the spacious sitting area off to the side. I reach down to adjust the strap of my shoe that's been cutting my circulation for most of the night. If I'm being honest, these shoes have had my feet in a world of pain since the moment I put them on, but I'm a sucker for fashion and they're Jimmy Choo's. Enough said.

The walls of the restroom drown out the club's music, giving way to the audible moans that echo from the cubicle behind me. There's a breathy sigh followed by a low, deep grunt, combined with the repetitive rattling of the cubicle door. Someone is getting lucky in here tonight.

Katerina will be mad she missed this. I can imagine her crouching at the door of the cubicle waiting to snap a pic of the culprits with her phone, or pulling some kind of cruel but hilarious prank. With the click of the lock, a man emerges momentarily, only to be dragged back in by his partner in crime for one last embrace. A woman laughs softly as he pulls away from the door. I recognise him. He's the bartender that served us our cosmos earlier.

I smile to myself. Good for her, whoever she is. The bartender is hot.

The woman says something undecipherable, to which he replies in a whisper. "Okay. I gotta get back to work. I'll see you soon."

Ignoring me, he beelines for the exit.

I rise unsteadily to my feet. The cocktails have definitely blurred the edges and I form a silent prayer that the drive home in the uber will sober me up. I let the wall take my weight until the head spin subsides.

The woman appears from the cubicle. Her cheeks are flushed, her eye makeup slightly smudged as she stumbles on a pair of too-high red heels.

I observe her, unnoticed, from the corner of the room, as though in a dream. Her air of confidence captivates me, demands my attention. I'm under her spell, both struck by the familiarity of her reflection in the mirror and baffled by my own sense of naivety.

I watch as she reapplies her lipstick, swipes at her uncouth mascara and tousles her messy blonde curls.

Curls that are identical to mine.

My lungs are empty of air. My feet are stuck, frozen in their place on the marble tiles below. I blink, desperate to dissolve this vision before me, but she remains, unable to be unseen. My heart battles with my sceptic mind, for although this woman seems completely foreign to me, she is no stranger.

A crack rips through my chest.

A shrill sound echoes off the granite walls. My iPhone. A text from Katerina.

Did you get lost in there? LOL! I'm ordering another round.

As I inhale sharply, I realise I've been holding my breath. The woman looks up, her wide hazel eyes meeting mine in the reflection.

"Olivia," she gasps, her voice barely a whisper.

"Mum."

Chapter 2

LIV

I walk the esplanade aimlessly, as I've done every other day this week. Cliff Haven is quiet today, even more so than usual. I slouch down lethargically onto the bench seat at the end of the pier, welcoming the warmth of the late afternoon sun on my face. A gentle breeze sweeps orange leaves from the ground, whisking them in lazy circles, entwining a small piece of crumpled paper in their midst.

Curiously, I lean forward and retrieve the wrinkled note. Smoothing out the creases from the middle to the edges, I hold it closer to read the fine print. It's a job advertisement for a local café, The Haven. I recognise the name and know exactly where it is too, just a few blocks from where I now sit, back up on the esplanade.

The community noticeboard stands a few feet away, so I stroll over to it, pull a tack out of the cork, and stab it precisely through the centre of the top of the small page.

There. I was saving the environment, and now some lucky person would get a job. My good deed for the day. I wonder how many honourable deeds it would take to erase all the bad I've done.

I stare at the words on the advertisement. "Seeking wait staff for busy seaside café. Must have a positive attitude and a friendly demeanour. No experience necessary."

I don't have experience. Positive and friendly? I'd have to work on that, but of all the words on that flyer, one of them stands out.

Busy.

It would be nice to be busy. If there's one thing I need most right now, it's a distraction. Without another thought, I rip the paper from the notice board, tearing the top of it in the process and march back up the esplanade to the Haven Café.

A petite woman with a blonde pixie cut stands behind the kiosk, counting money from the till. Her head snaps up when she hears the little bell ding above the door as I enter. "Sorry, we're about to close."

For a second, I hesitate, unable to form words. I seem to have lost my vigour on the way up the hill. "I know. Are…are you the manager?" I look back down at the flyer, searching for the contact name. "Carla?"

"Yeah," she answers, matter-of-factly.

"I'd like to apply for the waitressing position." My voice is smaller than I intend it to be.

"Oh, I see." She closes the till, leaving her position behind the counter and gestures for me to sit down at a table with her. "Do you have a resume I can see?"

I feel more comfortable standing, but out of respect, I take the seat across from her. The metal legs scrape unpleasantly along the terracotta tiled floor.

"Uh, no. I actually only just saw the ad. I can bring you one though." I mentally scramble for things I could write on a resume that doesn't exist yet.

"That's okay," she replies with a smile. She has a sing-song voice and certainly embodies the friendly demeanour stated on the ad. "What's your name?"

"Liv," I reply automatically, folding my hands nervously in my lap.

"Liv," she repeats. "That's pretty. Is it short for…?"

"No," I cut her off, a little too abruptly. "No, it's just Liv. Liv Peters."

She seems stunned by my rudeness and I immediately feel guilty for snapping. I didn't mean to.

"Sorry," I mumble, tucking a stray, espresso brown tendril behind my ear.

"Well, Liv. Why don't you tell me a little bit about yourself?" She folds her toned tanned arms across her chest, which only heightens my anxiety.

Fantastic. If she's waiting to hear about my greatest achievements, she's about to be sorely disappointed. I pick at my fingernails nervously under the table, wondering where I should begin. What do I tell her? That I killed my social status so now I have no friends? That I flunked high school and can't get into university?

Or I could lead with my favourite one. That I, single-handedly, destroyed my own mother.

"Well," I begin. "I finished high school last year."

"Okay. So, you went to Cliff Haven High?"

"Uh, yeah." Great. Add 'liar' to that list of qualities.

"And do you go to university now? Are you looking to work part time?"

"No. I'm not a student. I can be available to work whenever you need me."

Busy. That's what I want to be.

She studies my face as I speak. I sense some austerity under all of that friendly, though I guess that's probably appropriate criterion for a café manager. I'm afraid she can see right through me, see all the damage.

"Okay. Well, we work on a rostered system here, so it's generally just part time, but there are extra hours every now and then. We've been getting a little busier lately, which is why I've decided to hire an extra person."

"Okay," I reply, not sure what else to say.

She eyes the Chanel handbag resting in my lap. God, what was I even thinking coming down here? I wonder briefly how many other twenty-year-olds have walked into her café asking for a job sporting a bag that costs more than a waitress's monthly salary. I stand, ready to get the hell out of here, but just as I think she's about to dismiss me, she does the complete opposite. "The café opens at 8am tomorrow, so I'll see you at half past seven to set up."

"Really? You're hiring me?"

"If you still want the job, yes."

It will never cease to amaze me how quickly life can change. One action, whether it's your own doing, or left up to fate, can set you on a whole new path.

"Thank you," I stammer. "I won't let you down." And strangely enough, I half believe myself.

The drive back home to Hampton Ridge takes about forty-five minutes, thanks to the frequent windy bends and low speed limits on the way up the cliff, but I quite enjoy it. For me, driving alone is an opportunity to increase the volume of my rock music of choice and zone out for a while. It's my favourite way to escape reality. I try to tell myself that I don't mind spending so much time alone.

In my experience, people are overrated anyway.

Once I reach the top of the ridge, the sun has almost set and the bright city lights of Milton are becoming visible below. Milton lies to the right. Cliff Haven, although I can't see it in the dimming light, way further down on the left. Milton Hospital is lit like a beacon and I think of my dad, who would be down there somewhere, performing surgery or holding meetings, or whatever else he does that keeps him away from home for hours on end.

I drive down the main boulevard. The deciduous trees that line the streets sway in the wind, their ochre leaves contrasting with the purple, orange glow of the sunset.

There's no denying that Hampton Ridge is aesthetically a gorgeous place to live. It's a sanctuary between the city and the sea, full of beautifully landscaped gardens and spacious parks.

Too bad the people here suck.

Mayfield Boulevard runs through the centre of Hampton Ridge, a street lined with picturesque mansions. They're the kind of houses you find in dream home magazines, complete with manicured lawns and enormous swimming pools.

At the end of the boulevard, my family home rests on the back of the highest cliff. I use the term 'family home' loosely. In actual fact, my family home is a seven-bedroom, five-bathroom Victorian style mansion, with a grand upstairs balcony held up by stone columns, and a tennis court that I'm pretty sure has never been used. 'Family' is now just me and my father.

Pulling into the long cobblestone driveway, the sheer grandeur of this place stirs a loneliness within me. The external lighting, designed to create a soft hospitable glow, somehow makes me feel anything but welcome.

Fumbling with my keychain, I locate the button on my garage remote and raise the wide panelled door of the six-car garage, which is way too big considering we only own two cars. My dad had always planned to buy a project car, but he would have no idea what to do with one and no time to learn.

I round the end of the hall, entering the kitchen, lit only by the crystal pendant lights above the stone benchtop. A figure sits perched upon a bar stool.

"Tessa! Oh my god, you scared me!" I shout as I clutch at my chest.

Tessa usually leaves at six and it's now almost six thirty. I wasn't expecting her, although I'm grateful for her presence. There's something really depressing about coming home to an exceptionally large, empty house.

"Tessa, what are you still doing here? It's late." I place my handbag and keys down on the bench.

"*I* scared *you*!" she exclaims. "Liv, I've been so worried! You scared the hell out of me. Where have you been?"

As I near closer, the concern on her face becomes apparent. Guilt wraps me with its iron fist at the thought that I've made her worry. It was never my intention. Tessa is the kindest person I've ever known, and God knows, she's had her fair share in putting up with my shit over the years. In the past, our relationship could have been described as tumultuous at best, but now I consider her the one true constant in my life.

"Why? Did something happen?" A sense of panic rises in my chest, my eyes fixating on the soft frown creases that appear on her forehead when it's wrinkled with worry.

A lump forms in my throat as I remember the last time she'd worn that expression. It had been the night she told me my mother was gone.

"No. Nothing has happened." She shakes her head and with it the concern evaporates. "You didn't answer your phone when I called! I tried four times already! I didn't know where you were!"

I let out a long breath of relief. It was easy for me to forget that I had someone looking out for me, someone who worried about my whereabouts, when my parents previously had so often never been present to care. I pull my phone from my handbag. Sure enough, there's a notification illuminating the screen. Four missed calls. Disappointment floods me at the realisation.

"Oh. I was driving. It looks like I must have turned the Bluetooth off by accident." Truthfully, I never really bother to check my phone that much these days because no one ever calls me. "Oh, Tessa. I'm sorry."

"You're starting to worry me, Liv. I don't want to sound like your father, but you can't keep wandering through life. You've been through so much and I understand that, but you …"

"Tessa! Calm down. I'm okay." I hold her steady by her petite shoulders and look her straight in her chocolate brown eyes. "I'm actually glad you're still here. I have some news."

"Well, it better be good," she teases.

"I got a job!" I say, the hint of excitement in my voice surprising even myself.

"A job? Where?" she asks.

"At this café in Cliff Haven. It's really cosy. It has this little nook off to the side where you can read books. You would love it." I pluck an apple from the fruit bowl on the counter and take a bite. "I start tomorrow."

"Cliff Haven? What were you doing down there? I thought you hated that place."

"I don't mind it. It has a certain charm about it," I tell her.

I don't bother explaining that I've been going down to Cliff Haven almost every day for the past couple of weeks. It was Katerina that hated going to Cliff Haven. She'd said it was a dump full of townies that would never make anything of themselves. It's the one place in the world that she will never go, which makes it the perfect place for me.

"Well, that's great! Congratulations!" There's nothing but kindness and pride in Tessa's eyes as she holds out her tanned, olive arms, pulling me in a huge, comforting hug. "See, I told you, Liv. You are destined for wonderful things!"

"Settle down, Tessa!" I laugh. "It's just a waitress job." I roll my eyes and wrap my arms around her.

"No, my dear. This is the start of things to come. You'll see. I have a good feeling about this!"

To say Tessa was an optimist would be an understatement. Her sweet nature and ability to be genuinely happy for other people make her a rare find in this town. These are some of the many reasons why I love her. To be honest, she is, without a doubt, the reason I'm not a self-indulged brat. I've come a long way with her love and guidance, but I have no idea if I can live up to this vision she's created of me inside of her mind.

"What's wrong, Liv?" she asks me, sensing the dismay that must be written all over my face.

"What do you think my dad will say?" I ask her.

She gives me a look that says, "Come on, we both know what your father will say." She's probably right. Even though it's just a waitressing job, it could be a step in the right direction for me because at least I will no longer be standing still, but convincing my father of that won't be easy. He expects more of me. He's been dreaming of me following his footsteps into medicine since I got my first doctor's playset at five years old and I've shattered those dreams into oblivion.

"Let's not worry about it right now. What you need to worry about is that you are doing what's right for you. Are you doing what's right for you?"

"I think so," I reply. "For now. I just need some time. You know, to figure things out."

"Good," she says, snatching the half-eaten apple from my hand and waving it dramatically in the air. "Now, this is not dinner! Come on. I'll fix you something to eat."

Chapter 8

OLIVIA

The blindfold is uncomfortable and scratchy, flattening my eyelash extensions and smudging my makeup.

"Seriously! Do I have to wear this thing?" I complain, aware of the whiny high-pitched tone in my voice.

"Not for much longer," my father booms as he directs me down the driveway with firm hands on my shoulders. Then, as he unties the blindfold and lets it slide off my face, he shouts excitedly, "Happy birthday!"

His arms are splayed out in the direction of my birthday present. Parked in front of me is a brand-new, A-Class Mercedes convertible, my reflection staring back at me from its glossy sheen.

I jump up and down a few times and scream, "Oh my God! Is it for me?"

Of course, I know it is. I've been expecting it.

"Absolutely. I can't believe my little girl is finally turning eighteen." My father squeezes me in a tight hug and plants a kiss on my forehead.

"Ugh! Dad, you're going to ruin my makeup." I pull away from him, checking myself in the side mirror and tucking the blonde tendril of hair that has come loose from my braided updo during the unblindfolding.

"Men, huh?" My mother reaches out, attempting to touch the back of my hair. "They have no idea how many hours we sit in the salon chair."

I know she's only half kidding but considering how true it is, having spent the entire day perfecting my platinum blonde colour at Luxe Hair and Co, her joke irritates me.

"Just don't touch it, Mum!" I slap her hand away, then swiftly pull it back in to catch a glimpse of her watch, purely to see what time it is, not to admire her taste in jewellery. It's the watch she bought on one of our many shopping trips together. I'd told her the Chanel one was classier, but for some reason she'd opted for a plainer, less expensive option. "When are you guys leaving?"

Half of Hampton Ridge College will be here any minute and the last thing I want is my parents lurking around at my eighteenth birthday party.

My mum conceals her disappointment at my eagerness for her departure under a hostile demeanour. "Now, actually," she snaps. "Our driver is almost here. Call us if you need anything."

I can't help being particularly aggressive toward my mother. Who could blame me after that night at the Salt Factory? She'd told me that she wouldn't cheat on my father ever again. She'd tried to justify it by saying that Dad hadn't been showing her how important she was to him and that there were other 'things I didn't know about.'

She'd basically bribed me. I would keep her secret if she kept quiet on the fact that Katerina and I had been partying at the Salt Factory. I doubt there was anything my father could do to punish me if he found out, but I couldn't let

Katerina take the fall. It wasn't fair, but I couldn't do that to my best friend.

I continue playing with the strands of loose hair, torn between whether to leave them down or pin them back up.

"Olivia, did you hear your mother?" There is irritation in my father's voice, though I don't know what his problem is. I'm the one trying to pull off the greatest party of my life. My parents need to get out of here already.

"Yes! I heard you! I'll be fine," I retaliate, challenging his impatience.

"Okay, we're staying at the Shangri-La. Call us if you need anything."

"I will. Has the housekeeper organised the caterers?"

The housekeeper hears my question and shuffles over. "Yes, Olivia. They will be here at seven."

"Great. But you won't be. Right?" I know I'm being rude, but I don't really care. No one ever seems to react to the way I behave. As it turns out, Olivia Petersen can say and do pretty much whatever she likes.

I catch the housekeeper rolling her eyes as she turns away from me. "I'm leaving now," she mutters, then glancing back at me she adds, "Oh. And, Olivia?"

"Yes," I respond, without looking up.

"I do have a name you know," I hear her say.

I ignore her and shift my attention back to my parents, flashing my best fake smile. "Okay, bye, Mum. Bye, Dad! Love you!"

"Goodbye, sweetie," they both say, each giving me another hug, although not as tightly this time.

"Oh, I almost forgot!" exclaims my mother, reaching into her Birkin bag and pulling out a flat package wrapped with designer paper and an impeccable silver bow. "Happy birthday, my darling girl. I hope you'll use this."

"Thanks, Mum." I smile half-heartedly as I take the package, with no intention of opening it immediately. Whatever it is will have to wait because Sean's BMW is coming up the driveway. "I'll open it later."

"Oh, okay." It's not hard to detect the disappointment in my mother's voice, but she turns nonetheless and with my father by her side, heads for the black, stretch limousine that awaits them on the curb.

Sean strolls toward me, then wrapping himself around me, he lifts me up and kisses me roughly on the cheek. He whispers in my ear. "Happy birthday, sexy."

"Put me down, Sean," I say, unable and unwilling to hide my annoyance.

"Nice ride!" he says, skimming the roof of my new car with his fingertips.

"Yeah, it's nice, but he didn't get the right colour." I'd asked my father for a custom red, but I guess he thought he knew better.

"Gunmetal is sleek. I like it," he replies, as he follows me into the house like a lost puppy. "That's unfortunate that I missed your dad. I wanted to talk to him about the benefit next week. He said he was going to put in a good word with the professor for me."

"Yeah. How unfortunate." I say, sarcastically, as I reach for my mother's vodka bottle on the top shelf of the glass cabinet.

"Don't be like that, Olivia." There's that tone again. It's the same tone I hear constantly in my mother's voice, in my father's voice. Disappointment.

"Like what?" I shrug.

"Every time I mention Milton you get all defensive and moody," he answers.

"Because it's all you ever talk about. Seriously, who are you dating? Me or my dad? It's like you only ever come over here to talk to him."

It may sound harsh, but it's true. I've only invited Sean here a handful of times and every single one of those times he's wound up talking to my dad about his dreams of a career in medicine.

My father is the best cardiac surgeon in the state and a director on the board at Milton Hospital. A recommendation from him would provide Sean with a better chance of being accepted into the medical program there, and he knows it.

I understand that he's looking out for his future, and maybe I'm being petty, but I can't help feeling upset that all his attention is focused on his career prospects, instead of on me.

"Come on, you know it's not like that," he says, snaking an arm around my waist.

"He's already writing you a reference. What more do you want?" I don't want to start an argument before everyone arrives, but he's making it impossible.

"Nothing. Just you," he leans into me, attempting to plant a kiss on my lips, but I push him aside.

"Everyone will be here soon. I have to go check on the caterers." I already know that the caterers won't be here till seven. The housekeeper told me so, but it gave me an out.

It annoys me that Sean can't see the real reason I'm upset. I know he can't read my mind, but I wish he would make more of an effort to understand me.

The truth is that I'm torn between my mother and father's aspirations for me, while having no idea what my own are. My dad has always wanted me to follow his footsteps into medicine, but my grades will never be enough to get me there and that fact left me feeling like one huge failure. My mum believes I could get early acceptance into the Milton Conservatorium of Music, but lately, she pisses me off so much I want to take a sledge hammer to my piano as a big 'fuck you' to her. Besides, we're young. Are we really meant to have it all figured out already?

"What's that?" Sean asks, pointing to the ornately wrapped giftbox I'm still carrying.

"Oh, just a present from my mum." I toss the box onto the kitchen counter. "I'll open it later."

"That reminds me," he says, pulling a small box from his jacket pocket. "Happy birthday, babe."

Sean holds out a Tiffany blue box, his chestnut brown eyes boring into mine. I instantly feel guilty. Maybe he does care about me after all.

"You went to Tiffany's for me?" I lift the lid on the small giftbox, revealing its contents. A Tiffany bow bracelet, a dainty platinum chain with a diamond encrusted bow in the centre.

"Well, you did tell me how much you liked it about three hundred times." Sean cups my face and kisses me on the cheek, then his mouth moves over mine. This time I let him.

"Thank you," I say, as I squeeze him tightly. "Help me put it on. I wanna wear it right now. Katerina is going to be so jealous!"

Chapter 4

LIV

My phone resonates maddeningly from my bedside table. I set my alarm to a tone called 'charming bell', but at five thirty in the morning it is anything but charming.

Waking up at this hour feels completely foreign to me. I slam my hand down on the touch screen. A number of different apps open up as my fingers fumble to shut off the sound. With my eyes only half open, I finally find the snooze button and the incessant bleeping ceases.

Resting my head back onto the silk pillowcase, I'm overcome with a strong urge to stay in bed and ignore the alarm. Then I remember that this is my life now. I'm a responsible, employed adult and I'm determined to function as one. Tessa's voice replays in my head as I remember our conversation from the previous night.

You are destined for wonderful things.

Maybe she's right. Maybe she's insanely delusional, but nonetheless I reluctantly stumble into the shower.

Although I don't need to be at the café until 7:30am, I plan to arrive a little earlier to prove my commitment to my new boss. And to myself. And if I could impress my dad, that would certainly be a bonus. I want to show him that I can actually function as a person again. That I can survive on my own.

Dad arrived home from work at a reasonable hour last night and I was able to have a very brief chat with him before he strode off to the shower and then bed.

It wasn't uncommon for us to go a few days without seeing each other. We're often like two ships passing in the night. When we talk, it's rarely about anything that actually matters. Never about how we really feel.

And never about Mum.

But at least last night I was able to tell him about my new job. As I'd suspected, he hadn't been too thrilled but for different reasons than I'd thought. Although I'm sure he wasn't over the moon that his only daughter was now a lowly waitress, he'd genuinely seemed concerned about my wellbeing. All this time I've been anxious about disappointing him by doing nothing with my life, but last night he seemed more concerned that I was launching myself out into the world before I was ready. It's nice that he cares, but it kind of makes me feel like a needy child.

I never thought to ask Carla about what she considers appropriate attire for work. I'd taken note that yesterday she'd been wearing jeans and a t-shirt so I figure as long as I look neat and presentable, casual wear will be okay. I slip into a short, black denim skirt, throw on a white tank top, and layer it with a light grey, cable-knit cardi, which I guess I won't need for long. Cliff Haven is usually warm and sunny during the day, but up here on the ridge, it's always windy.

I pull my deep brown hair into a half up style. The edgy shoulder length bob I've adopted doesn't quite allow for a full ponytail. I'm not big on wearing a lot of makeup these days, so I apply a tinted moisturiser to my lightly freckled complexion, accentuate my hazel eyes with a slick of black mascara and wipe a light sheen of clear gloss over my lips.

I pause for a second, remembering how my mother would never even go as far as the mailbox without a full face of makeup. Tessa had told me that she hadn't always been like that. In her younger days, when I was just a kid, my mum had rarely worn makeup. She didn't need it. She was a natural beauty, but over time the housewives of Hampton Ridge had worn down her self-esteem.

I stare at the girl in the reflection. She stares back. She still holds sadness within her expression, but there's something dancing in her eyes that wasn't there yesterday.

Hope.

She hasn't given up yet. There is still fight left in her. For the first time in a long time I hold onto the belief that just maybe, she's going to be okay.

I lean down to put my lip gloss back into the dresser drawer when my eyes drift over the music books my mother gave me on my eighteenth birthday. I hadn't known it then, but it would be the last birthday I'd ever get to spend with her. Not that I'd devoted much of my time to her. I was too preoccupied with impressing the people I'd called friends.

Now those people are gone, and so is she, and all I'm left with is a handful of papers bound in soft, black leather.

What I wouldn't do to relive that day, how different I would spend it. If only I had another chance to tell her that I loved her and I accepted her.

I lift the book from the drawer, running my hands over its smooth cover and tracing the embossed letters with my forefinger. I open it and read the inscription inside, written in my mother's elegant handwriting.

My dearest Livvie,
Always follow your dreams. They know the way.

Love Mum

Sorry to disappoint you mum, but it's not always that simple.

I slam the book shut. I know now that my mother had her own battles to fight, but these words were still useless coming from her. Even so, it's the only piece of her that I have left and I feel compelled to have it close to me. I stuff the book inside my handbag and tiptoe down the staircase quietly, in case my dad is still sleeping.

I arrive at the Haven at ten past seven. The town is practically empty at this hour. Apart from a couple of early morning joggers sprinting toward the pier, I can't see anyone else. The only sound comes from the cawing of birds near the foreshore. A sense of tranquillity permeates the atmosphere, with the sun having not long ago risen from the water's edge in the distance.

My plan to arrive early seems to have backfired. Carla hasn't arrived yet, and without keys to get inside, I have no choice but to wait for her out the front. I peer through the window, mentally preparing myself for what tasks may lay ahead for me.

As I step back, a movement in the reflection catches my eye. I spin around, scanning the opposite side of the street. A guy leans against a run-down shopfront on the corner across the road. I've never really paid much attention to it before on my day visits to Cliff Haven, but looking at it now, I can see it's a pub. The sign above the door reads 'Steve's Tavern.'

I wonder what has brought this guy to be standing outside a pub at this time of the morning. I contemplate the fact that maybe he's trying to break in, but then the sound of metal ringing travels across the street and I realise he's holding a set of keys.

It's hard to tell from a distance, and with the morning sun penetrating my line of sight, but he looks like he couldn't be more than a couple of years older than I am. He wears a black leather jacket and his brown hair is almost shoulder length. He glances over in my direction and I turn away, not wanting him to think I'm watching him. Even though I am.

Whatever.

Carla's voice startles me from behind. "Hello, Liv. You're here bright and early!"

I gasp, clutching my chest in shock as I twist around. "Good morning," I say, politely, and slightly out of breath from being scared half to death. I was so focused on the guy across the street I hadn't heard her coming.

"Sorry, I shouldn't have snuck up on you like that," she says, apologetically.

I laugh nervously. "That's okay." I will my heart rate to return to normal. "It's just so quiet around here."

"Yeah," she agrees. "But the customers will be pouring in soon." She plucks a set of keys from her small, blue messenger bag and begins unlocking the door, delegating my tasks as she does so. "Okay, let's get to work. I need you to take all the chairs down from the tables while I set up the registers. Kristen should be here any minute to help you out."

"Okay, great!" I say, probably a little too enthusiastically. I am both nervous and excited to get to work.

To be busy.

"Dammit," Carla says, as she fumbles with the lock. "The lock is stuck. I keep telling Charlie to replace it. He's our chef, but he also comes in handy when things need fixing. That is, when he actually remembers to fix them." There's a loud click as the lock releases and Carla pushes the door open. "Ah, there we go! Just close that door behind you. We'll open up at eight."

As I gently press the door closed, I notice the guy across the street is still there. His gaze lingers on me for a few seconds until he realises I'm watching him too. He averts his eyes to the ground, and with his hands in his pockets, he walks off in the direction of the beach. I try not to read too much into it as Carla helps me find a place for my belongings. Then I begin pulling the chairs from upon the tables.

"Sorry, I'm late! I must have somehow accidentally turned my alarm off and only woke up, like, fifteen minutes ago. Can you believe it?" A young woman barges through the café door, sending the bell above it into a frenzy.

And no, I can't believe it, because the first thing I notice about her is her beauty. No one should look this gorgeous fifteen minutes after waking up. She's stunning, even without makeup, with long dark chestnut hair cascading down her back.

The second thing I'm aware of is her confidence. It exudes from her in a way that demands the room's attention. Not in an arrogant way, but in a way that suggests she's unapologetically herself. I know who she is, although we haven't met. This is Kristen. And I instantly like her.

She smiles as she approaches me, her hand extended in a welcoming handshake. "Hi, allow me to introduce myself. I'm Kristen. You must be Liv. Carla told me she found our newest team member!"

"Hi," I reply, awkwardly. "Yes. That would be me."

"Awesome. Now, let me help you with that." Kristen catches the barstool I'm attempting to lift from the counter as it slips through my grip.

"Oh, God! I'm so sorry!" I cry out, half expecting her to be impatient with my clumsiness, but she only laughs which makes me laugh too.

After taking all of the chairs down from the tables, we help Carla prepare fruit salads, yoghurt, and muesli. I'm introduced briefly to Charlie, the chef, as he fusses around in the kitchen, organising things for the day ahead. When Carla reverses the 'Closed' sign on the café window to 'Open,' the first customers begin filing in like bees swarming to pollen.

Things become so hectic at the cafe that Carla, Kristen, and I (mostly I), struggle to keep an efficient pace and I have to wonder if this is considered exceptionally busy, or if this is what I'll be subjected to on a daily basis.

Kristen does her best to train me on the basics while holding down the fort, but the breakfast rush seems to run directly into the lunchtime rush and I find myself getting flustered. When my own stomach starts to rumble, I regret my decision to skip breakfast this morning. The blueberry muffin I'd scoffed during my short morning tea break hadn't been enough to curb my hunger for long.

When the lunch time customers have finally dispersed, I hurry over to clear a large table, where previously, a group of eight people had been sitting.

Lifting the stack of food crusted plates between my wrist and the crook of my elbow requires strength and balance, as well as some serious concentration, but it only takes one single person to waltz in through those open stacker doors to throw my entire world off its axis.

The world slows. My mind races in overtime to put this picture together. It doesn't make sense.

He doesn't belong here, with his black suit pants and silver-grey tie, the expensive dress shirt with its sleeves rolled up to the elbows a blinding shade of white. His dark eyes meet mine as he rips a pair of Prada sunglasses from his chiselled face.

Everything is all wrong.

www.ingramcontent.com/pod-product-compliance
Lightning Source LLC
Chambersburg PA
CBHW050113120726
47904CB00004B/1327